"HELL OR HIGH WATER" IN THE INDIAN TERRITORY

THE ADVENTURES OF THE DODSON BROTHERS, DEPUTY U.S. MARSHALS

TERRY GROSZ

WOLFPACK PUBLISHING

Print Edition

© Copyright 2018 Terry Grosz

Wolfpack Publishing
6032 Wheat Penny Avenue
Las Vegas, NV 89122

ISBN: 978-1-62918-702-0

CONTENTS

"HELL OR HIGH WATER" IN THE INDIAN TERRITORY

TERRY GROSZ

CHAPTER ONE

"STARS AND BARS", EVIL EYES AND EVIL HEARTS...

CAPTAIN ALBERT DODSON, late of the Pennsylvania 3rd Cavalry, patriarch of the Dodson clan, new landowner of 4,000 acres of rich farm and ranch lands near the town of Booneville, Arkansas, sat quietly in his saddle overlooking 30 prime head of registered Angus cattle isolated out in his pasture. Seated on their horses alongside their father, sat Joe Dodson, oldest son, James and Lewis Dodson, and David, the youngest, also quietly surveying those same 30 head of registered cattle belonging to the ranch and ready for shipment and sale to a local neighbor and fellow cattleman.

"Alright, Boys, I need you to drive these cattle over to Joseph Meek's place in Blue Mountain, give him a bill of sale, collect what he owes me

1

in coin of the realm, and then get your tail-ends back here so we can get our brands on the rest of this year's calves before they 'wander' off into the hands of those less than honest neighbors around us," said Albert, as he began surveying the remainder of his herd of cattle gathered up at the south end of the pasture awaiting branding. "Boys, try and remember we are Yankees from Pennsylvania now living out here in a southern state that was on the losing side in the late Civil War. I suspect a number of the locals don't 'cotton' to us newcomers, especially since we migrated of late into this area with some money in our pockets and most of them are war weary and now as poor as a mess of church mice. Then we probably did the unthinkable in their eyes and bought up this prime piece of bottomland from one of their locals with hard cash and did so right out from under their suspicious noses. I would also imagine if these southern folks are a lot like those rural folks we left back in Pennsylvania, we will need to prove ourselves up before we are accepted. That is, if we ever are, being that we came from 'Yankee-land' far to the north. So, be polite to everyone that you meet on the road regardless of which side they fought on because they are our new neighbors now, and I expect that we all need to make an effort and get along because of the war losses suffered on both sides of the flag," said their father, Albert.

"As I figure it geographically, being new to

this area and all, it is just a little over ten miles to Meek's place. With a little luck, the four of you should be home in time for supper if you get with it and don't stop or dawdle along the way looking at any of the ladies you four may run across. We all may be Yankees but we all still have manners when it comes to the fairer sex, so act like all of you were raised right and proper like. Remember, we have a full hard week ahead of us branding and castrating that needs doing with the remainder of the calves in this herd, so you boys need to get with it," said old man Dodson, as he continued carefully looking over the remainder of the cattle in his herd in the south pasture.

"OK, Dad," said Joe. "Come on, Guys. We are burning daylight and if any of you want to sample any of Ma's pies come suppertime, we best get along with our chores." With that and spurs tapped slightly to the flanks of their horses, the four young Dodson men moved the 30 head of cattle set aside for sale easily out the open gate and headed them easterly down the dirt road toward Joseph Meek's place over at Blue Mountain so he could add new registered stock to his own herd of cattle and improve their bloodlines.

Watching his boys move the cattle down the road, Albert couldn't help himself from being overly proud of his four young sons. They had all turned out to be hard workers, ranch-smart, crack rifle and pistol shooters, excellent horse-men, tough as a horseshoe nail when they had to be, outstanding cattlemen, and good Christian men. No two ways about it, both he and his wife had done a good job in raising their children. Quietly sitting there on his horse, he proudly watched his young sons move the cattle expertly down the road until they had moved out of sight and sound. Then Albert dismounted, closed the gate to the pasture, re-mounted his horse and spent the next hour moving in and among his large herd of cattle, inspecting all the remaining heifers with their new young calves making sure each calf had an accepting mother to nurse.

However, Albert's eyes were not the only set of eyes looking at his herd of cattle quietly feed-ing in the south pasture. Sitting on his horse on a nearby hillside out of sight from the eyes of the rancher below, was Lieutenant Colonel Timothy Jackson, late of the 5th Arkansas Cavalry, Jones's Regiment, McDowell's Brigade… Jackson's dark eyes were quietly surveying the valuable 80 plus cows and calves below him still left in Albert's pasture with avarice in his heart. To him, those cattle, although not his, represented many good times if he and his men could safely make off with them and take them out of Arkansas into the Indian Territory just a few days travel to his west, where local Arkansas law had no jurisdiction or authority. There he figured the stolen cattle could be sold to any willing buyer, white man or Indian, who could overlook the 'small' fact that they came without any ownership papers or Bills of Sale!

Behind their ex-Confederate commander quietly sitting on their horses that morning were eight other men who were nothing more than renegade guerillas of the insidious "Quantrill" variety, one and all! 'Guerillas' who had for several years since the end of the Civil War been roaming the rural areas of Arkansas still 'fighting the late war'. In so doing, they had been terrorizing anyone who they suspected were northern sympathizers and taking from those people what the raiders figured they had coming for the service they had rendered for the "Stars and Bars" during their losing part in that war. The way Jackson and his men figured it, cattle were an easily disposable commodity once they got them into the essentially lawless Indian Territory and that would go double for those registered cattle of high quality quietly feeding in Albert's pasture. Cattle which just happened to belong to a recently transplanted and much hated wealthy Yankee farmer and rancher from Pennsylvania! From where the guerillas sat on their horses, those cattle represented nothing more than many future good times with loose women and almost unlimited drinks of whiskey over in the lawless Indian Territory once they were sold. Sold in Indian Territory where the long arm of the law hardly reached and then only with difficulty because of the over 70,000 square miles of lawless land in which any bad man could find succor and lack of attention from those pesky individuals wearing a silver star, carrying a Winchester rifle and sporting a Colt revolver. Additionally, that lawless land was basically ruled over by others of their kind with dark eyes and evil hearts, where the 'rule of law' depended upon whoever toted the fastest gun and knew how to accurately use it.

Jackson, tired of being broke and from sleeping on the cold ground for the last few days out at the old Curnow farm, saw nothing but opportunity in what he was looking at below him, namely over 80 head of prime cattle being watched over by now just one man once the other four riders had ridden off down the road and out of sight pushing another smaller herd of cattle. Because it had been over an hour since those four other heavily armed riders had ridden off with the smaller herd of cattle, they now would be out of hearing range if any gunplay ensued below once he and his men made their appearance and their desires known to the individual rancher inspecting his cattle. So Jackson felt it was now time to strike if they were going to rustle all of those cattle and make their get-away with over 80 slow-moving head before darkness set in, making quick pursuit then by the local law problematic until the day following.

"Come on, Men. Let us go on down and show this Yankee son-of-a-bitch some good ole southern hospitality, courtesy of the "Stars and Bars" and let him know that the 'war' is not yet over and that he and his kind don't belong in the great State of Arkansas," uttered Jackson with a sinister look spreading across his face.

As Jackson's men picked their way off the low, brush-covered hill upon where they had been sitting hidden from view, Albert, totally involved in examining the condition of his cows and their new calves, failed to notice the string of suspicious looking men picking their ways across the nearby hillside. A group of men, with a number of them still sporting parts of their southern military uniforms from the conflict now since past for several years, picking their ways suspiciously towards Albert's cow pasture. Finally looking up from his cow-calf inspections, Albert noticed a number of dismounted men at the far side of his cow-calf pasture, calmly cutting his new barbed wire fence so they could bring their horses into the enclosure holding his cattle!

"Hey, what the hell are you men doing?" yelled Albert, as he spurred his horse towards the men cutting an ever-widening gap in his new four strand barbed wire fence!

Riding across his pasture and being grounded in military experience, he noticed that a number of the mystery men now riding his way were wearing parts of uniforms from the southern army's recent conflict in the war between the north and south... Moments later, Albert was confronted by nine men, riding boldly and sinisterly line abreast right at him in a threatening manner!

Reining up, Albert waited for the men to make their intentions known so he could see who they were and what the hell they were up to. However, as he waited for their arrival and being suspicious of nature under similar previous military circumstances, he unsnapped the leather 'catch' on his pistol as his ex-military training kicked in and had taught him to do in like situations. Then Albert realizing the nine men riding at him were not slowing down and possibly meant him harm, quickly withdrew his Sharps carbine from his rifle scabbard, just as the closest three oncoming riders increased their horses' paces and broke into a gallop heading right at the rancher! As they did, Albert could clearly see that they were ominously holding their reins in their left hands and had 'cleared leather' with their handguns in their right hands!

"Hold her right there!" Albert yelled, as he swung his rifle towards the first of the three men obviously now meaning to 'ride him down', shoot and unhorse him...

BOOM! went a pistol shot from one of the three men riding right at him, and ZZZZIIPPP! went the bullet right by Albert's head so close that he felt the wind of its closeness! That shooter had missed but Albert did not, as he cleared that shooter from his saddle with his .50 Sharps with his first deadly shot!

BOOM-BOOM-BOOM-BOOM — BOOM! went five more quick shots being fired by the now remaining eight onrushing men and the impacts from that fusillade of bullets cleared Albert from his saddle, dropping him to the ground! With that, Albert's horse then bolted out of the way from the now hard-charging eight 'horsed' men, as Albert, being the leather tough Irishman that he was, upon hitting the ground and not yet dead, managed to get one shot off with his pistol, clearing another close at hand onrushing man from his saddle! Albert was then stomped to death by the remaining arriving seven horsemen!

Whirling their horses around after riding their horses over Albert, the remaining men rode back to the now inert rancher whereupon Colonel

Jackson took his pistol and shamefully emptied it into the corpse of the rancher from just feet away! "Take that, you Yankee son-of-a-bitch!" yelled Jackson, as he stared down at the more than dead man lying alongside that shooter's now nervously snorting horse upon smelling the fresh blood from the dead rancher so close at hand.

Then other than the rumble heard from the fleeing herd of cattle running across the pasture over all the nearby shooting, the now seven ex-Confederate guerillas sat there on their horses looking down at the rancher who had unflinchingly stood his ground in the face of initially nine hard charging men and had killed two of their kind in the uneven exchange that had just occurred before his untimely demise.

"Now what do we do, Colonel? That bastard managed to kill Cole and Jessie before we got him. What do you want us to do with their bodies?" asked one of Jackson's men.

"Leave them where they fell. It will be a reminder to all the other Yankee sympathizers in this area to steer clear of our kind in the future. In fact, it may even run off those other four men who came into this pasture with him right at daylight as we were getting ready to rustle all of their cattle before anyone intervened," replied Jackson, as he slowly reloaded his now empty 'pin-fire' revolver.

Then Jackson continued, "I would bet the home at the end of the hollow is this guy's house. Since we are short of grub, what say we all make ourselves right at home, raid the place, get ourselves something to eat, and then sack it for anything else of value that we can use? Then after that, we can return to this here field, recover all the cattle and start driving them over to the town of Poteau in the Indian Territory. There we can sell them to that Choctaw renegade Indian named Samuel July and let him worry about what to do with them," said Jackson.

With those suggestions, several of the men rode back and repaired that portion of the pasture fence they had cut so the cattle would not in the interim find the opening in the fence and wander off. Then the bodies of Cole and Jessie were stripped of their weapons and other useful items and left where they fell after Albert had shot them out from their saddles. Then all of the dead men's horses were rounded up and trailed over to the farmhouse Colonel Jackson figured was the just-killed rancher's homestead.

When the remaining seven ex-Confederates drew their horses up abruptly into the front yard of the ranch house, there they were greeted by a young woman who appeared to be in her late teens saying, "Good Morning. My name is Linda and welcome to our home." Then Linda spotted

her father's horse being led by one of the unknown men and said, "Is that my Dad's horse?
What has happened to him?"

Those were her last words as one of the ruffians quickly stepped off his horse and before
she could say another word or run, had his hand
covering her mouth so she could not shout out
a warning to those still inside the house! With
that, the rest of the men dismounted, tied off
their horses on the rail of the front porch, and
then streamed unannounced through the ranch
house's front door and into the kitchen area of
the home. There they discovered another young
teenaged woman removing freshly baked bread
from their pans and a middle aged woman placing a pie into the wood stove's hot oven for baking.

Surprised over the intrusion of the ragged
looking lot of unfamiliar men, all three women
were moments later quickly hustled into the bedrooms of the house by six of the men. As that was
occurring, Colonel Jackson sat himself down at
the kitchen table, cut himself a slice of homemade
bread just removed from the oven, slathered it
with freshly churned butter from a nearby crock
and began calmly eating. As he did, he could hear
screams followed by many groans and some crying from the teenage girls and the older woman,
as the six men took turns sexually with the now

terrified and defenseless women! Those screams continued as the men alternated with each of the hapless women, as the 'good' Colonel, unfazed by his men's animal-like behavior, calmly helped himself to a large slice of homemade blackberry pie freshly removed from the oven and set out on the table to cool...

Forty minutes later, three muffled shots could be heard and with that, there was complete silence coming from the bedrooms of the ranch house. Moments later, the six ruffians exited the sleeping area adjusting their clothing and then entered the kitchen eating area as well!

"We didn't save you 'any', Colonel, because we knew you are still a married Christian man. But that sure as hell didn't stop the six of us from having our ways, especially with them 'fresh' young ladies," said Corporal John Atkins. "They sure were good but a little bloody afore we were finished," said John with a sly smile crossing his face. "However as you could tell from all the shooting, we made sure they will be telling no tales on us and what we did in any court of law," continued Atkins, as he nonchalantly helped himself to a piece of freshly baked pie like he and his kind had done nothing out of the unusual or ordinary with the women in the back rooms of the ranch house...

However, in their 'gluttony' with the three

women and all the freshly baked goods scattered about in the kitchen, the men failed to realize that the sixteen-year-old hired hand who had been working in the nearby barn, had witnessed some and heard a lot of what was going on in the bedrooms of the house! Now, his 'flying feet' were carrying him to the next house down the lane so he could borrow a horse and ride to alert Sheriff Del Garrison over in Booneville as to what evil things were ongoing over at the Dodson's place! Twenty minutes of hard riding put Sam, the hired hand, at the Sheriff's Office in Booneville. Bursting into the office, Sam quickly blurted out what was happening over at the Dodson's! It took a few moments for Sheriff Garrison to get Sam calmed down so he could be understood and then a few more minutes to round up his closest three deputies and quickly 'swear in' eight additional armed townsfolk. Soon the thirteen men were riding 'hell bent for leather' for the Dodson place in order to put a stop to the reported violence and apprehend those doing the evil things going on that Sam had just described to Sheriff Garrison!

Meanwhile, Colonel Jackson and his men were now ransacking the Dodsons's home looking for spare ammunition and any additional weapons that they could use in their future depredations. Then the men hurriedly left with all of their horses and several more that were in a nearby corral, as they sped back to their herd of cattle of interest. When they arrived back at the pasture, several men began herding the cattle over to the now reopened break in the back of the pasture's fence and drove the cattle off and on their way via numerous back roads and lanes south towards White Oak Mountain, and along the north side of the east-west ridges running towards the Arkansas-Indian Territory border. Then from there, the rustlers and killers planned on heading north to the town of Poteau in the Indian Territory and renegade Indian Samuel July's place. There they planned on selling the rustled cattle and horses and after a few days of celebration in Poteau over their rustling successes, head deeper into Indian Territory in case anyone from Arkansas was hot on their trail and looking for those who had done this 'evil thing' to several members of the Dodson clan...

In the meantime, Sheriff Del Garrison and his newly formed posse rode hard to the very outskirts of the Dodson place, then reined up and quietly examined the ranch house setting from a short distance away so they would not alert any evildoers that may have still been in the house. In so doing, they could not see any signs of what Sam, the hired hand, had described to them earlier as to what evil things had been going on inside the ranch house by a large number of unknown men. Ever careful because Sam had said there were seven men violently storming the Dodson ranch house, the sheriff led his men quietly near the side of the house, hid their horses in the trees and then carefully stalked the house proper looking for evidence of the seven men. Seeing or hearing no sign of any kind of activity, Sheriff Garrison prepared to enter the house through the back door looking for any signs of the violent behavior that Sam had described as occurring inside between the unfortunate Dodson women and the unknown men.

Sheriff Garrison and his lead deputy carefully entered the Dodson house after arranging for the rest of his posse to surround the premises in case they 'smoked' out the culprits causing all the chaos as they tried to flee out the front or side doors. Upon entering, all the two lawmen could smell was a pie burning in the oven and not a single sound could be heard coming from the rest of the house. Carefully searching the house, the two lawmen soon discovered the scene of death in the two back bedrooms of the home!

In the main bedroom lying on her bed was Mrs. Dodson, who from all the signs on her naked body, had been brutally raped and then shot in the head! In the second bedroom on the bottom floor, the two lawmen discovered an equally grisly scene in the girls' bedroom. Both girls had also been brutally raped and from the physical evidence on their naked bodies, numerous times! They too had both been shot execution style in their heads and left where they lay violated on their beds!

The two lawmen could find no further evidence of deadly foul play in the men's bedrooms and it quickly became apparent that they had been away when the raping and killing had occurred. Sheriff Garrison then dispatched his lead deputy to ride back into town and have Clem Watkins the mortician, dispatched to the scene of multiple murders. Additionally, his lead deputy was told to organize a larger posse and head back to the Dodson place so they could start following the tracks of the murderers just as soon as they could even though it was getting late in the day and darkness would soon be upon them making tracking of the killers all but impossible.

Two hours later, the lead deputy and his 15-man deputized posse arrived at the Dodson place. They had brought the mortician along with them and leaving him to do what he had to do, the rest of the now very large posse began following the culprits tracks leading away from the home place. Shortly thereafter, the posse following the fleeing culprits' horses' tracks arrived at the cattle pasture. There they discovered the body of Albert and two unidentified ruffians that from all appearances, Old Man Dodson had done in before being killed by a number of the remaining cattle rustlers. That they deduced from all appearances of the numbers and placement of horse tracks scattered throughout the disturbed ground in the pasture and the numerous spent rifle and pistol cartridges lying scattered about what had earlier become a killing field.

Then it was just a matter of making a simple deduction by Sheriff Garrison that the unknown men had tried to rustle Albert Dodson's cattle, he had caught them in the act, a fight had ensued and being outnumbered as evidenced from all the other horse tracks present in the pasture, that Albert had put up and lost one hell of a fight! But in the process, the tough old Yankee Army Captain had taken two of the culprits with him, as evidenced by the two dead men left behind where they had fallen by the rest of the cattle rustlers and killers.

That was when Sheriff Garrison got a break in the case. One of the men in the posse, one Dee Barbea, an ex-Army scout and tracker during the Civil War, recognized one of the dead men. He quickly told the sheriff, "Sheriff, I know that dead man. That was Jessie Odums and he was riding with Colonel Jackson and his bunch of cattle stealing ruffians who last that I had heard, were staying out by the old Curnow place. I rec- ognized him because I had to re-shoe his horse last week after his animal had thrown two rear shoes. That bunch he rode in with was nine in number and I know that since they all had hung around while I shod Odums's horse. Looking here on the ground and what we have been track- ing since leaving the ranch house, there are only seven horses leaving deeper hoofprints showing that they are being ridden. All the rest of the horse tracks are showing that they are not being rid- den but trailed because of shallower hoofprints. Lastly, there were originally nine men riding in Jackson's bunch when I did the shoeing, with two dead ones lying here in the pasture, one of whom I recognize, so that would make sense that is was the Jackson bunch with only seven horses now being ridden off!"

"Makes sense, Dee," said Sheriff Garrison. "Since I knew that Albert had almost 100 head of expensive registered cattle in this here pasture and now there are none, we know what happened and why. Let us get after them boys before they leave the country. Because it now looks like that the Jackson bunch rustled all of Albert's cattle and must have ransacked his house and 'taken' all of his women in the process. Dee, it looks like those cattle were taken out through that break in the fence over yonder. You get after them and stay on the trail of those seven horses and me and the boys will back you up even though it is getting a little late in the day for tracking these killing bastards," advised Sheriff Garrison.

"Wait, Sheriff. Here come the rest of the Dodson boys down the road. You had best get to them boys afore they get up a killing heat over what has just happened and decide to take the law into their own hands," said Deputy Peter Becker.

About then, the Dodson boys rode into their cattle pasture with questioning looks spread across their faces over why all the local men were in the middle of their now empty cow pasture. Seconds later, the four men reined up by the body of their dad lying face up in the pasture and all of them bailed off their horses and rushed to his side. It didn't take the boys but a few seconds to realize with a dozen bloody holes in their dad's shirt, that he had been riddled with bullets from very close range by a number of shooters and was now beyond any help!

Looking away from his dad's body and up at Sheriff Garrison sitting on his horse for answers, Joe strode over to the lawman and coldly said, "What the hell happened here, Del?"

"Before you boys blow up, let me tell you what has happened from as near as I can figure it. It appears your dad caught a mess of what we have since identified as ex-Confederate ruffians in the act of rustling his cattle. He obviously tried to stop them and in the process, was gunned down by about seven men as near as we can tell. I say seven because out of a gang of nine rustlers initially confronting him as evidenced by all of the horse tracks scattered around and confirmed by Dee who is one hell of a tracker, it appears he managed to kill two of them. It is from those bodies that we have come to identify the dead from an ex-Confederate Colonel who has been hell raising and stealing cattle from hereabouts for the last several years. Looks like today, they picked on your dad's herd of cattle and were after the whole herd. Your dad caught them in the act and they had a shootout. Albert got two of them right off the bat and then he was gunned down and killed. Then it looks like the remaining bunch of cattle rustlers, not content to just steal all your cattle, rode over to your home, invaded it, raped and killed your two younger sisters and your mother! Sam, here, heard all the hell being raised over what was going on in your house from his place of hiding in the barn and, not being armed and outnumbered by those causing the evil, ran off, borrowed a neighbor's horse, rode over, and got me and the boys to come back and try and catch the rustlers and evildoers in the act. We got here too late, discovered what those bastards had done and now are in the process of tracking them down and after a trial, hopefully hanging the lot," quietly replied Sheriff Garrison, as he could see that all four boys upon hearing of the death of almost their entire family, were now badly tearing up and understandably getting very emotional over their losses...

Since it was now beginning to get dark and trying to trail a number of killers in the dark would be futile and possibly just getting ambushed in the process, the sheriff took the boys back to their home so they could see for themselves what had happened. By the time they arrived back at their home, mortician Clem Watkins had all three of the dead women laid out in the back of his buckboard in preparation for burial and had thoughtfully covered up all of their naked and desecrated bodies with a blanket. Upon seeing their dead mother and sisters, all four of the sons broke down and could hardly be consoled over their family losses.

An hour later, Joe, the oldest, had recovered as best as he could in light of the situation and was now planning a killing of his own of those responsible for his family's deaths! He had already organized the three remaining boys in the family group that would pursue and hopefully bring the killers to justice. He had also, after a lot of persuading, gotten his younger brother David, to remain home and look after the place with the help of Sam. After all, they still had a small herd of horses, a dozen milk cows and another 40 head of cattle in the north pasture to look after and care for. That would take someone from their family and young David was selected as the stay-behind brother to look after their rather extensive ranch and farm holdings. Plus, they would be leaving all of the money they had received from Joseph Meek from their cattle sale to him earlier in the day. That amount of funding would be more than enough to allow David, if he was careful, to last until the boys came back from the hunting of their family's killers.

Lastly, Sam had briefed the boys on who he had observed riding off after they had left the ranch house. Sam indicated the leader of the group was about six and a half feet tall, had long blond hair with curls, was very slight of build, almost skinny, and wore a long and very distinctive looking 'handle-bar' mustache. As for the remaining men riding with the 'tall one', they all looked alike wearing their old Confederate Cavalry jackets with a distinct red stripe on their left sleeves (McDowell's Brigade) and like their leader, had all been riding matching 'grays' when he had last observed their horses tied off in front of the home ranch before the raping and killing had occurred.

Then promising Sheriff Garrison that they

would remain at the homestead until the next morning and not go running off after the killers by themselves, the posse was pulled back into town so they could prepare for what figured to be a long, hard and dangerous pursuit after the cattle rustlers, horse thieves, rapists and killers.

Daylight the next morning found the three Dodson brothers quietly sitting a-horse, trailing two packhorses with extra clothing, provisions and some cookware. They were prepared to pursue the killers until hell froze over or the killers were in hell themselves. Shortly thereafter, they were joined by ten other serious looking men from town who had been deputized and were also ready for a long pursuit if necessary for the killers of the Dodson family from Logan County, Arkansas. Leading the posse was Sheriff Del Garrison, who was there to see justice done and make sure a 'neck-tie' party was not prematurely in the offing if the killers could be run down in the process as they trailed a slow moving herd of cattle, were apprehended and brought back to stand trial.

CHAPTER TWO

THE DEPUTY U.S. MARSHAL ODYSSEY BEGINS...

BIDDING THEIR YOUNGER BROTHER David, and Sam the hired hand, good-bye, the three older Dodson brothers remounted their horses and swung in with Sheriff Garrison's grim faced posse. Heading out to where darkness the day before had cut short their tracking pursuit, the obvious trail left by the stolen cattle was once again rather easily picked up. Heading westerly as they ran along the northern side of White Oak Mountain, the posse made good time in their pursuit of the rustlers and killers. The trail of 80 plus cattle was easy to follow as Dee Barbea, the ex-Army tracker made sure they stayed on the track and the rest of the posse rode 'shotgun' at the edge of the track to make sure they were not ambushed in their pursuit of the killers.

It soon became evident to the pursuers that the killers were pushing the stolen herd with as much speed as possible, suspecting that maybe pursuit was close at hand. So much so, that it was not long before the posse began finding calves too young to make such an exhausting trip, dead and left along the trail. Figuring they were close at hand to the killers and rustlers, the posse redoubled their pursuit efforts. But as it turned out, the killers had too big a lead on the posse and soon the lawmen's horses began showing signs of stress from being pushed so hard in trying to catch their fleeing quarry still heading westerly toward the Indian Territory.

Stopping to let their horses 'blow', Sheriff Garrison rode over to the three grim faced looking Dodson brothers saying, "Boys, they appear to be heading 'hell bent for leather' for the Indian Territory. If we don't catch them before they cross that line into the 'Territory', I am afraid that is where our chase must officially end. I do not have any arrest authority in the Indian Territory nor do any of my deputies. Jurisdiction over there in that lawless land belongs to the Tribal Police when it comes to Indians breaking the law, and to the U.S. Marshal's Office out of Fort Smith, Arkansas, when it comes to dealing with any white men operating outside the federal laws. If they get into the Indian Territory before we can catch them, I am afraid we all must turn back at the border. That does not preclude you boys from carrying on after them killing son-of-a-bitches as ordinary civilians. However, it sure as hell ties my hands officially as a local sheriff and makes it a bit dangerous legally for you three to act without any authority other than what God gave you under the circumstances."

"Win, lose or draw, Sheriff, we three intend to pursue these bastards until it kills us or we kill them. What they did to our kin was not Christian and my brothers and I do not intend to be Christian if we get our hands on them either," said Joe Dodson quietly, but with steely authority in the tone and tenor of his voice.

"Well, these horses have rested enough, Boys, so let us get on with it before those outlaws cross over into Indian Territory," said Sheriff Garrison as he spurred his horse back onto the trail of the stolen cattle once again with an urgency now more than ever in his pursuit of the killers.

Four more hours of hard pursuit suddenly found Sheriff Garrison reining up his horse and stopping his trailing posse with an upraised hand. "This is as far as we can legally go, Boys. Over yonder by that grove of trees is the start of Indian Territory and here is where we must stop. It is pretty apparent that our outlaws have gotten away from us by the looks of that cattle trail crossing over into Indian Territory and disappearing out of sight beyond those rolling hills. But by damn it, I sure wanted to catch those bastards and after a trial, watch them swing from the gallows back in Booneville," he quietly said through clinched teeth.

"What are you boys carrying for rifles and pistols?" asked Garrison, all of a sudden looking over at the Dodsons.

"We all are shooting .50 Sharps and Colt .45 pistols," advised Joe Dodson.

"Alright, Boys, any of you carrying a .50 Sharps rifle sidle over to these boys and share some of your cartridges with them so they can continue the chase. That also goes for those of you who are carrying Colt .45's. Leave some of your extra cartridges with these Dodson boys so they don't have to worry about 'running dry' if they run to ground the killers of their kin and get into a shoot out with them," said Garrison.

For the next few minutes, a number of riders rode their horses over to where the Dodson men sat on their horses and shared some of their .50 Sharps and .45 Colt cartridges. The Dodsons in turn, placed the extra rifle and pistol cartridges received from their fellow neighbors into their saddlebags for safekeeping. Then with a number of encouraging comments from their fellow posse members, the Dodson brothers turned their horses and pack animals westward and were soon in Indian Territory, alone in their pursuit of those who had all but wiped out most of their entire family.

Come nightfall, found the Dodson brothers still following the trail of stolen cattle in the Indian Territory as their tracks continued heading towards the nearby town of Poteau. Finally stopping alongside a small creek as darkness finally overcame the men making tracking all but impossible, the men lit down for the night. As James Dodson unsaddled their riding horses and Joe unpacked their two pack animals, Lewis made a fire and prepared their campsite for the evening. The riding and pack saddles were brought into the men's campsite for safekeeping as their horses were hobbled and let out to water and graze adjacent to their sleeping area. Soon the men had a fire going and Joe was cooking up their dinner of fried ham along with chunks of freshly made homemade bread previously taken from their dead mother's kitchen...

Shortly after finishing their meager supper, the men, physically exhausted after the long ride and still emotionally drained over the deaths of their family members, crawled under their bedrolls and drifted deeply off to sleep. Soon their campfire burned low and soon only hot coals glowed eerily in their first night in the lawless Indian Territory.

Watching the fire as it was slowly reduced to burning embers, three sets of eyes betraying their evil intentions, closely scanned the unmoving mounds of the sleeping men. Satisfied those men were fast asleep, three men who had been watching the Dodsons's campsite slipped out from the nearby underbrush and began silently moving in and among the horses and removed their hobbles. Then all of the riding and packhorses belonging to the Dodson brothers were quietly secreted away!

Ten minutes later after walking back to their nearby hidden picketed horses, the three horse thieves who had been watching their stolen cattle's back trail on the look-out for any pursuers, as their military smart Colonel had anticipated and ordered, mounted up and trailing all the Dodsons's stock, quietly drifted through the darkened forest towards the faint light of another distant campfire on a creekside flat over a mile away. Once there, the three horse thieves dismounted and reported to Colonel Jackson that the posse that had been trailing them and their herd of stolen cattle had turned back at the boundary of the Indian Territory. That was except for the three men from the original posse who had continued following their stolen cattle trail, and were now without any riding or pack stock in which to continue their pursuit...

Daylight the following morning, found the stolen cattle again on the move along with Colonel Jackson and his band of killers. Soon they would be arriving at July's ranch, home of a Choctaw Indian, just south of the town of Poteau. Once Colonel Jackson and his men were there, the slow moving cattle could be sold off as well as the five Dodson horses that had been spirited away in the dead of night by three of Jackson's men. Three 'Jackson men', who a military wise Colonel Jackson had earlier detached from his main group of cattle rustlers to watch their back trail and take any action they deemed necessary to preclude any followers from catching the escaping band of killers or their stolen slow moving herd of cattle...

Rolling over in the warmth of his bedroll, Lewis Dodson, now awake, out of habit looked over to where he had tied off their horses the evening before. The sight that greeted his eyes caused him to blink his eyes again to make sure of what he was 'not seeing' and then jumping up from his sleep-site, he yelled for his two brothers to wake up! Soon there was total consternation in the Dodson camp over the absence of their horses! Their horses, all of them, were nowhere to be seen and now the brothers realized that they were afoot in Indian Territory!

Running over to where he had tied off their

string of riding and pack animals the night before, Lewis examined the ground beside the tree to which he had tied off their horse string. There were two sets of unfamiliar boot prints that did not match anyone in their camp and then the realization set in. They had been watched the whole time they had been slow-trailing the tracks left by the cattle by those who had stolen them and had killed off most of their family! *How foolish of me*, Lewis thought, not to have someone watch their valuable stock animals through the night, especially now that they were deep in Indian country!

About then, Joe had pulled on his boots and had run over to where Lewis was standing looking off in the direction the horses' hooves were leading in the soft forest soil. "What do you think, Brother?" asked Joe. "Did they just wander off by themselves or were they taken?" he asked.

"They were stolen right out from under our noses," Lewis replied as James, now dressed, ran up to his brothers with a questioning look over their lack of horses on his face as well. Then realizing they were in deep trouble, James said, "Well, if Pop was here he would say let us get after them before they get into the next county, so let us roll."

Without another word, the brothers tied their packs and sleeping rolls up into several nearby trees for safekeeping, then shouldering their riding saddles, began following the trail their stolen horses had left. Six hours later, the three boys lying behind a small rise in the landscape, were watching a nearby ranch into which the trail of their stolen cattle and horses had directly led. There they spied about 60 head of cattle in a corral, minus the calves that had died along the way, and tied to a hitching post in front of the ranch house were their five riding and packhorses!

Without a word between them since none were needed and following Joe, a natural born leader, the three Dodson brothers, still embarrassed over doing something stupid like losing all of their horses, somewhat later walked into the front yard of one Samuel July, a Choctaw Indian. As the three brothers cautiously walked into the ranch's front yard with their rifles at the ready in case they were not welcome, they visually confirmed that the five horses tied off to the ranch's hitching rail, were in fact their horses that had been stolen the night before by what appeared to have been three men! Not finding anybody in the ranch house proper to answer for what the brothers figured were the thefts of their cattle and horses, they smelled smoke from a wood fire. Following their noses and ears upon hearing a number of bawling, hungry cattle behind the ranch house, the three brothers moments later came upon two Indians in a large corral with what they figured was their father's herd of stolen cattle. One Indian was roping out cattle one at a time, dragging them over to the fire pit, dogging them down and the other Indian was using a 'running iron' and in the process, altering the Dodsons's legally Arkansas registered cattle brand!

Having seen enough, the three men entered the corral unseen from the far side and approached the two Indians totally intent upon changing the brands on the Dodson cattle. Finally upon seeing three armed men with Sharps rifles approaching them rather menacingly, one Indian bolted and sprinted for the other side of the corral, leapt over the fence and was last seen running like the wind across the grasslands. However, the Indian holding the running iron dropped it back into the fire and slowly raised his hands realizing that to run would only get him shot clear full of holes, if the grave looks on the faces of the three approaching men meant anything to one caught red-handed using an illegal running iron on someone else's stolen cattle…

Five minutes of questioning by a rather intense Joe Dodson soon provided a wealth of information from the remaining Indian. As the Indian talked rather freely under the withering gaze of three heavily armed men not looking like they were any too happy over what they had discovered, he initially advised that his name was Samuel July, a Choctaw Indian. He then further advised under Joe's questioning that this was his ranch and that he had just that morning purchased all the cattle in the corral. He further advised that the one selling him the cattle went by the name of "Colonel" by his group of men, many of which were still wearing parts of Confederate States Army uniforms and were a rather rough looking lot. July further advised that the men did not have any papers on the cattle and since that was the case, he was happily able to get the animals for a much reduced price. He also advised that the Colonel had sold him the five horses tied up out front as well and those, like the cattle, also did not have a Bill of Sale from their previous owners.

When asked by Joe in which direction the Colonel and his men had gone, July refused to say because the men had threatened his life if he divulged such information. However, figuring out the killers and cattle rustlers' direction of travel did not turn out to be a problem. Lewis with a bit of close looking discovered that one of the outlaws had a horse with a loose shoe. Their horse tracks, including the one horse with a bad shoe, led in the direction of Poteau! Shortly thereafter, the Dodsons and one Samuel July, riding with tied hands, were en route Poteau. As it turned out, the Dodsons were now hot on the trail of their family's killers and July was en route the local Indian jail for purchasing obviously stolen cattle and horses from the Colonel and his gang of killers!

Arriving shortly thereafter in the small town of Poteau, the Dodsons finally located where the local Indian Police were stationed and presented one Samuel July for them to incarcerate for purchasing their stolen cattle and horses. Then enlisting the aid of the Indian Police, the Dodsons, realizing the police could not help them in arresting any white men under Indian or federal laws, just requested they quietly assist the brothers in locating the killers who they figured were somewhere in town. That was soon done when the Indian Police determined that seven men, not local to the area and easily identified as white men, had gone into the local saloon and whorehouse about an hour earlier.

That information was all the Dodson brothers needed as they unlimbered their Sharps rifles and quietly entered the saloon and whorehouse like regular customers. However, upon closer examination of the three men, one could see in their faces that they did so with the look of having 'blood in their eyes' and a serious score to settle with someone! But as was many times the case with civilians not being skilled in hunting down their fellow man, they let their emotions get the better of them. Emotions which clearly showed as they boldly went in through the front door of the saloon and whorehouse as heavily armed men after the individuals who had killed off most of their family and had rustled their cattle. Men, who from the looks on their faces, were not to be toyed with…

Fortunately or unfortunately, depending upon which side you were on, they were inadvertently detected by one of the outlaws who had just finished up with his 'business' with the female owner of the whorehouse. Just as he began leaving the lady's room, through a partially cracked open door, he witnessed the three Dodsons sneaking up the stairs to where all the bedrooms of the 'ladies of the night' were located, carrying their rifles at the ready! Putting 'two and two together', since he had been one of the men who had robbed three sleeping men of their horses and seen those three men who had been in the posse earlier, he carefully shut the door and went out the back window and onto the roof of the whorehouse. As he did, he sneaked by each of the bedroom windows alerting the rest of his henchmen as to the danger close at hand. As the alerted men quickly dressed and made ready to escape, the first man having by now jumped off the roof, had brought around all of their horses and was waiting below the second story windows of the whorehouse for his partners in crime. As the Colonel, who had now decided married or not, he wanted to partake of the 'riches' from the sale of the horses and cattle with the 'fallen doves', he bailed out the window on the backside of the house of ill repute with the rest of his men and ran across the rooftop. Looking over the side of the roof at their horses below, they leaped from the edge of the roof, then leapt onto their saddles and quietly left town. When they did and having been there before, they headed off into the 70,000 square miles of what was known as the lawless Indian Territory.

Meanwhile back at the house of ill repute, the Dodson brothers quietly went from room to room looking for their quarry. Once again, not skilled in any kind of law enforcement related to hunting their fellow human beings, they had allowed their quarry to sneak off unmolested to live and sin another day! Additionally, they had also now alerted their quarry that they were being pursued by three very unusual and determined men with deadly intent in their hearts and eyes...

Frustrated when they realized their quarry had so easily escaped, the Dodson brothers could do nothing but mount their own steeds and head back to their earlier campsite in order to retrieve their provisions so they could continue the chase. But before they did, they talked to all of the 'ladies of the night' that had been visited by the seven killers and in so doing, received a small bit of information overheard between two of their clients talking about where they were heading next, once all of them had 'finished their business' with the ladies.

That information revealed that one of the men had a brother-in-law who owned a small spread near the town of Red Oak located adjacent the Sans Bois Mountains. According to the lady, the men had talked about heading in that direction and 'holing up' until things had 'cooled off'.

Later back at their previous camp, the Dodsons retrieved their gear still tied up in several trees and being that it was now late in the evening, once again threw out their bedrolls and without eating any supper, called it a day. However, this time their horses were picketed right in the area of their campsite, right next to where each of the men would be sleeping...

The following day, the three brothers rode back into the town of Poteau and arranged for the legal sale of all their cattle to an Indian rancher named Blue Duck. Little did the boys realize that Blue Duck was an outlaw of the deadliest kind and they would run across him later on while acting in a law enforcement capacity as Deputy U.S. Marshals. However, with the money from the sale of their father's cattle, they ventured into Poteau and purchased additional provisions for the trip to Red Oak in order to follow up on their 'Red Oak' lead from a 'lady of the night'. However, before leaving town, they visited the local Indian Police and received directions to the location of the small town of Red Oak. Then Joe remembered the cautionary words spoken to them from their local sheriff back in Arkansas, namely one Delbert Garrison. Those cautionary words being related to not going out and looking to initiate a 'neck-tie' party if the boys managed to capture the killers of their family members, but bring them back and turn them over to the law. With those cautionary words still ringing in his ears, Joe requested from the Indian Chief of Police and received shortly thereafter eight sets of leg irons, manacles and keys…just in case.

Then the brothers were surprised over what happened next. Before they headed westerly to the small town of Red Oak on their quest to apprehend their family's killers, they were assigned by the Indian Chief of Police in Poteau an Indian Police Officer who would act as the Dodsons' guide and interpreter. As it turned out, the Indian Police Officer assigned to the Dodsons, who was named Indian Tom, was a highly educated man who had been raised in a Quaker missionary school back in Poteau when he was just a boy. The Dodsons were also soon to discover what a learned resource Indian Tom would prove to be, especially when it came to knowing the lay of the land and being able to utilize his innate law enforcement abilities which came to light many times in their coming relationship.

That first night on the trail, found the three boys and their Indian guide camped several miles outside the small territorial town of Red Oak. Sitting around their campfire after eating a small supper, the men discussed their strategy for the next day's entrance into Red Oak. As a group they figured that to barge into town as strangers on the hunt would more than likely allow the hunted to once again slip away. Finally their Indian guide, older and more skilled in the hunting of human beings, suggested that he go into Red Oak first. There he would inquire around using some of his Indian sources and try and ascertain if the seven hunted men were in fact in town and if so, where they were staying.

Agreeing to that plan, the men soon slipped into their bedrolls and found sleep an easy 'partner' to accept. Daylight the next morning, found the four men gathered around a roaring campfire trying to get warm and waiting for their coffee to boil. Later around several cups of coffee, the men went over their plans for the day. Shortly thereafter, their Indian guide slipped away from their camp and with that, Joe grabbed his Sharps rifle and left camp hunting for the group's supper that coming evening. An hour later the other two brothers who were carrying for their livestock heard a single shot and the look they gave each other signaled that there would be fresh venison for all come suppertime.

Around seven that evening, the three brothers heard the unmistakable sounds of a shod horse walking across the rocky ground coming towards their campsite. Soon their Indian guide rode into view and dismounted. As he did, he had a cup of hot coffee thrust into his eager hands and as he took a welcome sip, the three brothers held their tongues respecting the reserved ways of an Indian when it came to talking, as they waited for any information he possessed regarding his trip into Red Oak and the seven killers they were seeking.

Finally Indian Tom spoke to the Dodsons in his clipped way of speaking in the white man's tongue. "I have good and bad news. My Indian sources advised me that the seven bad white men are indeed in the area. They are now at one of the men's brother-in-law's home just about a mile out from town. However, my Indian sources say the brother-in-law so described is also a bad white man. He is fast with a gun, has a 'hair-trigger' like temper and is known to many of the local Indians as one who does not like the law or any Indians on his land."

Then Indian Tom, having run down on what he had to say for the moment, motioned that he needed another cup of coffee. Joe was fast in getting their Indian friend another cup and after he had taken another sip of the hot brew, began speaking once again. "The bad news is that the brother-in-law, one called "Badlands Bob", is currently running with his two other pals in crime. As is spoken quietly among my people, they don't dare let any of their horses stray over at Bob's ranch for if they do, they up and 'disappear' into his horse corral. That being the case, if one then goes over to Bob's and asks for his horse back, he and the stolen horse are never seen again! So as I now see it, we are not facing seven bad white men, but ten of them if they are ever riled up by the likes of us. The other bad news is that Bob's place is much like a fortress. His home is out in the open so no one can sneak up on him or his horse corrals and it is a log home closely surrounded by a three-foot-high adobe brick wall, making it almost fortress-like. Additionally, its roof is covered with about two feet of dirt so if we were to attack the place, we cannot set it on fire either. So, there you have it and say, that venison cooking over the fire sure smells good. Do you think I can have some supper now? I haven't eaten since breakfast and could not be served any food in town because they do not cater to any Indians in places where the whites eat. So, not having anything to eat all day, I sure could use something to keep my 'slats' from collapsing in," said Indian Tom with a hungry looking grin of anticipation.

Sitting around the fire after a supper of roasted venison and coffee, the talk continued on how best to separate out the seven bad men from Badland Bob's crew. There was much talk about ways in which to attack the issue but all of them kept coming back to the fact that to go directly after the seven would probably get a number of their kind killed in the process. Throughout the discussions by the three brothers on how best to address their burning issue of capture or killing the seven white men, Indian Tom said nothing but just sat there among the men in typical stoic Indian silence.

Finally Indian Tom got up, walked over to his saddle and from its saddlebags removed a bundle of something wrapped up in a towel like rag. Walking back to the three brothers, Indian Tom said, "I have a solution to our problem. I want the two half-breeds that are reported to be running with Bob for stealing other Indians' horses and the rape of several ten-year-old Indian girls. The three of you want the other seven white men in this group, so I propose we work together in order to get done what needs doing. I can't help you with your own people because I have no authority to touch any bad white man. But by working together we can even up the odds somewhat and all of us can get what we want. Back in Poteau when you three arrived and the Chief of Law Enforcement ordered me to accompany you boys, I figured it soon would come to 'hell or high water' if we four got involved and were not careful about how and what we did. So I took from our supplies at the jail and brought along a little 'friend' that always seems to do the trick no matter how tough the situation is when it comes to convincing someone to come along peacefully."

With that, Indian Tom carefully unrolled the dirty towel holding his mystery bundle and exposed a large number of sticks of 20% dynamite! For a second the Dodson brothers recoiled back just a bit realizing what Indian Tom was holding, and his being so close to the fire made all three of the brothers instantly nervous. Then James Dodson got a huge smile on his face and said, "Damn, Boys! We got just the trick for what we need but how the hell do we get close enough to plant that damn stuff alongside Bob's cabin if he will not come out and give up the seven killers we are after? I damn sure do not want to be the one trying to run up to that fort of a cabin through a hail of bullets all aimed at me and launch that bundle of joy onto the side of their cabin. That is just asking to get one shot all to hell or blown all to bits, whichever comes first and neither option really appeals to me and my miserable carcass."

"Well, here is how I am looking at it. My two Indian rapists that I am pursuing are looking at being hung once I get them back to the jail and after their trials in Poteau. So, I doubt they will surrender to me or any of my kind any time soon. I would also imagine, after what the three of you have told me about the other seven men and what they did to your kin, that they are none too eager to surrender to the three of you either. No matter how one looks at it, all nine of the men, not including Badlands Bob, we are after are looking at hanging offenses if they are ever taken alive. That being said and seeing that the three of you are carrying those long range shooting Sharps rifles, I suggest we give the lot of them a chance to surrender right off the bat. Figuring that will get us nowhere, I suggest you three let those Sharps 'buffalo guns' speak for themselves. If nothing else, any men we kill in such an exchange, reduces the odds of bad men that we are facing. Then I would imagine the remaining live ones after our initial fire fight, will flee into that fort of a cabin, hole up and try and wait us out. Wait us out that they can easily do because they have the water from that little creek flowing right by their cabin, I am sure they have provisions inside their cabin and with that, there is no way we can get at them short of using the dynamite. So, I guess that is our plan. We surprise them, shoot those that don't surrender and come nightfall, sneak up to their cabin and blow them all to hell," said Indian Tom with more than just a touch of Indian reality in his voice.

Just the way Indian Tom spoke and in such tones of finality, the three Dodsons could easily tell that he had seen and been a part of a lot of 'hell' in the Indian Territory during his time as an Indian Police Officer, and a little more was not going to make much of any difference to his way of thinking.

The following morning, the four men made ready at their campsite, put out their fire after cooking up a mess of venison steaks for their breakfasts and some extra to eat later on in case regular meals became an issue, saddled their horses and pack animals and rode out from their camp in single file behind Indian Tom. There were no words spoken among the men and none were needed because of the momentous events of the deadly moment soon to be faced by all of the men at Badland Bob's 'built like a fortress' cabin site...

Shortly thereafter, Indian Tom stopped their little party just outside the town of Red Oak and spoke in his native tongue to several Indians walking along the dusty road on their way into town. After receiving the answers to his questions from the Indian travelers, the four men proceeded on towards town. A short time later, the four men split up into two pairs, the men rode through the town separately and at different times so they would not arouse any undue suspicion being strangers and all. Following that ruse, the men got together again once out of sight of those in Red Oak, then rode out to Badland Bob's ranch without further incident.

Setting up their hidden campsite a short distance away overlooking Bob's ranch house, the men picketed their horses unseen and out of the way in a small draw. Leaving their horses and crawling up onto a small hill overlooking Bob's cabin, the four men spent the rest of the day watching the activity of the ten men below at Bob's ranch house in order to determine their patterns of activity. That night, the men slept in a cold camp and went without eating any supper other than some of the cold venison steaks they had brought along from their previous camp. The next day was more of the same when it came to watching all the men's activities down at the ranch house and looking for any kind of weakness one could exploit during any arrest procedures attempted. As it turned out, all ten men at the ranch house spent the entire day in the cattle corrals branding cattle, dehorning a number of them and castrating a number of the calves.

The next morning way before dawn, the four men moved in closer to Bob's ranch house and set up in predetermined positions whereby they had commanding views of the entire area as well as open shooting lanes and then waited out the cold that came with the predawn. Right at dawn, the back door to the ranch house opened and two of Colonel Tim's ex-Cavalrymen staggered out and walked over to the nearby outhouse holding wiping papers in hand. Being that the outhouse was one with two holes, both men entered at the same time and when they did, little did they realize that they had just forfeited any further chance of freedom…

Behind the outhouse lay Joe and Lewis Dodson with their Sharps rifles in hand. With Joe now watching the back door to the ranch house as a precaution, Lewis quietly threw open the outhouse door catching both men with their pants down around their ankles taking care of business. He then drew down on the men from about four feet distant with the 'business end' of his Sharps rifle! As he did, Lewis made sure through hand signals that both men had best remain silent as to the situation they now faced or hell would be coming their way in the way of a .50 caliber, one ounce rifled slug! That being the case, both men previously 'taking care of business', realized to not obey the command for silence would soon land one or both of them in a lot hotter place than the cold and smelly outhouse they currently occupied...

Making another hand gesture, Lewis made sure the two men removed the pistols they had worn to the outhouse, dropped them into the 'bore-hole' of the outhouse and then had them pull up their britches. Both men were then quickly marched outside and behind the outhouse and there they were shackled with leg irons and manacles and then had pieces of their shirts ripped into rags and tightly tied around their mouths so they could not sound out their alarm of capture if given the chance. Then the two men were laid face down out of sight behind the outhouse and told in no uncertain terms to be still and quiet. Then Lewis and Joe once again took up their nearby defensive positions watching the back door of the ranch house for any more activity from those men still inside. This they did because there were no windows on the backside of the cabin in which to observe any inside activities.

About twenty minutes later, another man exited the back door of the ranch house, walked over to the front of the outhouse, knocked on its door and informed the occupants he believed to be inside that breakfast was ready. When that chap turned around to walk back to the ranch house, he was surprised to find himself facing the rather large bore of the serious end of a Sharps rifle leveled at his belly! When his eyes looked up from the end of the rifle barrel to its holder, he could see that the man's index finger on his strong hand was upon the trigger and the index finger from his off hand was on his lips indicating 'silence'! Within minutes, that man was also disarmed, shackled, and manacled, and had a part of his shirt torn off and wrapped firmly around his mouth for the silence it engendered. Then that man was also laid face down in the dirt and out of sight behind the outhouse as Joe and Lewis once again returned back to their nearby places of hiding waiting for what was to come.

As it now stood, the odds had been reduced from ten outlaws to just seven with the capture of the 'outhouse three', compared to the three still very determined Dodson brothers and one Indian Tom policeman from the Indian Police in Poteau. But the stillness of the morning was then shattered when Joe and Lewis heard the loud voice of their brother James coming from the front of the nearby ranch house barking out orders to "Stand down, lower your pistol belt and lay down upon the ground!"

The stillness that followed those commands

was quickly broken with the sound of a quick pistol shot fired by a surprised and wanted Indian half-breed followed by the telling booming report from a .50 caliber Sharps being fired in anger by James from his concealed place of hiding! When that shot was fired, Joe heard a very distinct 'thud' of a .50 caliber lead bullet smashing through soft human tissue! No two ways about it, their dad Albert had taught the boys well when it came to accurately shooting with his words of "aim small, miss small"! Seconds later, the still morning air was once again rent with the sounds of many pistols being discharged at real and imagined targets from the six remaining men now trapped inside the cabin from out the three window openings in the side and front of the cabin and out the open front doorway! Those lighter reports were then followed by the heavier sounds of rifles being fired back in response by James and Indian Tom from their places of concealment in front of the ranch house. It was then that the back door to the ranch house burst open and out sprinted two of Colonel Jackson's men at a dead run as they headed for the cover and escape they figured the nearby outhouse provided.

"Hold it right there!" yelled Joe at the two men sprinting his way from the back of the ranch house. Surprised at now being faced by two other men, both of Jackson's men reached for their pistols only to find themselves instantly being spun around and dropped to the ground as heavy .50 caliber rifle slugs violently tore through their bodies, blowing huge chunks of flesh and bits of bone out their backs! As was the case, both Dodson brothers using the outhouse as cover, who were also trained in the art and use of firearms by their father Albert at an early age, killed the two running for cover Cavalrymen before they even 'cleared leather'! Both fleeing men were dead before they even hit the ground and in so doing, joined one of their half-breed Indian compatriots from the front of the ranch house who had just run afoul of James's .50 caliber Sharps when he had failed to obey the order of 'standing down'.

Then all shooting stopped as the remaining four trapped men in the ranch house, failing to see any of their assailants within shooting range, held their fire in order to conserve ammunition. Then the booming voice of Indian Tom rent the air telling the trapped men in the ranch house who he was, that they were surrounded, under arrest and for all of them to come out and surrender or suffer the consequences.

"You can go to hell! If you want us, come in and get us," boomed out the voice of Badlands Bob from inside the solidly built and fortified cabin.

"I will tell all of you one more time to drop your weapons, raise your hands and come out or we will see to it that you wished you had," yelled back Indian Tom from his place of concealment over by the nearby horse corrals.

"Like I said, you and yours can go to hell!" yelled back Badlands Bob. "Come to think of it, if you want to start your journey to hell, why don't all of you try and rush us. If you do, we will be waiting for you and sure as all get-out can start every one of you on that journey to hell," he bellowed back, sounding like that of a gored bull.

Indian Tom leaned over and said to James, "We don't dare try our hand at rushing them. They have us over a barrel by being barricaded inside that fortified cabin. Near as I figure it, your brothers have already killed at least two of the outlaws from the sounds of rifle fire coming from behind the cabin. But that still leaves a passel of them behind those thick walls and us at a stand-off. Looks like we wait until dark and when they can't see us moving around, we get back together with your brothers and plan our next move."

Lewis just nodded as he kept a sharp eye peeled on the front door of the cabin, as he slipped another cigar-sized cartridge into his Sharps rifle and kept his cover behind a large horse watering trough next to the corral.

For the rest of the day, the men trapped inside

the cabin kept looking for any sign of a target at which to unlimber their artillery upon, while those men on the outside just held their position in hiding since they held the 'high ground'.

Come darkness and using their pre-arranged gathering call of a great horned owl, Indian Tom summoned together the other Dodson brothers and their prisoners from behind the ranch house for a powwow on what they were going to do next to root out the outlaws hiding inside the cabin. It was only then that Indian Tom and James realized that Badland Bob's numbers had been reduced by two killed at the back of the cabin and another three captured.

Once together and out of view from the trapped men still inside the cabin, Indian Tom laid out his next plan of attack to the Dodson brothers. This he did outside of the hearing range of the three still shackled, gagged and manacled prisoners the Dodson men had brought with them from the outhouse. As Indian Tom laid out his plans for getting the four outlaws from inside their fortified cabin without any harm befalling the attackers, his reasoning found all of the Dodsons nodding in agreement to his daring plan. Then with the Dodson brothers guarding their prisoners, Indian Tom quietly slipped away and off into the darkness. An hour later, the Dodsons heard the almost inaudible approach of Indian

Tom as he returned with the 'makings' of their next planned move on how to capture the four remaining outlaws still safely ensconced within the fortified walls of their cabin. The rest of the night, the four men on the hunt took turns fitfully sleeping awaiting the coming dawn and their next move calculated to bring the outlaws still hidden in the cabin 'to bay'.

Finally came a reddened dawn-colored sun the next morning, followed by the typical chill in the air that comes with the day's arrival. As the sun continued rising casting its rays earthward, it found the Dodsons still surrounding the cabin. Minutes later saw Indian Tom quietly moving toward the windowless side of the cabin holding the remaining four outlaws with a mysterious looking, 'baby-sized' bundle cradled in his arms. Moving up along the windowless wall on the north side of the cabin, Indian Tom removed a sizeable object from the bundle's cloth wrapping, knelt down and was doing something to the contents of the bundle as it now lay out of sight. Then Indian Tom gave an 'alert' hand signal to his compatriots watching and waiting, stood up quickly and tossed his mysterious and now smoking bundle up onto the center of the fortified cabin's rooftop.

With that hurried movement, Indian Tom took off running as he headed for the cover of a horse trough next to a set of corrals. Diving over the horse trough and remaining out of sight, Indian Tom waited for the second stage in his plan to 'evict' the four outlaws into the Indian lawman's hands and those of the waiting Dodson brothers.

BOOOOM! went a thunderous roar in the early morning's normally quiet air, spooking off a mess of black-billed magpies into the air which minutes earlier had been sitting on a nearby corral enclosing a number of resting cattle! That explosion was immediately followed by a huge plume of whitish-gray smoke, flying dirt and a large number of roof timbers erupting high into the air! Simultaneously, great clouds of smoke blew out through the now blown open back door of the cabin and out every window's opening with the force and effect of a small 'Oklahoma spring twister'!

Immediately out the front door of the cabin burst four men yelling at the top of their lungs and holding their ears with both hands from the downward concussive blast from the just thrown bundle of dynamite, which had just blown a huge hole in the cabin's roof! Jumping up and down in eardrum pain like a mess of Indians doing a war dance, the four men hardly noticed being quickly surrounded in the process by three serious looking brothers holding Sharps rifles leveled at the temporarily disoriented but still heavily armed outlaws.

It was about then that the still-in-pain outlaws noticed the three armed men moving closer in on them with their rifles leveled! Colonel Jackson seeing the close at hand danger, went for his pistol and immediately was 'rewarded' by having his mouth smashed inward with the butt of a heavy Sharps rifle meeting his mouth at a rather high rate of speed! When the Colonel hit the ground, one of his men, named John Atkins, the man who had initiated the earlier gang rapes and killing of the Dodson women back at their home place by all of the Colonel's followers, realized the trouble they were facing and went for his pistol regardless of his still loudly 'ringing' eardrums!

Seeing John's threatening action, Joe Dodson swung his rifle barrel toward the man making such a threatening move for his Colt .45 revolver. Joe, not being a small man, swung the rifle barrel upward with such authority, that upon impact with John's head, it lifted the struck man clear off his feet and deposited his crumpled form some six feet away with nary a movement of life! Observing those two deadly actions being committed on his fellow henchmen, Badlands Bob and an Indian renegade, "Herschel Tulley", jerked their arms skyward in order to avoid any like 'rifle metal to the head' actions taking place on their miserable carcasses...

It was at that moment in time that Indian Tom

slipped into the melee, jerked Herschel's pistol from his holster, dropped him to the ground with a knee to the back, and then slipped a set of manacles onto the man's wrists without any further fanfare. Standing back up, Indian Tom coldly said, "Now, Herschel, try raping another ten-year-old girl after killing her mom. The last thing you will see after your trial is me standing in the crowd of folks happily watching the hangman slipping the noose around your neck and the hood being placed over your head just before you swing into the air and go off to meet the rest of the 'Cloud People'!"

"Don't hit me! Don't hit me," yelled Badlands Bob, now that he didn't have the stout walls of his cabin protecting him so he could shoot off his mouth without any fear of retaliation, and after observing the physical actions violently taken against his cohorts in crime.

"I have no immediate plans for you, Bob. Especially since these men are taking the Colonel and the rest of his men back to Fort Smith to stand trial for the raping and murdering of their kin back in Arkansas. However, I am aware that a federal warrant has been sworn out for you by the court back in Fort Smith for cattle rustling. With that in mind and since I have no authority over any white man in the Indian Territory, I am sure that the Dodsons will see to it that you are delivered into the hands of the proper authorities right along with the rest of their prisoners," said Indian Tom, with a 'glad to be rid of your kind' smile on his bronzed and weathered face.

"Turn around," said Lewis, as he jerked Bob's pistol from his holster and, handing his rifle and pistol off to his brother, placed the manacles over Bob's wrists to prevent any further danger to the group. Then Lewis walked over to the still inert form of John Atkins, one of the rapists of his two sisters and his mother although unknown to Dodson at that moment in time, placed a set of manacles around his wrists, lifted him bodily up and dragged him over to the pile of now squirming, other manacled men.

About then the four men realized that the dynamite blast had set the cabin's inside timbers afire and now it was merrily blazing away! Dragging the four manacled men further away from the fire's heat now being generated, Joe and Lewis walked over to the nearby corral of now loudly bellowing and terrified cattle, opened the gate and let the panicked animals flee from their confines, as they ran out onto the nearby grassy plains.

With Lewis and Joe watching over their prisoners, Indian Tom and James walked over to the barn, and together dragged out a wagon with high-walled sides that Badlands Bob had stored inside. As James searched the barn for harnesses and such, Indian Tom walked over to the corral where the horses were kept, removed several bridles from a corral post and brought back to the barn two hell-for-stout looking horses. With that, both horses were hitched to the wagon and it was then driven over to where their four prisoners were seated or in the case of Atkins, still laid out. There those four outlaws and the three previously captured were bodily loaded into the back of the wagon, which had been previously partially filled with hay from the barn's haymow by James so the men could comfortably ride or sleep on their journey back to Poteau. Then the four men returned to the horse corral and bridled up Colonel Jackson's seven Cavalrymen's horses which the Dodson brothers figured they had coming as a result over what their riders had done earlier to their family. Joe then opened up all the corral gates and let the rest of Badland Bob's livestock contained therein out so they could run wild and not starve inside their corral after everyone had left the area. Additionally, Joe did so because where Badlands Bob and the rest of his cohorts were going, namely jail and trial in Fort Smith Arkansas, they would have no use for any riding stock for a long time, if ever...

Lewis then drove the wagon and prisoners

back to their 'spike' camp while Joe, Indian Tom and James walked the distance. Once there, the men retrieved all of their horses and camp gear and, with the black curls of smoke from Badland Bob's furiously burning cabin and now some of his close at hand corrals as a backdrop darkening the sky, began their long ride back to and through the small town of Red Oak.

An hour or so just before dusk, the Dodsons and Indian Tom rode into Red Oak along with their prisoners riding sullenly in the back of the wagon. When they rode onto the main street in the small town, curious people rolled out from the only saloon to watch the caravan of men and wagon full of obviously manacled prisoners roll on by.

It was then that Indian Tom noticed another Indian named Blue Duck closely watching his party roll through the streets of town. He also noticed two of Blue Duck's confederates intently looking on as well, as the wagon with its seven prisoners slowly rolled on by. Without letting on what he had just observed, the experienced Indian Policeman let his horse drift slowly back to the end of their party and quietly advised Joe that they had best make camp outside of town. Joe looked over at Indian Tom realizing he had seen something sinister in the group of men tumbling out from the saloon looking on, and did not let on that a quiet warning had just been passed from one man to another.

Once outside of Red Oak and away from peering eyes, Joe rode up alongside Indian Tom and asked, "What the dickens did you see back in town, Tom, that set you off and made you uneasy?"

Indian Tom was quiet for a moment and then said, "Joe, those two heavyset Indians next to the other Indian with the red shirt standing by the hitching post watching us go by were outlaw confederates of 'red shirt'. That red shirt-wearing man is known to me as Blue Duck and he is a bad one, and it is just a matter of time before I catch him breaking the law. He is a known killer and rustler of horses and cattle from not only his own people but anyone else who is not on to him for what he represents."

"Damn, Tom, are you sure about that fellow Blue Duck? Because if you are, that is the fellow my brothers and I sold all of our cattle to in order to be quickly free of them so we could hunt down the killers of our family! If we had known he was such a 'bad actor', damned if we would have sold him a single steer."

"That is OK. You not being familiar with some of our bad Indians out here in Indian Territory, just did what you thought was right at the time. But Blue Duck is a close friend of Badlands Bob and that could mean trouble for us if we are not careful. Knowing him, I think we had best keep a sharp eye peeled because I can see him sending his henchmen to waylay us along the trail and try and release his friend and fellow confederate, Bob," said Indian Tom quietly.

An hour later found the Dodson brothers, Indian Tom and their four prisoners camped along a small stream running through some low foothills several miles east of Red Oak. As James and Lewis carefully watched the four prisoners just let out from the wagon so they could relieve themselves, Joe and Indian Tom began setting up their out of the way campsite.

Prior to arriving at their campsite, Joe had jumped a small buck from out of a small draw and with one well-placed shot from his rifle, had dropped the animal. While Indian Tom built a fire, Joe dressed out the deer and removed a number of steaks from the animal for the men's supper. James and Lewis then seated their four prisoners around the fire as their supper was roasting over the fire, while Joe and Indian Tom laid out their bedrolls nearby. As for the seven prisoners, they would be sleeping in the hay in the back of their wagon where they could be shackled to the wagon's oaken floorboards and closely watched.

After supper, the seven prisoners were reloaded back into their wagon and the Dodson brothers and Indian Tom retreated to their bedrolls and talked over the day's events. Then remembering that his brother James snored loudly when he slept, Joe moved his bedroll about ten yards away from the rest of the men and placed it under a juniper tree. Just before the men went to sleep, Indian Tom and Joe made sure each of their prisoners was still properly manacled to the oaken ribbing along the inside of the back of the wagon in order to prevent their escapes.

Then as the fire slowly burned down to its embers, the tired men drifted off to sleep after a long and hard day knowing their prisoners were firmly secured on their bed of hay inside the wagon and their horses were double hobbled and feeding nearby. When they did, just as Joe had figured, his brother James began snoring so loudly that he even woke up God... With that, Joe was glad he was sleeping a distance away from his noisy brother because he suspected that tomorrow would be another long and taxing day.

BOOM! went the blast from a ten gage shotgun into the three men sleeping together in the same area not far from the wagon! The two ounces of buckshot from the shotgun blast tore into one of the three sleeping men, namely Indian Tom, exploding into his chest area and killing him instantly! The explosive report of the ten gage shotgun going off just feet away from where the men had been sleeping, caused James and Lewis to explode from their deep sleep into wide awake, straight up from their bedrolls in fear and surprise! When they had settled down and had gathered their wits about them as to what had happened, they saw they were now faced by two Indian men standing just feet away holding two double barreled shotguns leveled at their bellies!

"Hold it right there, unless you want what that damn Indian Policeman got, you sons-a-bitch-es!" growled The Apache Kid. "Kick those guns away from your bedrolls," growled another man named Johnny Crow, as he held the barrel of his ten gage shotgun menacingly level with Lewis's belly from just six feet away!

Both Lewis and James toed their gun belts and Sharps rifles away from their bedrolls, with their hands raised as high as they could stretch to avoid getting what Indian Tom had just received from the shotgun blast from one of the two rough looking Indian men. "Either of you men makes a move and I will see to it that you have your guts splattered all over this ground for the ants to enjoy come daylight tomorrow!" growled The Apache Kid through his heavily stained tobacco colored teeth. With those words of warning, James and Lewis tried to even breathe shallowly so as not to set off the evil looking men holding a shotgun on the both of them. But both of them did manage a knowing smile over what they were seeing and what was about to happen…

WHOOMP! went the barrel of a Colt .45 across the side of The Apache Kid's head from behind, as he was 'buffaloed' with such force that he dropped to the ground and out cold like a stone! Johnny Crow, taken by surprise over what had just occurred to his partner in crime from an unseen assailant moving up on them from behind, quickly turned his head to see what had happened, only to have the end of a Colt .45 revolver barrel thrust into his right eye socket with such force that he screeched out in intense agony, dropped his shotgun and clutched his now madly bleeding and rapidly discharging eye! In fact, that revolver barrel had been thrust so violently into Johnny's eye that the front sight had just ripped open his eyeball, releasing all of its eyesight-giving fluid!

"First one of you who makes any kind of a move and I will kill him where he stands," yelled Joe, who upon hearing the shotgun blast that had killed Indian Tom moments earlier, had bailed out from his bedroll unobserved from a number of yards away where he had been sleeping under a juniper tree. Then observing what had just happening, had sneaked around behind the two armed men in the dying light of their campfire, had 'buffaloed' one man and had thrust the end of his pistol barrel into another man's eye socket with such force that it had exploded the man's eyeball, blinding him forever in that eye!

As Johnny Crow rolled around on the ground in extreme pain over having one of his eyeballs ripped open and with The Apache Kid laid out inert on the ground, Lewis and James hustled over to their previously kicked away firearms, quickly armed themselves and prepared to meet with deadly force anyone else who planned on invading their campsite and causing them harm. Seeing no further danger from outside sources of humanity, Lewis grabbed up The Apache Kid, dragged him over to the wagon, removed his gun belt and manacled the still unconscious man's right hand to a wagon wheel spoke. Their last set of manacles went around the wrists of the still screaming out in pain Johnny Crow over his madly bleeding and rapidly draining eye-fluid exploded eyeball!

Realizing the two men now manacled were the same two Indian men who had been watching them from the saloon closely as they moved through Red Oak earlier in the day and been seen talking to Blue Duck, and were the only two culprits in country around their campsite, they turned their attention to their friend, Indian Tom. It quickly became apparent due to the location in which Indian Tom had suffered the full force of the ten gage shotgun blast that he was now with what he had earlier called deceased Indians' Cloud People!

Figuring the Blue Duck person had sent the two men to kill the Dodsons and Indian Tom, not to mention releasing his friend Badlands Bob, James and Lewis were instantly hell bent on saddling up, returning to Red Oak, looking up Blue Duck and killing him where he stood! Fortunately, older brother Joe was able to drum some sense into his two hot-headed brothers and in so doing, a semblance of calm once again returned to their campsite.

Joe then realized they now had nine prisoners to turn over to the proper Indian and federal authorities and that he was duty bound to do so. Especially in light of the killing and loss of his friend and helping hand Indian Policeman, Indian Tom. That was the least he figured he could do in order to right the wrongful killing of his friend and he was damned sure that chore would be carried out come 'hell or high water'!

Shortly thereafter, their fire was built up once again and now all three brothers were on high alert just in case anyone else had any ideas of intervening and releasing any or all of their now nine prisoners. To the brothers' way of thinking, especially after the untimely death of their friend, Indian Tom, anyone harboring such ideas would now be facing three Sharps .50 caliber rifles, three Colt .45's, along with the associated firepower that would come from the acquisition of the two culprits', now prisoners, double barreled ten gage shotguns! In short, the 'hellfire and brimstone' befalling any future prisoner-releasing miscreants from the now alert, heavily armed and renowned shooters of the highest degree Dodson brothers, spoke sheer volumes of the deadly violence to come to any and all actions by such ill-advised mere mortals...

Come daylight the next morning, found the three brothers heading for the Indian Territorial town of Poteau with their nine prisoners jammed into the back of their wagon. James now drove the wagon trailing his riding horse, their two packhorses and Indian Tom's horse carrying his now dead master slung over and tied down on the back of his horse. Riding 'shotgun' alongside that strange caravan with a wagon full of manacled men trailing several horses, one of which was carrying a dead man, rode the other two brothers, Joe and Lewis.

As Joe rode alongside the prisoner-loaded wagon, he figured the two Indians who had invaded their campsite the evening before and had killed Indian Tom, and Herschel, the Indian rapist caught back at Bob's cabin, would be handed over to the Indian Police in Poteau for adjudication in their tribal courts of law for the crimes they had committed. As for the remaining six white men, five of whom were Colonel Jackson and his ruffians who had killed off most of the Dodson clan back in Arkansas and the remaining white man was Badlands Bob already wanted by the federal authorities in Fort Smith, Arkansas, for rustling. Hence, that was where they all were headed to be delivered as per Sheriff Del Garrison's earlier cautionary words to the Dodson brothers regarding that justice be served and that it not be in the form of a lynch mob's request.

Little did the three brothers realize at the time, that they had just gotten their first 'taste' of what it felt like to hunt and catch the 'most dangerous game', namely their fellow human beings. Nor did they share those thoughts with each other about those revelations, that they liked what they were experiencing in what they were doing for their fellow man… In short, as a result of their most recent experience, each brother discovered unto himself, that they truly enjoyed 'hunting his fellow man' and doing so for those less fortunate in their time of need…

Two days later, the wagon full of prisoners and three tired brothers rode into the town of Poteau in Indian Territory. However, that entire journey chasing the killers of their family members now evidenced subtle changes in the attitudes, psychology and behavior of the three brothers. For some reason, they sat differently in their saddles, like they knew what they were doing and in so doing, rightfully belonged there doing for others. Additionally, they unknowingly found themselves trusting no one when it came to riding into a strange town while transporting hard case killers, rapist and livestock rustlers. Unlike when they had ridden into Red Oak with their prisoners, the three brothers now rode and remained vigilant of anything and everything that looked like it was unusual or out of place when it came to their presence among the lawless. Henceforth, the three brothers would work as a team and trust little of anything or anyone that looked suspicious or unusually interested in their presence or what they were doing.

Riding up to the Indian Police Station in Poteau, Joe dismounted and entered the building while his two brothers provided 'shotgun' coverage over any events occurring back at their wagon load of hard case prisoners. For to bring such hard cases that far and then lose them at that juncture in time because of their carelessness, was not an option in the minds of the brothers. Shortly thereafter the front of the Indian Police building emitted several Indian Police officers who immediately and happily took possession of The Apache Kid, Johnny Crow and Herschel Tully for the illegal deeds all those men had committed. Those three Indians were briskly escorted into the building and quickly placed in their cells to await their forthcoming trials for previously committed illegalities in the Indian Territory. Then the Indian Police returned and escorted the six white prisoners into the building and jailed those men as well at the request of Joe so they would be safely confined for the night.

Joe just figured that he and his brothers needed a decent night's rest in the town of Poteau without the intervention of other outlaws trying to free the rest of their prisoners before they headed for Fort Smith, Arkansas. That the Indian Police Chief had acceded to and with the white prisoners safely locked up in the Indian jail, the brothers headed for the local boardinghouse for a much needed bath, a good supper and a decent night's sleep.

The next morning after their six prisoners had eaten breakfast, they were manacled once again, put back into their leg irons and loaded into the wagon for transport to Fort Smith, Arkansas. All six prisoners, realizing they had not outrun the long arm of the law by now being en route the federal lockup in Fort Smith, remained sullen and uncommunicative. In fact, their self-confident attitudes were almost like the prisoners knew they had outlaw help on the way that would see to it that they would be soon released and away from the physical control of the Dodson brothers...

However, a serious physical and mental change had occurred within the ranks of the three brothers. First, they had telegraphed their telegraph office in their town of Booneville, Arkansas, with a message for their younger brother and Sam to meet them in Fort Smith for the trial of Colonel Jackson and his henchmen killers of their family members so they could testify at the upcoming trials. Second, the outside appearance of the brothers had changed after just one day in Poteau. All three brothers now wore gun belts and holsters holding not one but two Colt .45 pistols! Further, brothers Lewis and James now sported in addition to their coveted Sharps rifles in scabbards, the two ten gage shotguns seized from The Apache Kid and Johnny Crow as extra artillery in case close-in work was needed in order to see their prisoners safely to Fort Smith. Last, all three brothers, now realizing that justice would soon be close at hand, wore the looks of men more than determined not to be deterred in their legal and moral missions.

Heading northeast towards the small town of Panama in the Indian Territory, older brother Joe led the prisoner wagon being driven by Lewis with James riding 'shotgun' in the position as an 'outrider'. That evening, the men finally pulled up in front of the Indian Police building in Panama and had that Chief of Police place their prisoners into several of his jail cells for safekeeping as had been done in Poteau. Relieved over the fact that the almost final leg of their journey was over, the three brothers celebrated at Ma Perkins Boardinghouse in Panama with several drinks and a good old fashioned dinner with homemade bread and pies like their mother used to make.

However sitting there in the front dining room of the boardinghouse by a window, Lewis chanced seeing an Indian walking by the front door of the eating establishment for just an instant. That Indian looked familiar and then Lewis all of a sudden jumped up and ran for the front door like a man on a mission! Racing outside, he looked both ways up and down the boardwalk and did not see that Indian previously observed walking around anywhere. But he knew he had seen that man somewhere else and that did not sit well with him as he looked both ways once again in the off chance he had just missed seeing him walking in among the general population. But alas, the mystery Indian that was sticking in Lewis's craw was gone from sight. Walking slowly back into the dining area, Lewis was met with questioning looks from his two brothers over his rather strange antics.

Sitting back down to his meal, it was then that the mystery person's identity was solved in his mind. "Damn, I am sure that I just saw Blue Duck walk by the front of the building on the boardwalk! However, by the time I got to the front door, I looked both ways up and down the street but did not see him again. But I damn well know it was the same man we saw in Red Oak wearing that bright red shirt that Indian Tom identified as Blue Duck, a 'bad Indian'. Then shortly after that, we got ambushed by The Apache Kid and Johnny Crow and that was when Indian Tom was killed."

"Are you sure over what you saw, Lewis?" asked Joe, who was now starting to get concerned.

"Damn right. I never forget a face, especially that one after what happened to us later that evening at our campsite outside of the town of Red Oak," Lewis slowly responded.

"Well, if that bastard is in town, I do not think he is here to see the sights. My guess is he has been trailing us looking for the opportunity to get his friend Badlands Bob released from our custody. Was he with anyone else?" asked Joe.

"No, he was all by himself. But I got a damn good look at him as he peered through the window looking at us as we sat here eating our supper. I swear Blue Duck knows we are here and if we are here, he knows his friend is close by. He must also suspect we are heading for Fort Smith because that is where all the federal law emanates from that is found operating in the Indian Territory, and I wonder if he thinks we three are federal lawmen," said Lewis slowly.

"Well, that means if he is to take us on, it will have to be along the way somewhere tomorrow where an ambush can be successfully pulled off. Because after that, barring our wagon breaking down or a horse going lame, we will be in Fort Smith late tomorrow and then his chances of springing Badlands Bob are not going to be possible with all the lawmen surrounding that area plus the type of secure lockup he and his cohorts are going to be placed into," said Joe.

The following morning way before daylight and before the prisoners had eaten their breakfast, they had been manacled, leg-ironed and loaded into the Dodsons' wagon. Then Joe paid the Indian jailer for the prisoners' previous evening's meal and the men set out heading for the small town of Spiro which was still just inside the Indian Territory. There they planned on resting their horses, letting the prisoners out to relieve themselves and then continuing on to Fort Smith, still a long day's ride away.

Arriving later in the day at the town of Spiro, the brothers took care of business and then once again headed out for Fort Smith. That they did with an urgency because the time for Blue Duck and his allies to ambush the brothers if they planned on doing so and allow the prisoners to escape was drawing nigh, especially if they wanted to do so before the Indian Territory with its lawlessness was left behind.

BOOM-BOOM-BOOM! went three quick rifle shots around noon from a small glen of trees, as the brothers slowly passed by on the deserted road with their wagon and horses! Lewis, who was driving the wagon, had a large chunk of wood blown from out of his wagon seat just inches away from his rump as the shot taken missed! James, who was riding alongside his brother, had his horse shot out from underneath him, with the bullet passing clear through his horse and lodging painfully inside his leather boot! As for Joe, the bullet shot at him passed so closely to his head that he felt the air's displacement as the heavy slug screamed by!

Scrambling off his staggering horse and jerking his Sharps rifle out from the scabbard all in one fluid motion before his horse fell, James snapped off a shot at the puff of black powder smoke in the brush near the glen of trees from whence the shot had come. "OOOWEE!" screamed a voice from the stand of dense elderberry brush behind the smoke cloud, as James's accurately placed slug had found a 'home' in his mystery ambush shooter!

"Duck!" yelled Lewis to James, who was standing alongside their now stopped wagon, as he unlimbered his ten gage double barrel and let fly with both barrels loaded with buckshot at the brush from whence had come the shooting as evidenced by the still lingering cloud of black powder smoke. That double load of buckshot elicited another louder scream and then silence!

Then the crap really hit the fan as Badlands Bob, even manacled and leg-ironed as he was, rose up from the back of the wagon and tried to drag Lewis over backwards from his seat in the wagon and into the rest of the prisoners' eagerly reaching hands, so they could disarm him by taking his pistols and shotgun!

Seeing what was happening to his brother, James jerked his double barreled shotgun from the scabbard on his now dead horse and smashed its heavy barrel down upon the head of Badlands Bob as he tried wrestling Lewis from off his front seat on the wagon! That blow dropped Bob onto the floor of the wagon, as John Atkins then lunged forward towards Lewis and grabbed for one of his revolvers!

BOOM! went James's ten gage from just four feet away, blowing John Atkins, Colonel Jackson's man who had engineered the raping of all the Dodson women when they had raided the home place many days earlier, COMPLETELY

IN HALF! That close at hand blast stunned and cowed all the rest of the prisoners in the back of the wagon and displaced any further thoughts of escaping, realizing that James still had one more barrel with a live round of buckshot contained therein and was prepared to use it on whomever wished to 'receive' 2¼ quarter ounces of hot lead...

Joe in the meantime, had dismounted and spotting a man running through the brush carrying a rifle, drew down on him and with one shot, sent him sprawling onto the ground in death. As Joe quickly reloaded his single shot Sharps rifle, all the while mentally praising his dad, Albert, for teaching him to be such a good shooter, saw another Indian-looking man vaulting onto the back of his horse and briskly riding off. An Indian rider who obviously did not want any further part of the action back on the road near the wagon full of prisoners. Lewis still continued looking from atop the wagon box for any other ambush assailants with one eye, while keeping the other on his now five cowed and terrified prisoners. James was also looking from his position alongside his dead horse for any other shooters and finding none, began removing his saddle and tack from his dead horse and pitching it into the back of the wagon.

Joe on the other hand was now riding through

the forested glen with his Sharps rifle held at the ready, looking for any other ambushers lurking nearby. Riding by the man he had just shot with his Sharps rifle earlier, he stopped and looked down at the body. As it turned out, the man lying on the ground was obviously an Indian! As he did, Joe just shook his head at the lethal damage a Sharps rifle bullet could do at fifty yards! Then he rode his horse over to where Lewis pointed out from whence the first shooter had fired at them from his place of concealment in the elderberry bushes adjacent the roadway. Once again riding over and looking down, Joe could see where the man had been initially hit in his right shoulder and then when Lewis had unlimbered both barrels from his shotgun from such close range, that had been the final ticket. It was obvious that at least a dozen of the buckshot fired by Lewis had lethally found their marks, as evidenced by the bloody wounds on the man's face and body! Once again, the dead man lying alongside Joe's horse appeared to be of Indian descent! The thought that Blue Duck, an Indian, had once again orchestrated the ambush in order to allow the escape of his friend, one Badlands Bob, had come to naught!

Realizing the ambush action was over, James walked back to Lewis's horse being trailed behind the wagon along with their other horses, adjusted the stirrups for his leg length, placed his rifle and shotgun in the scabbards' on his new mount and then mounted up so he could continue riding 'shotgun'.

Then all the deadly action around the wagon box full of prisoners was over. All the prisoners were accounted for except for John Atkins. He was in two parts, one half bloodily contained inside the wagon box and the other lying on the roadbed, attached by a length of intestine leading from the remains of his carcass back in the wagon! Lewis had the prisoners toss John Atkins's bottom half out from the wagon and then Joe and James dragged those remains off into the brush and left them for the 'little people'. Then with the aid of Lewis's horse dragging, James and Joe moved the dead horse off the roadbed so their wagon could continue on its way to Fort Smith.

Those chores out of the way, the three brothers continued on their way towards Fort Smith without further incident. Arriving later that evening, the three brothers were met by several U.S. Marshals at the combination courthouse and jail. There they advised the lawmen as to what had occurred, what U.S. violations of law their load of prisoners individually represented, and requested that the men be formally arrested after just receiving a citizen's complaint regarding their alleged crimes.

Shortly after the brothers had administratively filed their complaints of criminal wrongdoing with the court, the remaining prisoners were escorted down into the jail portion under the courthouse complex, released from their manacles and leg irons and placed into the cell along with a number of other 'hard case' prisoners awaiting trial. As that was being done, the three brothers could not help but noticing the absolutely terrible smell emanating from the jail complex located under the court's administrative offices which were located upstairs!

Two days later, David Dodson, the youngest brother arrived in Fort Smith, as did Sam the ranch's hired hand, after receiving a telegraph from Joe Dodson relative to the capture of the men who had raped and killed most of the Dodson clan and the need for David and Sam to testify. After a brief Dodson family reunion, Colonel Jackson and the remainder of his men were tried on murder, rape and rustling charges by William Clayton, District Attorney for the Western District of Arkansas. Sam was the main witness during the trials because he had personally observed Colonel Jackson and his men entering the Dodsons's ranch house and heard all the screaming and yelling when the Dodson women were being abused and raped. Sam had also heard the shooting that had gone on inside the ranch house during the time when the Dodson women had been killed by some of Colonel Jackson's men. Then Joe, Lewis and James testified as to their part in pursuing and retaking their rustled livestock, and being able to personally assign the degree of blame on Colonel Jackson and his men for the cattle's illegal movement across state and territorial boundaries and the subsequent sale of said illegal cattle to the Indian rancher named July in the Indian Territory.

As it turned out, Colonel Jackson had a close military friend who was an attorney who took up the Dodson case and represented his old military commander in his defense. After all the trials had run their course, the Colonel and his men were only found guilty of cattle rustling! That was because no one had actually observed the killing of Albert or the actual raping and murdering of the Dodson women, so the 'good' Colonel and his men walked on the most serious of the charges lodged against them! However, Judge Isaac Parker did sentence Colonel Jackson and his men to serving 40 years in a federal prison over the cattle rustling and illegal sale charges after finding them guilty of the same.

Suffice to say, the Dodson clan was understandably upset over the fact that the most serious charges against the Colonel and his men were found wanting for lack of any witnesses. But in so doing, the Dodson men learned a valuable lesson regarding the law and its many avenues of construction. They also learned there were many ins and outs when it came to enforcing the laws of the land, and that only determined and exacting law enforcement work would yield the results sought after by those parties so 'injured'.

As for Badlands Bob and his trial, he too was found guilty over the cattle he had rustled in the Indian Territory and was also sentenced to 40 years in a federal prison. Shortly thereafter, the Colonel, his remaining men and Badlands Bob were shackled and made the trip in a prison wagon to the nearest federal prison where they began serving their sentences for cattle rustling.

Resting up for a day in Fort Smith after the trials, the four Dodsons and hired hand Sam made preparations to leave and return to their home near Booneville. However, fate stepped in and on the afternoon of their last day in town, a U.S. Marshal interrupted the men's supper. The Marshal advised Joe, Lewis and James that Federal Judge Isaac Parker, also known as the "Hanging Judge", wanted to see all three men bright and early the next day in his chambers! When Joe asked why the judge wanted to see all of them, the Marshal advised that when Judge Parker requested that someone meet with him, that was what one so asked had better do…

Since there were still livestock needing to be managed and looked after back on the Dodson ranch, David and Sam left the next day to attend to those animal husbandry duties, leaving Joe, Lewis and James to remain and ponder why Judge Parker had so pointedly ordered a meeting with them for the very next day...

CHAPTER THREE

JUDGE ISAAC PARKER AND LEARNING FROM BASS REEVES

The following morning found Joe, Lewis and James Dodson waiting in the Clerk of the Court's Office as they had been instructed to do so by a U.S. Marshal the evening before. Moments later, the Clerk's door burst open and in walked Chief U.S. Marshal James F. Fagan. The Dodsons quickly noticed that Fagan was a large and stout looking man, with an 'all business'-like look and appearance on his heavily mustached and weathered face.

"Are you chaps the three Dodson boys who brought in a load of prisoners yesterday from the Indian Territory?" boomed out Marshal Fagan's voice, as he carefully examined the men standing to his front.

"Yes Sir," responded Joe, thinking that the

marshal's manners and overall bearing reminded him of his dad Albert in his earlier days, when he was a Captain in the U.S. Cavalry during the late Civil War between the southern and northern states.

"My name is James Fagan and I am the Chief U.S. Marshal for the Federal Judicial District for the Western District of Arkansas. You fellas follow me into this unused office next door so I can prepare you for your meeting with Federal Judge Isaac Parker," continued Marshal Fagan as he turned and abruptly walked into an adjacent empty office.

Getting up from their chairs, the Dodsons trooped into the adjacent office behind the marshal as they had been so instructed, as a number of questions now spun crazily around in their heads as to why they were even there, having already testified against all of their prisoners they had brought in earlier in the week.

Marshal Fagan walked over to an unused desk, sat down heavily behind it and instructed the Dodsons to close the door, grab a chair and sit down. Once the door had been closed, the Dodsons could see that the marshal was closely scrutinizing each of the three men sitting before him as if examining them for some sort or degree of 'fitness' for what he had in mind that he felt needed saying. Seemingly satisfied over what he was seeing sitting before him, Fagan began speaking in a tone of voice that betrayed the fact that he did not want to be interrupted with any questions until he had finished with what he had to say.

Fagan began by saying, "You fellas are about to meet one of the most powerful men in this here United States. His name and he is to be addressed as such, is Judge Isaac Parker and he is the Federal District Judge for the Western District of Arkansas. He is the youngest federal judge in the United States and was given a life-time appointment to that position by President Grant. He was appointed to such a powerful and far-reaching position because of the ongoing degree of lawlessness found in this here Indian Territory. This here Indian Territory of which I am speaking is over 70,000 square miles in size and is 'home' to every kind of lawless individual found and known to mankind. Additionally, this Indian Territory is home to just about every kind of lawlessness, such as killings, robbery, horse and cattle rustling, rapes, whiskey peddling, selling illegal whiskey to the Indians, bootlegging, and renegade Indians of every kind and manner, most of whom are wanted by the federal authorities here at Fort Smith so they can be hung for their individual crimes committed against humanity or sent off to federal prison! State law does not carry any authority in this here Indian Territory, and that is why every type and kind of outlaw on the run from the law in the United States either lives here or is en route so they can duck the law that is trailing them for the crimes they have committed."

With that information out and on the table, Marshal Fagan seemed to run down a bit and paused in what he was saying or had to say. Then getting 'his second wind', he began once again with more information that seemed to be important in impressing upon the Dodson men for some reason known only to him but necessary to do so before they met the judge in his chambers.

"Judge Parker's Chief Federal Prosecutor is one William Clayton, whom you all have already met and he too was given a lifetime appointment in the Indian Territory by President Grant as well. Lastly within this group of federal officers is George Maledon. George is Judge Parker's hangman and is known locally and throughout the Indian Territory as the "Prince of Hangmen". He is a unique and efficient individual who always wears two pistols when hanging some son-of-a-bitch for his crimes committed against humanity, is a crack pistol shot with either hand, and gets his special hanging ropes from a firm in St. Louis that makes the finest hanging ropes available to mankind. George is very skilled as a hangman and he ties his knots in his ropes so they break the neck of those he is hanging instead of letting them slowly strangle to death," said Marshal Fagan sounding somewhat proudly.

Once again, Marshal Fagan paused in what he had to say as if collecting his thoughts for what he still had to say next and by so doing, not wanting to forget to pass on any of the necessary information the three men sitting before him needed to hear. "Judge Parker is aware of what happened to you boys' family members and what you did in running down and bringing to justice those who did to you and yours so wrongly. It is because of the brave thing that you boys did, that the Judge wants to meet and speak with you this morning. Just remember that when you meet him that you show great respect and under no circumstances use any off-color language around him or in his court. Judge Parker is a very religious man and you men need to respect that in him and in all of your actions now and in the future when officially around him. Now, with that bit of history under all of your belts, let us go up and meet His Honor because he has been expecting you to meet with him in his chambers."

With that information out and on the table, Marshal Fagan abruptly rose from his chair and led the three brothers from the room and upstairs as they all headed for the judge's chambers. Stopping outside the door leading to the judge's chambers, Marshal Fagan paused, turned and said, "Remember, no off-color language while in the judge's chamber and in front of this honorable man." With that, Marshal Fagan knocked on the judge's door and was asked to enter by a voice from inside. Opening up the massive oaken door and marching the men before him, Marshal Fagan marched the three Dodsons in front of the judge's desk, introduced them to the judge and then stepped back several paces, leaving the stage to that of the judge and the Dodson brothers.

"Good Morning, Gentlemen. My name is Judge Isaac Parker and I asked Marshal Fagan to bring all of you up to meet me this morning so I could talk to the three of you. I am aware of what those ex-Confederate soldiers and outlaws, one and all, did to your family and what all of you had to do in order to run down those killers and bring them before me and my court. What the three of you did was admirable and darn foolish all at the same time! None of you had any binding legal authority other than that from God to go after and apprehend those killers, and then bring them before me for adjudication for the ills they perpetuated upon society and you and your folks in particular. It is with that thought in mind and in recognition of your fine accomplishments, that I asked my Chief Marshal to bring all of you before me today for a specific reason."

"My officers of the court and I are faced with an unbelievable task in what awaits us in bringing the law of the land and its justice into this Indian Territory for all of its subjects. The area we are to bring law, justice and order into is so large, that our tasks in doing so are a heavy burden for all of us to bear. Yet all of humanity within that area of our responsibility is crying out for peace and justice in every corner of this land called the Indian Territory. In order for me to carry out my legal responsibilities, I have been authorized by the United States Government to hire 200 Deputy U.S. Marshals to enforce the federal laws applicable to the area of responsibility I now oversee. As such, I have instructed Marshal Fagan to hire any and all good men found honest, ethical, willing and capable to enforce the laws of this great country of ours called the United States," said Judge Parker stridently and with feeling.

"Now for my reason in bringing the three of you Dodsons before me today. The marshal and I liked the mettle we saw in the three of you and how you handled yourselves in pursuing, apprehending and bringing before me the men who did such an evil thing to your family members. It is with those thoughts in mind that I would like the three of you to consider working for your United States Government and me as Deputy U.S. Marshals in this lawless land called the Indian Territory! What brave, good and ethical behavior all of you showed in what you did tells me that I need to seek your employment into my ranks of officers in order to assist me and mine in bringing order and peace into this lawless land. As such, I would like to propose that the three of you put your domestic lives on hold for a while to be determined, and join our ranks in this dangerous profession of bringing good law enforcement and justice to this lawless land. I realize this proposal is sudden and unexpected so I propose the three of you take a day, think it over and get back to me by no later than by noon tomorrow. Regarding what I just said, do any of you have any questions for me?" asked Judge Parker.

The three Dodson brothers just stood there in front of His Honor thunderstruck over the possible change of life's events just laid at their doorstep! Here they had earlier thought of just going back home to their ranch and becoming gentlemen farmers and cattle ranchers in Arkansas. Now lying before them was an unprecedented challenge of a magnitude never ever imagined or considered among the three brothers.

All three brothers just looked at one another in amazement and then finally Joe spoke up. "Judge

Parker, none of us ever thought of becoming law enforcement officers until you suggested it in this moment in time! We just contemplated on going back to our ranch, quietly settling down, raising our families and living out the years the good Lord has given to us. But I think all three of us have changed inside somewhat since we began hunting down those who perpetuated such a heinous crime against our family and then subsequently went through all the trouble in bringing them to justice. We all have changed somewhat when it comes to our thinking about taking care of those who are less fortunate than we are since this series of events have taken place. Your Honor, give us a day to think over your proposal and we will get back to you by noon tomorrow with our collective answer. Because we are brothers and have such a strong love for each other, our answer back to you will have to be one that is collective as well. If we are to do what you have requested of us, we will only do so as three brothers working together as federal officers for the good of those less fortunate than us. We have already lost most of our family to the lawless ones and care not in having to work singularly instead of as a family unit. So, we all come as a package deal if we are to accept your surprising and generous offer. Our bottom line has to be one where we all live together and if

God willing, we all die together as a family," replied Joe.

With that and after thanking the judge for his time and rather unusual offer, Marshal Fagan escorted the three brothers from the judge's chambers and then they headed for their hotel and some late morning breakfast. Sitting down at their breakfast table, the brothers ordered their meals and a bottle of good whiskey with three glasses for the memorable discussion that was to follow among the three of them as per the judge's instructions regarding a dangerous life change into that of federal law enforcement in a lawless land called the Indian Territory. A career change among the brothers, that was one in which their father, were he still alive, would more than likely support because it would involve service to one's country and its humanity...

Just before noon the following day, found the Dodson brothers following Marshal Fagan up to Judge Parker's chambers. There they were warmly greeted by the judge, who followed up with his inquiry on whether or not the three brothers were going to accept a highly dangerous position with his Federal Court System as Deputy U.S. Marshals in the Indian Territory.

For the next few moments in the quiet of the judge's chambers after the question of becoming Deputy U.S. Marshals had been asked, for the longest time all one could hear were the chirping sounds made by some nesting English sparrows under the eaves of the courthouse.

Then Joe, being the eldest son, quietly spoke up for the three Dodson brothers. "Your Honor, we three Dodsons have decided to take you up on your offer to become Deputy U.S. Marshals and enforce the federal laws within the Indian Territory. However, as I requested yesterday, our condition of employment acceptance is that we never be separated but will work only as a family unit and team on any and all assignments. With our decisions to accept positions as Deputy U.S. Marshals in mind and you, your Honor, accepting the same, we took the liberty of tele-graphing our younger brother back home at our ranch near Booneville and advised him that he is to manage the family spread while we are in-volved as lawmen for the Federal Court System for the Western District of Arkansas for however long that takes. That he has consented to do and so here we three are at your service, Sir."

Smiling at the three Dodsons over their deci-sions in becoming Deputy U.S. Marshals, Judge Parker, not wanting to waste any more time or lose such an opportunity, asked the three men to immediately raise their right hands, and then and there swore them in as Deputy U.S. Marshals! Then the judge looked over at Chief Marshal

James Fagan and asked him to see to it that all the paperwork was executed in making the Dodson brothers official Deputy U.S. Marshals, and that any and all assignments made by his office would be in accordance with the understanding that the three brothers would always work together. Then looking over at the three smiling Dodsons, the judge said, "Gentlemen, for your information, there is no Sunday west of St. Louis and no God west of Fort Smith. May Godspeed to all of you in what you are now about to do and undertake upon yourselves!"

Then as if remembering something important, Judge Parker looked over at his Chief Marshal and asked, "Say, Marshal Fagan, isn't Deputy U.S. Marshal Bass Reeves in town?"

"He sure is, Your Honor. He just brought in five prisoners from the Wildcat Canyon Gang of cattle rustlers. Why do you ask?" asked Marshal Fagan.

"I would like to suggest that you hook these three new officers up with Bass so he can teach them some of his tricks of the trade and maybe then these men will last longer than a number of our other deputies, who have since disappeared once they ventured afield on a law enforcement assignment," suggested Judge Parker with a bit of hope in the tone and tenor of his voice.

"I know that Bass has gathered in another

handful of Writs for more cattle rustlers and planned on leaving shortly to go back into the field after he spends some time with his wife and family," replied Marshal Fagan.

"Good! Please see to it that these three new deputies are hooked up with Bass so he can teach them how to stay alive when out in the Indian Territory if you would, Marshal," asked Judge Parker.

Then a frown crossed Judge Parker's face and he said, "Wait, Marshal. I would like Bass to also get the Writs on the "Cherokee Charlie" Jones Gang of ex-Confederate soldiers (Cherokee Charlie was a white man so named because of his marriage to a full-blooded Cherokee woman). It has just been reported by the Indian Police in Oleta that he and his gang of outlaws have just killed Preacher Simmons, his three children, and raped and killed his wife, Betty. If that word from the field is true, I want Bass diverted to hunt down that bunch first and bring them before me for the hanging they so rightfully deserve. Since there are reported to be five of them in Charlie's gang of ex-soldiers, I would think with Bass having the Dodson deputies riding along with him as his posse, that would be the safer remedy for success in capturing or killing that bunch of evildoers," said Judge Parker with a degree of 'iron' in the tone of his voice.

Then looking back at the Dodsons, Judge Parker said, "Gentlemen, when you are doing your job out in the Indian Territory, I want you to bring your prisoners back to me alive so they can be tried -- or dead, as the circumstances or the good Lord so decrees! Welcome, Gentlemen, to one of the most dangerous professions in this here United States. I thank you and your country now thanks you for the service you are about to render for your fellow man!"

With the judge's words ringing in the Dodsons' ears, Marshal Fagan escorted the men back to his office in order to fill out the paperwork making the Dodsons official as the court's three newest Deputy U.S. Marshals. As Marshal Fagan began filling out the necessary papers on the three Dodsons authorizing them to carry the badge and execute the authorities and dictates of the court, Lewis offhandedly asked Marshal Fagan, "Who is this Bass Reeves fellow the judge was talking about?"

Stopping what he was doing filling out the necessary paperwork, Marshal Fagan took out his plug of chewing tobacco, bit off and plopped a wad between his cheek and gum, sat back in his chair, and smiled. "Gentlemen, Bass Reeves is one of the finest officers I have going! He is an ex-slave, is over six feet in height, weighs about 180 pounds, and is built like a stone outhouse. He is equally expert with a rifle or pistol in either hand, strong as a bull, absolutely fearless, extremely cunning, and when he gets on an outlaw's trail, the only way to get him off is to kill him on sight! To my knowledge, he is the first black Deputy U.S. Marshal west of the Mississippi River and as I have said, one of the very best."

Then turning in his chair and spitting a stream of tobacco juice over his shoulder and out his open second story window behind him, Marshal Fagan continued filling out all the necessary paperwork as the Dodson brothers just sat there silently, wondering what their new life as law enforcement officers would really be like compared to just being gentlemen farmers and ranchers back in Booneville, Arkansas.

Finally finishing up with all the necessary paperwork, Marshal Fagan opened up his desk drawer, pulled out three brand new badges of office, handed one to each of his new deputies, and said, "Welcome aboard, Gentlemen, and may the good Lord take a likin' to the three of you!"

Then Marshal Fagan got really business-like saying, "Gentlemen, you have now become Deputy U.S. Marshals in an organization that has been around since the organization of this country back in the late 1700s. Judge Parker is in the never-ending business it seems in hiring 200 new deputies like the three of you to enforce the federal laws within the Indian Territory. You will be enforcing the federal laws in an approximately 70,000-square mile area called the Indian Territory, which was established in 1830 under the Indian Removal Act. That Act passed by the U.S. Congress was done in order to house the many tribes of Indians moved off and displaced from their ancestral lands by the U.S. Government in the eastern part of our country in order to make room for the ever expanding white European populations. Currently there are five major tribes of Indians on the eastern side of the Indian Territory, namely the Cherokee, Creek, Seminole, Choctaw, and Chickasaw, with a number of other tribes slated for entry into other parts of the Indian Territory as we speak."

Shifting his mass to a more comfortable position in his swivel chair, Marshal Fagan continued briefing the Dodsons saying, "For your information, our federal laws do not apply to the Indians in the Indian Territory. Their own tribal people are responsible for keeping their own kind in line in accordance with their various tribal laws. However, you will be enforcing all federal laws against the thousands of white men, outlaws and white renegades who have fled from the other states seeking refuge from those state laws by hiding in the Indian Territory. Your jobs will entail receiving and serving Writs from this court authorizing arrest of white individuals in the Indian Territory, securing witnesses, securing evidence of the crimes, and subsequently providing testimony against the prisoners you apprehend and bring in, so the juries can convict those you have captured and returned to this court's jurisdiction."

Then after pausing to re-load his mouth with a fresh chew of Brown's Mule chewing tobacco, Marshal Fagan commenced once again, as the Dodsons tried to assimilate all the information being provided to them, saying, "All of you must remember that every bad man you cross swords with and try to arrest is for the most part and has been on the run from the law for some time. Many realize they are going to hang if they are ever returned to Fort Smith for their crimes. So those criminals will have nothing to lose in resisting your arrest or try killing you in the process to avoid going to trial!"

Now with a mouth full of spittle from his most recent chew, Marshal Fagan turned in his chair and spit a black stream of tobacco juice out the open window behind his desk. Following that effort by wiping some of the tobacco spittle from the corners of his mouth, he said, "Deputies, you do not draw any salary but you will be compensated six cents for every mile that you ride in your quest to secure evidence, arrest individuals, serve various court papers, and return to testify in a court of law. You will receive two dollars for every summons that you deliver to an individual, two dollars for every prisoner that you deliver to the jail, and you can collect any outside reward money that is offered for the arrest and conviction of every prisoner that you apprehend that is provided by the stage companies, railroads and banks. You must furnish your own weapons and horse, however; the court will supply you, as appropriate and depending upon the circumstances, extra horses and mules, a cook, a chuck and/or prison wagon as needed, and sometimes extra deputies as members of your posse. In addition, in accordance with various tribal laws, an Indian Policeman will ride with you in the case there arises a need to assist in the enforcement of tribal laws."

Then spitting his old chew of tobacco out his window because it possessed too many stems in the cud making it a rough 'chew', Marshal Fagan commenced with his long list of instructions saying, "If anyone resists your arrest, he is looking at a year in jail and if you kill a suspect, you are personally responsible for his burial. Additionally, if you end up killing a prisoner, you will receive no pay for his capture. Judge Parker's court is both a Circuit and District Court, and the only recourse for anyone so convicted in his court is a Presidential Pardon. However, all of you must remember, your goal is to capture and bring back your prisoners alive if at all possible."

"Now," began Marshal Fagan again, "I need to get hold of Bass Reeves and let him know he will be taking along the three of you as his posse in his next assignment. Also while he is doing so, I will expect that he will be teaching you some of his many techniques that he has used successfully in capturing and bringing back his many prisoners. I know he was on the trail of his last prisoner for about a month, so he is more than likely as we speak, spending time with his wife and family. I will fetch up another deputy who knows the area and send him to fetch Bass and have him stop by and pick up his latest Writ to arrest Cherokee Charlie and his gang for killing Preacher Simmons, his three kids, and gang raping and killing his wife. When he comes to my office to fetch up his Writs, I will see to it that you three are here and can meet him at that time and begin to get acquainted with each other."

With that, Marshal Fagan had run down on what he had to say to the Dodsons and sent them back to their boardinghouse so they would have time to provision up with their personal necessaries, purchase fresh ammunition for their rifles and pistols, and have all of their horses reshod for the many long days and rough trails they would be traveling with Bass Reeves in his pursuit of Cherokee Charlie and his gang of four killers and rapists. Killers and rapists who would now more than likely be on the run for cover in the wilds of the Indian Territory to avoid pursuit and apprehension from Deputy U.S. Marshals.

Several days later, a deputy marshal summoned the Dodson brothers to Marshal Fagan's office to meet Bass Reeves. Walking into Marshal Fagan's office, the Dodson brothers were met by a well-dressed Deputy U.S. Marshal wearing a black hat and introduced to the brothers as the renowned throughout the Indian Territory, Bass Reeves. All of the brothers later commented that when they shook his hand during their introduction, they were amazed at his tremendous hand strength. Then the men got down to the business at hand, as Marshal Fagan laid out the particulars as reported to him regarding the killing of Preacher Simmons and his family by ex-Confederate soldiers from Cherokee Charlie's Gang. Bass, not being able to read or write, had Joe read the Writ just handed him by Marshal Fagan to be served against Cherokee Charlie and his four henchmen for the killings. As Joe read the Writ out loud, he could just see that Bass was committing to his memory the words being read to him off the Writ of Arrest so he could recite them back to any prisoner so arrested and named for arrest by the Writ.

Following that, the deputy marshals were introduced to their cook and chuck wagon driver, a Mexican named Chino, and their tribally required Indian Police Officer 'tag-along' named Tom Johns. After the introductions had been made all around, Bass Reeves wanted to be on his way just as soon as they could before the vastness of the Indian Territory 'disappeared' the Cherokee Charlie Gang into much of the vast unknown wilderness of the territory.

Leaving the Chief Marshal's office, Bass took a quick inventory of the chuck wagon's provisions, examined his wagon's team of horses, checked on the supply of manacles and leg irons, and examined for their fitness the extra replacement horses and mules tied to the back of the wagon. Satisfied over what he had just examined, the men mounted up and began heading for the last known location of Cherokee Charlie's gang after they had left the preacher's home and their deadly human destruction behind. However, as the posse of men left, the Dodson brothers were quick to learn from watching Bass Reeves that after he had checked out his resources, he then, without a wasted effort, hit the outlaw trail. The Dodsons, having been raised in a military family, quickly learned to appreciate Bass Reeves's quick and efficient attention to detail and his outlaw hunting cunning and ethic. Their lessons in how to become a good lawman by watching one of the best in the business in the Indian Territory in 'motion', were not lost on the Dodson brothers and would go on to serve them well over their coming years of law enforcement service as Deputy U.S. Marshals.

As they left Fort Smith, the Dodsons noticed that Bass carried a Winchester 1876 rifle, caliber .40-82, as his main long range weapon and a pair of Schofield pistols, caliber .44, worn in the cross draw fashion. Bass being a large man for that period of time was riding a grayish white horse of substantial size and wearing a very distinctive and stylish black slouch hat. They also noticed that just as soon as they left the Fort Smith area and hit the 'outlaw trail', his eyes never stopped moving along the nearby ridges, tree lines, draws or brush fields, because he was a black man who was well known among the outlaw gentry and a much looked for target by all of those he was hunting with his Writs of Arrest in hand.

Riding alongside Bass, the Dodsons made every effort to become familiar with their more experienced deputy and gain from whatever law enforcement knowledge and or arrest techniques he commonly used that he would casually share with them as they rode along. Looking over at Lewis one morning while on the trail, Bass said, "In this business you always want to remember that a good and quick mind is every bit as good as your Winchester." Later in the day when the men were resting their horses while on their way to the town of Oleta where Preacher Simmons and his family had been killed to question any witnesses, Bass was heard to utter that one of the keys to his survival all these years was his detailed preparation and knowledge of his surroundings before he ever made a move in rounding up his outlaw targets. Those words were committed to 'stone' and undertaken by the Dodson brothers in every future law enforcement operation they would undertake. When Bass's posse was still five miles from the town of Oleta, home of the recently killed Preacher and his family, they were drawn up short alongside a small out of the way creek and adjacent meadow.

"We will make our camp here and operate out from this location on a daily basis so as not to arouse any undue suspicion as to our real law enforcement mission," said Bass as he surveyed their potential campsite.

With those words, Chino swung his chuck wagon into a small grove of trees, dismounted and began unharnessing his team of mules so they could rest and put on the 'feed bag'. Then Indian Patrolman Tom Johns and Chino began laying out their fire pit and the rest of their campsite, while Bass and the Dodsons dismounted, unsaddled their mounts, hobbled their horses, and then let them out to feed nearby as well. Following that, Bass surveyed their surroundings making sure they were in a good defensive posture in case they were attacked by any of the numerous roving bands of Indian Territory ruffians, while the Dodsons gathered up several armloads of firewood for their campfire.

That evening after a supper of beans, fatback and Dutch oven biscuits, Bass gathered together the men of his posse for a powwow. There Bass told the men that he planned on going alone into Oleta the following day for a look-around while posing as an out of work cowboy. By so doing, he allowed that his non-threatening appearance and being a black man would allow him to gather up some intelligence as to Cherokee Charlie's movements. Especially those movements made after committing the crimes he had been accused of when it came to killing the preacher and his family earlier in the month. In the meantime, he wanted the rest of the posse to stay low key at their campsite, posing as out of work cowboys and wait for Bass's return. Before dawn the following morning, Bass was up, had two cups of coffee for his breakfast and was gone on his informational gathering mission.

Come dark, the men in the posse heard the sounds of a horse's hooves approaching as they sat around their campfire. Soon a tired Bass Reeves rode into camp, dismounted and straightaway asked Chino for a cup of coffee and a couple of his great tasting Dutch oven biscuits. Respecting Bass's silence as he hungrily ate his biscuits and drank some of his coffee, the other lawmen waited for any news Bass had gleaned from the local people in Oleta.

Finally Bass leaned back against his saddle, which had been removed and lay alongside the fire pit, took another sip of his coffee and then said, "Tomorrow we ride for Hugo to our south, just this side of Texas and the Red River. Word I picked up in the "Dog's Leg Saloon" in Oleta was that Cherokee Charlie and his bunch of cutthroats were rumored to have been last seen heading in that direction. Also, the liveryman reported that he had replaced a shoe on one of Charlie's men's horses and he had mentioned they would be heading in that direction in order to lay low for a while. Charlie's man had also volunteered, that way if they ever discovered they were being pursued by the law, they would easily slip across the Red River and head deep into Texas to shake any pursuing law off their trail. That is pretty big country down there and finding someone on the run in that state can be somewhat of a problem because many of the Texans have a tendency to hide outlaws on the run in that neck of the woods. Lastly and the best news is that Charlie's Cherokee woman is heavy with child and expected to 'drop it' within the month."

Bass paused in his intelligence report long enough to grab another biscuit and another cup of coffee, then he said, "Since that is the case with Charlie's old woman that is the area in which we will set up shop. I can't see him not returning before she 'calves' and being with her when she does. So all of us will find ourselves setting up shop a mile south of Apple where she lives nearby with her older son and a mess of 'young-uns'. I took the time to ride near her place and located an old and abandoned dugout whereby we can pull in our wagon, make a new campsite and be out of the way from any casual observers. Then each day until she 'calves', we can set up shop and watch for Charlie's return from a distance away with our binoculars. If and when Charlie does, we will slip in on their homestead at night, round up the bunch and bring them back to Judge Parker's court for trial." With that, Bass helped himself to Chino's last Dutch oven biscuit, leaned back against his saddle lying on the ground next to their fire, closed his eyes and just visibly savored his biscuit.

Breaking camp right at daylight, Bass's posse and wagon headed for the area of the small town of Apple. Turning off before arriving in Apple and maybe setting off a mess of suspicions as to who the six strangers were, Bass headed them off to an abandoned dugout on an old home site that he had located earlier that was off the beaten trail. Once there, the men again set up their campsite so they could be as comfortable as possible while staking out Cherokee Charlie's wife's homestead located about a mile distant, waiting for his hoped for return for the 'birthing' of his newborn baby.

For the next five days at a distance, Bass's posse staked out Cherokee Charlie's heavily pregnant wife's homestead and cabin waiting for any sign of the outlaw's return. In staking out the suspect ranch house, Bass broke the men up into teams so they would not burn out their patience when it came to such long and boring stakeouts. This stakeout regimen went on for the next two weeks with no results as far as Cherokee Charlie returning home so he could be with his Cherokee Indian wife when she was having their newest baby.

One afternoon while Indian Patrolman Tom Johns, Chino, Bass and Joe lounged around their campsite waiting for their turn at night stakeout duties, Joe got impatient saying, "I like Chino's cooking but I am getting tired of fatback and beans for almost every meal. I am going to grab our shotgun and see if I can't kill a couple of those prairie chickens flying in every evening we have been seeing over by that little spring-seep near the hills."

"I could use a little change in my diet as well," said Bass with a grin over Joe's suggestion.

With Bass's grin as a sign of approval, Joe grabbed his shotgun out from the back of the wagon, removed the double ought buck brass shotgun shells from the double barrel, inserted some number six sized shot shells into the shotgun's two chambers, closed the barrels with a loud click, and began walking over towards the distant hills to where the spring-seep was located in the hopes of 'bagging' a couple of prairie chickens for their supper. Two hours later found Joe returning to their campsite, only to find four unknown riders sitting on their horses talking to Bass Reeves who was standing beside them.

Walking into camp, Joe pretended to ignore the four unidentified riders, but his ears were 'flapping' for anything being said between Bass and the four riders just as Bass had taught him to do when one needed information.

"Yeah, there are the six of us waiting until our cattle boss arrives next week with a herd of beeves being driven out from Texas," he overheard Bass telling the four unidentified men looking suspiciously down upon him. As they did, Chino and

Tom Johns were messing around the campfire like nothing much was going on, but Joe could see that both of those men were more than alert without making it obvious in case things turned ugly. Their 'alert' was made even more obvious to Joe's eyes as he checked out Chino's and Indian Tom Johns's holstered handguns. When one did with his practiced eye, he could see that they had unsnapped the holster's small leather loops normally carried over the hammers of their pistols to keep them from falling out from the holster during routine activities. This 'leather loop removal' was normally done when one figured there might be a call for their quick withdrawal and use in a self-defense situation...

Taking his 'remain casual' cue from the two men around the campfire, Joe placed his shotgun back into the wagon and then holding up the four prairie chickens shot earlier said, "Hey, how about you two giving me a hand in cleaning and picking these here chickens for our supper tonight?"

"Bring them on over and we will give you a hand," said Chino as he placed several more limbs of firewood into their burning campfire.

With that word, Joe headed over to the campfire without looking directly at the four new arrivals, loudly saying for the strangers' benefit, "With these going into the pot, we will be eating 'high on the hog' and something other than just your damn old beans, Chino," he said with a laugh in the tone and tenor of his voice. With that and his arrival at the campfire, Joe sat down, handed a prairie chicken to each of the two men and then the three of them began picking and throwing their feathers into the fire, stinking up the area. But as they did, Joe, whose back was turned towards the four strangers, checked again and in so doing, could definitely see that Chino and Johns had loosened the 'leather catches' over the hammers on their pistols…just in case.

Then Joe heard Bass invite the four strangers to light down and have supper with the rest of the men in his camp, which was the neighborly thing to do in that day and age. The leader of the new arrivals, who had been doing most of the talking, thanked Bass and declined his offer with the words, "We need to get back to Charlie's place. His wife is about to have another kid and we would like to be there to congratulate Charlie. That and we need to pick up an Indian midwife for Charlie's wife this afternoon and take her over to his place for when the baby comes."

It was then that Joe realized what Johns and Chino had known all along. The four new arrivals were members of Cherokee Charlie's gang who were just checking out Bass's camp of strangers to the area! He then wondered why Bass had not snatched up the four gang members right on the spot since he had Writs for their arrests as well. But realizing that Bass was in charge of this posse, Joe 'held his milk' figuring that Bass would later share his reasoning for not grabbing off the four men right on the spot and kept on plucking his prairie chicken like it was the normal thing to do. However as Joe did, he continued keeping a 'cocked' eye and a 'tuned ear' on the four men in case things went downhill and defensive action was called for 'posthaste'.

Finished checking out Bass's camp of reported 'out of work' cowboys, the four members of Cherokee Charlie's gang, whirled their horses about and rode off to pick up a midwife for Charlie's expecting wife. Bass just stood there until the four men rode out of sight and then walked over to the campfire where Johns, Chino and Joe Dodson were sitting plucking their prairie chickens.

"Well, you passed your first test as a Deputy U.S. Marshal," said a smiling Bass Reeves. "I was hoping you would not blow our cover and give us away when you walked into our camp 'stone-cold' over what was occurring in light of who those strangers were in reality," said Reeves with a smile of appreciation for the actions of his young novice officer. "I half expected you, not knowing what was going on, to give us away and start a shooting not to my liking, time or place. But you did good and kept your mouth shut and even more importantly, did not let your feelings of suspicion show over who those chaps really were. Since I did not know where Charlie was, I wanted to wait until I had the entire nest of killers close at hand and then capture the whole 'kit and caboodle' in one fell swoop. They were suspicious as hell when they rode up, but my 'out of work and waiting for our old cattle boss on his way up from Texas with a herd of cattle to take us in' story finally sold them in believing we were OK. It is a damn good thing that a lot of Texas drovers come this way from the Red River Valley in Texas on their ways to the stock pens in Kansas City. Otherwise, my story of out of work 'cow-pokes' would not have held a single drop of water in their suspicious eyes. Now, hand me one of those prairie chickens and I can pluck it along with the three of you so we all can have a feast for our suppers this evening when the rest of our crew comes back from their afternoon stakeout," he said.

Come nightfall when Lewis and James Dodson returned from their all-day stakeout, they had good news. They reported that they had observed a single man ride up early in the morning to Charlie's ranch house and that rider had put his horse in a nearby barn and was still there.

They also reported that later on in the day, they had observed another four riders riding up to the same ranch house leading a buckboard being driven by a single Indian woman. The Indian woman had then gone inside the ranch house after gathering up an armful of items from the back of her buckboard. Moments later, the earlier rider they had observed, exited the ranch house and met briefly with the four still mounted riders. Then the four men dismounted and with the fifth man leading the way, they all adjourned for the barn and it appeared they were staying for the night and were going to sleep in the barn, not the ranch house for some reason.

Around ten in the evening, Bass advised the men in his posse that it was time to saddle up and leave. Bass also advised that by leaving so late in the evening, that by the time they arrived at the suspect's ranch house, the men they were hunting and would hopefully arrest, would be in their deepest of natural sleep in the barn. In so doing, that would reduce the danger to the arresting officers of a bloody confrontation if they could catch the outlaws 'dead to the world'. After all, Bass advised, Judge Parker wanted all of his suspects back at Fort Smith alive to stand trial, if at all possible. Additionally, Bass reminded the men that the horses could find their ways in the dark without the use of any light, making their sneak up to the suspect ranch house complete. Suffice to say, the Dodsons had just learned another set of good lessons from one of the Indian Territory's best federal officers and were soon to realize the fruits from his night-stalking wisdom.

Leaving their horses picketed a good hundred yards from the suspects' barn which was far enough away so their horses would not give the lawmen away with a friendly whinny to another horse smelled at the ranch house, the men removed their rifles from their scabbards and began their walk towards the darkened barn. As they did, Bass Reeves was hopeful that the barn still held Cherokee Charlie's gang and the killers of Preacher Simmons's entire family from a month earlier in Oleta, Indian Territory (I.T.).

Thirty minutes of careful stalking through the countryside brought the four men to the side of the barn suspected of holding Cherokee Charlie's gang of killers who were still sleeping inside. As the posse paused, the men could hear the faint squalling of a newborn baby coming from the nearby ranch house...

Bass whispered for James and Lewis to enter the hay barn from the rear of the building and once inside, wait for him to call them forward so no one would be mistakenly shot if their attempt at arrests went sour. Then Bass and Joe would enter the front of the building and attempt to quietly locate the five sleeping men and make the arrests. When they did, they would call James and Lewis forward to further cement in the outlaws mind the futility of trying to escape because of the overpowering numbers of officers present all around them.

The men than quietly split up into two groups and disappeared toward their entry points into the barn. Lewis and James soon found a door that allowed entry into the rear of the barn and quietly entered. As they did, they noticed a faint light burning toward the front of the interior of the barn from what appeared to be that of a light cast from a burning coal oil lamp. Sliding next to a horse stall, both men waited for Bass or Joe to give them the OK to move forward, surround the outlaws from their side of the barn, and join any fracas that may occur as a result of the impending arrests.

Meanwhile, Joe and Bass quietly opened up a squeaky and noisy front barn door and quickly slipped quietly inside. Once inside, they noticed the nearby faint light being emitted from a coal oil lamp whose wick had been turned down to low so the men could still sleep but see if a need arose. Next to the coal oil lamp Joe and Bass could see the blanket-covered mounds of five men sleeping soundly on the barn's floor on a bed of hay.

Careful not to alert the five men, Joe slipped

off to one side of the group of sleeping men and Bass to the other. When they did, both men simultaneously became aware of the fact that all five of the men had removed their gun belts and had laid them near their heads where they lay sleeping for quick retrieval if necessary. Without a word being spoken between the two lawmen, Joe began quietly sneaking by the first man nearest him in the row of sleeping men, reached down and quietly removed his gun belt. Standing back up, he quietly looped the gun belt around his off gun hand's shoulder and then looked over at Bass. Bass seeing that Joe was now in the position to guard him in his gun belt removal attempt, quietly reached down, lifted up the gun belt from near his sleeper's head and looped it around his off gun hand shoulder as well. In the faint oil lamp's glow, Bass nodded for Joe to go for his next in line sleeper's gun belt. As Joe bent over, the previously retrieved outlaw's gun belt looped over his off gun hand shoulder, suddenly slipped off and dropped down to the floor alongside the next man in line still sleeping in the bed of hay with a soft sounding THUMP! Joe quickly grabbed up the gun belt and then froze in his bent over position to see if the man had heard the gun belt softly drop onto the barn's hay-covered floor next to his head. The second man in line to Joe's side of the group of men stirred somewhat over the slight noise by his head but then continued on in his deep sleep. It was as Bass had so predicted earlier regarding the men being in their deepest of sleep at that time of the morning. In so far that being the normal sleep pattern for most people, that made it the best and safest time for an arrest to be made to avoid any deadly altercations...

Seeing his man had not awakened when the gun belt had landed quietly near his head, Joe reached over and quietly removed that second heavy sleeper's gun belt from near his head where he had laid it before going to sleep. Then he slowly and oh so quietly, raised back up to his full standing position in order to make ready for his next move. It was then that both Joe and Bass stood there silently for a few moments letting their hearts return their heartbeats back to a normal rhythm, after an almost disaster when the first seized gun belt had slipped off Joe's shoulder and dropped its holstered firearm onto the wooden, hay-covered barn floor near the sleeper's head before he could grab it midair!

Now the two officers had quietly disarmed three of the five sleeping men lying close at their feet without deadly incident. That left only two more outlaws' gun belts to retrieve before they would have full control over the five deeply sleeping outlaws by virtue of the fact they all would be disarmed. That was when the 'wheels came off their wagon of luck' and the two federal officers' hoped for peaceful arrest success ran out!

SQUEEEAK! went the front barn door as it was abruptly opened and in walked the Indian woman who had been acting as a midwife to Charlie's wife and as she entered the barn, she was observed in the faint coal oil lamp light holding a newborn baby all wrapped up in a woolen blanket! "Charlie," she happily announced, without really knowing what had been going on just moments before, "wake up so you can meet your newly born son."

All five previously sleeping men woke up with a start, first over the noisy barn door being opened up unexpectedly and second, the Indian woman announcing in a loud and proud voice the arrival of a newly born baby boy! When that series of events played out, the five men, not expecting any interruption in their sleep, exploded up off the barn floor where they had been sleeping in surprise! They did so coming from such a deep sleep over the unexpected opening of the barn's noisy front door, the abrupt arrival and surprise entry of the Indian midwife with the newborn baby, and then over the fact that there were two heavily armed strangers nearby standing almost over them, covering them with drawn pistols!

Instantly all five men went for their guns where

they had left them on the floor by their previously resting heads, realizing the two armed strangers standing next to them meant extreme danger!

Three of the men instantly discovered that their gun belts were missing and had been taken while they slept! However, the other two outlaws quickly grabbed their gun belts up from off the floor, reached for their revolvers, jerked them from their holsters, and then things went from peaceable to deadly in a heartbeat!

Joe grabbed the closest now-armed man to him by the head and flung him to the floor before he could get a shot off. But that didn't stop him from jerking himself away from Joe's headlock in a heartbeat! That man rolled off to one side, jumped up to his feet, quickly drew down on Joe from just five feet away and jerked back the hammer on his single action revolver, all in the same fluid practiced motion common among gunfighters of the day, when there was a BOOM! With that sound of shooting, that gunfighter had his head exploded in a bright red spew of blood! Lewis hearing all the commotion and not waiting for a call to assist those officers in the front of the barn, had run forward into the melee, realized what was exploding all around him, quickly swung his rifle up and 'head-shot' the man from just a few feet away who was just about to kill his older brother!

In that same instant, Cherokee Charlie, over

the screaming of the now-terrified Indian woman who had walked into such an instant explosion of humanity and shooting, swung the barrel of his pistol at Bass Reeves's belly for a close in 'gut-shot'! That was when Bass Reeves 'buffaloed' Cherokee Charlie with his pistol barrel across the side of his head and Charlie's 'lights' went out! However, not before Charlie fell over backwards after being struck violently in the head and, in the process of falling, his trigger finger involuntarily jerked off one shot from his now poorly aimed Colt revolver...

That sound of Cherokee Charlie getting one shot off as he was falling over backwards, totally unconscious after being head-smashed by Bass, simultaneously brought forth an inhuman scream from the Indian midwife! That she did, as Charlie's errant shot blew his new son out of her arms killing him instantly! However, not before that errant bullet went clear through the baby's small body and mortally wounded the Indian woman holding the child as well!

When that happened, for a moment time stood still in that hay barn smelling of freshly mown hay, horse manure and the acrid smell of freshly burned black powder. Then the realization sunk into all the men standing there as to what had just happened. Joe was covered from head to toe in gray matter, bits of splintered skull bone and more blood than he cared to be covered with, as a result of being so close to the outlaw whom his brother had just head shot from three feet away with his heavy caliber Sharps buffalo rifle! Lewis on the other hand, being so close to the outlaw he had just shot who was about to kill his brother, was spotted with 'blow-back' blood from head to toe! James bringing up the rear in a race from the rear to the front of the barn so he could assist in the arrest going badly was also spotted with blood from Charlie's errant .45 caliber slug. A .45 caliber slug which had slammed into the belly area of his newborn son, spewing blood about from his little body with the same explosive reaction like would happen when someone had shot into a watermelon from just a few feet away! The only man untouched by the gore was Bass Reeves. But once again, the Dodson brothers got a real lesson in life when it came to that 'law enforcement thing' and its possible explosive end result happenings when trying to enforce the law of the land in the Indian Territory…

Afterwards, Bass Reeves had the unfortunate job of informing Cherokee Charlie's wife about the death of her newborn son by her husband's errant bullet. A bullet fired from his own gun as he fought to retain his freedom and outlaw way of life. As for Joe, Lewis and James, they got the job of burying the man head shot by Lewis, as was in keeping with the policy set by Judge Parker when a prisoner was killed in the process of being arrested by the court's deputies. That policy being if one of his Deputy U.S. Marshals killed one of the people he was trying to bring in, he had to personally take care of the dead man's burial… Bass Reeves also later took care of informing the dead Indian woman's family of her unfortunate loss and giving her husband information on how to contact Judge Parker's court in Fort Smith, Arkansas, to see if any government compensation for the loss of his wife would be available.

As the four Deputy U.S. Marshals finally rode away that morning, they were trailed by a sullen and head still throbbing Cherokee Charlie from the pistol whipping he had taken from Bass Reeves, and the surviving three members of his gang. All of those very bad men were not only manacled but had their feet shackled underneath their horses bellies as they rode away from that violent scene after being placed under arrest by Bass Reeves and restrained in the maximum degree in order to prevent any further unfortunate events from occurring.

The Dodsons were unusually aware of the fact that the wails and screams from the extremely distraught new mother who had just violently lost her newborn son, could be heard for the better part of a mile, as the lawmen rode back to their camp across a desolate and stone-quiet stretch of Indian Territory. Upon their arrival and with Chino taking a close look at the deputies when they arrived back in camp said, "Holy Mary, Mother of God, what happened to you three Dodsons? Are you guys all right?"

It took a few minutes to assure Chino that all was well among the brothers other than having their clothing blood and gray matter splattered. It also took a few more minutes to settle Chino down over what he had just observed, being a staunch Roman Catholic and in the process, making all of his many "Signs of the Cross" across his chest after hearing about the previous evening's violent events. As for Indian Patrolman and fellow posse member Tom Johns, he just grunted something under his breath and said nothing more over the recent events, because he had been raised in the bloody and lawless Indian Territory, seen its many ugly sides and that nothing more needed saying...

To avoid any locally aroused interference with the prisoner transport over the unfortunate events that happened back at the barn, Bass Reeves had his posse in the saddle and the wagon ready to be rolling on its way back to Fort Smith around four in the morning the following day. He made it very clear to the brothers that to linger in an area after arresting locals just invited outside intervention by sympathetic folks and possibly allowing one's prisoners the opportunity to escape with said outside help. Additionally, he was concerned over the fact that a local Indian woman had been killed in the melee and wanted to avoid any problems with local Indians who may have taken offense to the accidental killing and were out to seek justice by killing Cherokee Charlie for being the cause of their loss in the first place.

Bass Reeves had double checked his prisoners just moments before leaving and had made sure all four of them were now firmly shackled down to the bed of the chuck wagon in which they were now riding. Satisfied over what he saw, the posse was headed up and moved along on its way up the road towards the small town of Antlers and then north towards Poteau. From there he planned on heading northeasterly into the town of Fort Smith, Arkansas. There his prisoners would be jailed awaiting their individual trials, he would gather up more Writs of Arrest on more felons needing to be arrested, and then spend some time with his family before hitting the 'arrest' trail looking for more much wanted outlaws needing to be tried in Judge Parker's court…

As for the Dodson brothers, they would provide guard duty to Fort Smith with Reeves's prisoners and then as expected after testifying at the prisoner's trials, find themselves assigned Writs of Arrest for their own number of much wanted felons by Marshal Fagan, now needing to be hunted down and arrested so they could stand trial in Judge Parker's court as well.

For the next twelve days, Reeves's posse and prisoners traveled northward toward Poteau and eventually Fort Smith. The days on the trail turned into a blur of eating breakfast before daylight, feeding the prisoners under the watchful eyes of two armed guards, letting the prisoners out twice a day to relieve themselves again under armed guard, and then letting them out come suppertime to stretch their legs, eat some supper and then back into the rear end of the chuck wagon for the night. Then each evening, one man remained awake by the campfire on six-hour shifts to make sure there was no interference from outside sources when it came to safely keeping their prisoners and their own lives intact.

Finally came their day of arrival into the Fort Smith District Court and jail complex. There they were met by a number of jailers who took their four prisoners forthwith into the stinking dungeon-like jail under the courthouse and released from their shackles and chains into the jail cells. Reeves and the Dodsons then went into the court's administrative offices, returned their now served Writs and found out what the prisoner's respective trial dates were, so the deputy marshals could come back and provide testimony in the court of law. Reeves then dismissed himself from his tired posse and reported on the capture events to Chief Marshal Fagan. While there, he also reported on the behavior, performance and professionalism exhibited by the Dodson brothers as Marshal Fagan's newest Deputy U.S. Marshals.

After that, the posse was again reunited and had a much welcome noonday dinner of something other than fatback and beans with an occasional Dutch oven biscuit or prairie chicken thrown in for good measure. Following that, the Dodsons and Bass Reeves parted company, with Bass to see and spend some time with his family, and the Dodsons to meet once again with Marshal Fagan as he had requested. Meeting later as had been requested by the Chief U.S. Marshal, the Dodsons stood at a respectful attention while Fagan finished up with some other administrative business and debriefing two other deputy marshals fresh from off a successful trip arresting two federally wanted outlaws in the Indian Territory for cattle and horse rustling.

Than Fagan motioned for the three brothers to sit down in his office while he shoveled a partial plug of black-looking Brown's Mule chewing tobacco into his mouth with his grizzly bear paw-sized hands. Sloshing that wad of tobacco around in his mouth until he found a comfortable place for it to sit, he turned his attention to the three brothers sitting before him, saying with a big grin, "Well done! I spoke to Bass Reeves earlier and he had nothing but praise for you three and how you handled yourselves out on the trail and during what turned out to be a rather dangerous and deadly arrest situation. That being said and out of respect for what Bass had to say about the three of you and his following recommendations, I have before me another set of Writs of Arrest for an individual called "Three-Fingered" Jack and his gang of five accomplices for you fellas to serve. In accordance with Judge Parker's wishes that the three of you always serve together as a family unit, I am sending you three after a gang of six bad hombres! Jack's accomplices are five of the worst kind of raping and killing scum of the earth and if you are able to corner them, I don't imagine they will surrender or go with you any too peaceable like. In fact, I suspect that all of that bunch will fight you to the death versus being arrested and brought back to Judge Parker's court to stand trial for their reported crimes. The reason being for them to more than likely fighting you three to the death versus being arrested is simple. Once they are brought back here to Judge

Parker's court, they will be found guilty anyway and being hung will be their reward. So as you can see, they have nothing to lose by dying out in the field because they are going to die on the judge's gallows at some point in time anyway!"

Then turning in his swivel chair, Marshal Fagan spit a long spew of black-looking spittle out his open window and onto the bushes below. Then turning back and facing his deputies, he said, "Up until recently, we didn't have live witness accounts of such previous raping and killings done by these outlaws because such chaps don't apparently exist. That is because Jack's gang makes it a point not to leave any live witnesses around to testify against them for the crimes they have committed. All we have so far regarding their raping and killing escapades are a number of too scared to testify folks about the rumors they have heard from any surviving folks close to the violence being committed. Those unfortunates will tell us what they heard being whispered around as to what is going on but every one of them refuses to testify for fear of being killed themselves by those they testify against, so there you have it. Many of those folks will share with us information regarding that gang's cattle rustling and such but not much of anything else. So, remember what Judge Parker has ordered and that is to bring them back to his court alive so he can hang them here and not for you to shoot them out on the outlaw trail. That is unless they won't go quietly and if that happens, then the three of you do what must be done."

Pausing to spit a stream of tobacco juice out his second floor window again, Fagan then continued as the three Dodsons hung on his every word out of respect for their senior command officer and not wanting to miss anything in the way of orders given. This they also did because none of them expected to be turned loose on their own so early without more training being received from an experienced deputy marshal like Bass Reeves had been doing for the last couple of weeks with the three of them. "Jack's five accomplices are also all named in your Writ of Arrest documents, and there is a physical description of each man provided from the federal prison in Joplin, Missouri, in which each man served out a previous ten year sentence for cattle rustling. In fact, that is what each man is now wanted for in Judge Parker's District Court. They have been accused of rustling several smaller herds of cattle being driven up from Texas over the past few months. Then they bring the stolen stock up here into the Indian Territory and sell them to a number of willing hands, both Indian and white man alike. This time, we have a number of the Texas drovers who have agreed to testify as to the cattle they lost to this bunch, hence the Writs of Arrest you fellas will be asked to serve for the cattle rustling they have been doing over these last few months."

Then it was time for another stream of tobacco juice to be spewed out the window before Fagan could commence with what more he had to say to the brothers. "However, be aware that there are a number of unsolved reports of gang rapes and murders in the Broken Bow area in the southeastern tip of the Indian Territory that many surmise is related to Three-Fingered Jack's gang. Additionally, the sheriff in the town of De Queen, Arkansas, has informed me that he has a twelve-year-old girl who witnessed the raping of her older sister and mother while she hid undiscovered in their woodshed. This girl claims she saw her two kin raped repeatedly in their backyard by several men and then the two raped women were hung and strangled with the family's clothes line, while she remained hidden and terrified from her hiding place in their shed."

Pausing to spit out some bothersome tobacco leaves from his chew, Marshal Fagan began once again with his instructions by saying, "When those six killers fled the area, this girl fled to a neighbor's, who took the still terrified girl to the Sheriff's Office in De Queen and from there, this being a federal crime because it was committed in the Indian Territory, the local Arkansas sheriff contacted us with her information. However, this time Jack and his gang really screwed up. The girl's mother was a local and much beloved and respected school teacher, who had been teaching the Indian children to read and write. When she taught school, she also took her daughter along and not only home-schooled her but taught her to read and write in the Indian school as well. So for once, we have a really well educated and believable witness in which to testify and in essence, slip the noose around these killers' necks. And you can damn well bet that there is not a defense attorney alive that will badger that dear little girl in Judge Parker's court unless he wants to be sent to the gallows by my 'hanging judge' as well."

Then Marshal Fagan paused once again, turned and spat out his second story office window another spew of evil-looking black tobacco juice, wiped his mouth and then continued on saying, "Now here is the good part of this sad story. The sheriff was able to show this little girl some of his wanted posters that he had on hand and she was able to identify Three-Fingered Jack and two of his partners in crime. One of the men so identified, other than Three-Fingered Jack, was an old fur trapper from the early frontier days named William "Shite Poke" Kelly, and the other miscreant and curmudgeon was one ex-lawman and former Deputy U.S. Marshal gone bad named Larry Clinton. Both men are known accomplices of Three-Fingered Jack's gang, hence the Writs of Arrest you three are going to receive, fingering those three individuals for the raping and killing of this girl's mother and sister. Since we know who the other three men are running in that gang from previous reports from the area, known Indian Territory cattle rustlers one and all, those Writs you will be asked to serve are in the hopes you three can round up the entire gang, put them out of business, bring them back here for trial, and finally get them out of my hair once and for all time."

Then it was time once again to spit out some of Marshal Fagan's Brown's Mule thick black-looking chewing tobacco juice out the window. However, this time he slurped his spew and most of it went onto his inside window wall, joining a slew of other previous tobacco stains deposited thereon by poor aim as well. Wiping some residue spew from off his chin, Marshal Fagan began once again saying, "As for this little homeless girl, the sheriff's wife who was child-less, has taken her into their home and now the sheriff and his wife are looking at adopting her since all of her kin are now dead. Damn fine end-ing to this story of ruination if there ever was one, but I am not yet done. Under the care of that 'no-nonsense' sheriff and his many, local home-grown deputies, no one will dare touch this girl if she steps forth and testifies against Jack and his gang. I personally know that sheriff and of his service, and he has somewhat of a dark reputation for seeing to it that a lot of bad men that he and his deputies have captured over the years never seem to make it to his lockup in one piece! That in mind, I suspect after you interview her and get the facts of the killing and raping of her kin and she testifies back here in court, that entire gang is going to find themselves swinging from Judge Parker's gallows in fine style! So here are all of those Writs you three will need but before you do anything in serving them, I expect you to interview this little gal and get her testimony as to what happened. Then I expect you three to hunt down this gang of outlaws no matter how long it takes and bring them back to Judge Parker so he can try and hang the lot for their crimes against humanity. I also expect that the three of you will be out on the trail for this bunch of outlaws a long while because they are reported to be in the remotest part of the Indian Territory in our southeast. That being the case and with those outlaws being reported by the sheriff as operating so close to the Texas border, getting other folks from that neck of the woods to provide information on this bunch might be hard to come by. That being the case, I would suggest that you tell Chino to expect a several month detail and have him to pack his provisions for this trip accordingly. Lastly, don't none of you go and do anything foolish in trying to apprehend this bunch without 'going in after them full bore' and armed accordingly! This Three-Fingered Jack and his mess of killers and cattle rustlers are what I would call 'real bad men'. I would suggest, regardless of Judge Parker's policy of bringing them in alive, that the three of you be very circumspect in what you do if and when you get close to them. Remember, these men all know they are wanted for many felonious crimes and realize that if brought back to Judge Parker's court, they will more than likely swing from his gallows. So knowing that, they have nothing to lose in resisting being arrested by the three of you and as I said earlier, I imagine they will fight to the death versus feeling a noose slipped around their necks! Be especially careful around that chap William Kelly. He is alleged to be one hell of a rifle shot and carries and uses a Sharps .50-110 rifle and knows how to use it if you get my meaning, he being an old time buffalo hunter and all. So for Christ's sake, don't take any chances. If need be, you shoot that bastard between the eyes and leave him where he falls for the birds and beasts to enjoy what is left of his scrawny damn carcass!" With those words of instruction and warning, another spew of black tobacco juice went flying out Fagan's second story window onto the bushes and flowers below. "Now get the hell out of here and see what the three of you deputies can do for God and country," growled Chief Marshal Fagan, as he fumbled around in his desk drawer for another new plug of his 'strong as an angry mule's kick' chewing tobacco...

Chapter Four

"THREE-FINGERED" JACK'S GANG

OVER THE NEXT TWO DAYS, the Dodsons purchased the personal supplies they figured they would need for an extended trip hunting Jack's gang, including a new supply of pistol and rifle bullets, especially for their ever hungry .50 caliber Sharps buffalo rifles. Chino on the other hand, made sure he laid in a plentiful supply of flour for making biscuits, 50 pounds of dried beans, a 20-pound sack of rice, an extra 20 pounds of coffee and sugar, dried apples for his pie making, and a new 16-quart Dutch oven. The new Dutch oven was added because he had discovered on their first trip with Bass Reeves that the posse of deputies and Indian Policeman Tom Johns were all 'eager eaters' come every meal, requiring a larger cooking pot for those occasions.

Traveling almost due south through the Indian Territory after leaving Fort Smith, the men finally camped on the southern end of the Broken Bow Lake on the Mountain Fork of the Little River. There the men set up their camp on an out of the way, abandoned homestead, turned their mules and horses out to graze, and collected up a mess of firewood for what they figured might be a long stay.

Leaving Indian Policeman Tom Johns and Chino to man their campsite and guard the rest of their livestock, the three brothers split up and wandered into the town of Broken Bow separately, acting like out of work cowboys. This was a law enforcement trick they had picked up from Bass Reeves in which to gather information on the men they were seeking to arrest without arousing any undue suspicions on their part from the locals. In so doing, the brothers headed for a local saloon, purchased a few supplies from a local mercantile and talked with the owner from a local hardware store. Making sure they covered every base possible when seeking information as Bass Reeves had taught the brothers to do, Lewis even attended a local church service seeking information on Jack's gang from any 'loose-lipped' religious practitioners after the service and during the following church social.

Come nightfall, the three brothers wandered

back into their campsite one by one, to discuss their findings on the gang of outlaws they were tracking, eat some supper and get some rest. Brothers Joe and James had struck out when it came to finding out anything pertaining to the whereabouts of Three-Fingered Jack and his gang. To them, it seemed if anyone knew anything about Jack and his gang, they weren't saying much of anything to anyone, especially to a stranger out of fear of reprisal. However, Lewis in his visit to a saloon had managed to share several drinks with an unusually talkative local drunk well into his 'whiskey cups' by that time of the day.

That individual knew Three-Fingered Jack from his earlier days when they had served together on the range as cowboys, and had talked quite liberally, especially when furnished with several free drinks. In those discussions that followed, Lewis came to discover how Jack had lost two of his fingers in a shootout with another drunken cowboy early on in his career, about his two marriages that had failed, and how he came to be a cattle rustler.

In that 'cattle rustling' story, the man drinking with Lewis advised that Jack had tired of his hard work on the range 'punching cows' and figured he could work less and live 'higher on the hog' if he took someone else's cattle when they weren't looking, moved them into the Indian Territory and disposed of the same to those who would pay cash for the critters 'of many different brands' and could keep their mouths shut. As Lewis provided more free drinks to his talkative 'partner', Jack's old friend became looser with his information and finally divulged that Jack and his gang of five cohorts lived along the Indian Territory and Texas border near the nearby small town of Harris. That way, according to his loose-lipped friend, he could avail himself of a number of cattle moving out from Texas en route the railheads in Kansas. And many times doing so without the Texas drovers even becoming aware a number of their cattle had been rustled away from the main herd in the dark of night and then driven into the Indian Territory for sale to any buyer who had the money.

Then Jack and his gang would stay a week or so in the Indian Territory letting things cool off and having a good time spending the money they had made off the stolen cattle. Then when out of money, the gang would move south once again and help themselves by removing another small herd of cattle in the dark of night from those huge herds being driven north from Texas.

With two more supplied drinks, Lewis discovered that Jack and his gang had now moved into a small homesteader's abandoned cabin along the Red River to make their access easier when it came to lifting a small number of cattle from the larger herds being driven north and hiding them along the breaks until the main herd had been driven further north and chances of discovery had vanished. Then the cattle would be driven north into Indian Territory and sold.

Lewis also learned that the drunk at the bar had severed his relationship with his old friend Jack when he discovered that Jack and his gang, as had been whispered about, were now into raping and killing those isolated ranchers and farmers just south of the Red River. Then once those deeds were done, the gang would flee back into the Indian Territory where they could hide outside the reach of Texas lawmen and wait for their next criminal opportunity. Then Lewis advised the quietly listening group of lawmen at their campsite that he had left the man who had been doing all of the talking slumped over the card table at the saloon dead drunk and more than likely forgetful of the revealing conversation he had with 'an out of work cowboy' from another town about his old friend, Three-Fingered Jack.

Daylight the following morning, found the Dodsons saddled and out on the trail as they headed for the nearby Arkansas town of De Queen so they could interview the young girl who had allegedly lost her older sister and mother to the raping and killing of Three-Fingered Jack's gang. Arriving later in the evening, the three brothers holed up in a local boardinghouse in the town of De Queen after leaving their horses in the hands of a local liveryman.

The next morning, the three brothers reined up in front of the De Queen Sheriff's Office, went in and introduced themselves to the local sheriff. After a short discussion as to the deputy marshals' mission, the sheriff had one of his deputies ride his horse over to his home where the girl had been living and fetch her to the Sheriff's Office so she could talk with the marshals. When she arrived, Joe sat down with the young girl named Colleen, and gently asked her if she would tell him what she had witnessed from her place of hiding in the woodshed when her sister and mother had been raped and killed. However, realizing the innate sensitivity of such an event and before he started questioning Colleen, Joe had also requested that the sheriff's wife accompany him and sit in on the conversation by the young girl with the deputy marshals. Joe did so in order to lessen the sensitive cultural nature of speaking to strangers about such a violent and life-changing experience. Once again, another 'trick of the trade' he had learned from his time with Deputy Marshal Bass Reeves during some general law enforcement 'tricks of the trade' conversation.

Once Joe began questioning Colleen, he discovered she was not only a very strong willed young lady but was an excellent witness to her life-altering event as well. Colleen soon had not only described the deadly series of events in very graphic detail but did so with a thread of 'steel' in her young voice that just dripped of a desire for justice to be served for what had happened to her kin and her own life in general.

After about a half-hour of questioning the young girl, Joe and his brothers felt they had more than enough information as to the commission of the crime, with the additional bonus of Colleen being able to physically describe in particular the other three men who had also 'feasted' (her terms) upon her sister and mother. Additionally, Colleen was able to describe in her 'rich' choice of words the savage degree of involvement in the actual killing of the women by the men through strangulation with her mom's own backyard clothesline! Yes, Joe and his brothers felt Miss Colleen would make a very fine witness at any future trial, especially in front of the very religious and understanding Judge Parker regarding Three-Fingered Jack and his gang. Well, they felt so anyway for all those gang members who survived the actual moment of their arrest for the commission of their crimes of rape and murder…

Later that evening found the Dodsons riding

into their campsite back at the abandoned homestead, only to face an armed Chino and Tom
Johns when they came riding back into camp
unexpectedly at such a late hour. That late arrival situation was soon gratefully resolved and
Chino had some supper warmed up for the three
tired and now hungry deputy marshals.

Two days later found Chino driving his team
of mules pulling his chuck wagon into the breaks
along the Red River just south of Harris in the
Indian Territory. Making sure the wagon was
pulled deeply into the river's vegetation and hidden from the casual rider's view, the men disem-
barked, set up their camp and let their hobbled
livestock out to graze in the rich river bottom
grasses. The place they had selected was adjacent
a well-traveled cattle trail route commonly used
to trail one's cattle from Texas on the way to the
Kansas stockyards and markets. It was also adjacent the reported location provided earlier by
a drunk in a saloon to an inquiring Lewis while
out on an informational gathering detail as to
the whereabouts of Three-Fingered Jack and his
gang of killers, rapists and cattle rustlers…

For the next two weeks, the Dodsons rode
throughout the sparsely settled area getting familiar with the terrain, as well as from a distance
with their binoculars, the nearby location of the
suspected Three-Fingered Jack home site cur-

rently occupied by five unknown men. As it just so happened, three of unknown men observed at the old home site observed through the lawmen's binoculars from their hidden positions, pretty much matched the descriptions given by the sheriff of De Queen of Three-Fingered Jack and two of his known associates. Physical descriptions that the sheriff had derived from their prison records that had been provided to him from the authorities at the Missouri prison where the outlaws had been previously incarcerated for cattle rustling.

Then early one afternoon, the five men suspected as being Three-Fingered Jack's gang members were observed by the Dodsons leaving their home site and heading south towards the Red River. There they were later observed surreptitiously overviewing a large herd of cattle being driven up from Texas, as the animals were being herded northward up the well-traveled cattle trail presumably en route the distant Kansas stockyards. Later, those same five men were observed unsaddling their horses and letting those animals graze in the area, as the men bedded down by their saddles and slept through the rest of the heat of the afternoon.

Figuring the men were going to raid the herd of cattle that evening, the Dodsons made ready to intercept the cattle rustlers at some kind of a choke point and arrest the bunch, hopefully catching them 'red-handed' in the act of breaking the law in the act of felony theft of livestock. Little did the Dodsons realize in their limited experience as western lawmen that life could be a surprising son-of-a-bitch in the law enforcement world if not thoroughly enough planned out...

Come sundown, the Texas cattle drovers began circling their huge herd and stopping their northward progress for the day so the cattle could graze and water throughout the dark of the night along the luxuriant Red River valley area. Seeing that herd-circling action, the five suspects rose, saddled their horses and then stealthily rode them into the Red River bottoms adjacent the edge of the huge cattle herd. There they held up and waited for darkness to provide them some cover for what they had planned out in their minds earlier in the day on how to rustle a number of cattle from the near at hand Texas herd and not get caught doing so.

The three Dodson deputy marshals with the Writs of Arrest in their saddlebags for the whole gang for previous felony violations of the law and now anticipating what their suspects were planning, surreptitiously headed in the same direction as well. In so doing, the Dodsons figured they would ride down the five suspects hidden in the river breaks below, surprise them in the act, arrest the lot once final identification was made, and take them back to their camp as their prisoners. Sounded simple enough but maybe the Dodsons should have taken a chew of Marshal Fagan's Brown's Mule chewing tobacco before attempting to implement such a bold plan of arrest on five known and hardened criminals by three essentially rookie lawmen...

With Joe in the lead and his two brothers fanned out towards each side of the group of unsuspecting outlaw suspects and riding further in the rear, the deputies made their approach towards the five men still seated on their horses quietly watching the herd of cattle milling about just to their south. Quietly riding up to the front of the five unsuspecting men seated on their horses still partially hidden in the brush along the Red River, Joe acted surprised as he rode up upon the men out in the middle of nowhere, initiating the first part of his ruse.

"Hello, any of you men see a bay come by this way just moments earlier?" asked Joe, like some dumb 'dirt-farmer' out looking for a lost horse. However, as he did holding the attention of the men to his front in an unthreatening manner, Lewis was silently moving in on the bunch of men from one side, and his brother, James, the other.

"Get lost, you damn turd farmer!" bellowed

out Three-Fingered Jack, who Joe had instantly recognized from his previously provided prison records containing his arrest pictures therein.

Then William Kelly spotted Lewis quietly moving through the brush towards the group of men from their north side. "Let's get the hell out of here!" he yelled. "It's the law!"

With that warning, the five suspects exploded in five different directions like they had been there before and knew exactly how to react during such situations! Three-Fingered Jack tried to unhorse Joe as he blasted by on his steed, only to get a gun barrel from Joe's rifle laid across the bridge of his nose at a high rate of speed! "OOOFF"! grunted Jack, as his 'lights' went out and instead of unhorsing Joe, found himself flying through the air over the rump of his horse and landing hard onto the ground, unconscious!

Larry Clinton, Jack's half-brother, upon hearing Kelly's warning about the law being upon them, violently jerked his horse sideways away from Joe's location and blew his way through a mess of saddle-high brush as he tried escaping. However as he did, he found himself being confronted by Lewis coming his way on his horse at a dead run holding his rifle at the ready! Jerking his horse hard once again, only this time in the opposite direction away from Lewis, Larry found his horse losing his balance and falling over the two quick and violent directional commands just given! Down Clinton went only to quickly step out from the stirrups of his falling horse, and his reward for his fast action anticipating the oncoming horse wreck with a hard-charging Lewis was the steel butt of a lawman's Sharps rifle smashed down upon the top of his head, causing him to forget about escaping as he lost consciousness!

James on the other hand, riding hard from his opposite position of the 'hurrah', found his horse colliding with the flying horse of a madly fleeing William Kelly and was himself violently unhorsed and pitched painfully into a patch of beavertail cactus!

Within seconds, only brush violently whipping back and forth from numerous riders making fast entries and exits and the dust-filled air, were the sole evidence of the explosions of humanity and horseflesh that had occurred! As James tenderly picked himself up from the beaver tail cactus patch he had just been unhorsed into, Joe and Lewis found themselves afoot and quickly disarming their two still unconscious prisoners. Then it was a quick trip to their saddlebags on their horses to retrieve two sets of manacles. Those were then quickly placed around the wrists of the two still unconscious men lying at their feet, rendering them once and for all safely restrained.

Moments later, the three deputies had gathered together to survey the results of their actions. Both Jack and Larry Clinton were positively identified from the prison flyers carried in Joe's saddlebags, and then the Dodsons captured their prisoners' mounts so they would have some sort of transportation for their captures once they recovered consciousness from being struck in the face and on the top of the head by rifles. As for James, when the men figured the rest of the gang had 'vamoosed' for good, they took turns picking the painful cactus needles out from James's back, legs and his 'last part in the saddle'...

It was then that Joe realized the brothers now had a serious problem! There were still four very deadly alerted outlaws on the loose and they were now more than likely trying to figure out how to get their captured compatriots back. Then another deadly realization came flying home to all the brothers. They were now three against four and they had no idea as to where the four outlaws were and when they would strike!

Finally Jack and Larry came around and were helped up into their saddles for transport back to the deputies' campsite. Once there and still concerned over the four outlaws they had missed coming back to free their compatriots, the men broke camp and headed en masse to De Queen, Arkansas, with their two prisoners. Joe had ordered such a movement of their camp and prisoners because he felt having their captures incarcerated in the De Queen lockup was the safest thing to do in light of the fact that a number of the gang members were still on the loose.

That evening, the sheriff trooped Miss Colleen by Three-Fingered Jack and Larry Clinton and she positively identified both men as being involved in the raping and actual killing of her older sister and mother! Knowing that identification sealed their doom, especially if they were ever before the 'hanging judge', Three-Fingered Jack rushed the bars of his cell scaring the hell out of Colleen who had been standing on the other side of the bars making the identifications. When he rushed the bars of his cell, it caused Colleen to recoil in terror! Then Jack said to Colleen in a scorching tone of voice, "You testify against us, young lady, and the rest of my men will come for you in the dead of night when you least expect it, gang rape and kill you, and if you do not believe it, you just wait!"

With those words of warning and before the marshals could react, De Queen Sheriff Conklin quickly opened up the door to Jack's cell and taking his hammer-sized fists, the bearish-sized sheriff pummeled Jack so hard, that Joe heard Jack's teeth clatter like a muffled pistol shot from the impact of the monster-sized sheriff's fist violently striking his face!

Finally getting the maddened sheriff under control for what Jack had said to Colleen, Joe had to remind him that Jack, or what was left of him after being struck numerous times in the face with hammer-like fist strikes, was a federal prisoner and subject to federal control and protection.

The sheriff, still in anger over what had occurred, slowly turned and facing Joe said, "As long as he is in my jail and continues to threaten my new daughter, he will pay the price!" With that, he turned and gathered into his arms his new daughter and together they left the jail much to Joe's relief. However, Joe remembered back to what Marshal Fagan had said to the brothers earlier in his office about the De Queen Sheriff. A sheriff who had a reputation for bringing a number of his prisoners in who looked like they had gone through a dog-fight with a big dog and had lost... Then Joe just shook his head over what 'the law' could really 'look like' in the Arkansas outback...

That night the marshal's posse stayed in the local boardinghouse enjoying a nice supper and then a hot bath was had by all. The next morning at their breakfast table, the marshal's posse was interrupted by a sheriff's deputy rushing into the eating area and breathlessly advising Joe and his brother deputies that their prisoners had escaped in the dead of the night and in the process, their night jailer had been killed by those effectuating the escape!

Storming out from the boardinghouse, the men ran the short distance to the jail to survey the scene. When they arrived, they found the sheriff livid over what had happened and suspecting Three-Fingered Jack's gang had effectuated the prisoner's release and they had all now run back into the Indian Territory where he had no jurisdiction. With that realization running through his mind, the sheriff blew his stack! About then another deputy rushed into the jail and told the sheriff that the gang had taken their only town doctor prisoner, presumably to treat the injured Three-Fingered Jack's damaged mouth, face and jaw from when the sheriff had lambasted him the evening before after Jack had threatened his new daughter, Colleen, from his jail cell!

Breakfast now forgotten, the posse paid the boardinghouse owner for their night's stay, retrieved their horses and mules from the livery and were soon hot on the trail of the escaped prisoners. As they followed the trail left by the escapees and the rest of their gang, Joe had an 'outlaw capture' plan spinning around in his head that he had 'borrowed' from Poteau Policeman Indian Tom. A plan that they had successfully used when he and his brothers had captured Confederate Colonel Jackson and his outlaws for the raping and killing of many of their family on their farm near Booneville.

Without mentioning anything about his crazy idea on what he planned on doing regarding his pending outlaw recapture effort, Joe and posse headed back into the Indian Territory after Three-Fingered Jack and his cohorts. Finding a place that was somewhat out of the way, Chino, Tom Johns and their wagon was ditched, and the two of them stayed back with the rest of the horses and mules to keep an eye on them. They also stayed back because neither of the two men had any federal enforcement authority allowing them to actively assist the three deputy marshals. With their wagon and their livestock secure, the three marshals continued on into the interior of the Indian Territory to a suspect hideout destination previously discovered by the deputies when their search for Jack's gang had initially started.

Stopping after the posse had ridden deep into the Indian Territory, Joe held them at bay for a while in order to give the tired horses a 'blow'. By then, Joe had finalized his recapture plan and shared his idea with his brothers on where first to look for the gang of outlaws they were chasing. He began by saying as they sat on their resting horses, "Look, those guys do not know that we know where we suspect they have been living. What say we sneak over to where we first discovered them by that abandoned homestead and see if that is where they are now staying in that old cabin. If they are, we need to come up with a better plan than we had earlier down by the river in order to capture the entire gang. Plus when we do, we had better see to it that De Queen's only doctor is not injured, or I have a feeling that that sheriff will do to us what he did to Three-Fingered Jack back in his jail cell when he mouthed off to Miss Colleen. Now with that in mind, I have a plan to capture the lot of Jack's gang if that is where they are hiding at the old abandoned homestead. Or at least those who will decide to peacefully surrender to the three of us anyway. Indian Tom gave me an outlaw capture idea on the first law enforcement trip we took together in the Red Oak area chasing Colonel Jackson and his bloody lot of outlaws. I liked that 'trick of the trade' so much that I learned from it and decided to put it into my Deputy U.S. Marshal bag of law enforcement tricks. In fact, before we left Fort Smith, I saw to it that I purchased what I needed from the mercantile store in order to help us in capturing the worst of the worst of the outlaws that we ran across. In so doing, I took the liberty of stashing what I figured we would need for such law enforcement details into my saddlebags. With that little 'trick of the trade' in the back of my mind, here is what I propose the three of us do in the case of capturing Three-Fingered Jack's gang..."

Later that afternoon as the sun was setting in the west, found the three deputy marshals looking down at the abandoned homestead where they had originally discovered what they suspected was Three-Fingered Jack's gang hideout. Lying belly down on a small hillside a short distance away, the three men glassed the cabin below with their binoculars and discovered there were now seven horses located in the corral next to the cabin! Sure as 'frog's hair is fine', the six outlaws were all back in their original cabin with what the deputy marshals figured was also the kidnapped doctor from De Queen. That was most certainly so if one counted that seventh horse as the one that the doctor had been forced to ride when he had been abducted from his home in De Queen right after the outlaws escape from the jail! Having previously discussed the tenets of his outlaw 'trick of the trade' capture-plan with his brothers, the men left their horses and began their sneak toward the cabin with the sinking sun at their backs. That was another one of Joe's learned 'tricks of the trade', so anyone looking in their direction into the bright rays of the setting sun would not see the three men carefully sneaking in towards the targeted cabin holding a number of suspected outlaws and hopefully the still safe and sound De Queen town doctor.

Finally managing to sneak up to the close-in outskirts of the area without being discovered, the deputy marshals took up their individual capture-positions around the log hut so they could safely corral the outlaws once they were ultimately forced from their cabin. Then Lewis and James quietly remained hidden, waiting for Joe to execute his plan on 'outlaw-capture' using a modification of a strategy he had learned from Poteau Policeman Indian Tom on their first law enforcement detail working together in the Red Oak area in an attempt to capture Colonel Jackson, Badlands Bob and the rest of the band of ex-Confederate outlaws on the run in the Indian Territory.

Joe, from his place of hiding behind a large, filled horse trough in front of the suspect outlaw cabin by the corrals, when he saw that his brothers were safely in place ready to provide covering fire, yelled out to the outlaws inside the cabin who up until that moment in time, were unaware of the close at hand presence of the three federal lawmen.

"Hey, you inside the cabin, you are surrounded by U.S. Marshals! Come out with your hands in the air and not wearing your gun belts. If you don't do as I say, I have 20 sticks of dynamite and will blow you and that damn cabin clear into the Red River!" yelled Joe.

Upon hearing those shouted commands, the next few minutes were filled with the sounds of surprised men scrambling around inside the cabin so they could cover the three windows and open front door of the cabin against what they now knew was threatening them from the outside. Then the brothers heard one of the men inside say, "If you bastards want us, come in and get us!" Then a heavy rifle blast boomed out through the open front door of the cabin from a shooter hidden somewhere inside the cabin, and a huge splash of water was seen to erupt from the horse trough Joe was hiding behind for protection! With that shot, it was obvious to Joe that the shooter was only shooting in the general direction from whence he had heard the voice of the deputy marshal demanding the group's surrender. But to Joe's way of thinking, the shooter had pretty well pinpointed the 'sound of the voice's' exact location, which was too damn close for his comfort! Upon the bullet's terrific impact into the side of the horse trough, Joe realized that the killer inside known as William Kelly, the old buffalo hunter with the huge caliber .50-110 Sharps rifle, had to have been the one doing the shooting at his horse trough.

"I told all of you, if you want to live, throw down all of your weapons and come out with your hands held high, or I will throw this bundle of dynamite at your cabin and blow all of you clear into the State of Texas," yelled Joe from behind his protective horse trough, still full of gallons of 'bullet-stopping' water.

Once again, the big caliber Sharps rifle was fired from inside the darkened cabin by an out-of-sight shooter through the open doorway, blowing another huge hole into the side of the horse trough behind which Joe was hiding. In so doing and smashing another large hole into the side of the horse trough, it once again let out a stream of water where the heavy bullet had entered through the wooden side of the trough. Joe then realized it was just a matter of time until the horse trough was drained of all its protective column of 'bullet-shielding' water and then the huge .50-110 bullets would easily come tearing through the wooden sides of the trough and out the other side and maybe into him! With that realization in mind and now aware of the dangers he would soon be facing hiding behind an empty wooden horse trough, Joe put the final stage of his plan into motion while it was still safe for him to do so from his protective place of hiding.

"OK, you asked for it!" yelled Joe as he lit the fast burning fuse, quickly stood up and hurled his bundle of dynamite sticks right at the cabin's open front door! When he did, it was a perfect throw, landing in plain view right within inches of the cabin's open front doorway! There it menacingly laid with its fuse madly smoking and continuing to burn down towards the 20 sticks of 'cabin-blasting all to hell' dynamite! Then Joe immediately ducked back down behind his protective water trough before one of those big 50-110 buffalo gun slugs found him as its target instead of the horse trough…

With the dynamite lying there in plain and menacing smoking view, nothing happened for the longest few moments. Then one could hear lots of excited and panicked loud talking coming from inside the cabin over what was now lying in plain view just outside the cabin's open front door! Moments later, out the front door burst a heavily bearded man with a Winchester rifle in hand, shooting every which way at any object that could be hiding a marshal! When he did, there were so many bullets flying through the air every which way, that it caused the brothers to instinctively duck back down behind their protections because of so many flying bullets being randomly sprayed about. Then the madly shooting rifleman quit shooting, bravely reached down in order to grab and toss the menacing bundle of dynamite away from their cabin.

BOOM! went Joe's Sharps rifle, blowing the man violently backwards inside the open doorway of the cabin and out of sight, as the impact of the heavy bullet caused the mortally wounded man to drop the bundle of dynamite sticks now directly in front of the open doorway! Joe had placed his bullet squarely into the man's chest when he had stood up with the bundle of dynamite in hand and now figured there were only a total of five outlaws to deal with… As Joe ducked back down once again behind his protective water trough, his mind ran back to his earlier days as a young man when his dad, Albert, had taught him the finer points of shooting a rifle and a handgun. From the way the man trying to pick up the bundle of dynamite had reacted to Joe's rifle shot, Albert had done his teaching job on the accurate aiming and shooting of a rifle rather well when it came to his eldest son's shooting abilities…

Then out the door burst William Kelly, the man previously responsible for shooting the deadly Sharps .50-110 rifle. As he did, he blazed away with his buffalo rifle in the direction of Joe's now quickly draining horse trough as he exited the cabin! After firing his single shot rifle in Joe's direction towards where he had been last seen when he had stood up and just moments earlier, shot the man with the rapidly firing Winchester, Kelly quickly leaned down to grab the bundle of dynamite with the still madly smoking fuse and died where he stood! That move on the part of William Kelly trying to pick up the smoking bundle of dynamite and toss it away from the cabin was all it took for Lewis from his defensive position by a stack of loose hay, to 'head shoot' the deadly adversary and dropped him 'smack-dab' onto the top of the smoking bundle of dynamite!

The rest of the outlaws still inside the cabin upon seeing the 'Winchester man' and Kelly shot dead and realizing the fuse leading into the deadly bundle of dynamite was burning itself shorter and shorter, lost their nerve and burst out from the open front door like they had been shot from a cannon! When they did, out streamed four unarmed and desperate outlaws, all running for their lives, trying to avoid being blown all to smithereens by the 20 sticks of dynamite laid smoking at the front door of their cabin! When they burst forth from the cabin, sometimes two at a time through the same narrow open doorway in a panic, they found themselves covered by three serious looking Deputy U.S. Marshals holding their rifles at the ready! But that did little good in the physical control department, as the escaping outlaws tried running far enough away from the bundle of dynamite to avoid getting blown to pieces that the Dodsons now had trouble corralling the thoroughly panicked bunch of killers.

Finally getting the remaining four outlaws rounded up and under control in addition to one very terrified looking innocent town doctor, Joe then casually walked over to the bundle of dynamite with what was left of its still-smoking fuse, picked it up and carried it under his arm back to where his brothers had all the outlaws now seated in a group. As he did, he casually cut off the end of the burning fuse with his knife, which upon closer examination, only led by itself into the bundle of dynamite and NOT into any fuse cap, which would have been needed in order to set off the explosives...

"Damn!" said Three-Fingered Jack angrily, upon seeing that Joe had just lit a fuse that led nowhere into the bundle of sticks of dynamite that had been tossed at the outlaws' cabin front doorstep! "That bastard tricked us into thinking the dynamite was going to blow us all up!" he fumed loudly upon seeing Joe's 'trick of the trade'.

Joe just grinned over hearing Jack's words of frustration and grinned even more when Lewis returned somewhat later with the marshals' horses toting sets of manacles in their saddlebags. Moments later, all of the outlaws were safely manacled, as Lewis and James began saddling up the outlaws' horses for the long ride back to De Queen, Arkansas. Since there was a telegraph office in De Queen, Joe hoped to telegraph Chief Marshal Fagan back in Fort Smith to alert him as to the capture of Three-Fingered Jack and his merry band of killers, cattle rustlers and rapists, minus those killed of course, who had refused to surrender and tried shooting their ways to freedom...

Later on their way back to De Queen and the local lockup, Joe had the town's doctor ride on ahead so he could get back with his still very worried family at the first opportunity and let them know that he was all right. Then he and his posse continued heading northeast towards the town of De Queen with his prisoners so he could telegraph Chief Marshal Fagan for any further instructions as to what he wanted done with the prisoners and any future orders he wanted his posse to execute since they were already in that remote part of the Indian Territory. In tow as his prisoners were Three-Fingered Jack, leader of the gang of killers, rapists and cattle rustlers; one Ernie "Skunky" Eaton, considered a half-crazy desperado of the worst degree who seldom ever changed the clothes he was wearing or took a bath; Jack's half-brother, one Larry Clinton who had a thirst for the women of a younger age; and lastly one Jacob Pitts, a man who never found a woman that he didn't like or a cow that was too damn tough to rustle.

But, just south of Broken Bow as the posse and their prisoners made their ways towards the jail in De Queen, Ernie Skunky Eaton, even though manacled, broke away in a surprise move with his horse and raced off towards a small nearby farming settlement. Catching the marshals by surprise, Lewis finally also broke away after the racing-off Ernie in hot pursuit. Ernie was a good horseman on a fast horse and it took Lewis some time to close the distance between the two riders. However, Ernie, seeing Lewis catching up to him, raced his horse towards a large hay barn and rode in that direction like the devil was on his tail. Arriving in a cloud of barnyard dust, Ernie jumped off his lathered-up horse and ran into the open-doored barn looking for some sort of a weapon in which to attack Lewis once he arrived on the scene.

However, that fast move into the barn and quick grab of a nearby pitchfork sticking up in a loose pile of hay where it had been left by the farmer, got Ernie more of a surprise than he had bargained for! Little did Ernie realize that prior to his arrival at that loose pile of hay, a deadly battle between a house mouse and striped skunk was in its final throes from within! Then all of a sudden, the striped skunk was interrupted in his life and death struggle with the aggressive house mouse by someone rapidly removing the pitchfork from 'his' pile of hay. Pissed off over being interrupted during his 'hunt for breakfast', the skunk did what he did best during such times of disturbance and travail. Running out from under the pile of loose hay, the skunk spotted Ernie kneeling several feet away next to the pile of hay, ready to put his pitchfork now in hand into the body of that of the fast arriving in pursuit, Lewis.

Ernie, totally intent in waiting to strike once Lewis got within range of his pitchfork, had failed to see his 'little black and white buddy' just two feet away, stamping his front feet in irritation over being surprised and then robbed of his house mouse breakfast! As it turned out, Ernie disrespected the skunk's stamping front feet warning because his attention was now focused on the fast approaching Lewis. Not one to be ignored, the skunk, bring so highly disrespected, stamped his front feet one more time over the intruder's rude manners, evil behavior and badly smelling body, raised his hind end or 'business end' up into the air in one last warning!

Once again, Ernie neglected to see or understand the striped skunk's warnings and just coldly waited for Lewis's arrival so he could stab him with the pitchfork, disarm him and then he would see 'who was in charge' of the impending 'hurrah' with the remainder of Deputy U.S. Marshals!

SPISSSIS! went a 'full fathom five' spew of skunk piss along Ernie's entire side, a man who had yet to see and acknowledge his 'friend' "Mr. Skunk" raised up on his hind legs alongside and aiming Mother Nature's 'double barrel' and letting his essence fly directly onto his crotchety smelling body!

"UGGGHHH!" bellowed Ernie as the skunk's piss went all over his entire side, into his eyes and open mouth all in one encompassing spew of essence! As Ernie was jumping to his feet and wiping his now inflamed eyes with one of his hands, Mr. Skunk then gave Ernie the other barrel of Mother Nature's perfume since Ernie had disrespected Mr. Skunk so badly! "UGGGHHH!" yelled Ernie once again, as he now dropped his pitchfork, fell to the ground and rolled over and over along the barn's floor in eye-pain and unbelievable stench! That was when Ernie rolled right over several fresh, still warm and very liquid, fly-covered 'cow pies' left by a cow in the advanced stages of one of the worst cases of cow-diarrhea known to man! Now with a face utterly covered with sloppy wet and horribly stinking cow manure, Ernie continued rolling back and forth, thrashing about in pain, smell and now with a mouth full of still warm 'cow poo' to go along with his earlier mouthful of skunk piss!

It was then that Ernie's luck, all of which had been of the worst kind that morning, continued unabated and getting worse by the moment in fine style! SNAAAP! went the steel jaws of a trap that had been set in the barn in order to catch troublesome skunks, ACROSS ALL FOUR OF HIS FINGERS ON HIS SHOOTING HAND! All of those events culminated in a crescendo as Ernie continued to thrash about on the floor of the barn from the double load of skunk piss previously received into his eyes and mouth, having rolled over three fresh and still warm diarrhea-induced cow pies with the 'full' of his face 'meeting' each pie as he rolled along, along with his gun hand loudly 'clanking' with its skunk trap still firmly attached, as he thrashed about on a dried horse manure-covered barn floor!

As if the man's luck was not yet bad enough, when the steel-jawed skunk trap had slammed closed across Ernie's extended and flailing about fingers, the power of the trap's jaws broke four of his digits in the process! "OOOWEEE!" screamed Ernie now in even more pain than ever, as he jerked his hand violently against the end of the trap's chain, which had been anchored to a horse's stall post and in so doing, separating the broken finger bones in his damaged hand as a result of his violent thrashing around and about! In so doing, Ernie's little surprise that he had planned for the close at hand pursuing Deputy U.S. Marshal was lost in the 'horse manure dust' of the events taking place around him…

It was a sorry looking and smelling Ernie Eaton, appropriately nicknamed "Skunky" by his cohorts in crime because of his aversion to taking a bath, when Lewis exited the farmer's barn pushing ahead of him a very different looking prisoner than he had looked prior to associating himself with the barn and its other 'associates'.

Suffice to say, Skunky rode at the end of the prisoner caravan for the rest of the way to De Queen. Once there, the prisoners were jailed into the jail's cells and Joe went off to telegraph Chief Marshal Fagan for further orders since he did not have a jail wagon to transport his charges such a distance back to Fort Smith. An hour later, Marshal Fagan telegraphed back to Joe with orders to leave the four prisoners in jail at De Queen because as a matter of policy, he would be sending a jail wagon to transport such dangerous outlaws all the way to Fort Smith so they could remain properly manacled and chained while in transport. Additionally, Joe was further advised to wait there in De Queen for another set of instructions to arrive the following day via telegraph, regarding another federal law enforcement issue that had just been reported as having taken place in his neck of the woods that dictated a Deputy U.S. Marshal's quick and timely intervention.

With that information in hand, Joe returned

to the De Queen jail only to find one of his federal prisoners missing. Fearing that the missing prisoner named Skunky had mouthed off to the mean as a snake local sheriff and had been 'taken care of', caused him to look around for an explanation as to the why of his prisoner's disappearance from the jail cell into which he had been originally placed by the marshals.

Once asked the question by Joe as to the disappearance of his federal prisoner, the sheriff gave a resoundingly loud laugh over the question. Then with the sheriff still chuckling over the question about the disappearance of the federal prisoner, he got up from his desk and gestured for Joe to follow him out to the back of the jail's complex. There Joe observed an outhouse made of stone sitting off by itself because of its smelly contents. On its door was a huge padlock and inside he could hear Skunky pleading to be let out from the cold and stink of the outhouse and be allowed to join the rest of the prisoners in a cleaner smelling jail cell...

Finally getting over his laughter regarding his unique placement of the federal prisoner, the sheriff told Joe that his prisoner smelled so badly from all the skunk piss and cow manure that he had stunk up his entire jail. Having had enough of such bad smells, the sheriff had decided to place Skunky in the jail's old stone outhouse and let him remain there until he smelled better. That the sheriff had done after the local doctor had splinted up the broken fingers on Skunky's shooting hand. Joe figured the old sheriff had a point and since it was his jail, he let sleeping dogs lie and the two men went back inside the jail and shared some old, boiled all to hell strong coffee, as Joe shared his 'dynamite tale' and how he had captured Three-Fingered Jack's gang using a trick he had learned from a Poteau Indian Policeman during an earlier pursuit of the outlaws that had raped and killed a number of his family's kin.

After the old sheriff had finished laughing over Joe's clever use of a learned 'trick of the trade', he smiled and said, "Son, if you ever decide to leave working for those damn federals and need a job, I could use a good man like you. Between the two of us, we could raise enough hell that we could make that damn old devil move over and give us both a decent place in hell…"

CHAPTER FIVE

THE BURNING OF "TEN CROWS" BY TEXAS COWBOYS

THE FOLLOWING MORNING, Joe left his brothers to finish their breakfasts and walked over to De Queen's telegraph office to see if the telegraph operator had any further instructions for the Dodson Deputy U.S. Marshals from the Chief U.S. Marshal from Fort Smith. As it turned out, the Chief Marshal's reply was just coming through the telegraph when Joe arrived, so he sat down in the office and waited for the message to be completed and translated. There he found himself waiting for about ten more minutes while the lengthy telegraph from his boss in Fort Smith was being transmitted, translated and copied by the telegraph operator.

Upon completion of the message being sent and copied, the telegrapher handed Joe a piece of paper holding a rather lengthy set of instructions thereon. In those instructions, Joe was advised that a jail wagon would be dispatched from Fort Smith the following day en route De Queen, take on his prisoners and return the lot back to Fort Smith, so they could stand trial and be prosecuted for their crimes committed in the Indian Territory against a number of its citizens.

Then Marshal Fagan instructed that Joe and his deputies were to contact Chief Buffalo Calf of the Caddo Tribe, a man who was located in the small southeastern town of Bokhoma in the Indian Territory. According to the marshal, one of the chief's tribal members named Ten Crows, had been a prosperous rancher and farmer in that portion of the Indian Territory. Days earlier, Ten Crows had discovered a herd of Texas longhorn cattle being driven up from the Red River Valley, which had been deliberately driven onto his fields full of growing crops and were in the process of destroying all of the same. Ten Crows, upon discovering the cattle in his fields destroying his crops, according to Marshal Fagan, had confronted the Texas drovers demanding to be paid for the damage the cattle had caused to his crops and the livestock's immediate removal. According to Ten Crows's wife who had been riding with him at the time, for his troubles in confronting three of the drovers over the damage their cattle had done to his crops, he was tied up to a nearby cottonwood tree, set afire and burned alive! Then the three Texas drovers moved their cattle away from Ten Crows's land, but not before taking a 100 or so head of his personally owned cattle grazing in another of his fenced pastures, and then continued on their way to the Kansas stockyards on one of the trails commonly used by the Texas herds coming up from the Red River Valley area. Marshal Fagan instructed Joe and his brothers to immediately go after those three drovers who had allegedly burned Ten Crows alive in front of his wife and had rustled his cattle. He then wanted them quickly arrested and personally brought back to Fort Smith to be tried in Judge Parker's District Court for cattle rustling and murder.

Continuing, Marshal Fagan's telegram further advised that Joe and his brothers were to pursue the drovers as soon as possible or the entire Caddo Indian Nation was going on a warpath and that would be bad for all future white cattlemen driving their cattle up from Texas, as well as the many local whites living peacefully in the Indian Territory and even the nearby surrounding State of Arkansas! The marshal further advised where Chief Buffalo Calf of the Caddo Nation could be located for any further information regarding the matter, with an admonishment once again to get moving on the problem no later than the next day to preclude an Indian uprising over the brutal burning of Ten Crows while he was still alive!

The next day right at daylight, found the Dodson posse's chuck wagon re-provisioned with bacon, beans, flour, dried fruit, and a five-gallon tin of lard (for cooking), and moving to the southwest towards the small town of Bokhoma to meet with Chief Buffalo Calf from the Caddo Indian Nation. The following morning on their second day of travel, the three Deputy U.S. Marshals rode into the cabin area of Chief Buffalo Calf, only to find it surrounded by at least 100 armed and mounted Caddo warriors obviously ready to go on the warpath for the wrongs committed against one of their people, namely Ten Crows! As the three deputies rode closer towards Chief Buffalo Calf's cabin, once the white men were observed riding into the area, they were immediately surrounded by the hostile Caddo warriors, who made many threatening physical and verbal gestures towards and at the time and unknown to them, white man deputies.

Joe, now the recognized leader of the posse because of the leadership traits he had commonly shown throughout their juncture in the federal law enforcement arena, stopped the movement of his posse, raised his badge of office for all the angry warriors to see, then placed it back onto the front of his shirt and rode into the immediate cabin area showing no signs of fear. Lewis and James did the same, realizing how much the Indians respected a show of bravery in the face of suspected danger and superior numbers. However, upon seeing such a mad swarm of Indians when they had originally ridden into view, all three brothers had unsnapped the leather 'catches' on the hammers of their handguns just in case they had to shoot their ways out from an obviously intense and troubling situation.

Riding up to the front door of what turned out to be the chief's cabin, Joe found himself faced with a rather tall and imposing Chief Buffalo Calf standing there looking him dead in the eyes. Joe dismounted, strode over to the imposing figure of the chief, opened up the flap on his vest so the man could see his badge of office, and then extended his hand in a sign of friendship. For the longest moment, the chief refused to shake Joe's hand but finally his hand slowly moved out and clasped Joe's hand in a sign of friendship. When he did, Lewis and James, still surrounded by a mess of angry warriors, each breathed a sigh of relief and came to respect their older brother even more for the bravery he had just shown and in the wisdom of his actions in what could have been a rather troubling and ugly situation.

"Chief Buffalo Calf, my name is Joe Dodson and these two men are my brothers, James and Lewis. We three are Deputy U.S. Marshals sent here by Chief Marshal Fagan in Fort Smith, Arkansas, to investigate the killing of one of your tribal members named Ten Crows by some Texas cattlemen, and the rustling of a number of his cattle by those same individuals. I need to start my investigation into this matter by interviewing Ten Crows's wife to get her side of the story so she can tell us in her own words what she witnessed and in the process, have her physically describe the men doing the killing of her husband and the rustling of their cattle. The quicker that we can get that done, the quicker we can get after those guilty parties before they get lost in the wilds of Arkansas or Kansas. May I have your help and cooperation in this matter, Chief?" asked Joe.

For the longest time, Buffalo Calf just looked hard at Joe after he had spoken and then finally said, "I have already sent for Ten Crows's wife so I could hear in her own words what happened, so my warriors and I might know better what to do if something needed doing. She should be here within a short period of time. Yes, you will have my cooperation, but if you cannot find these bad white men who killed Ten Crows, I can. My warriors upon hearing of this killing from Ten Crows's only son, dispatched a number of men to find the bad Texas white men. They did so not to attack and kill them, but are now trailing them so the proper authorities will know where they are located and can catch and arrest them. My warriors have reported to me just this morning that these men and their cattle are moving slowly and can easily be found just south of Muskogee. They will continue trailing this herd of cattle and those three bad white men who burned Ten Crows alive until I tell them to do otherwise. But if you do not catch and arrest these men and take them before the Federal Judge in Fort Smith who hangs all bad white men, then we will kill the bad white men ourselves, and stampede their herd to the four winds for all to catch, have and enjoy as they please."

"Well," said Joe, "since we are here, we will investigate this issue and if we find that the three drovers from Texas did as you say, they will be arrested and transported to the jail in Fort Smith for trial. So if your warriors want to trail those bad white men so they can keep an eye on what they are doing and their daily locations, that is fine with us. However, just let us do our job and if the drovers are in the wrong, they will be punished by the federal authorities."

About then, a small buckboard was driven into the chief's front yard carrying a young man driving the wagon's single horse, with an older woman seated on the other side of the seat. When it stopped, Chief Buffalo Calf walked over to the woman and spoke to her in the Caddo tongue for a few minutes. As he did, Joe could see that she looked over at the brothers several times, as if the chief was explaining to her that the three white men were lawmen and it was all right to talk to them and explain what had happened to her husband and the rest of their herd of cattle that they had in another pasture.

Moments later, the chief turned and gestured for Joe to walk over to the wagon's seat upon which the Indian woman quietly sat watching him as he approached. When Joe arrived, the chief introduced Joe to the late Ten Crows's wife who was named Lily White Grass.

Joe, not one to mince any words even during delicate situations such as the one he now found himself facing, began speaking straightaway. "Miss White Grass, I am Deputy U.S. Marshal Joe Dodson and these other two white men are my brothers, who are also Deputy U.S. Marshals. We have been sent here to investigate the killing of your husband Ten Crows and the rustling of your cattle. Would you explain to the three of us what happened when your late husband was killed and what you remember about what the bad white men physically looked like who did the killing and rustled your cattle." With that,

Joe physically backed off a bit from where he was standing and let the Indian woman have her space, as she explained to him what had happened out on the range that day her husband was tied to a tree, burned alive, and their small herd of cattle taken by her husband's killers and intermixed into the Texans' herd.

"Me and my man heard a lot of cattle bellowing in our south wheat field and rode out to see if they were ours and had gotten out from their enclosure. When we arrived at our wheat field, we saw that a large number of strange longhorn cattle were grazing in our unharvested wheat field! When my husband tried to run them off our land, three cattlemen rode up and demanded to know what we were doing. My husband tried telling them that he was trying to get the strange cattle away from his crops and if he could not, who was going to pay for the damage to his wheat field? When he said those words to the cowboys, one of the men threw a rope around my man, dragged him over to a cottonwood tree and then wrapped him up with the rope by riding his horse around and around the tree, until he had my man all wrapped up to the tree. Then the men laughed at me as I tried to get my man untied and one of them even struck and knocked me down, telling me to stay there on the ground or I would get more of the same as my husband!

Then they piled up brush around my tied-up husband and set him afire before I could help him! I
can still hear his screams as he burned up by the
tree and now he is with the Cloud People." Then
she paused as the tears just rained down from
her weathered and grief stricken-looking face.

Catching herself moments later over the public
airing of her grief, she sat up straighter on her
buckboard seat and then continued saying in a
strong and firm voice, "My husband was a good
man. Those three cowboys killed him and took
away my son's father before the Great Spirit was
ready for him. I will never forget those three men
for what they did to my man, my son's father
and our family. All three of the men who killed
my husband spoke different than the rest of us
living around here. In fact, they spoke kind of
like many of those black people talk who have
escaped from the south and came here in the
Indian Territory to live and escape capture. All
three men spoke like that and wore those funny
looking Confederate Army hats like their soldiers
used to wear during the great war fought between the 'white-eyes'. As for how they looked,
all three had long mustaches that curled up at the
ends and tiny little beards on the ends of their
chins. One of the men was older, walked with
a limp and had a big belly. He was the one who
roped up my man to the tree so he could not es-

cape. The other two were younger and were the ones who gathered up the brush placed around my husband and set him afire. All three men chewed the tobacco leaf and spit on my man as he screamed and burned to death in front of me and them. Those cowboys all rode matched gray horses and then as my husband burned, rode off laughing to our enclosure in our north pasture, let our cattle out and mixed them in with their longhorns still feeding and milling around in our wheat field. Then the three men rode off laughing as they herded all the cattle from our wheat field back towards their large herd, which was still moving slowly towards where one finds the North Star in the sky at night. That is all I know and I do not want to speak of the dead anymore because to do so causes their beings to wander aimlessly forever," she said as she grew silent, and then looked dead ahead as if no one was standing around her signifying she had nothing more to say.

Joe, realizing that Miss Lily White Grass was through talking about the incident regarding the death of her husband and the theft of their cattle, thanked her and then moved back towards where his brothers were standing off at a respectful distance from the buckboard and the ongoing interview. "I think I have heard enough so we can get on with the investigation and the arrest of those three drovers. With her descriptions and testimony, it looks like we have three mustached with goatees, ex-Civil War veterans from a southern state by the manner of their speaking, who all are riding matched gray horses. With those descriptions and her first hand testimony, I think we have enough to ride like the wind and try and intercept those three killers before they ride off into the sunset or into some frontier cattle town and disappear. What makes it even nicer, we have a mess of Caddo Indians shadowing the slow moving herd and once we arrive, they can fill us in on what has been happening as well. So I suggest you two mount up and I have a few more things to say to the chief, and then I will be along directly to join you," said Joe.

As Lewis and James headed for their horses, Joe walked back in order to talk with the chief. Once again as Joe approached the chief, he could see that he was suspiciously eyeing him as much as Joe was eyeing the chief. To Joe it was obvious from the chief's body language that he just as soon wished that he had the 'white-eyes' out of and away from his neck of the woods and off his land…

"Chief Buffalo Calf, I have a request to make of you. Could you provide several of your braves to act as our guides so we don't waste any time in running these killers and cattle rustlers to ground?" asked Joe.

"I have already selected four men to accompany the three of you, so you can ride directly to where this Texas herd of cattle is currently bedded down on a new feed ground so they can put on some more weight before being moved on and later sold at the stockyards," Chief Buffalo Calf stated in a matter of fact, deadpan tone of voice.

"Good," replied Joe, "that being the case, me and my brothers are ready to leave right now if that is alright with the four men you have selected to ride with us."

With Joe's words, Chief Buffalo Calf raised up his arm in a come hither gesture and immediately four fierce looking warriors detached themselves from the main group of Indians surrounding the chief's cabin and rode towards the chief and the deputy marshal.

"You four are to see that these marshals are quickly guided to where this herd of Texas longhorn cattle and the bad white men are currently located near Muskogee for a few days where they are resting up from their long days' ride on the trail. There you will not get involved with any of the white men unless these marshals request your assistance. However, if the marshals need any kind of help, you are to give it, even if that means you have to kill some of the bad white men," coldly directed Chief Buffalo Calf. Then

Chief Buffalo Calf turned to Joe and looking him hard in his eyes said, "Marshal, you and your men must get these bad men who burned Ten Crows alive. If you are not able to arrest these killers for some reason, then my men have orders from me to take care of them so they never burn anyone alive ever again..."

Not letting Chief Buffalo Calf's seminal words be lost on him, Joe nodded his understanding of what had just been said, shook the chief's hand again and joined his brothers who were already mounted and ready to ride. Soon the seven men, three marshals and four determined Caddo Indians, rode back to where Joe had left Chino, Indian Policeman Tom Johns and their chuck wagon. Soon nine men were heading north towards the town of Muskogee where the suspect Texas cattle herd and its three killers were under observation by ten other previously dispatched by their chief, Caddo Indians.

Seven days later found the marshals and their Indian escorts still hot on the trail of the Texas cattle herd, as it now had once again resumed its travels northwesterly towards the Kansas border, en route the railhead and stockyards. It was then that Joe detached their chuck wagon and Indian Policeman Tom Johns, who was required to travel with them while in Indian Territory in case they ran across Indian-on-Indian crime, and told Chino to meet them later at the livery in the nearby town of Drumright. Then the posse and their Caddo Indian escorts made haste after the northward bound herd of Texas cattle and their three suspects of federal interest for the burning of Ten Crows and the stealing of his herd of cattle.

Heading northwesterly after leaving the Muskogee area, the posse and their Indian guides finally 'ran to ground' the herd of Texas cattle they had been hotly pursuing, hopefully still holding the three suspects who had burned Ten Crows alive days earlier. As the posse approached those drovers riding 'drag' on their herd, their Indian escort without a word being spoken since their work was done as they had been instructed by Chief Buffalo Calf, melted off into the surrounding landscape, joining the ten other Caddo Indians who had been silently following the Texas herd ever since it had left Ten Crows's land back near the small town of Bokhoma, Indian Territory (I.T.).

Tired, dirty and hungry after their many hard and long days riding after the suspect herd of cattle, Joe made the decision to ride right into the night camp now being constructed, announce to the Trail Boss why they were there, make the arrests of their three suspects if they were still with the herd, and then head for the nearby town of Haskell and the local jail in order to incarcerate their three prisoners. There they would safely lodge their prisoners for the night, find a place to stay and get a good night's rest before they headed back to Drumright to pick up their chuck wagon crew and then on to Muskogee to leave their prisoners with U.S. Marshal Bennett for him to arrange their transport over to Fort Smith in a safer form of travel, namely a federal prison wagon.

That thinking and what happened next was when 'the wheels came off Joe's wagon' in a manner of speaking! Slowly riding into the cattlemen's night camp in the process of just being set up by the Texas drovers, the three Deputy U.S. Marshals identified themselves. That they did to avoid the chance of getting shot riding in totally unannounced in the twilight.

With his brothers holding all the deputies' horses, Joe walked over to the cook standing by the chuck wagon looking on, identified himself with the badge of his office, and asked if the Trail Boss was in camp or close at hand.

"No Sir, Deputy, but I expect him in right shortly 'cause he knows I will be making my special Dutch oven biscuits this evening for our supper which he dearly loves," replied the cook, as he suspiciously eyeballed Joe.

"That is good," replied Joe. "We have some business with him so if you don't mind, we will wait for him to arrive so we can discuss that business," said Joe.

"Suit yourself," said the cook rather brusquely, as he turned and gave a set of instructions to his helper regarding several Dutch ovens cooking over the fire.

"Say, do you care if we have a couple cups of that good smelling coffee a-boiling away over the fire?" asked Joe.

"No, go on over and 'hep' yourselves, Deputy. The extra cups are over there in that camp box full of utensils, so go on over and 'hep' yourselves," replied the cook, as he commenced hanging several large Dutch ovens on the hanging forks over the campfire so they would commence cooking up their contents for the drovers' evening meal. Then the cook and his helper began mixing up biscuit dough and greasing several more Dutch ovens in preparation for the baking of biscuits to come.

About then, several riders rode up to the chuck wagon, dismounted and began removing the saddles from their horses. Then as two riders began currying down their horses, the cook ambled over to an older and much graying man and quietly said something to him that Joe could not hear because of the distance separating the group of men and the marshal. However, Joe just figured the cook was faithfully reporting to his boss the presence of several Deputy U.S. Marshals, who were residing in camp and wanting to talk with him about some 'marshal business'. With those words of warning from the cook, the gray-haired man looked up over the back of his horse at Joe and said, "The hell you say!" Then the Trail Boss spit a long spew of tobacco spittle over the back of his horse in Joe's direction like he wasn't much impressed with or over Joe's presence…

With that, the gray-haired man dismounted and walked briskly over to Joe. As he did, he extended his hand in an all-business sort of way and shook Joe's hand saying, "My cook here tells me you have some business with me. What might that business be regarding, Marshal?" asked the Trail Boss.

"Well, Sir, I'll be direct. Several days back, three of the men from this herd tied up a Caddo Indian man named Ten Crows to a tree on his property near Bokhoma, set him on fire and of course, killed him. As near as we can tell from a female witness and wife who was there when all of this occurred, she advised that this land-owner, her husband, was trying to run off a mess of your steers from his unharvested wheat field and tangled with three of your cowboys. They apparently took umbrage with what the man had to say, tied him up to a cottonwood tree and set him a-fire. Then the witness further advised your cowboys rode off to the Indian's nearby cattle enclosure, let them out, inter-mixed those cows into your herd, and then rode off with the rest of the Indian's animals," said Joe rather flatly.

"Why hell, Marshal, you are saying that all of this fuss requiring you presence is over killing some damn thieving 'Injun'? You mean to tell me that you are taking the word of an 'Injun' woman over a white man and a damn old squaw at that? Damn, Marshal, I think you rode all this way from wherever you came from over a no account 'Injun' and that means nothing to me or my men! What say you and your men have some damn good homemade chow with me and my men this evening and then you and your deputies can commence along on your way back to wherever you came from. 'Cause you ain't got no reason to stay and harass me and my cowboys over having a little fun as near as I can see it," replied the Trail Boss with a 'good ole boy' grin spread clear across his whiskered face…

For an instant, Joe saw 'red' over what and how the Trail Boss chose to address the felonious taking of a human life and the rustling of cattle issues just laid before him! Then quickly cooling down and getting control of his inner self, Joe made another attempt to bring to the Trail Boss's attention the seriousness of the issue at hand and doing so without getting into some kind of a shoot-out with him or a number of his cowhands over what he had to officially say or do. But 'Joe being Joe', that meant the issue would be faced dead-on and without any fancy fanfare sooner than later, 'come hell or high water'...

"Well, Sir, regardless of what you think, three men from this herd allegedly committed a serious federal offense in the Indian Territory and that is why I am officially here. Before this night is out, me and my men mean to have three of your men in custody for murder and cattle rustling, both of which are serious federal crimes," concluded Joe in a tone and tenor of voice meant to convince anyone of the importance and seriousness of the official mission he meant to carry out, 'come hell or high water'...

"The hell you say! I can't believe what an impudent prick you are over such a small issue! Well, Marshal, where I come from, if a man kills a damn maggot-infested 'Injun', he is looked up to as if one had just killed a stinking ole rat or a too damn close at hand rattlesnake! As for taking the word of a woman regarding this matter, I don't know what part of this here United States you came from or what 'rock you crawled from under', but in the great State of Texas, that kind of testimony don't carry any weight any more than a good spit of tobacco juice," replied the Trail Boss, who was now verbally evidencing that he was fast approaching a 'rock-hard wall' when it came to wills over the matter at hand!

About then, three cowboys rode their horses into camp, dismounted and began unsaddling their matched set of gray horses prior to them being curried down and let out to graze while tied onto the picket line! All three of those men wore Confederate Army kepis, spoke in a slow southern drawl, were graced with long and curled mustaches, and sported a goatee one and all, just as Ten Crows's wife had described to Joe earlier!

As they did, Joe could see his two brothers recognizing their 'arrest targets' and quietly began moving in the direction of the three newly arriving, obviously ex-Confederate soldiers. Ex-Confederate soldiers, who fit to a "T" the physical description Miss Lily White Grass had provided to Joe and overheard by his two brothers days earlier when she described her husband's killers and rustlers of their cattle!

About then, four more cowboys rode into camp, making a total of eleven rough-looking Texas drovers now in camp and that didn't count the camp cook and his helper! No matter how Joe looked at what was happening around him, especially in light of the demeanor the Trail Boss was now evidencing over what Joe had said to him earlier, an explosion of sorts appeared to soon be forthcoming! To Joe, that was an obvious forthcoming event if he chose to enforce the federal law in the Indian Territory and do so in the Texas drovers' camp against superior odds.

Realizing the odds facing him and remembering all of the lawlessness he and his brothers had not only personally experienced with their family back in Arkansas but throughout their stay in the Indian Territory, Joe typically dug in his heels, 'Bass Reeves style'! "Well, Boss, those three men who killed Ten Crows back on the trail, just rode into your camp. I say that based on an eyewitness account as to their physical characteristics, and what I am seeing and hearing coming from those three riders off to your left who just rode in riding those matched grays."

As he did, Joe saw that his two brothers had steeled themselves as to the dangerous situation at hand, outnumbered as they were and yet were quietly moving into position knowing what was coming next, either an arrest, cowboy-camp explosion or both, whichever came first once Joe 'made his play'!

Walking over and facing the three surprised drovers, Joe said, "Gentlemen, my name is Joe Dodson and I am a Deputy U.S. Marshal. A number of days back on the trail further south of here, the three of you confronted a Caddo Indian man who was upset over the fact that your cattle were eating and trampling into the ground portions of his wheat crop. Then as a result of that confrontation, did the three of you tie that Indian man up to a tree and burn him to death?" This he asked as he looked the men steadily into their eyes looking for any kind of a sign that would indicate 'fight or flight' emanating from the three men upon hearing those pretty damn searing accusations.

"What if we did?" said the oldest of the three men with a very pronounced pot belly and sharp tone in his response.

"You didn't answer my question," responded Joe.

"What's it to you?" asked one of the other men. "He was just a stinking Indian and down where we come from in south Texas, killing one of those bastards is no crime. In fact, our kind of people considered it a good deed to get rid of them before they steal one of your horses or rape our women," said the young cowboy with a sneering look now spreading clear across his face. Then he continued saying rather coldly, "Yeah, I torched that bastard after he gave the three of us a bunch of guff about who was going to pay for the damage our cattle did to his wheat field. So, he got what he deserved and if his old lady had been better looking, we would have had our way with her as well before we headed off on down the trail," he proudly bleated out.

That was when that cowboy hit the ground

with a resounding THUD!, as Joe 'buffaloed' him
with the barrel of his hastily drawn pistol! The
instant Joe 'pistol-whipped' the mouthy young
cowboy, his two partners in crime instantly went
for their pistols. When they did, they found a pair
of cocked Colt .45's instantly stuck in their ears
by Lewis and James, who had quietly slipped in
behind them, realizing Joe was going to arrest
the lot, 'come hell or high water', regardless of
the odds now facing him in that cow camp that
evening!

"All three of you men are under arrest for the
murder of Ten Crows and the rustling of his
cattle," quietly said Joe. He then waited for the
next 'shoe to drop', which he figured was soon to
come from the rest of the Texas drovers in camp
who were now up on their feet and ready to do
battle… Well, as for that next 'shoe to drop'; Joe's
concerns were as 'right as rain'.

"You ain't taking any of my men, especially
those three experienced hands, you government
son-of-a-bitch!" yelled the Trail Boss as he went
for his six-shooter. When he did, Joe was standing close enough to the Trail Boss that he quickly
redrew his cocked pistol in a blazing move and
roughly jammed the end of his barrel under the
Trail Boss's nose, shoving it painfully upward in
order to make a point saying, "Your move!"

When that happened, it was absolutely amazing just how fast the Trail Boss changed his mind and "flew' his hands high into the air! Then he bellowed out, "The rest of you men, take these 'law dogs' down! Don't any of you bastards back down either jest 'cause he is a damn federal marshal, 'cause if you do, you can draw your pay and hightail it out of here right now afore I really get on my 'high horse' and go to kicking a mess of cowardly cowboy asses all over this campsite!"

Before any of the other cowboys in camp could make a move to back up their boss upon hearing his bellowed-out command for their actions, the cook reached up under the "boot" of the nearby chuck wagon, drew out a double barreled ten gage shotgun, quickly cocked both hammers full-back and started to swing it around in Joe's direction, only to have an arrow slam into the spice box of the chuck wagon right next to his head where he had been standing! In fact, that arrow hit so close to his head, that it took a 'nick' of flesh out from his right ear lobe!

Yelling out in surprise, fear and pain all at the same time, the cook dropped the double barreled shotgun and grabbed his damaged and now badly bleeding earlobe! When he did, the shotgun he had drawn from the chuck wagon boot and had cocked back both hammers, hit the ground, went off with a terrific BOOM!, and its two ounces of shot from a fired brass shot shell went directly into one of the nearby 16-quart Dutch ovens hanging over the fire cooking supper! When that occurred, the Dutch oven exploded into a dozen pieces of flying cast iron, and a bucket load of hot bean and beef stew flew all over the rest of the cowboys standing there in amazement over how quickly things were happening so closely around them! Cowboys, who just moments before had been quietly observing the arrest action at hand and had now been splattered with hot bean and beef soup and chunks of hot flying cast iron from the blown all to hell Dutch oven!

Like Joe had said earlier, 'hell or high water', only this time, it had been flying hot stew and pieces of hot Dutch oven cast iron, which upon bodily contact, further dissuaded all the Trail Boss's cowboys from getting involved. That was especially so if one took into consideration of the fact that they were all too busy rubbing off the hot pieces of metal and sticking, steaming hot stew that had just then been blown all over their bodies…

That moment in time then stood still, as the entire camp of cowboys found that they had been quickly surrounded with fourteen heavily armed and fierce-looking Caddo Indians with their trusty Winchesters, bows and arrows in hand! Once again like Joe had said, even though he had not prepared for this moment in time to occur, 'hell or high water' was the result of his actions, or was it hot flying stew or fourteen pissed-off and heavily armed Indians eyeballing everyone from close at hand quarters! Soon every cowboy within reach of the fierce-looking Indians covering them with their rifles and the like, were like their boss and reaching for the sky!

Then Joe took it upon himself to holster his pistol, walked over to the deputies' horses, removed three sets of manacles from their saddlebags and returned to their Texas cowhand prisoners. Once manacled, Lewis re-saddled all the men's horses and helped the three prisoners up into their saddles. As those sullen looking killers sat there quietly in their saddles under the armed and watchful eyes of Lewis, Joe walked over to the Trail Boss and told him to lower his hands but in so doing, not to try anything stupid. Walking over to his saddle once again, Joe removed a piece of paper, walked back to the Trail Boss and handed it to him to read by the flickering light from the cow camp's two fires, as almost total silence reigned over the cow camp.

"What the hell is this?" asked the Trail Boss.

"It is a Bill of Sale for the 103 head of Ten Crows's cattle that those three prisoners of mine rustled and were then co-mingled into your herd. The way I figure it, I can hold you up here for several days while we try to sort out Ten Crows's cattle from yours, or you can buy them at the going Kansas City stockyard price per head. If you do that, I think that will satisfy Ten Crows's widow and make it all legal-like. That will be your call, but I will only accept coin of the realm and not a note from you or your cattle company if you decide to buy those cattle at what I consider to be a fair market price. That is because once you are back in Texas, you can void the Promissory Note and Ten Crows's wife and her son will have nothing to show for their loss. So, Mr. Trail Boss, what you chose to do is your call regarding this purchase of 103 head of cattle from Ten Crows's widow, or you can sit here for how many days it will take to separate his cattle out from yours. Your call to make, Mr. Trail Boss," said Joe quietly…

Later with $309.00 in gold coin taken from the Trail Boss's strong box carried in the chuck wagon, Joe took it upon himself to sign over the cattle to him with a legal Bill of Sale in exchange for his payment in coin. That payment of $309.00 made being based on the going rate for that many of cattle ultimately being delivered at the Kansas railhead, at $3.00 per head. With that piece of business settled and with his three prisoners manacled and in tow riding on their three gray horses, Joe and his posse quietly rode out from the cow camp. As they did, Joe looked back into the light from the cowboys' two campfires and noticed that their surprise and protective shield of fourteen Caddo Indians had quietly vanished back into the darkened timber, never to be seen by the Trail Boss and his crew of drovers again... However, as Joe, the posse and their prisoners rode off into the darkness he could not help but notice the wonderful smell accompanying his group of riders. Their supper that night once they were safely away from the irate Trail Boss and his crew of Texas drovers, was the still warm, golden brown biscuit-bounty carried in two towels which had been removed from two Dutch ovens prior to their leaving the cow camp... After all, the Trail Boss HAD offered for Joe and his men to stay for supper and then take their tail-ends and ride off into the sunset, hadn't he?

Several days later, Joe, his posse and their three prisoners were back at the federal lockup in Muskogee. There the prisoners were turned over to U.S. Marshal Bennett for official transport with other waiting federal prisoners from his jail facilities via a jail wagon back to the lockup at Fort Smith, Arkansas. While there in Muskogee, Joe telegraphed Marshal Fagan for further orders or future assignments. Additionally, Joe also telegraphed his younger brother David back in Arkansas to see how he and the family's home place was faring.

Following that, the posse adjourned to the

nearest hotel for a much-needed bath, some good home cooking other than that found on the trail and a good night's sleep in a bed instead of under the stars, lying under a single blanket, covered with mosquitoes and using a saddle smelling strongly of horse sweat for a pillow.

Returning the following day to the telegraph office, Joe found two telegrams awaiting him. One was from his brother back on the home ranch advising that all was well, that the ranch was prospering and that he missed his brothers and hoped they were all right. The other telegraph was from Marshal Fagan requesting the return of the posse to Fort Smith. Return, so the deputies could testify in Judge Parker's court during the trials of their previously delivered prisoners, receive their next assignments, pick up the pay owed them, and refit their chuck wagon as well as re-provision it for their next assignment. A week later found the Dodson brothers back in Fort Smith and for the next ten days, testifying in their case when they had assisted Bass Reeves, as well as those from their most recent assignments regarding Three-Fingered Jack's gang and the Ten Crows burning investigations.

At the conclusion of the various trials, Judge Parker found Three-Fingered Jack and his entire gang of outlaws guilty of rape, murder, escape from jail, and cattle rustling. All the members from that gang soon discovered what 'hell or high water in the Indian Territory' was all about when the hangman's trap was sprung from beneath their feet... As for the three Texas drovers and where they 'went', they never again were able to eat Dutch oven biscuits, sing cowboy songs or hear the lowing of a herd of cattle being moved along a 'trail' to the Kansas railheads or stockyards. That is because 'Eternity' can be a quiet place and does not require that anyone eat three meals a day...

CHAPTER SIX

THE CAPTURE OF "GRIZZLY CREEK" BARNES AND JUDGE PARKER'S SURPRISE

FOLLOWING THE SUCCESSFUL culmination of the Dodson brothers' trials in Judge Parker's District Court, since there was no appeal process during that period of time of any of Judge Parker's rulings (only President Grant could grant a pardon to anyone found initially guilty in Judge Parker's court), as said earlier, the entire number of men were hung over the next seven days for their felony crimes against the Indian Territory subjects! Prior to Miss Lily White Grass's leaving after she had testified against the three Texas drovers, Joe saw to it that she received $309.00 in gold coin for the sale of her small herd of cattle to the Texas drovers. That was a small return for the loss of her husband and father to her only son, but a sort

215

of recompense just the same seldom found in or around the harsh Indian Territory frontier.

The following day after all of the hangings, found the three Dodson Deputy U.S. Marshals sitting in Marshal Fagan's outside office awaiting a meeting with him, in order to draw their recently earned six cents per mile pay (standard payout for Deputy U.S. Marshals), payout monies for successfully bringing all the federally wanted men to trial at $2.00 per head, and their next arrest assignment.

As the three brothers sat in the Chief Marshal's waiting room awaiting their meeting with their Boss, a rather unique discussion ensued among the brothers. They now discovered among themselves in the discussions that followed that they truly enjoyed 'hunting their fellow man' and being able to provide a modicum of justice to those downtrodden human beings living in the Indian Territory, a most lawless land. The brothers also realized that they were not only enjoying what they were now doing for a living, but were good at what they did and getting better with each and every investigation they conducted! That, coupled with the realization their younger brother was doing rather well running the home ranch by himself, they decided to continue on with their work as deputy marshals until they tired of the good work they were doing or something rather catastrophic befell the brothers. Something so catastrophic that the occurrence of such an event would take away their hearts, souls and desires when it came to enforcing the laws of the land in the Indian Territory...

"Good Morning, Gentlemen," said Marshal Fagan, as he greeted his deputies when they were finally ushered into his office. After congratulatory handshakes all around with his men for the successful duties so rendered, Marshal Fagan immediately launched into discussing the quality of their work to date. Suffice to say, Marshal Fagan was more than satisfied with his deputies' performance and heartened by that, now informed the men that he was going to assign them a completely different kind of needed investigation with an arrest to follow if they were successful in their newly assigned endeavors. In short, Marshal Fagan was assigning the brothers a different type of investigation that required an unusual amount of cunning on their part in order to 'run' their latest subject to ground and eventually bring him to trial in Judge Parker's court of last resort. Upon hearing what Marshal Fagan had to say pertaining to the potential challenge in order to be successful in running such a rascal to ground, all of the brothers really 'tuned' into what their boss had to say regarding the 'hunt that was in the wind'.

As they soon discovered, the brothers' latest subject of investigation was a man named "Grizzly Creek" Barnes, who was reportedly a major, very savvy, illegal bootlegger of 'moonshine' whiskey, operating in the Jackfork Mountains area near the small town of Daisy, which was located smack dab in the Indian Territory. As they were soon to learn, several other Deputy U.S. Marshals had been previously assigned this case and in every instance, they 'were found wanting' and unsuccessful in being able to capture and arrest the savvy 'moonshiner'…

Continuing, Fagan said, "Grizzly Creek Barnes, whose real name is Rufous Barnes, is operating under the moniker of "Grizzly Creek" Barnes for the creek where his reported stilling operation is located. From all reports, Rufous was an ex-Confederate soldier on the run from the Tennessee authorities for bootlegging whiskey from the western part of Tennessee where he once lived near the small burg of Crockett Mills. Shortly after starting up in his bootlegging business, jealous neighbor informants reported him to the authorities and he was arrested. To avoid being taken out from the local jail and hanged by his 'Yankee' bootlegging competition of mountain folks that he had bested in quality and overall production of corn liquor, caused him to flee once he was freed on bond to the Indian Territory several years earlier in order to hide out from the law."

Halting with his briefing for just a moment, Marshal Fagan turned in his swivel chair and spit a long stream of tobacco juice out his second story window onto the bushes and flowers below. Turning back around, Marshal Fagan began his briefing once again by saying, "There near the small town of Daisy, Rufous found work on a small ranch that also served as a local stage stop named "The Chase Place". There he served as a 'buckaroo' breaking horses for the local stage lines that ran through the area. Somewhat later, Barnes fell in love with the ranch's female cook for the stage lines, a woman named Martha Gee, who was only 14 years old at the time. Those two were eventually married and moved out to a place called North Arm, settled down on a hardscrabble piece of ground and tried to make a go of it as small farmers and ranchers."

Pausing once again for a moment, Marshal Fagan reloaded his mouth with a fresh chew of Brown's Mule chewing tobacco and then commenced with his briefing once again by saying, "However, once Martha got pregnant, Barnes realized he could not make a good enough living as a small-time rancher with all the extra mouths to feed as his family quickly expanded in numbers. With that concern in mind, he decided to return to his old family business of making high-quality bootleg corn liquor. Being from western Tennessee, he was more than familiar with making really good bootleg whiskey as his family had done for many years previously, and soon had a flourishing business making and selling his brand of whiskey to a goodly number of the local Indians as well as many of the white men residing in the area."

Having said about all he wanted to say for the moment, Marshal Fagan turned heavily in his swivel chair and spit a long line of tobacco-laced spittle out his open office window onto the bushes below. Then he leaned forward and spit out his old cud of chew out the window as well. Without any word of apology for the break in what he had been saying to his three deputies or his rather coarse manners, he reached into a vest pocket and removed a black, ugly-looking plug of Brown's Mule chewing tobacco. Taking a small penknife from his vest pocket, Marshal Fagan cut off fully a third of the plug and plopped it into his mouth and then placed his much-used 'plug cutting' knife back into his pocket.

Following that bit of action, he then visibly moved the lump of chewing tobacco around in his mouth until he found a comfortable place for it to reside and then commenced talking once again like nothing out of the ordinary had just occurred, saying, "Where were we? Oh yes, back to the business of Barnes selling his bootleg whiskey illegally to the local Indians and such. Now as you three know, that bootleg making and whiskey-selling business in the Indian Territory is illegal as hell and does nothing but debauch every Indian who lets that 'devil's brew' cross his lips. From what has been reported to this office by a nearby local white rancher who is not happy with what he is seeing, 'Barnes's Brew' is a hit with most of the local Indians and a large number of the local, tough as a hickory nut lumbermen, who are always seen flocking over to Barnes's ranch to purchase some of his hooch every time he makes it or returns from the sheltering mountains after making a whiskey run. According to our rancher source of information, Barnes has his still hidden somewhere high up in the Jackfork Mountains near the mouth of Grizzly Creek below Kettle Rock near his ranch."

Marshal Fagan then took a break from his bootlegging case instructions, turned in his swivel chair and spit a long, black-looking spew of tobacco juice out his window, then turned around and faced his three deputies again saying, "We have been told by his rancher neighbor that Barnes's bootlegging method of operation is to take a couple of well-trained, hell-for-stout mules carrying the bags of sugar, yeast and sacks of corn and heads out in the dead of night for his still, hidden high up on Grizzly Creek. Once there, he spends the next few days at his campsite making his whiskey and watching his back trail. Then when the new batch of whiskey is ready, Barnes loads it into four five-gallon Redwing earthen crocks, loads two jugs onto each mule in panniers, slaps them on the ass and they being trained, head out back to his ranch. Barnes then comes home by another route via horseback so no one ever catches him with the illegal whiskey in his possession or is any the wiser as to what he is doing. As we have been told by our complaining rancher source of information, the mules move down off the mountain in the dead of night and walk back into Barnes's open-doored barn and wait by their stalls for him to return so they can be unloaded and fed. When Barnes comes home by another direction, he unloads his mules and hides his five-gallon jugs of illegal hooch under the loose piles of hay in his barn. The main reason we know all of this in such detail is that his rancher neighbor living right next door, is an ex-Yankee soldier who hates 'Johnny Rebs', of which Barnes was at one time late in the war. That plus the nearby rancher, every time Barnes returns with more whiskey for later sale, the local Indians swarm all over the neighbor's property and steal everything not nailed down and use what they steal as barter with Barnes for his whiskey. So I guess he is tired of losing all of his chickens, lambs, bridles, tools and such to the roving bands of thieving Indians because of the whiskey-making actions of a 'Johnny Reb' and is blowing the whistle. But we need to keep that quiet because if we don't, the neighbor may end up at the end of Barnes's fists or worse. As I have been told, Barnes is an Irishman from the old school and if you cross him or let your guard down, he is quite a pugilist, not to mention, a crack rifle shot!"

Then it was time for another long spew of tobacco spittle to fly out the window and then the Marshal continued as if nothing unusual had just happened. "We are not sure how the Indians discover the exact time Grizzly Creek Barnes returns with a fresh batch of his whiskey, but they darn sure know or find out, and flock to his small ranch to either purchase or barter for the stuff before it is all gone. That is where you three men come into play. I want you to get Chino in on this trip and have him set aside enough provisions for at least another month's long trip. As I see it, you men are going to have to camp out in some out of the way spot, stake out Barnes's ranch house, and then try to follow him to his still and catch him in the act. But I am also told that may be damned hard to do. For it seems Barnes has the Indians on his side and any time any stranger comes into the North Arm area, he is alerted to that fact and seems to go to ground, making himself and his whiskey making operation scarce until he can 'truth out' the new arrival." Then it was time for another long spit of his used tobacco juice out the window by the Marshal.

Wiping off his mouth, the Marshal continued with, "Now as I see it, you boys are going to have to make yourselves known in the area as out of work cowboys or something along those lines and try to worm yourselves into the local fabric of the area so the Indians, farmers and lumber-men drop their guards regarding your presence and any questions they might have regarding your backgrounds. Either that or maybe you could pose as market hunters in the Jackfork Mountains, kill off a mess of deer and sell them to the locals for a 'song'. That way, they take a liking to the three of you for being so generous and once again drop their guards. Then as I see it, that allows you to move about more easily without Barnes being suspicious of your actions or just generally any the wiser as to your true intentions. However, I need to give you three a word of caution regarding this detail when deal-ing with this Irish bootlegger with a Tennessee backwoods bent and with him facing the possi-bility of an arrest and long imprisonment for his illegal actions. Grizzly Creek Barnes is known as a very clever backwoods man and one hell of a fine shot with a rifle. Sure as God makes green apples, he will not go gentle into the night if faced with an arrest for his illegal actions. That goes double when he realizes there is an arrest close at hand and upon that occurrence, he will be leaving his young wife and their kids home alone and without much in the way of a means of support. I am sure that he realizes what he is doing is illegal as hell, but he flies in the face of that federal issue and continues making illegal boot-leg whiskey and selling it to anyone who has the price of a quart or two as his main source of making a living. Additionally and I can't emphasize this enough, he now has several children as I am told and I am sure that will cross his mind, especially if and when you fellas arrest him, put the manacles on his wrists and haul him back to Judge Parker's court. Bear in mind if you grab him off and arrest him, there will be no one to take care of his family. With that in mind, he could very well make for an extremely deadly adversary! Lastly, I want that damn still blown clear to kingdom come when you men finally round this chap up and place him under arrest. By so doing and making it known to all concerned, you men will make an example of the man for what he is doing illegally and maybe someone else with the same intentions will take heed and not follow in Barnes's footsteps after he has been removed from North Arm's local society." With those words of caution ringing in the three brothers' ears, another spew of tobacco juice went flying out the open window and then Marshal Fagan handed the Writs of Arrest over to Joe, the now acknowledged leader of the group, to be served against one Rufous Grizzly Creek Barnes, maker of bootleg 'shine' and whiskey peddler.

Following that meeting with the Chief Marshal and gathering up the Writs of Arrest issued by Judge Parker for Rufous Grizzly Creek Barnes for illegally bootlegging whiskey and selling the same in the Indian Territory, the men left his office. Meeting with Chino somewhat later, Joe laid out their plans for the upcoming trip to the Daisy area of the Indian Territory. As Chino headed over to the local emporium to gather in the supplies he figured they would need for another month long trip, the three brothers headed back to the local boardinghouse in which they had been staying. Once there, they all three took a hot bath then adjoined to the dining room, and with their newly acquired pay for previous services rendered as Deputy U.S. Marshals at six cents per mile traveled, bought themselves steak dinners with all the trimmings. As a part of those 'trimmings', Joe saw to it that a bottle of legal whiskey was ordered and on the supper table as well. When the whiskey was delivered and after each brother had a full glass, they had a good laugh over Marshal Fagan's parting words to them as they left his office. Those words spoken by the Marshal being, "You damn boys had better bring me a goodly sour mash sample of what Barnes is making if any of you want to escape my wrath with any hide left on your backsides for mission failure!"

For the next two days, the Dodsons and Chino made ready for their trip to the Jackfork Mountains and the small town of Daisy. Provisions were loaded into the chuck wagon for at least a month-long trip, all the horses and mules were reshod, and worn out leather strappings on the chuck wagon, for the pack animals and the two-span of mules pulling the wagon were repaired or replaced. Additionally, since the posse was going only after a white man, Indian Policeman Tom Johns was to be left behind since he was not tribally required to accompany the deputies on such a mission involving non-Indians.

On day three after receiving their new assignment, Joe led the posse out from Fort Smith, Arkansas, and headed his group to the south and west towards the small town of Daisy, which was near the home of one Rufous "Grizzly Creek" Barnes, maker of bootleg whiskey. One week later, the posse arrived in the small town of Daisy posing as out of work cowboys, just laid off from an obscure ranch somewhere deep in Texas. By so doing, they hoped to find work in the local area and help perpetuate their cover. Parking their chuck wagon near a small stream in Rabbit Gulch, the posse set up their campsite and then the brothers went into town looking for any kind of work that would allow the men to blend into a rather tight-lipped and conservative community, yet still allow them the latitude to gather intelligence regarding their target and his illegal bootlegging operations.

Right off the bat, the men discovered there was no work on any of the nearby ranches for any out of work cowboys. However, the local Meadow Valley Lumber Company was always looking for skilled horse or mule skinners for their logging show, so there the brothers went looking for work the following day after their arrival. As it turned out, Woods Boss Cal Cole had need for two experienced mule skinners who were familiar with logging operations. Since both Joe and James had been the ones dragging in the logs used to build their new ranch house back in Arkansas and were experienced in such endeavors as mule skinners, they were hired immediately. Lewis on the other hand, based on a referral from Cole, found work at Meadow Valley's local lumber mill by the end of his third day in town.

Finished up with their successes in seeking work in the local community, the three men went into town to the local butcher shop in order to purchase some fresh meat for their camp. There they discovered that the butcher at the "Grosz and Grandson James — Purveyors Of Fine Meats Butcher Shop", had need for any amount of big game meat they could supply if they chose to go into the big game market hunting business on their days off from working at the mill and in the logging 'show'. Joe, realizing they could cover more bases in meeting and gaining the confidence of the locals by working in several arenas, advised Rich Grosz the butcher, that they would be trying their hands at market hunting big game, as well as working in the lumber and logging business because they needed to amass a small fortune so they could buy their own spread and go into the cattle raising business. If they did, Grosz advised he would buy any and all of the meat they were able to supply his shop, providing it wasn't blood shot and had been properly cared for. This the men agreed to do among themselves and on their ride back to their campsite, the Dodsons were pleased with their efforts at hiding in 'plain view' in order to round up and put one illegal whiskey maker named Grizzly Creek Barnes, out of business.

Chino had the Dodsons up at four in the

morning their first work day and after making all the men what he considered a 'lumberjack' breakfast of fried spuds, deer steak, eggs, Dutch oven biscuits and coffee, he then commenced quietly making the men their lunches while they ate their breakfasts. By five-thirty in the morning, Joe and James were being introduced to their mule teams preparatory to beginning their work in the nearby pine forests. Work that involved using mule teams to drag out the 'bucked-up' logs left behind by the 'double buck saw-wielding timber fallers' and onto the nearby 'landings'. There the logs were loaded onto specialized heavy duty, oxen-drawn wagons, then by winch and pulley-operated 'steam-donkeys' for transport to the local mill so the green logs could be made into lumber. Then after a period of time out in the mill yard in large, aerated stacks, the green lumber would be used in the building of structures in the growing town of Daisy. On the other hand, Lewis was at the mill boss's shack at five in the morning getting lined out on what his duties would be while working as a 'green chain-puller' (pulling green, fresh cut lumber off a moving steam-driven chain, then stacking that lumber on a wooden pallet for transport out into the 'yard' where such lumber could be set out to air dry to prevent undue warpage).

For that first week of work, the three men

worked hard at their jobs and found little time other than during their short lunch hour, to meet other people and gather intelligence on Grizzly Creek Barnes. Chino on the other hand, in order to keep busy, went from local North Arm ranch to ranch, including that of Rufous Barnes's, buying up live chickens, eggs, fresh vegetables, canned fruits and vegetables, along with the occasional lamb for his and the Dodsons' suppers when they came home from work in the woods and at the lumber mill. In so doing, Chino, in making those 'rounds' buying up food items, soon found that he was quickly becoming known and accepted locally as the cook for a bunch of now hard-working cowboys recently employed in the logging and lumber businesses. Chino made sure everyone whom he met was made aware that he and his three partners, who were working at the mill and in the logging show, were doing so in order to make enough money to buy a small ranch and get settled into the cattle business locally. Additionally, Chino made sure everyone, as part of the deputies' cover, knew that his three friends were soon also going into the market hunting for big game business on their weekends and if they were successful, there would soon be fresh big game meat for commercial sale at the Grosz and Grandson James Butcher Shop in Daisy.

After their first week of hard work, Joe and

the rest of the posse, in order to maintain their cover as big game market hunters, found the four of them up at the crack of dawn on their first Saturday off and out into the nearby forests hunting mule deer and bear. As by design, that first week found the four men hunting the lower Grizzly Creek drainage for big game because that was the reported general area of Grizzly Creek's whiskey still. As they did, all the while pretending to be hunting any big game animals that 'crossed their rifle sights', they kept their eyes peeled and on the lookout for any oddball sets of mule tracks leading up from the North Arm lowlands that led higher up into the head-waters of the Grizzly Creek drainage. (Author's Note: Mule shoe prints are distinctly different than that of a horse, namely narrower.) That they did based on the information Marshal Fagan had received and supplied to his deputies, because that was the drainage in which Barnes allegedly had his whiskey-making still located, and was the only way in which to efficiently haul heavy sacks of sugar and corn either by horse or mule when traveling through such rugged mountain-ous and heavily timbered terrain.

Over that first weekend of looking for their subject while masquerading as market hunt-ers, no such tracks other than those made by the deputies' own horses and pack mules were discovered entering into or in evidence along the stream bottom of Grizzly Creek. This exacting type of 'track' examination was done because Barnes was reported to be highly suspicious, extremely woods-wise and elusive in his travel habits when conducting his illegal whiskey-making operations. As such, Joe figured any savvy type of individual breaking federal bootlegging laws would do everything that he could to camouflage any trace of such illegal activities. That included using an old Indian trick of hiding one's horse or mule tracks by having them walk in a moving stream of water in order to camouflage their entry or exit in an area. Then one day later when Lewis had stopped alongside Grizzly Creek to let his horse drink, he noticed old yet faint sets of mule and horse tracks in a slow-moving pool of the creek bed leading upstream! The posse then followed the 'off and on' tracks of the horse and two mules being ridden upstream for about a mile until the tracks exited the stream and headed even further upstream into the heavily forested and rocky high country known to hold the Grizzly Creek headwaters.

It was about then that Joe spotted a large four-point mule deer buck and shot him so they would have some meat to sell back in the town of Daisy, which would help the lawmen in maintaining their cover as legitimate market hunters in addition to being local loggers and lumbermen. As they gutted out the deer, Joe just happened to notice a stout-looking man far above them partially hidden in the brush, looking down at them through a pair of binoculars! Making it look like he had not observed the individual partially hidden in the mountain mahogany far up on the mountainside spying on the activity below, Joe slipped by each of his brothers as if helping them with the gutting of their deer. As he did, he quietly advised each brother that a rather stout-looking individual was closely watching them from up on the hillside with binoculars, and for them not to let on that they knew they were now being watched.

Finished with the gutting of the deer and placing the heart and liver back into the thoracic cavity for their supper that evening, the men loaded the animal onto one of their pack mules, tied the critter down so it would not slip off in the rugged terrain, and then without any suspicious looks backward, headed off downhill like they were on their way out of the woods with their deer. However as they did, they all figured they were finally on the right track of Rufous "Grizzly Creek" Barnes and his whiskey-making still's location based on the horse and mule tracks observed earlier in Grizzly Creek, the reported use of that specific area as his whiskey-making site, and now the mystery man surreptitiously watching them from out in the damn middle of nowhere.

The next week while the three brothers were hard at work maintaining their cover as loggers and lumbermen in the eyes of the local population and trying to quietly pick up intelligence on Grizzly Creek's whiskey-making operations, Chino made a chance discovery. While making a fresh egg, butter and vegetable purchase from Martha Barnes, wife of Rufous Barnes, he noticed out of the corner of his eye two heavily loaded mules walking by themselves across the lower pasture below the Barnes's ranch house. Keeping a 'cocked' eye on those heavily loaded mystery mules, Chino eventually saw them moving through the open doors of the adjacent hay barn and quietly disappearing inside. As they did and when Martha wasn't keeping a close eye on him, Chino also noticed that each mule was carrying what appeared to be five-gallon jug earthenware containers on either side of their pannier pack sets when they had walked through the adjoining pasture and into the nearby barn!

Moments later when Chino was in the process of loading his two dozen, just purchased fresh, brown-shelled chicken eggs, two quarts of churned butter, a half-gallon jug of homemade buttermilk loaded with gobs of yellow-orange butterfat for his Dutch oven biscuits, and a crock-ful of pungent, freshly ground, 'strong as an angry mule's kick' horseradish, he noticed that Martha was now in her backyard hastily gather-ing in her fresh laundry from off her clothesline. Little did Chino realize at the time that clothes on that clothesline was a key to be used in the capturing of one Rufous "Grizzly Creek" Barnes, and putting an end to his illegal bootlegging and sale of an illegal alcohol product to the local Indians and white men in the North Arm area.

Suppertime the next day back at Chino's campsite brought forth even more evidentiary information when Joe and James returned home from their daily logging activities. During their lunch period as they ate with some of their new logging buddies, they reported that they had hit pay dirt. Two of the timber fallers, when they ate their lunches with Joe and James during that day's noontime period, unknowingly shared an illegal surprise with the two undercover depu-ties. Upon finishing their lunches and just before the men went back to felling timber and skid-ding the logs out to the landing, one of the fallers named Jenkins broke out an earthenware jug and shared some fine homemade Tennessee sour mash whiskey with the two deputies...

Acting surprised over the type of brew being offered during the lunch hour, Joe after taking a sip and acting pleased over what was being shared, asked Jenkins, a local Indian, where he had gotten such a fine-tasting whiskey. Jenkins with a broad grin said that a 'friend' had given him a jug of the fine whiskey and there was more of the same from where that had come from. Joe, continuing to act surprised over the obvious homemade liquor being in country, asked how that was possible since he had heard whiskey was illegal to make, possess or sell in the Indian Territory. Jenkins just laughed over Joe's innocent-sounding question saying that, "For those of us who have an 'in', we can always come by such fine sipping whiskey." Then looking up in an alarmed fashion, Jenkins said, "Wait, here comes the woods boss! We best get back to work before he gives us our walking papers because we should by now be hard at work." With that observation and words of warning, the jug disappeared back into Jenkins's buckboard and the men hustled around like nothing out of the ordinary had occurred to avoid 'getting their walking papers' from their hard-working woods boss and expecting the same…

However, Joe and James now had more than just suspicions that Grizzly Creek Barnes's whiskey was commonly making the rounds in the hands of the locals. As such, they had to find a way to locate the still itself or get in on the marketing ground floor by purchasing a jug or two of the whiskey that seemed to be flowing fairly easily among the known and trusted folks of the North Arm area, in order to put a stop to such illegal actions.

Arriving back at camp later that evening, Joe and James were further surprised and encouraged when Lewis handed each man a half-pint of some of the finest tasting sour mash Tennessee whiskey they had ever tasted! As Lewis's story went, he had observed a rather stocky, middle-aged man riding a mule up to the mill boss's shack, stepping off the animal and when he did, was seen carrying an Redwing earthenware gallon jug. That jug was then delivered to the mill boss, who in turn handed the stocky-built man another earthenware gallon jug that was apparently empty by the way he easily handled it. When he did, the mill boss also handed some paper money over to the man delivering the jug. There were smiles of knowing and trusting one another, and then the unknown man boarded his mule and rode off toting the empty gallon jug. Shortly thereafter, the mill boss brought out several glasses of a clear liquid and handed one to each of his hard-working men on the 'green chain'. Soon there was much merry laughter along the work site as Lewis just took small sips from a pint jar that had been handed to him in lieu of a drinking glass. Then later when no one was watching him, he put the lid on the pint jar and smuggled it into a rolled-up dirty shirt that had been taken off when he had gotten hot and sweaty from the hard work that was required. Later, upon completion of his workday at the mill, Lewis took his rolled-up shirt, mounted his horse like he did every day and headed for Chino's campsite. With that information now in hand, it quickly became apparent to the deputies that Barnes's bootleg whiskey was more than making the rounds in amazing quantities as well as quality!

The following weekend, the three brothers worked their ways back into the area where they had killed their four-point mule deer buck the week before and had been observed by a mystery man from afar high up on the hillside towards what they now suspected was Grizzly Creek's still site. Joe figured that since they had been seen there the week before hunting deer and then they had later sold that deer at Rich Grosz and Grandson James's butcher shop in town, with that word making the rounds, they were safe being that close to what he figured was Barnes's still site in an obvious commercial hunting capacity again. So with all the evidentiary facts they had developed, the three men began hunting on foot in the same suspect area and soon had two doe deer down and in the process of being gutted. As his two brothers finished gutting out the two does, Joe kept a cautious watch out for the man who had been eyeballing them the week before from the timber-covered mountainside high above. However, that day they remained the only chaps obviously in that area of the forest, so Joe took a gamble at being nosy and made his move.

"Come on, Guys. Grab your rifles and follow me," said Joe. With that, the three men began making like they were hunting their ways up the mountainside towards the direction where they had observed the stranger overlooking them from the week before when they had gutted out the four-point buck. An hour later found the three brothers near the headwaters of Grizzly Creek and spread out below them near a small creek's rivulet some thirty yards away, stood a tent, a campfire now long gone out and a stoned-in copper still, mash pots, cooling coils, and all the other necessary parts needed to make a size-able quantity of fine Tennessee corn liquor!

Leaving his two brothers acting as lookouts, Joe took off his shoes so he would not leave any easily seen strange boot tracks in the immediate area and then gingerly walked down to the still site. Arriving on site and careful not to leave any easily discernible foot prints in the soft dirt around the base of the still, Joe walked all around making mental notes in his head as to what he was observing. Then peering inside the tent, he discovered two sacks of sugar, three gunnysacks of dried corn, and two empty Redwing five-gallon jugs like Chino had described being seen earlier in panniers on the two mules walking across the Barnes's lower pasture and into the barn, along with several canisters of yeast. Having seen enough and feeling that had to be Barnes's still site, the brothers carefully backtracked their ways out from the area, making every effort to hide their tracks or any other signs that strangers had been there in the area close to the still site.

Pleased over their discovery, the three men were making their ways off the mountain hunting deer as they went, when Lewis spotted a man riding his horse in the waters of Grizzly Creek far below while trailing two heavily loaded mules coming up the mountain in their direction! Quietly alerting Joe as to what he had seen, all three brothers hastily dismounted and fled quickly from the immediate area, but in such a manner so as not to leave any clouds of dust in the air as they ducked back into the heavier timber. Then with his brothers holding their horses far back in the deep timber and holding their noses so they would not whinny if they smelled the other horse or mules approaching, Joe quietly watched the stranger from a short distance away from behind the base of a large pine tree where he would not be inadvertently seen.

Soon, the rather stocky man hove into sight and continued on past Joe's hidden observation point up toward the recently reconnoitered still site and then eventually out of sight. Leaving his brothers behind to watch their animals, Joe quietly sneaked back up the mountainside to a secluded spot overlooking the still site from a roundabout way and was soon lying on his belly watching the man below cautiously approaching the campsite by the still. Once there, the man unloaded several sacks of sugar and corn by his tent and then commenced dumping out his previously used mash tank into Grizzly Creek and washed it out. Once that chore was done, the tank was re-set into its original position, filled with corn, sugar, creek water and yeast.

Having seen enough and not wanting to be inadvertently discovered as a stranger and betrayed by one of the man's mules, Joe back crawled away from his hiding spot and then took off down the mountain towards his two waiting brothers. Joe did so because he did not figure he nor his brothers were in a good enough position to successfully capture the armed still operator and avoid being shot in the process by the reported straight-shooting Tennessean as they made their approach to place him under arrest.

Arriving, Joe said, "Let's get the hell out of here. I will fill you in on what I saw when we get further away so we won't be discovered," and quickly the three men rode off. Once safely out of the area, Joe filled his three brothers in on what he had observed. That was when Lewis advised both of his brothers that the man they had seen that afternoon riding into the area, was the one and same who had brought a jug of 'moonshine' and sold the same to his boss at the mill. The same 'shine' that his boss had shared later on with all of his men pulling the green chain in glasses and pint jars! Now the deputies knew for sure that they were on the right track of catching one Grizzly Creek Barnes, especially since a physical identification had now been made of the man to be arrested. Then the three men rode back to their camp, skinned out their deer on their meat pole, took the animal to the Rich Grosz and Grandson James's Butcher Shop for sale, adding more 'cover' for what they were doing and about ready to do.

Taking the next Sunday off, the brothers slept in after experiencing several damn hard weeks of not-used-to-labor as loggers and lumbermen. But that downtime was not to be for Chino, as he saddled up his mule and pack mule and then rode off once again towards the Barnes ranch and several other North Arm ranches on his weekly 'groceries shopping trip'. Arriving at the Barnes ranch, he was greeted by Martha, young wife of Rufous, and requested that he be allowed to purchase more chicken eggs, this time a gallon of her homemade buttermilk, another quart of her powerful 'nose-catching' homemade ground horseradish with the 'angry mule's kick', and a sack of potatoes, if she had any for sale.

"Darn, you boys sure do go through a mountain of my eggs and the like. I am sure glad my hens are laying and not going through a molt or anything," she said, as she ambled over to her chicken coop to check on her hens' egg inventory. Minutes later, she returned carrying two dozen eggs in the front of her rolled-upwards apron. Once back at the house, she put the fresh eggs into the cloth sack that Chino had brought for just such a purchase. Then Martha, being a big woman, ambled off towards her spud cellar for the potatoes, jug of buttermilk, and another quart of her hotter than all get-out, ground homemade horseradish the Dodson brothers dearly loved as they smeared it all over their breakfast eggs. As for the buttermilk rich in globs of butterfat, it had now become a necessary staple for Chino's pancakes and Dutch oven biscuits. When she returned, Chino paid her $3.00 and made casual small talk as his practiced eyes casually made the 'rounds' looking for any kind of clues as to

Martha's husband's illegal activities back at the ranch, like his returning mules or clothing hanging on her clothesline.

When Martha returned she said, "I don't have any change on me at this time. My husband cleaned me out when he bought some more sacks of sugar for my cooking and sacks of corn to grind for my ever-hungry chickens," she continued, not realizing what clues she had just provided for Chino to bring back to the brothers relative to her husband's illegal bootlegging activities.

"That is OK, Martha. Your eggs and the like are the best in the valley and my guys, now that they are employed, do not mind paying top dollar for the food they are eating. You keep the change and buy some candy for those little kids next time you are in town at the store," said Chino with his trademark friendly smile. Saying good-bye, Chino noticed that Martha did not have any clothes drying out on her backyard clothesline as he loaded his pack mule with all the groceries he had just purchased. He knew that was strange having a number of small children around, especially the babies and their constant need for clean diapers. Chino also noticed that her husband's two mules and riding horse, many times found grazing in the south pasture, were absent the ranch that day as well...

Arriving back at his campsite, Chino unloaded

the items he had purchased from Martha, got the brothers out from under their sleeping blankets and began preparing their noonday meal. As he did, he cut off a number of steaks from the two deer brought back into camp and then informed Joe as to what he had learned when over at Martha's purchasing some more fresh supplies for their meals.

Once Chino had briefed Joe as to what he had observed over at the Barnes ranch, the deputy just sat there nursing a cup of coffee while he was mulling over what Chino had just told him. "You know, Chino, we still do not have a clear picture of what the face of this Barnes fellow exactly looks like and that bothers me. That bothers me because if we spring our trap and he is not the man we are after, we will be done in this area working undercover. True, we will have a 'man' for running an illegal still but maybe not the man we were sent to arrest and fetch back to Judge Parker's court of law. Suffice to say, if that were to happen, that would not suit me or Marshal Fagan either," said Joe concernedly.

"I know what the man at the still site looked like and by-damn his description sure fits with what Lewis described to me about the man who delivered the jug of whiskey over to the mill boss's shack. Damn. the more I think about it, I am obliged to think the man I saw and the one

Lewis observed must be the one and same based on his size and build. Furthermore, that is evidenced by the mystery jug of liquor he delivered to the mill boss. Damn, the more I think about this, the more I think this Barnes fellow is one and the same and before someone finds us out and why we are here, I am thinking we need to spring our trap. I also think that clothesline with or without a load of clothes hanging thereon back at the Barnes ranch is a clue of some sort or a signal to Grizzly Creek, but I haven't just yet figured it out. However, I am leaning toward that it must be some kind of a signal that all is clear when the clothes are hanging on it, or it means that is the day that Barnes is arriving home from his stint at the still with a fresh load of bootleg whiskey."

Then Lewis and James arrived, served themselves some coffee and sitting around the campfire, discussed what Chino had observed at the Barnes ranch and the fact that they needed to get the two doe deer over to the butcher now that the animals had hung long enough to properly cool out and glaze. Besides, the yellow jackets had discovered the meat and were making the most of it. So, before one or all of they got bitten and stung by the winged pests, they had to take the carcasses down and get them to the butcher shop.

Finishing their lunches, the three brothers rode

into town trailing on their pack mules their two doe deer to be sold at the butcher shop. However, as the three men rode into town, Lewis leaned over to James saying, "Look at our brother, Joe. He has hardly said a word since we left camp. That means he is thinking and the three of us will soon be in some sort of 'hell or high water' if Joe has his way about what is soon going to happen."

Later on their way back to the campsite, Joe finally shared with his two brothers what he had been thinking all along that afternoon when they had ridden into the town with their deer. "I think for the sake of continuing our covers, we need to show up for work tomorrow and all of us collect the pay we have earned. That way, things with the three of us will look all normal-like. Then the day following, we need to 'mash our asses' into our saddles and head back up on that mountain, sneak into that still site and see if we can arrest the man we think is Barnes in the act of running an illegal still in violation of federal law. The time is about right since we saw him last and if I were a betting man, I would say his latest batch of bootleg whiskey is just about ready to 'come off' and be 'jugged' up for transport back to his ranch. If we are successful, we can catch him in the tail end of his bootlegging activities and capture him while he is all intent in filling up those jugs with his precious whiskey and getting it down off the mountain for sale. That way, we will have met what Marshal Fagan calls 'closing the ring' on our investigation by catching our still operator right in the process of his illegal trade with all of his illegal goods in hand. Let us just hope we catch Barnes with 'his pants down' and before he can get his hands on his rifle. What say you my brothers to that plan?" asked Joe.

Lewis, looked over at his brother James, and grinning said, "That sounds like a plan to me. Like you said earlier little brother when we were taking our deer over to the butcher shop, when Joe is thinking, we are soon to find ourselves in 'hell or high water' before the sun sets on the day after tomorrow." The following day, Joe and James, at the end of their day of work as mule skinners, were paid off in gold coin for their previous week's work as were the other loggers. At the end of his week's work at the lumber mill, Lewis, like all the other Meadow Valley employees on payday, were also paid off in gold coin for their previous work.

The next morning way before daylight found Chino up, his campfire blazing and breakfast cooking away. That morning, Chino fixed the deputies another of his famous 'lumberjack' breakfasts of buttermilk pancakes slathered in homemade butter and honey, all covered with five eggs 'sunny side-up' and all the coffee they could stuff down, full well knowing it may be the only meal his friends got for a long time once the hunt for Grizzly Creek Barnes was full on...

Checking over their gear before making ready to leave for a long trip up Grizzly Creek to a hoped-for capture of one Grizzly Creek Barnes, Joe made sure he had loaded in his saddlebags a 'trick of the trade' he had learned from Indian Policeman Tom from Poteau before he was killed on an earlier adventure near the town of Red Oak. Satisfied that they were ready for whatever came their way, the three deputies saddled up, bid Chino good day and headed off into the awakening day for the 'hell or high water' the good Lord had in store for them. However as they headed out in the pre-dawn darkness, Joe was really hoping they were now headed for the right man, namely one Rufous "Grizzly Creek" Barnes or he would have to face an all-business, tobacco-spitting Chief Marshal back at Fort Smith. Little did Joe realize the unique turn his latest adventure in the Indian Territory was about to take...

Four hours later found the men tying their horses off in the dark timber just below the known still site, with Lewis and James removing their rifles from their scabbards as Joe pulled his 'trick of the trade' from his saddlebag and tucked it gently under his arm. Then huddling together one more time, Joe laid out his final capture plan and then the three men went their separate ways as they approached the still site from different directions to ensure a safe capture if Grizzly Creek decided to run or fight once he became aware of the deputies' presence and their mission at hand.

About thirty minutes later, found Joe overlooking the still site some 30 or so yards below his sneaked into concealed position. Looking on, Joe could see the man below removing a bucket from below a pipe trickling a clear liquid from the large still that appeared to be brim full of a clear liquid. Then the bootlegger, after quickly placing another empty bucket beneath the freshly stilled whiskey-draining pipe, walking over to a mule standing nearby and began pouring the liquid from the full bucket into a funnel leading into a five-gallon jug inside a pannier attached to the side of the mule's pack saddle. On the other side of that mule was another five-gallon jug apparently already filled with the liquid from the still, as was evidenced by a cork stuffed into its spout. Shortly thereafter, that second jug was filled to the 'moonshiner's' satisfaction and was corked off as well. Then the man brought forth his second mule already loaded with a pack saddle holding a pannier on each side carrying two more, empty five-gallon earthenware jugs. For the next hour, the man continued filling those two remaining jugs with the clear liquid slowly draining from the still as well. When those jugs were filled, they were corked off as well. Then as the man snuffed out his fire from underneath his now run-dry still, Joe observed his brother Lewis sneaking up to the still from one side and his other brother James, from the other side nearest the two fully loaded mules.

That was when the proverbial 'wheels came off Joe's capture planning wagon' when the two mules spotted a stranger sneaking towards them. All of a sudden a loud mule's bray rent the cold clear mountain morning air, causing the man cleaning up around the still to run around the still's huge pot to see what had caused his well-trained mule to sound the alarm when strangers strode into the area. When he did, he saw James near his mule and without a moment's hesitation, grabbed his rifle lying propped up against the side of a nearby sack of corn, raised it to his shoulder 'in the blink of an eye', only to have Lewis immediately rise up from his place of hiding at the rear of the man's tent from behind some elderberry bushes!

"DROP THE RIFLE OR YOU ARE A DEAD MAN!" yelled Lewis, whose rifle barrel muzzle was now less than ten feet away from the now-threatening man's head!

Hearing those deadly words coming from behind him and being so close at hand, caused the surprised 'moonshiner' to spin around and look directly into the big bore of a menacing rifle barrel! Standing there in utter surprise, the 'moonshiner' found himself looking into the muzzle of a rifle barrel from a Sharps now not five feet distant from his face, as Lewis continued his advance towards the man with his rifle at the ready! On the other end of that unwavering rifle barrel, was a determined-looking man staring him dead-cold in his eyes over a set of open rifle sights!

Grizzly Creek Barnes, realizing there were no good odds in what he had been about to do with his own rifle, slowly lowered it to the ground as he continued looking right into the muzzle of the rifle being leveled right at his head and then raised his hands slowly skyward in resignation. Lewis never lowered his rifle aimed at Grizzly Creek Barnes's head until his brother James had placed the manacles he had been carrying around the stocky Irishman's wrists, making their arrest of a bootlegging whiskey-making legend in the North Arm area of the Indian Territory complete and now just a part of history…

Finally lowering his rifle, Lewis said, "Grizzly Creek Barnes, I assume?" When Lewis uttered those words, the 'moonshiner' under the gun slowly nodded in the affirmative. Then he continued saying, "My name is Lewis Dodson, Deputy

U.S. Marshal and you, Sir, are now under arrest for making and being in possession of illegal whiskey in violation of federal law in the Indian Territory. The man who was next to your mules and the one who placed the manacles on your wrists is my brother James, who is also a Deputy U.S. Marshal. Now, I need you to walk over to that stand of timber with me if you would please, Mr. Barnes, because we have some work to do before we leave this illegal whiskey-producing still site and you need to meet my older brother, Joe, who is also a Deputy U.S. Marshal."

Walking Barnes over to a distant stand of Douglas fir trees, Lewis silently seated the quiet man onto the ground, placed his brother James over him as an armed guard, then walked back and brought the man's 'moonshiner's' mules and now saddled riding horse over to the distant copse of trees where the prisoner now quietly sat. Seeing that all was secure over at the far stand of fir trees, Joe walked down to Barnes's tent and began stacking all the bags of corn and sugar around the base of the still. Once all the bootlegging materials had been stacked around the whiskey still, Joe began doing something out of sight around its base. Lewis and James could not see what Joe was doing because his back was turned to the two men and their recent capture, but they knew what he was doing, so they waited patiently for him to finish his business. But his brothers knew it was Joe's 'hell or high water' moment manifesting itself, when it came to those associated with breaking the federal laws and his own special brand of treatment when it came to addressing the causative agent of the wrongdoing...

Then all of a sudden, Joe took off running for the distant fir trees where his two brothers, Barnes, the two mules and the 'moonshiner's' riding horse were waiting a goodly number of yards away! Minutes later, the Grizzly Creek headwaters and the mountain morning's quiet was 'greeted' with a tremendous explosion, immediately accompanied by numerous flying bits and pieces of a blown all to hell still, sacks of whiskey-making ingredients and other assorted paraphernalia associated with the illegal whiskey making business!

Once the three brothers, Grizzly Creek Barnes, two mules and Barnes's horse had settled down over the surprising explosion brought forth from twenty sticks of 20% dynamite, a grinning Joe, pleased over his 'trick of the trade' handiwork, said, "Just as Marshal Fagan had ordered us to do, one still blown all to hell." Then for the next hour, the deputies combed the area making sure there were no remaining bits and pieces of burning material associated with the blast of dynamite lying around in the forest to cause a forest fire.

An hour later found all the men back at the location where they had left their horses prior to sneaking up on the still. There they mounted up and trailing their prisoner, manacled and riding on his horse, and his two fully loaded pack mules, the group made their way off the mountain and back towards the Barnes ranch. As the men approached the ranch site, they noticed that there was a 'flurry' of clothes drying on Martha's clothesline… Joe looked back at his brothers over the fact and puzzle that the 'sign' that Rufous was on his way home to all his buyers had finally been solved. Simultaneously realizing the same about the meaning the clothing drying on the clothesline represented, the deputies all had to grin.

Continuing on their way towards where they had been camped with Chino and their chuck wagon, a serious issue now arose on Joe's mind kept causing him a mountain of increasing humanitarian concern! Oddly enough, after the fact of Grizzly Creek Barnes's successful capture, he himself had not uttered one word! Even more surprising, when they had bypassed the Barnes ranch house, even though he knew that he was leaving a young wife and a number of small children behind, one of which, the youngest, Larry, had polio and was crippled, even though now heading off into the legal unknown, Barnes had remained silent...

That silence on the part of Grizzly Creek bothered Joe and now he found that he had a serious humanitarian concern in the back of his mind relative to Grizzly Creek's capture. Joe's original plans were to load up their campsite and head back to Fort Smith that same day with their prisoner, just in case a large number of the friendly to Barnes locals tried to intercede and take the prisoner away from the marshals. However, Joe now found that he had another, what he considered more pressing concern mentally dogging him as well. A concern that was becoming so paramount in his general nature, that it was almost as if he could hear his long dead father quietly speaking to him about what needed to be done to rectify this most serious of situations that was now front and center to Joe's manner of thinking...

Loading up their campsite somewhat later, the marshals, their prisoner and Chino made ready to leave. When the group of men and Chino's chuck wagon hit the main road, instead of heading on their way toward Fort Smith, Joe surprisingly headed them back toward the Barnes ranch! Arriving a short time later, Joe dismounted and walked over to the front door of the Barnes ranch house and knocked. He soon was confronted by Martha Barnes, who when looking over Joe's shoulder at her husband sitting upon his horse wearing a set of manacles and realizing the worst had happened, burst out into uncontrollable tears! Tears Joe was sure reflected her deep worry on how was she going to be able to raise her numerous small children without her husband at her side as the family's provider and protector?

After Joe had finally gotten Martha calmed down over her pending family loss, he formally identified himself and his brothers and explained to her why they had come all that way from Fort Smith, namely to arrest her husband for his whiskey-making activities, all in violation of federal law. Finally getting hold of her racing emotions, Martha asked what was to become of her husband now that he had been arrested for making illegal whiskey. Joe explained the trial process that Rufous was facing back in Fort Smith and the possible outcome as it related to Barnes's long incarceration in a federal prison if found guilty of the pending charges. That explanation brought forth an even greater flood of tears on the part of Martha, realizing that she may never see her husband again for a very long, long time!

Getting Martha calmed down again, Joe asked if she would like to talk to her husband before they took him to jail back in Fort Smith to be held for trial for 'moonshining'. With those words, Martha burst from her front door, ran to the side of her husband still calmly sitting on his horse and once again burst out into a flood of tears as she clutched at his leg!

With that emotional scene unfolding in front of him, Lewis helped Barnes from his horse so he could at least hold and try talking to his now very distraught wife. When he did, that was the first time they had heard the stoic Barnes say even one word since his arrest. In fact, when Lewis helped him off his horse, he turned to Lewis and politely said, "Thank you!" to his captor.

Still keeping a close eye on their prisoner, Joe let the couple move a few yards away so they could talk in private. Then once again, almost as if his dad was speaking to him, Joe had a revelation! Gathering his men around him, Joe broached an idea that had been floating around inside his head for the last few hours and without a single word of opposition to Joe's proposal, the men of the posse responded positively to Joe's suggestion.

As Joe's men began responding to a new mission at hand, he walked over to Grizzly Creek Barnes and asked him to leave his wife for a few minutes so they could talk. Once aside so they could talk in private, Joe made a proposal to Rufous that brought tears to the stoic prisoner's eyes, which he quickly wiped away with his manacled hands so that his true emotions could not be seen by his wife or the rest of the men. Then Rufous was allowed to go back to his wife and hold her while Joe and company put his earlier proposal into operation.

Moments later, most of the chuck wagon's food supplies had been piled up onto the front porch of the ranch house so that Martha and the kids would have at least a month's supply of bacon, beans, rice, sugar, salt, lard, and two pounds of hard candy, a favorite of the deputies, now released for the kids to enjoy! Then Joe gathered all the men together for the final part of his plan and after a few moments of gathering up what he had proposed they do, he walked over to Rufous and said, "Here is $113.75 for you to give to Martha so she can buy any kind of supplies that she needs for her and the kids for as long as it lasts. It is all of the money that we four men collectively had in our possession. It is the money we have earned from the sale of deer meat to the local butcher shop, our salaries for the last two months as Deputy U.S. Marshals, and the money we made working in the woods and at the lumber mill while here on assignment looking for you. If we had more we would give it to you but that is almost every dime between the four of us. So here, take it and go over and give it to Martha for her and the kids."

Once again, tears welled up in Grizzly Creek's

eyes as he thankfully took the money and then walked back over to Martha who was standing on the front porch looking on at all the supplies lying at her feet in amazement. There he handed her the two handfuls of gold and silver coins, gave her one last hug and kiss, and then calmly like the tough old Irishman that he was, walked back to the marshals and surrendered himself to their wishes.

"Thank you for taking care of my family. I won't forget what you men have done for me and mine even though we are on opposite sides of the law," said Barnes quietly and with conviction in the tone and tenor of his voice. Continuing, Barnes said, "I also have some close family friends in the Toscanni Family at the head of North Arm. Knowing them the way I do, they will help and keep an eye on Martha and the kids for as long as is necessary."

Then Lewis helped Rufous up into the saddle and the marshals without looking back at a very distraught woman standing all alone in the yard, began their long trek back to Fort Smith and their next assignment. For the next four days, Chino, the marshals and their prisoner had nothing but beans for their breakfasts, dinners and suppers because they had left behind all the rest of their provisions for Martha and the kids. The only change was when the men could kill a deer or antelope and then the beans-only meals improved immeasurably. But to a man, they all felt good about giving everything they had to the woman of their prisoner they had left behind without her man around to help and now, with a number of small children to care for...

Day five dawned miserable, as the rains and cold swept across the Sans Bois Mountains through which the posse was now traveling. As the caravan trudged ever northeasterly toward Fort Smith, they finally had enough of the bad weather and cold rains, so they stopped early in the day and built a roaring fire to dry out and warm up. Thankfully, the rains had stopped but the harsh winds blew cold out from the north, as the men huddled around their campfire until late in the night, drinking the last of their coffee in an effort to warm up. Throwing down their canvas tarp covers upon the ground under the chuck wagon, the men rolled out their damp-feeling sleeping blankets, crawled inside and then drew their rain tarps over them for whatever fitful sleep overcame them.

"DON'T A ONE OF YOU SONS-A-BITCHES MOVE, OR ME AND MY PARTNERS WILL BLOW YOU ALL TO KINGDOM COME!" bellowed out a voice from the darkness at the edge of the marshals' dying campfire! Joe, not sleeping very well because of his blankets being so damp and cold, sprang to his feet only to be hit on the head from behind by a man sneaking up unseen and the lights went out!

All the rest of the men awoke with a start, as did Rufous who was shackled to a prison-ring (a steel ring fastened to the floor of the chuck wagon onto which prisoners were shackled for the night) inside the chuck wagon. Moments later, two men emerged from the darkness just outside the dying light from the marshals' camp-fire carrying leveled Winchesters, while a third man moved into the feeble light of the fire from behind the chuck wagon with a double barreled ten gage shotgun with the hammers fully cocked back and ready for any action that came his way!

Upon hearing the rattling of Rufous's chains from inside the chuck wagon, the man carrying the ten gage shotgun used his gun barrel to move the end of the wagon's canvas flap aside and peered inside into the darkness of the wagon's interior. "Well, well, well, what the hell do we have here?" said the man. "Boys, get that damn fire a-going. I need more light to see what the hell we have here shackled to the floor of this here wagon," said the man who had slipped up behind Joe earlier and had 'whanged' him on the back of his head with the butt of his shotgun, knocking him unconscious.

Moments later as the fire was rekindled by one

of the men, it began flaring up providing more light to illuminate the area and with that, the scene and situation around the campsite slowly came into focus for the armed men controlling the scene and those now being held as prisoners. Standing alongside the chuck wagon was Chino, Lewis and James holding their hands skyward. Lying at their feet was the inert form of Joe who had been knocked unconscious when he had stood up upon hearing the 'ominous command from the dark'. Behind those men stood the man holding the shotgun and all the while nervously eyeballing the inside of the still darkened chuck wagon. Soon, enough light from the campfire faintly lit up the interior of the chuck wagon, allowing the man with the shotgun to more clearly see what was contained inside and solve the riddle of the clanking chain sounds.

"Holy Ned, Boys, there is a prisoner shackled to the inside of this here wagon! These bastards must be lawmen of some sort if they have some poor bastard shackled to the floor of this here wagon! Keep a sharp eye peeled on these gents, Boys. If they be the law, we may have our hands full of trouble with a capital "T" if we let them get out of hand and get hold of their 'smoke-poles'," said a man named Gratt Peters!

Then the man with the double barreled shotgun began kicking Joe until he finally was able to

rouse himself from having been knocked unconscious and slowly crawled unsteadily to his feet.
As Joe was steadied by Lewis, the two men by
the campfire moved forward and made sure they
had all of the marshals' weapons picked up and
stacked over by the campfire under their control
and out of the lawmen's easy reach.

"Well, look-ee here. We have a mess of lawmen by the looks of these here badges, "said
Dingas McGee, as he flipped open James's vest
exposing the marshal's badge pinned to his shirt.
Soon, McGee had located the badges on all three
of the marshals! "Well, looks like the horses and
mules we hoped to steal from these men belong
to the U.S. Government, Boys," said McGee, with
a killer's crazy-sounding, high-pitched lilt of
laughter to his squeaky-sounding voice.

"Can I kill 'em? Can I kill 'em?" said Rince
McGee, younger brother to Dingas and one who
was considered by his companions to be a bit
daft in the head.

"Naw, not yet till we find out why they have
this poor bastard all chained up and be taking
him somewhere," said Dingas, as he kept his
Winchester squarely aimed in the direction of
the three still grouped together marshals. "I am
not sure what this other fellow without a badge
is," said Dingas out loud in reference to Chino.
"Who the hell are you, Man?" asked Rince.

"I am just a poor Mexican who they employed for me to drive their wagon," said Chino, trying not to let his loyalty to the marshals now under the gun, show.

"Well, we kill damn poor stinkin' 'Messicans', as well as any damn lawman!" said Dingas, with a whole lot of 'ugly' rising up in the high-pitched tone of his voice!

"Can you guys let me go?" asked Rufous. "They caught me making bootleg whiskey and have me arrested and on the way to Fort Smith for trial by that damn old hanging judge, Judge Parker," continued Rufous. "You boys let me go and I can tell you where you can find some of the finest Tennessee sour mash whiskey around," continued Rufous in a hopeful tone of voice.

"Where the hell is one going to find some of that damn fine Tennessee whiskey way out here in these stinking mountains?" asked Rince with the clear sound of hope now rising up in his voice.

"Get the keys out of that marshal's front pocket that you 'whanged' on the head and let me go and I will show you fellas," said a now happier sounding Rufous.

"If you don't come across with that whiskey, Stranger, I have a bullet in this here rifle with your name on it," said Dingas in a threatening tone of voice. Then he said, "Rince, get the keys from that lawman's pocket and be careful about it, so we can let this poor bugger go so he can show us where these lawmen are keeping that sour mash he keeps talking about."

Then Dingas ordered the man with the shotgun, a man named Gratt Peters, to get Joe's keys and let the man in the wagon loose so he could get them some of that whiskey he keeps talking about. "The quicker we can get some of that talked-about sour mash into our empty guts, the warmer we will be able to get in this damn cold and wet weather," continued Dingas. Gratt did as he was told and soon Rufous was free as a bird and happy as a hog eating shit, being no longer a prisoner and manacled to the bottom of a cold and wet chuck wagon!

With that, Rufous walked over to where the marshals had piled up all their saddles and such and had covered them with a tarp to keep them dry if it rained anymore during the night. Struggling with one of the five-gallon jugs of evidence 'moonshine' as he removed it from one of the mule's panniers, Rufous struggled over to the fire and sat the heavy jug down with a resounding 'THUD'! Then he walked over to the chuck wagon, extracted four cups from the cook's utensil box, walked back to the jug, pulled the cork and tipped it over slightly so the whiskey could flow freely. As he did, one could almost see the eyes of Dingas glowing with the expectation of something wonderful to come into his drab and wet from the last rains, life just moments away. Then he poured four cups clear full of whiskey and realizing that Dingas was the boss of the group of previously stated horse thieves, handed him his cup first. Then Rufous stood back as Dingas took a small sip as if he could not believe his good luck in finding a drink of good sour mash whiskey way out there in the mountain remoteness that time of the night.

After that first careful sip, Dingas announced to the rest of the men looking on with extreme interest, that the corn liquor that he had just drunk was as smooth as 'frog's hair'! Soon all the men, including Rufous, were into the cups of bootleg whiskey like there was no tomorrow, with a lot of happy talk now flowing between the four of them like they were all long lost brothers cut from the same illegal cloth.

Then things turned ugly! Dingas turned to Gratt and said, "Smoke those lawmen son-of-a-bitches with that ten gage shotgun you are always bragging about. Just take them over behind the wagon and kill them so I don't have to look at 'em no more. Rince, you go with Gratt to see that he stays out of trouble. There are four of those bastards that need killing including that damn Messican, and Gratt only has two shots in that hand cannon of his. So you keep them covered while he reloads so he can kill the mess of then. Then get your ass back here and let us see what we can rustle up in the way of some grub from these soon to be dead bastards' chuck wagon. Killing them is giving me a powerful thirst for some more of this good whiskey and a hunger for some beans and biscuits. So let us get on with the killing of these bastards and the sooner the better."

With that, Gratt gestured with the end of his shotgun barrel for the marshals and Chino to move around behind the wagon. Then all of a sudden, Rufous chimed in with, "Mr. Dingas, can I kill the lot of them? They arrested me and took me away from my wife and small children. Left them to starve without a man in the house, they did. I would consider it a real treat if I could be the one to blow these bastards clear into hell and beyond," said Rufous with a wicked smile of glee plastered clear across his face, now that he had the upper hand and was no longer a prisoner shackled onto the bottom of a chuck wagon!

"Go ahead, I don't care. Rince, give this man your pistol and let him kill this bunch of bastards. Gratt, you go with them so if he only wounds any of them you can finish 'em off with that cannon you are always carrying around with you and carrying on about," said Dingas, as he began pouring himself his second full cup of whiskey from the five-gallon jug.

With a big grin on his face over the role he would play in the killing, Rince handed his pistol to Rufous, telling him that there were only five shells in the pistol's cylinder, not six, so don't miss. Then he too headed for the whiskey jug so he could refill his cup as well. With that, Rufous gestured with the end of his pistol barrel for the four men to walk around behind the wagon so he could shoot them out of sight from the two McGee brothers as Dingas had ordered.

Walking around the wagon, all Joe could think about was what good he had done for poor Martha and the kids in the way of leaving them their food and all of their hard-earned money so they would have a chance at survival, and this is what he gets for his thoughtfulness and his men's generosity in return...

Walking slowly around behind the chuck wagon, Lewis and James were in the process of saying good-bye to each other as they turned and faced their surprise executioner, just as Rufous raised his pistol AND SHOT GRATT IN THE HEAD FROM JUST TWO FEET AWAY! As Gratt dropped like a stone from an 'exploded' head, Rufous anticipating how he would fall from being head-shot, quickly reached out, grabbed his ten gage shotgun and all in one fluid motion, tossed it over to Joe! Then he ran around the rear of the wagon, drew down on Dingas and Rince who were in the process of greedily filling their cups again, saying, "Put those cups down, Boys! I didn't make such good whiskey only to have it being wasted on the likes of you two. First man who does not do as I say, will die with a gutful of good whiskey and a .45 slug in there floating around with it," said Rufous in such a tone that both Rince and Dingas quickly realized that death was just a trigger pull away, and that gun pointed at them was in the hand of someone who knew how to use it and relished doing so if called upon...

As Rufous held his pistol on the McGee brothers, Joe raced around the other side of the wagon and drew down upon the two outlaw brothers as well with the ten gage shotgun. Seeing they were dead men to do otherwise than what they were being told to do, both brothers slowly dropped their gun belts at their feet. Then Joe, still in surprise over the momentous change in events, ordered the two men to kick their gun belts over towards him, which they did posthaste.

Then Joe was joined by Lewis and James who picked up their gun belts and with those actions, peace and quiet once again returned to the night in the Sans Bois Mountains. Moments later found both McGee brothers in manacles, searched for any hidden weapons and shackled down to the floor in the back of the chuck wagon. As that action was unfolding, Chino refueled the camp-fire, got out the coffee pot and set it to boil once again using the previous evening's old grounds because they were out of fresh beans. However, all was not lost because into each man's cup of boiled once-over coffee went an ample supply of good sour mash Tennessee whiskey, courtesy of one Grizzly Creek Barnes, 'moonshiner'…

Somewhat later after the men's second full cup of much whiskey-addled coffee, Joe announced that the last time he had been in Marshal Fagan's office he had glanced over several of the wanted posters posted on his walls. Then with a big grin he said, "One of those posters was for the arrest, dead or alive, of the McGee Brothers for steal-ing horses from the local stagecoach line and robbing their coaches and passengers as well." Then taking another sip of coffee 'sweetened' with sour mash whiskey that was smoother than 'frog's hair', he announced with a smile, "Guess which posters had a reward posted on them by the stage lines for $1,000?" Then with an even bigger grin, somewhat induced by his previous two cups of sour mash mixed with his coffee, he said, "Gentlemen, that is one reward by policy we can collect even as Deputy U.S. Marshals, because it is offered by an outside entity and not the United States Government! In fact now that I think about it, that is a reward that is going to be split five ways since we all had a hand in executing its request for capture of the McGee brothers!"

"You ain't got us in jail yet, you bastard!" yelled Dingas from the back of the chuck wagon where he and his brother had been shackled to the oaken floorboards upon hearing Joe's words regarding the reward for the McGees.

Turning, Joe replied back quietly in such a manner that Dingas could clearly understand the implication of what he was saying, "Dingas, that poster says 'dead or alive'. I suggest the two of you brothers remember those words because I have just committed them to memory..."

Later that night aided by three cupfuls of Grizzly Creek Barnes's excellent sour mash Tennessee 'moonshine', Joe found that he slept well regardless of his still damp and cold blankets from the previous afternoon's rainstorm. As he drifted off to sleep almost like the rest of his now deeply snoring posse, he heard Chino quietly swear under his breath, "I am getting a dog! This is the last time that I will allow anyone to sneak up on me and almost make my dear sainted mother a childless woman..."

Right at daylight, Joe awakened to a slight scraping sound that did not register. Lying as still as death in his sleeping blankets and listening, Joe once again heard the slight unrecognized sound coming from the bed of the chuck wagon just overhead from where he had been sleeping. Quietly reaching for his revolver that he always kept alongside his head in case of emergencies, he quietly removed it from its holster and slid it beneath his blankets. Joe then cocked his single action revolver, so that 'cocking' sound would not be a dead giveaway that he was now awake and armed. With that, Joe unobtrusively withdrew his Colt .45 from his covers, laid his blankets aside and quietly rose to his knees. As he did, he could still hear the faint scratching sounds coming from the chuck wagon box overhead. Quietly standing up and moving to the rear of the wagon, Joe slowly peered around the end of the wagon box only to see Rince McGee quietly holding all the chains of his and his brother's shackles so they would not be heard making any clanking sounds when the two of them were mysteriously moving around. Clearly seen beneath Rince was Dingas quietly cutting away a hole with a six-inch knife into the oaken floorboard holding the bolt to his chains which were attached to his manacles!

Slowly drawing down on the duo with his pistol so his movement would not become readily apparent in the predawn light, Joe quietly said, "Dingas, drop your knife and slide it towards the rear of the wagon where I am standing. If you make any other move than that, I will kill you where you are kneeling!" When Dingas heard those unexpected words coming out from the pre-dawn darkness at the end of the wagon, he made a startled move! That was when the end of the barrel of the ten gage shotgun, once belonging to the late Gratt Peters, poked its way through the side of the partially upraised canvas cover on the wagon and slammed into the side of Dingas's head! It now appeared that James, who had been sleeping on the other side of the chuck wagon, had also heard the strange scratching sounds coming from the wagon box and had decided to investigate those mystery sounds as well.

"OOOFF!" went Dingas, as the cold end of the shotgun barrel slammed into the side of his head with such force that it smashed shut his left eye in an instant! Then all hell broke loose as the entire camp flew awake and alert to the possibility of the prisoner escape danger close at hand! However, Joe's quieting voice assured the posse that all was under control, as he reached into the wagon and withdrew the knife that Dingas had been using in his attempt to cut away the bolt base inside the wagon in his attempt to escape from the clutches of the lawmen.

Then it occurred to Joe that the two outlaw brothers had been searched before they had been manacled and shackled onto the floor of the chuck wagon to prevent any escape attempts. About the same time, Joe remembered an old trick used by many Mexican Nationals that he had dealt with over the years, who always seemed to carry hidden knives inside their cowboy boots.

"Both of you brothers remove your boots," said Joe, with a tone and tenor in his voice meant to be clearly understood and backed up by the end of his still leveled pistol barrel.

Slowly both McGee brothers removed their cowboy boots and sure as hell, Joe's latest defensive thinking had been right on the money. Out from Rince's boot dropped a six-inch bladed knife! As for Dingas's right boot, it revealed an empty six-inch knife holder sewn onto the inside of his boot! Taking both of the men's sets of boots and their knives, Joe walked over to a fire now re-stoked by Chino and dropped them into the fire — boots, knives and all!

Walking back to the rear of the wagon holding their two prisoners now under the watchful eyes and the end of the barrel of a ten gage shotgun of his brother James, Joe quietly said, "One more wrong move and I will strip the two of you bare-assed naked, burn your clothing and make you ride all the way back to Fort Smith in the heat and cold dressed like the day you were born. Is that clear?"

Both brothers sullenly nodded that they understood Joe's final words of warning. Then under the watchful eyes of James, Chino made several more holes into the walls and flooring of the chuck wagon with a hand-held drill, and double manacled and shackled the McGee brothers tight to the oaken planking so their chances of any further escape attempts were between slim and nothing...

After a breakfast of beans once again and letting the now bootless McGee brothers, one at a time, out from the wagon to go to the bathroom, the posse made ready to continue their travels to Fort Smith with their two prisoners. That's right, just TWO prisoners! Riding along like the rest of the posse was one Grizzly Creek Barnes on his own horse and riding without being manacled! He had given his word that he would not try to escape, and Joe had ordered that he be released and allowed to ride back to Fort Smith like everyone else. However, the McGee brothers remained bolted and shackled to the rough riding chuck wagon for the duration of the trip back to Fort Smith amid a world of grumbling and 'cat-a-walling'.

Days later, the tired and hungry group of men rode into Fort Smith and over to the federal courthouse. There the two McGee brothers were jailed into the holding facility located beneath the District Court. As for Barnes, he was only 'constrained' under the watchful eyes of Lewis and James at the local boardinghouse, where the rest of the posse, minus Joe, went for some much needed chow other than a belly full of beans out on the trail. Joe on the other hand, reported to Marshal Fagan on the success of their trip and filled him in on the story of the capture of Grizzly Creek Barnes, and how he had saved the entire posse after they had been surprised in the dead of the night and captured by the deadly McGee brothers.

It was then that Joe presented to Marshal Fagan a surprise proposal and asked for his backing in the matter. Marshal Fagan just thoughtfully looked at his young-in-law enforcement experience deputy marshal, then broke out into a wide, tobacco-stained toothy grin saying, "Let's the two of us go over and meet with Judge Parker relative your rather unusual proposal. He is not in court just yet and now would be the time to approach him with your proposal. In so doing, I have a feeling he will have a counter to your suggestion that will surprise and tickle the hell out of you, if it can be carried out as well."

Twenty minutes later found the Chief Marshal and his deputy, hats in hand, standing in front of the fearsome and no-nonsense but highly religious, Honorable Federal District Judge, Judge Isaac Parker. A no-nonsense judge who was also known as the "Hanging Judge" because of many of his lethal judicial decisions. After greetings and salutations had been made all around, Marshal Fagan began by bringing the judge up to speed on his deputy's latest sets of adventures. The success of the story and the captures of three known felons in his judicial district brought a big smile to the normally stern looking judge. Then Marshal Fagan advised the judge that his deputy had a special request and would like to present it to His Honor for consideration. After those lead-in words, Marshal Fagan turned to Joe saying, "It is your show, Deputy."

For a moment, Joe's heart just sank, as the stern looking judge looked down at one of his just returned from a successful manhunt in the lawless Indian Territory deputies who was still alive and well. Then 'gathering up his skirts', Joe commenced with his story of the capture of Grizzly Creek Barnes, a major illegal whiskey maker in the southern part of the Indian Territory. That capture story was then followed with the rest of the story concerning the posse's return travels, their surprise capture and almost being killed by their captors because of the sole fact that they were lawmen. Keeping up his courage and head of steam in the telling, Joe finally laid out his very unusual proposal to the very all-powerful, stern faced-looking federal judge.

Finished with his presentation to the judge minutes later, Joe just watched the judge's face closely for any signs of acceptance or denial relative to his very unusual proposal. Initially, after Joe's proposal, the judge's face had clouded up and he appeared to be very upset over the rather off the wall request made by one of his very junior deputies. He then quietly advised his Chief Marshal that he wanted to see both him and his upstart deputy back in his chambers around two in the afternoon after his last case, and bring Grizzly Creek Barnes, the 'moonshiner' who had caused him so much trouble in the southern Indian Territory, along as well! Then both men were rather abruptly dismissed without any further judicial action being taken upon Joe's rather unusual request, as the judge rose up from his chair and headed off to court...

Somewhat later, Joe rejoined his posse at the boardinghouse where they were resting around the table after eating a much deserved meal, ordered some for himself and then advised the group on what he had proposed and how the judge had taken Joe's proposal. The quiet around the table after Joe had presented his version of what had happened in the judge's chambers spoke volumes of what the group thought about their chances for success regarding Joe's proposal... The only person quieter than all the rest of the lawmen was one Grizzly Creek Barnes. Not only was he as quiet as a 'mouse pissing on a ball of cotton', but his face showed nothing but total surprise in what Joe had suggested earlier to the famous 'Hanging Judge'...

Prior to two in the afternoon, the posse and Grizzly Creek Barnes were admitted into the judge's chambers and quietly waited for the judge to make his appearance. Finally Judge Parker strode into his office still wearing his official robes of office, sat down heavily in his chair and then took the time to closely stare at Grizzly Creek Barnes over the top of his desk, as Barnes stared right back at the powerful judge with the same hardheaded Irish intensity...

Then the quiet but authoritative voice of Judge Parker was directed at Barnes saying, "Mr. Barnes, you have caused me and my court a lot of trouble over the years with your illegal making and sale of whiskey to the Indians and anyone else I am told who would buy it. For your information, the making of whiskey and its sale is a felonious violation of federal law in the Indian Territory. That law is in place for a very good reason and you openly and knowingly chose to ignore the law of the land and deliberately violated it numerous times over the last few years, as I have been told by the Tribal Authorities and other sources of information. Because of your flagrant disregard for that federal law, I was forced to send some of my overworked deputy marshals to your area with a Writ of Arrest for you because of the bootleg whiskey you were making and then providing, not only to the Indians but anyone else who had the money to purchase such 'devil's brew'!"

The judge then paused, poured himself a glass of water from a close at hand pitcher and then commenced once again reading the riot act to Barnes, saying, "Now I am perplexed over what I am to do with you. My deputy tells me you were captured without violence in the act of making bootleg whiskey, but when they made that arrest that forced them to leave your wife and six children to make a go of it for themselves without you as their main provider. Then my deputy tells me that they were subsequently surprised one evening by several desperadoes wanted by my court for stealing horses and robbing local stages. Those outlaws got the drop on my men and were going to kill them just because they were federal lawmen. Then according to my deputy, that was when you stepped in and pretended to want to help the outlaws out in the killing of my deputies by your own hand because they had arrested you. Then as I understand it, you turned on the outlaws once they had you released from your manacles, took a proffered handgun to be used in the killing of my deputies, killed one of the outlaws and got the drop on the rest. Then you aided my deputies in arresting those killers-to-be and helped in bringing them to my court. Is what I have said so far correct to your way of thinking?" asked the judge.

"Yes Sir, what you have said is correct as far as I remember," quietly replied Barnes.

"What am I to do with you? You, Sir, are an admitted felon in the eyes of this court for making and selling bootleg whiskey in the Indian Territory contrary to federal law. A guilty finding by this court for such a heinous offense is at least a ten-year sentence in a federal prison! Yet, you took it upon yourself to freely assist my deputies when they were in danger of losing their lives when you did not have to, and saved not only their lives but the life of their cook and wagon driver as well. Well, what do you have to say for yourself?" asked the judge.

"You are right, Your Honor. I did in fact make and sell bootleg whiskey in violation of the law in order to help feed my family. And yes, I did help your deputies out from a tight spot when those McGees and their friend, Gratt Peters, got the drop on them and were going to kill them. I just did what I thought was the Christian thing to do, Your Honor," quietly replied Barnes.

"Now, I have another problem regarding you and this matter. I have a deputy marshal who has requested that I find you guilty of making illegal whiskey and selling the same in direct violation of federal law. Then he has asked that I pardon you from that violation because you saved my three deputies and their cook from being killed outright by a pair of common horse thieves and stagecoach robbers," grumbled Judge Parker as he paused in his statements.

For the longest time after the judge had spoken, one could only hear the rhythmic ticking of the giant grandfather's clock in the judge's chambers. Then Judge Parker said, "Rufous Barnes, raise your right hand!"

Startled over the judge's abrupt order, Rufous hesitated for a moment than raised his right hand as he had been ordered.

"Rufous Barnes, do you solemnly swear to tell the truth, the whole truth and nothing but the truth, so help you God?" asked the judge.

"Yes Sir, I do," replied Rufous, still confused over where the judge was going with his line of judicial actions.

"Rufous Barnes, did you make and sell illegal bootleg whiskey to the local Indians and other people in the Indian Territory?" asked the judge.

"Yes Sir," quietly replied Rufous, now caught up in his moment of time before the judge.

"Then Rufous Barnes, I find you guilty of making and selling illegal bootleg whiskey contrary to federal law and sentence you to ten years in the federal prison!" barked out Judge Parker in such a tone of finality, that time almost stood still for all those officers in attendance and looking on during the now surprise hoped-for change in the legal proceedings!

Upon hearing those words from the judge, Joe, Lewis, James and Chino were flat startled and dismayed by his rendering of the rather harsh, immediate and commanding decision! Then Joe, upon hearing those words and the finding of the court being so contrary to what he had earlier proposed to the judge, without thinking, instinctively rose from his seat as if wanting to be recognized so he could speak as to the rendering of such a harsh decision upon a man who had saved all of their lives.

"Sit down, Young Man!" bellowed out the judge and in so doing, the tone of his command literally froze Joe in his tracks.

Ignoring the still standing and now totally surprised deputy, the judge turned and, facing an also shocked Rufous Barnes, said, "Now, having found you guilty, I am suspending the entire sentence PROVIDING that you never again ever make one single drop of illegal bootleg whiskey and sell the same to those around you. Mr. Barnes, do you agree to that modified sentence?" asked Judge Parker.

For a moment, Rufous just sat there still in shock over just moments earlier being sentenced

to ten years in federal prison and then immediately being granted a full suspension of that
sentence! Finally gathering up his wits around
him so he could find his voice and speak, Rufous
finally said, "Yes Sir, I do."

"Good! Now there is one other part to your
sentence that you must fulfill and enter into, or
the entire suspension of the sentence for the illegal making and selling of whiskey in the Indian
Territory will be rendered null and void and
you will be required to serve out your full ten
years in prison for such felonies, so here we go!
I need good deputies who understand the 'how,
where and why' of the bootlegging business and
a clear understanding of those who do such evil
and vile things. Basically, I am of the school that
says, 'it takes a thief to catch one'. If you agree
to become one of my federal deputies in good
standing and promise to pursue with all your
heart and energies those who violate this set of
'bootlegging' laws within the Indian Territory,
and arrest and bring those violators before me for
trial, then Sir, you will be a free man to go forth
and do the biding of the Federal Government in
this matter so subscribed before me this day of
our Lord, in the year of 1890. Additionally, if that
occurs, this matter, although a matter of record,
will be suspended as long as you faithfully fulfill
your legal duties," advised Judge Parker to a

now 'quiet as a mouse pissing on a ball of cotton' room full of surprised and amazed people. It was just like Marshal Fagan had told Joe earlier when the initial 'off the wall' proposal had been made to him by his deputy, "You might just find the judge will have a surprising response to your proposal..."

Then the judge looked over at a still standing in surprise Joe Dodson saying, "How was that, Deputy? You may sit down now and wipe that look of worry from off your face."

Then turning back to Rufous, who was still sitting down in shock over the whirl of events flying about him, Judge Parker said, "Rufous Barnes, please rise."

Once again Rufous rose with a look of concern racing across his eyes fearing the judge would go back on his suspension and impose the entire sentence because he had now thought better of what he had just done for a now convicted felon.

"Rufous Barnes, raise your right hand and repeat after me," ordered Judge Parker.

Rufous Barnes's right hand shot up like it had been shot from a cannon and as he stared back at the judge, Judge Parker said, "Rufous Barnes, do you solemnly swear to uphold the laws of the United States, obey the Constitution, follow the Bill of Rights, and declare that you are a citizen in good standing and are a good Christian?"

"I do," said a still surprised Rufous Barnes over just how fast his life was spinning around him in the courtroom that day.

"Then I now by the authority vested in me and the judicial office I now hold, declare you to be officially deputized as a Deputy U.S. Marshal in good standing in and for this United States of America. Congratulations, Deputy Marshal Barnes," concluded Judge Parker with a wide smile on his face over what he had just accomplished. Accomplished for his judicial district and the Indian Territory in removing a federal violator who was a master illegal whiskey maker, and had transformed him into a much needed deputy marshal especially knowledgeable and perfectly suited to pursue those still operating within his previous time-honored trade of illegally making and selling bootleg whiskey...

"Marshal Fagan, will you please see to it that Deputy Barnes is registered within the U.S. Marshals Service as a Deputy U.S. Marshal in good standing with all its benefits, and arrange for him to be adequately supplied in the time-honored tradition of the Service?" asked Judge Parker.

"Yes Sir, Judge Parker. I will see to it this day and also lay out my next assignment for my other three deputies," replied Marshal Fagan.

"I must now leave for my next sentencing.

A process that will send its recipient into the next world as a result of his evil actions and my sentencing decision in his case," replied Judge Parker with a shake of his head. With that, the judge rose, walked over to a still very surprised Rufous Barnes over the whirlwind events that had just taken place in the judge's chambers relative to the man's new life, wished him well and was out the door with his robes of office flowing out behind him like the Indian Territory whirlwind he was...

"Alright, Men, we have some serious law enforcement work to get done sometime this day and right now is as good a time as any to start. Follow me to my office, please," said Marshal Fagan, as he too briskly exited the judge's office, obviously a man on a mission of his own as well.

Once in Fagan's office, the marshal busied himself in getting all the administrative work that needed doing when and for a new deputy who had just been authorized. As Fagan and Barnes accomplished the necessary administrative work, the Dodsons quietly waited their turn with the marshal in his office for their next assignment.

Finally finished with his new deputy's administrative sign-up duties, Marshal Fagan sat all four of the men down in his office so he could explain his next assignment, which had been initiated by a personal and aggrieved witness whose husband had been killed and their small ranch house burned to the ground over contested 'free grazing' rights. (Author's Note: Open government lands were for many years considered 'free grazing' for one's cattle herds and first come, first served, which led to many a violent conflict between those wishing to make use of the 'free graze'.)

However, having been without the benefits of having a good chew in his mouth most of the morning because of the 'Rufous Barnes affair' in the judge's chambers, Marshal Fagan set about rectifying that situation as the four deputies sat quietly by his desk in his office. Once again, Marshal Fagan took out his all too familiar plug of black-as-coal tar Brown's Mule chewing tobacco, bit off a large chunk, sloshed it comfortably around in his mouth for a few moments to savor its taste and relish its placement between his teeth and gums, then said, "Gentlemen, you have not only a dangerous but difficult assignment in store for you. We have a prominent Texas cattleman who is 'free grazing' his cattle in the spring of the year in the Indian Territory and when winter returns, brings his livestock back to Texas where the winters are not as severe and the grazing is then easier to come by. However, this cattleman is not only a bully but a criminal as well. In providing for better grazing for his stock, he takes it upon himself, his white and Mexican cowboys, and four of his special Indian renegade cowboys to terrorize the smaller cattle ranchers in the Indian Territory located along the northern reaches of the Red River. He does so because in order to get to the free grazing areas from his ranch in Texas to such lands in the Indian Territory, he must move his cattle over and through a number of the smaller cattle ranches en route. We have been told by witnesses that this Texas cattleman does so even if he has to cut the barbed wire fences on the smaller Indian Territory cattle ranches in order to reach the much sought after free grazing in the government lands lying to the north. In fact, it has been reported to this office that this Texas cattleman basically grazes over the smaller ranches with his herd of cattle and if anyone objects, he has his four Chickasaw Indian renegade cowboys kill the smaller objecting rancher, rape the man's females, plunder his ranch house, and then burn it to the ground as a warning to all the other close at hand cattle ranchers to yield to his wishes or they can expect the same kind of treatment."

Then it was time for a spit of tobacco juice to be lobbed out his open window behind where the marshal sat, and then once again he continued with the men's briefing as if nothing was out of the ordinary when it came to spitting out one's open window. "Now Gentlemen, I have interviewed a complaining witness who recently came to Fort Smith, one who lost her husband in such a manner, had her ranch burned down and her honor forcefully violated by those four renegade Indian son-of-a-bitches who to my way of thinking, need to be killed outright for what they are doing under the Texas rancher's orders!"

Again another spew of tobacco spittle was spat out his open window and then Marshal Fagan commenced once again with, "Now, we have a small problem. You are not legally authorized to operate in Texas as Deputy U.S. Marshals because of the highly political Texas Ranger issue. So, you cannot go into Texas to root this powerful bastard cattleman out from his hole and bring him back across state lines to Fort Smith for trial. If you do, we will have problems from local Texas politicians and the Texas Rangers which are kind of watching over this very highly politically connected cattleman. So here is what I need you to do. You need to go down to the small town of Hendrix along the Red River in the Indian Territory adjacent the Texas state boundary. Now, I have a short list of surviving wives from allegedly killed small ranchers, who were also raped by the Indian cowboys as well as by their Texas boss and "Cattle King", as he has come to call himself. That information was provided by a widow who came to Fort Smith to complain about what was going on down there along our border. Because of what she had to tell the judge and he being such a religious man, he was highly incensed and has issued a number of Writs of Arrest for these guilty parties so charged. I need you men to melt into the local cattle ranching communities in this area along the Indian Territory border and in so doing, quietly interview these surviving widows without being discovered as to your mission by those in the surrounding general populace. With those interviews in hand affixing the blame on those individuals committing such illegal deeds, you need to somehow ambush this Texas bastard when he is in the Indian Territory grazing his cattle in the spring and summer and then, he being under Judge Parker's authority, arrest that bastard! I want him grabbed off and brought back to Fort Smith to stand trial for not only fostering the killing of our white settlers, but for the rape of their women and destruction of their property! Now, I suspect that you will have some trouble with his Indian cowboys who I am sure will try and protect their boss from being arrested by the likes of you. If they get in the way and try to impede your duties as federal officers, kill the bastards! In fact, that may be the only way you will get their boss arrested and transported clear back here in Arkansas to see the judge. So be alert to those cowboys interfering with your duties as a Deputy U.S. Marshals and handle it accordingly."

Once again, Fagan paused to spit out his open window behind his desk, then he continued with, "Now make sure you grab this bastard off when he is clearly inside the Indian Territory where you have the authority to do so. That opportunity will more than likely present itself when he brings up his cattle from Texas in the spring to free graze in the Indian Territory north of the Red River. Then there is another problem rearing its ugly head on this assignment. You three brothers are going to be outnumbered when you tangle with this Texas cattleman and his regular cowboys, not to mention his merry band of four, hired gun renegade Chickasaw Indians. So here is what I am proposing that the three of you do under these somewhat trying and dangerous circumstances. I am assigning our newest deputy, Deputy Barnes, to you three as an extra man! I am doing so, so that you three can act as instructors to him while en route Hendrix and teach him the expected ways and behavior of the U.S. Marshals Service. That way, I can kill two birds with one stone. In so doing, I can get Barnes trained in the ways of the Service as well as teaching him some of the tricks of the trade utilized by experienced federal law enforcement officers. Also by sending Deputy Barnes along with you three, that will give the three of you another gun in case things get a bit sticky because of being so outnumbered if and when an arrest is attempted."

Once again, it was time for another spit of tobacco juice which the marshal did like it was old home week. Then beginning once again, he said, "Now, Joe, here is this Texas cattleman's Writ of Arrest for facilitating murder, arson, theft of cattle and rape of the wives of the deceased ranchers who were killed. Additionally, since there more than likely will be some Indians involved before all of this is said and done with his Chickasaw renegades, I am sending Indian Police Officer Tom Johns along with you four to specifically handle the Indian problem, plus that will give you another gun in case things get hot or out of hand. Now I suggest you four get together with Chino, tell him to lay in enough groceries for at least a three-month trip, get his animals and wagon up to snuff and get going. I figure you will need three months because you officers will need time to quietly infiltrate the local community of ranchers, gain their trust and wait for the Texas cattleman to seasonally bring his cattle north to the 'free grazing' grounds north of the Red River into Indian Territory. Also, when you interview the affected women who have lost their menfolk, try to keep such interviews on the "QT". The less that Texas cattleman and the locals realize what you four are up to, the better and the safer it will be for all concerned. Now I suggest you four get 'cracking' because you have a lot to get done before you can even leave town. Oh by the way, I almost forgot. The woman who came to personally complain to the judge gave him the names and addresses of two other aggrieved women who had lost their husbands, cattle herds, homes, and 'honor' to this Texas cattleman and his henchmen. Both of those addresses of the widowed and aggrieved women are now at local whorehouse! It seems that when those women lost their husbands, they lost the ability to make a living and had to resort to making a living in the whorehouse selling their bodies in order to survive. That is just another good reason why I want this bastard standing before me so I can see a 'dead man walking', especially once Judge Parker finishes with him! Lastly, congratulations, Deputy Barnes, on your new career. I am sorry you have drawn such a rough assignment right out of the box on your first detail but welcome to the U.S. Marshals Service and our standard way of doing business in the Indian Territory in the year of our Lord, 1890!"

With that, Writs of Arrest in hand and handshakes all around, the four deputies exited the

Chief U.S. Marshal's office, hearing him spitting his tobacco juice out his office window as they walked out through the open doorway of his office.

CHAPTER SEVEN

"HELL OR HIGH WATER" ALONG THE RED RIVER

SOMEWHAT LATER, Chino was given his orders to 'provision up' for a three-month trip, and then the four men made their way to the local emporium in Fort Smith in order to stock up on .50 caliber Sharps, .40-82 Winchester, .45 Colt, and ten gage double 00 buckshot munitions, just in case 'things got out of hand'! At the same time, Joe also quietly replenished his supply of sticks of 20% dynamite, just in case 'his wicket got sticky' also...

As Chief Marshal Fagan got back to his administrative business at hand after the men had left his office, he was unaware that earlier his deputies had brought two five-gallon Redwing whiskey jugs into his office that were full of Grizzly Creek Barnes's much-coveted 'moonshine' and had placed them out of sight behind an unused desk where he would discover them later. In so doing, Joe had ordered the placement of such jugs of fine sour mash whiskey because Marshal Fagan's parting words to Joe and his brothers when they had been sent out originally to catch Barnes was, "You three had better bring me some of that 'shine' back when you return or all of your hind ends will end up in a 'ringer'!" Suffice to say, when Marshal Fagan finally discovered the jugs of sour mash whiskey, his day trying to manage over 200 Deputy U.S. Marshals in a lawless area larger than 70,000 square miles, full of thousands of outlaws doing to humanity what they shouldn't be doing, all of a sudden got one hell of a lot easier to do…

Two days later, the posse, now compromised of four deputy marshals, one Indian Police Man, Chino, and his new recently purchased watch dog, which was part prairie wolf and part German shepherd (so they would never again be surprised by outlaws coming at them in the dark), left Fort Smith, Arkansas, as they headed south en route the small town of Hendrix located just north of the mighty Red River. Their assignment, to arrest one "Horsehide" Charlie Potter, also known as the Cattle King, a Texas cattleman and felon, wanted by the U.S. District Court in and for the Western District of Arkansas for murder, theft of cattle, arson and rape.

Four days later of hard winter travel brought the posse to the small town of Daisy in the southern portion of the Indian Territory. Joe had directed the posse in such a direction for one main humanitarian purpose. That purpose being so their mules and horses could rest and graze for several days and allow Rufous Barnes some time with his wife Martha and their children. That purpose, as per Joe's instructions, also allowed the men of the posse to assist Rufous in laying in a goodly supply of winter firewood and helping in the tending of his livestock, mending fences, laying up Martha's winter food supplies, and other household chores before they left for Hendrix and the great unknown that awaited each and every one of them.

Saying good-bye to his wife and children three days later, Rufous mounted his horse and three days of hard winter travel later found the lawmen outside the small town of Hendrix, just north of the fabled Red River, boundary between the great State of Texas and the lawless Indian Territory lying to the vast northern reaches.

Being new to the area and bound to arouse suspicions from the local populace as to their reason for being there, Joe decided the men would camp out a-ways from town and away from a goodly number of the locals. Figuring they would set up camp somewhere along the Red River bottoms and out of the way from most forms of general travel, the posse headed west along the river looking for a suitable long-term campsite. The luck of the Irish favored the men of the posse, when they discovered an abandoned homestead that had in existence two sets of corrals and a large dug-out into a hillside that was suitable as living quarters, instead of the canvas tents they had planned on setting up and using throughout the cold winter months.

The men spent the rest of that arrival day setting up their camp for the long-term living they had in mind. While Joe and Lewis cleaned up all the dried cattle dung and small animal refuse from inside the long-abandoned dug-out, the rest of the men strengthened up the corrals and then unloaded all of their gear into the newly cleaned out dug-out. Once inside the dug-out, the men arranged their individual sleeping and eating areas, as Chino set up an outside firepit and began making preparations for their evening meal. As Chino tended to his supper-making duties, James at the end of the day herded all the mules and horses from off their nearby grazing areas and into the refurbished corrals and shut the gate. As he did, Tom Johns, the Indian Policeman, built up the old fire pit inside the dug-out where one had originally stood years earlier, cut several arm loads of firewood from the nearby Red River breaks, and started an inside fire for the warmth it would later provide come nightfall. By so doing, that allowed the warmth from the inside fire to heat up the hard-packed soil from the roof and walls of the dug-out, which in turn, provided radiant heat throughout the evening and into the morning hours.

After a supper of fried bacon, Dutch oven biscuits and a pot of pinto beans laced with lard, the tired men headed for their individual sleeping areas within the dug-out with sleep in mind after a hard day of labors. However, not before Chino pulled the cork on a 'brought-along' Redwing whiskey jug, allowing each man to savor a full cup of some damn fine sour mash whiskey, courtesy of one Grizzly Creek Barnes. Grizzly Creek Barnes was a 'man' was no more, as Judge Parker had decreed when Rufous had signed on as Deputy U.S. Marshal Rufous Barnes of the U.S. Marshals Service…

That evening, instead of sleeping in the back of his cold chuck wagon, Chino slept near the entrance of their dug-out, bathed in the radiant heat supplied from an earlier inside fire from off the thick mud and brick sides and walls of their temporary home. Additionally, found sleeping alongside Chino was his newfound and recently purchased companion, a now totally dedicated wolf-cross German shepherd companion named

"Dog", ever faithfully watching the front entrance to the dug-out. Like Chino had said after almost being killed by their earlier capturers, the McGee brothers, "Never again will I be caught off guard by the forces of evil..."

Pre-dawn the next morning found Chino setting a pot of dried, cleaned and sorted beans off to soak for their supper while Joe saddled up his riding horse. As that was going on, the rest of the posse was stirring inside, washing their hands and faces in a cold pan of water and combing their hair as they made ready for their day of hard work ahead. After a breakfast of Dutch oven biscuits, coffee and fried bacon, Joe headed off for town as the rest of the posse prepared to gather in a large winter's supply of dry wood for their cooking and evening fires before the snows came, making such work more difficult. That was all except for Lewis, as he shouldered his .50 Sharps rifle and headed off into the tangle of brush and trees along the Red River hunting for a deer or elk for the posse's next set of meals.

Lewis had only been gone for about an hour when the booming sound of his Sharps rifle being fired could be heard echoing throughout the breaks. Without a word, Tom Johns saddled up his horse and a pack mule and then lit out following the tracks left earlier by Lewis. About an hour later, Lewis and Tom returned leading a heavily packed, hell for stout mule carrying a freshly killed five-point bull elk! Suffice to say, the woodcutting and gathering detail was quickly forgotten, as all the men turned out for the butchering and boning out of their many future meals. That was all the men except for Chino. He was now in the process of building a 'tee-pee' shaped structure from poles and covered with a sheet of canvas. Soon, fresh elk meat was smoking away on the inside racks of the newly built smokehouse so it could be preserved for many later meals.

Joe on the other hand, was sitting inside the "Cattlemen's Rest Saloon" in the town of Hendrix, helping himself to his second breakfast of pancakes and coffee. As he did in his undercover capacity as a Deputy U.S. Marshal, he visited with several of the locals asking about if anyone had any extra work for a group of out of work cowboys. As several ranchers also having breakfast listened, Joe advised that he and several of his brothers and friends were camping west along the river in an abandoned dug-out and looking for any kind of paying farm or ranch work to carry them through until they could sign on with a northward-bound cattle drive from out of Texas.

"What kind of work are you and your brothers familiar with?" asked a man at the next table who was a local rancher named Charlie Dennis.

"Me and my brothers can do most any kind of work," said Joe. "We come from a farming and ranching family back in Arkansas and we are ready to do anything, just as long as we can make enough for 'found' and a few dollars extra until we can find steady work on a summer cattle drive."

"You boys any good when it comes to butchering hogs?" asked another farmer named Albert Brazinni, a Swiss-Italian emigrant sitting with Charlie Dennis having his breakfast as well.

"Never butchered any hogs but we did a mess of butchering of our steers come fall as we grew up," replied Joe, "not to mention one hell of a mess of picking and cleaning chickens over the years when the thrashing crews came through our area to harvest our wheat."

"How many of ye did you say are looking for work?" asked Brazinni.

"There can be up to five of us, not counting our cook that we brought along," replied Joe.

"Gordon, bring me a piece of writing paper and a pencil," yelled Brazinni over at the bartender. Moments later, Brazinni was drawing Joe a map on how to find his farm so he and his brothers could come out and help the farmer in the annual killing, scalding a mess of his hogs and butchering out the same, so they could be made into hams, bacon, smoked hocks, sausage and the like. "I don't pay a lot but if fifty cents a day, dinner and supper and a mess of pork meat suits you to take back to your campsite, it suits me as well," said Brazinni, handing Joe the piece of paper with a map drawn on it showing the way to his hog ranch. Then he said, "I expect a day's work for a day's pay and I will need the mess of you from daylight until dark or until we finally finish. I also run a smokehouse and the work entails a lot of work with knives boning out and cutting up the meat in preparation for the smokehouse," he continued. Then as an afterword, Albert said, "I reckon we will be butchering at least 30 hogs and several old bulls who are no longer breeders for my four brothers' ranches those meats will support throughout the year. You see, me and my three brothers run our four ranches. One of us is responsible for supporting all of the ranches with meat, one provides all of the livestock we eat or sell, and the other two raise all the grains and hay we need throughout the rest of the year for livestock feed or sale. My brothers will be with us as well to help in the butchering, so you make sure all of your gang gets here in plenty of time so they can earn their keep."

"That would suit me and my brothers just fine, Mr. Brazinni. When would you like us to start?" asked Joe.

"This is good hog-killing weather. Good and

cold all day long, so how about we plan on getting started with the killing, scalding and butchering tomorrow right after breakfast?" asked Brazinni.

Joe glanced at the map and could see the Italian's hog ranch was just a few miles out of town and appeared to be easy to find. "That would be fine with us. Did you say that included breakfast as well?" asked Joe, as several other men walked into the saloon and listened in on the conversation between the two men. Having several other men listening in on the friendly conversation between Brazinni and himself suited Joe just fine. That way the word would get about town about the strangers who appeared friendly enough and who were going to work for 'Old Man Brazinni' in the killing and butchering of his hogs.

Finished up with breakfast and his business with Brazinni, Joe quietly asked Curtis the bartender where the nearest "crib" (whorehouse) was located and was given the directions. Exiting the saloon, Joe walked the short distance to the edge of town and noticed a number of buildings located along the road leading into Hendrix. Walking up to the front door of one building and walking in after seeing a lit red lantern placed conveniently inside the window as an advertisement for a whorehouse, Joe observed a small number of women sitting around in a sitting area quietly talking among themselves. Moments later an older lady and obviously Madam of the whorehouse walked up to Joe and asked if she could be of service with a charming smile and a bathrobe partially opened showing a lot of cleavage. Joe, who remembered the name of one of the widowed rancher ladies from Marshal Fagan's earlier briefing, who had lost her husband to Horsehide Charlie Potter, the Texas cattleman that they were after, asked if he could see Mrs. Jane Wilkins.

"You sure can, Honey," said the Madam with all the cleavage, as she turned to the group of ladies sitting around in plush chairs at the end of the cabin saying, "Jane, Honey, you have a visitor here to see you this morning."

Moments later, a dark-haired lady of medium build and smallish breasts presented herself at the front of the cabin saying, "Did you call me, Mrs. Roberts?"

"Shore did, Jane. This here cowboy has asked for you. Are you available this early in the morning?" Roberts sweetly asked.

"Yes I am," replied the woman named Jane, but in a sad sounding tone of voice.

"Well, here is your cowboy. And Cowboy, she is yours to do with as you see fit. However, that will be five dollars for no more than twenty minutes. And Miss Jane, you call me if anything is going wrong or getting out of hand, hear?" said Roberts sweetly.

"Yes, Ma'am," said Wilkins, as she reached out, took Joe's hand and led him into the back of the cabin and into a small room holding only a bed and a single chair. "What would you like, Cowboy?" she said in that same sad tone of voice of resignation obviously over what had become her new existence.

"Can we sit on the edge of your bed and talk?" asked Joe.

"Sure can, Cowboy. You are paying for my time and that means whatever you would like," said Jane, as she moved over to the bed and sat down.

Joe then sat down on the edge of the bed and said, "First, if Mrs. Roberts comes to the door and tells you my time is up, you tell her I am asking for more time and will pay the going rate so that she leaves us alone. Now, I am going to share with you a secret and I hope you can keep it. Because if you can't, it may get me killed and you tossed out on your ear."

With those words, Jane's eyes flew wide open in surprise and then she said, "Who are you any-way and what do you want? You are scaring me and I think I need to call Mrs. Roberts!"

"No! Don't do that! I am here because of you and what happened to you and your husband. But word of what I am doing here cannot get out. If it does, it may be bad for the both of us!" said Joe as he grasped Jane's hand in quiet assurance.

Jane then said, "Who are you? What do you want from me?"

"Jane, I am a Deputy U.S. Marshal investigating what happened to you and your husband. I am here to find out about the Texas cattleman named Charlie Potter who rode through your ranch last year with his herd of cattle, killed Darrel your husband, stole your cattle, burned down your ranch house, and had his four Chickasaw Indians rape you, and then Charlie I am told raped you as well. Your neighbor Mrs. Janet Berry, who was also treated the same way when the Texas cattle herd went south in the fall of that year across her property, filed an affidavit in Federal District Court in Fort Smith in Arkansas against Potter regarding what happened to her and her husband. When she did, she also mentioned that you and another woman named Carol Jackson were also raped by Potter and his Indian minions, and then the two of you were forced into sexual slavery because when you lost your husbands, you lost your means of livelihood and had to turn to this style of life in order just to survive."

Joe then took out his badge and showed it to Jane, whose eyes were now almost the size of Morgan silver dollars over the surprise revelations taking place in her 'crib'!

KNOCK, KNOCK, KNOCK! went three loud knocks at the door of their room and Jane almost panicked when she heard the knocking. "It is alright. I just need more time with Miss Jane and am willing to pay whatever is the price if you just give me some more time with this lady," said Joe loudly, hoping she would not burst open the door and see the two of them just talking as they sat on the bed.

"Alright, Cowboy, but you had better have another five dollar gold piece or five silver dollars when you come out or I have a shotgun that says you are in deep trouble!" bellowed out the voice of Mrs. Roberts from outside the door.

"I do and expect to pay whatever you say once I come out," said Joe loudly enough so there would be no misunderstanding, and as a result of that, Mrs. Roberts would come barging into the room and see the two of them just sitting there and only talking.

"Whatever I say to you, you cannot tell anyone else here in town! And you cannot tell that Potter fellow either because he said he would kill me if I ever uttered a word as to what he did to me and my husband. Yes, you are correct. Potter and his Indians burst into our home last year and shot my husband dead without saying a word as to why they did what they did. Then his four Indians and he raped me repeatedly until I passed out from all the pain of being handled so roughly. When I came to, I was outside lying on the ground, my home was aflame and my husband was still inside and burned up to a crisp! Since I had no close at hand kin and there is no law in the area, I was forced into this lifestyle in order to live. I have saved a little money and had hoped to go to the authorities someday, but I fear I will die doing this before I get the chance to tell my side of the story in court," said a now very worried Mrs. Wilkins.

"Do not worry. Your story is safe with me and what you told me here this morning is just what I needed to put Potter away for a very long time, that is, if Judge Parker does not hang him high instead for what he and his minions did to you and your husband," said Joe quietly.

"That would serve that bastard right for what he did to me, my husband and ruining our lives," said Jane, as tears quickly welled up in her eyes!

"Alright, I have what I need from you," said Joe, as he rose to leave. "But now tell me, does Mrs. Jackson work here in this place as well? If she does, either I or one of my brothers who are also deputy marshals, will try and visit her as well to get her side of the story as to what happened to her and her husband," advised Joe, as he stood up, pulled out the tail of his shirt and removed his gun belt, like he was just getting hurriedly dressed after having had sex with Jane in order to make his and her cover stories foolproof.

"Yes, she does work here. She is the woman in our group with the long red hair," said Jane, now with a slight tone of hope rising up in her voice. "I will tell her what happened here to me here today when the time is right and let her know that you or one of your brothers will be coming to 'see' her as well. That is, if that is all right with you?" said Jane with the sound of hope in her voice.

"That would be fine with me but be sure and stress to her that she must keep her mouth shut and not say anything to anyone! Additionally, when my work here is done, me and my men will come for you and Mrs. Jackson and take you away from here," said Joe, with a more than serious look on his face meant to emphasize the meanings of his words.

When he said those words, Jane rose up from the bed and threw her arms around Joe in delight and obvious relief. "I will be waiting for that day, but please do not wait long or get yourself killed in the process. This is a life of hell and I don't know how much longer I can live like this," she said in a tone and tenor of voice that read only of deep despair and desperation.

Joe then gave her a hug saying, "I will be back for you and now I must go and see Mrs. Roberts and cover for you and our time together here this morning."

With those words, Joe told Jane to wait for a few minutes before she came out and he would take care of business. Striding out the door and down the hallway like a very happy customer, Joe strode into the antechamber in the front of the cabin, took out a ten dollar gold piece and flipped it into the outstretched hands of Mrs. Roberts the Madam saying, "That should take care of your concerns and Jane was wonderful. It just took me longer than I figured." Then Joe strode out the front door like a new man, swinging his looped gun belt around and around his outstretched arm like a more than happy cowboy...

Riding back to their compound at the dug-out, Joe bailed off his horse, rounded up the rest of the posse and filled them in on his successes in town. Then Joe and James laid out their next set of interview plans for the morrow at the whore-house, at the end of their workday out on the Brazinni ranch. Following that, Joe took the time to fill in the rest of the men as to what they would be doing at Brazinni's ranch in order to maintain their covers until all the interviews had been completed, prior to serving the Writ of Arrest on Potter and his band of four renegade outlaw Indians once they had set foot onto the Indian Territory with their herd of cattle.

The following morning after breakfast, Joe, James, Lewis, Rufous and Tom saddled up and rode out to the Brazinni ranch. Chino and Dog stayed behind at the dug-out to take care of any camp chores that needed doing and to protect their remaining horse and mule herd from theft.

Once at the Brazinni ranch, Albert introduced Joe and company to his other three brothers, Ernest, Alpino and Diego Brazinni. Then the nine men rolled up their sleeves and plunged into the killing, scalding, hair removal, gutting, and hanging of the hogs to cool out. They also spent time in sorting out the leaf lard from the entrails, separating out for later use a number of the organ meats, and began flushing out and washing the intestines and soaking them in brine baths so they could be used as casings in the sausage-stuffing processes to follow.

Come the noon meal, Leah, wife of Albert, had all the men in for a homemade Italian dinner, and then back to work went the men killing more hogs and began processing the same. By day's end the men had earned their keep according to a very happy Albert and he invited all the men back the next day to continue their meat processing work, upon which they all accepted. Then once again, Leah had supper for all of the men as had been agreed to by Albert early on with Joe when the arrangements for work had been made.

Riding back into Hendrix en route their dug-out and some much-needed baths, the men

smelling like butchered hogs rode by the whorehouse with its prominent red lantern glowing
out through the front window. It was then that
Joe noticed for the first time the red lettering
painted above the doorway announcing for the
whole world to see, "The Lamb's Inn"! With a
nod of his head at brother Joe, James broke away
from the group of returning riders, rode over
to the hitching rack in front of the house with
the red lantern, dismounted, tied off his horse
and entered the whorehouse, while the rest of
the posse continued on their way towards their
dug-out like nothing out of the ordinary had just
occurred.

Entering, James noticed a middle-aged man at
the back of the anteroom with two scantily clad
women sitting on his lap, laughing and talking
up a friendly storm. Standing there for a moment, James was soon surrounded by a bevy of
'ladies of the night' all competing for his attention. Remembering what Joe had told him, James
spied the long-haired redhead also known as
Mrs. Jackson, sitting on the lap of the man at the
back of the room. So excusing himself from the
bevy of the 'ladies of the night' surrounding him,
James headed for the back of the room with the
man happily holding the two women on his lap.

"Say there, Mister. Is that red-haired beauty
available for this tired old cowboy?" asked James
in a light-hearted tone of voice.

"Sure is, Cowboy," said the man who rose, stuck out his hand and introduced himself as "Dean Mastel, proud owner and proprietor of The Lamb's Inn. But my friends in the German Mafia here about town just call me 'Lambkins'. What is your 'handle', Cowboy?"

"My name is James and I just finished a hard day's work butchering hogs out on the Brazinni ranch. Now if you don't mind, 'Mr. Lambkins', I would like to spend some time with this young lady with the long and beautiful red hair before I head on back to our campsite," said James in a spirited sort of way.

"Hold her there, Cowboy. I have a small spread and am getting ready to butcher out some of my hogs as well, since this is great hog butchering weather. If you ever need a job butchering hogs, let me know. I can always use a good man because my previous hired man up and ran off with my neighbor's daughter. He is now a hunted man and if my neighbor ever catches him, he will become magpie bait. Hell, now that I think about it, that fellow was as useless as teats on the side of bacon when it came to hard work. So, if you finish out at Brazinni's anytime soon, give me a call. Also, if you need a place to stay, I might just have a room up over my barn for you to stay while working for me," said 'Lambkins'.

James thanked 'Lambkins', then turning back

to the business at hand and looking down at the redhead, James could tell she was turned off by how dirty, bloody and snot covered he looked, not to mention how badly he smelled after spending a day butchering hogs. But he figured that was just the cover he needed as he turned and faced a Mrs. Roberts, whose nose was also turned up as well at how badly he smelled. Then with a measure of swagger, James handed Mrs. Roberts a ten dollar gold piece, pointed to the redhead and asked, "Do we have a deal?"

"Yes Sir, Cowboy. We have a deal. Carol, will you see to this gentleman, please?" asked Mrs. Roberts, with a smirk on her face over what Carol would more than have to put up with coming from such a handsome but rough-looking and badly smelling cowboy. With that, Carol rose and escorted James into her assigned crib and closed the door behind the two of them.

"What will it be, Cowboy?" she asked, fearing she would never be able to get all the smell of dead hogs from off her body when all was said and done.

"Mrs. Jackson, my name is James Dodson and I am a Deputy U.S. Marshal from Fort Smith, Arkansas. Did Mrs. Wilkins speak to you about my brother Joe and their meeting yesterday?" asked James.

"Oh my God, are you for real?" she asked in

amazement. Then tears welled up in her eyes and she flew into James's arms and quietly burst out into tears of joy! Thirty minutes later, James had her story down pat on what Potter and his Indian cohorts had feloniously done to Mrs. Jackson and her now dead husband. Finished with that needed part of the interview, James assured her that the marshals would be back for both sexually enslaved women once they had Potter in custody. Then James had Mrs. Jackson muss her hair up like she had had a real rough time with James, and then he exited her crib telling her quietly to stay put for a few minutes before she made her entrance back into the main sitting area. Walking down the hallway of the whorehouse, James took out a five dollar gold piece, flipped it to the Madam Mrs. Roberts, and said, "I will be back for more when I have more money." With that, he left the building for his horse and as he looked back down the long hallway in the whorehouse, he could see 'Lambkins' hurriedly running into the back room to see how one of his best girls had fared in the hands of the rough-looking and badly smelling cowboy…

Once back at the dug-out, James filled in the rest of the posse regarding how his interview had gone with Mrs. Jackson and how she had indicated just how badly she had suffered at the hands of Potter. Joe after hearing what James had to say, said, "I think we have enough personal testimony evidence now for our arrest to stick in any court of law once they are made. All we will need now is Potter to show himself in the Indian Territory and we can grab him off, serve Judge Parker's Writ of Arrest and slap him into a set of manacles and chains. Once we have him safely in chains, we will need to go back into Hendrix, grab up Mrs. Wilkins and Mrs. Jackson and take them back with us and away from the lifestyle they are now forced into living. That way, when back in Fort Smith, they can testify against Potter and maybe Judge Parker can send that killing son-of-a-bitch on his way to hell in a handbasket..."

For the rest of that month and into the first vestiges of spring, the men of the posse continued working undercover on the various Brazinni brothers' ranches, assisting them in farming and ranching in order to maintain their cover as Deputy U.S. Marshals. Finally once winter had left the land and the greening grasses again covered the grasslands of the Indian Territory, a number of Texas cattlemen began moving their cattle northward as they had done for years for the free grazing those verdant lands offered. But no matter how hard the deputy marshals watched, none of the Texas herds moving north proved out to be those belonging to their man

Potter they had been looking for. It was then that Joe surmised maybe the word had somehow gotten out that the marshals were in town and laying for Potter, his Chickasaw renegades and his herd of free grazing cattle.

Lying in his sleeping blankets early one morning, Joe awakened thinking he was hearing the faint sounds of shooting coming from east of their dug-out near the next small cattle ranch down the line from their campsite. Scrambling to his feet, Joe yelled for the rest of the men to get up and get dressed! Soon their camp was a frenzy of men hurriedly saddling their horses, all accompanied to the sounds of more shooting coming from the closest cattle ranch to their east!

Storming out from their camp, the posse rode hard for their neighbors further to the east and as they raced their horses closer, Joe reined up so quickly as they passed through a small grove of trees that he almost caused a number of the hard riding riders behind to have one hell of a wreck! Joe then wheeled his horse off to the south and raced for a tall cottonwood tree near the ranch house that held a struggling and obviously strangling man hanging from a rope from one of its main branches!

Racing his horse right up to the violently struggling and choking man, Joe drew his Bowie knife and slashed at the rope holding the man! In so doing, Joe's deadly sharp knife cut clean through the rope in the process, dropping the struggling man like a sack of rocks! Then Joe whirled his horse around, rode back, dismounted at a dead run, and ran over to the man still struggling on the ground with his hands on a length of rope still tightly cinched up around his neck. Grabbing the rope around the man's neck, Joe quickly loosened the noose as the man who had almost choked to death at the end of the rope was desperately gasping and drawing in huge gulps of air! Struggling as he was, the man desperately tried talking to Joe, who was leaning over the man's mouth with a lowered ear in an attempt to hear what he was trying to 'gasp' out.

All of that activity with the struggling man was occurring simultaneously as a huge herd of Texas longhorn cattle milled around the nearby ranch house and were streaming by into the man's cornfields heading north to the choruses of a number of cowboys yelling and herding the animals along! Finally the man was able to make himself heard over the sounds of a thousand cattle bellowing and tromping everything green and living underfoot into dust nearby.

"My house for God's sake, go to my house, HELP!" he choked out, as he pointed and then collapsed in choking exhaustion and began vomiting once again.

Hearing those words of desperation and seeing the man pointing towards a nearby ranch house, it was then that James, Lewis, Rufous and Tom Johns spurred their horses past Joe, as they finally realized what might be occurring as they made a mad dash towards the rancher's house! Riding up to the front of the house amidst a number of milling cattle trampling the small trees and flowers in the rancher's front yard after they had plowed through and broken down his picket fence, the posse members bailed off their horses among five other riding horses tied to the hitching rail. Close behind the posse ran Joe and then the five men stormed inside the ranch house to see what was causing the rancher almost hanged such desperation.

Bursting through the front door led by Lewis and followed by the rest of the posse, the men were greeted with a visible sight beyond their years! One Indian man had a young girl all of twelve years of age bent over the kitchen table and was forcefully raping her! In the immediate adjoining room, another Indian was observed in the process of rising up from the floor having just raped a middle-aged woman, as another Indian nearby prepared to descend upon and rape her as well! In that same instant, a scream from the back room brought Joe back into his fast action senses, as he ran past the other two women being raped but soon to be tended to by the following posse, and into the bedroom from whence had come the horrendous scream of a woman in intense pain! There on a bed lay a young woman in her teens being forcefully raped by an older white man! Racing into the room, Joe drew his revolver and smashed it onto the side of the rapist's head with such force, that he almost broke several of his gun hand fingers against the bone of the man's skull! However in so doing, he had struck the white man so violently that he instantly had streams of blood running out from his ears, nose and one eye!

Meanwhile back in the kitchen, where the very young girl was being forcefully raped by a tall and heavyset Indian, Tom Johns, the Indian Policeman assigned to the posse, had shattered the back of the man's skull with the butt of his pistol and in so doing, killed the rapist outright! Then he grabbed up the violently screaming young girl and tried comforting her in his arms, all the while letting her know he was a lawman. As for the middle-aged woman lying face down on the floor in the next room, a woman who had been raped by one Indian and was getting ready to be raped by another, both of those men now lay inert on the floor from having concussive blows rained down upon their heads with pistols by James and Lewis! As for Rufous, he had cold cocked a fourth Indian in the process of stealing items from a china cabinet adjacent the kitchen, and was still standing over the inert Indian hoping he would get up so he could get more of what he had coming from one damn furious Irish 'moonshiner'...!

Jerking the now injured white man up off the teenager lying fully naked on the bed, now covered with blood from the bleeding man who had been in the process of raping her just moments before, Joe tossed the rapist aside and then covered her nakedness up with the bedspread, as she continued crying uncontrollably.

About then the rancher who had almost been hanged by the four Indians and the lone Texas white man earlier, staggered into the house in a fury of worry borne of desperation for his family members. Seeing what he saw upon entry into his violated home, he jerked a handgun from Tom Johns's holster as he still held the rancher's youngest daughter in his arms trying to comfort her in her moment of terror and not realizing the Indian rapist on the floor with his penis still hanging out from his pants was already dead, shot him five times! In so doing, every bullet pumped into the dead man's body upon impact caused the carcass to hump up off the floor slightly, as if still in life and reacting to the shock of the bullets entering his body...

Finally the crying women were brought under control, as was the raging rancher with the terrible rope burns and skin tears around his neck from almost being successfully hanged. About then, Chino and Dog rumbled up towards the ranch house in their chuck wagon. Moments later, they rolled to a dusty stop in front of the hitching rack in and among a number of cattle still pouring up from Texas, crossing the Red River and heading onto the northern grasslands for the free grazing such lands offered.

Then the moment around the rancher's house turned ominously dark! About ten cowboys riding 'drag' on the end of the herd being pushed across the almost hanged rancher's property, now rode into view. Seeing and realizing their cattle boss's horse was one of those horses tied to the rancher's hitching rack with a number of strangers in the form of posse members moving about, they stopped and just looked on trying to figure out what the hell was happening and if they should get involved. Their hesitation did not last long when their cattle boss and three of his Chickasaw renegade Indian bodyguards were pushed staggering out from the ranch house, led over to the chuck wagon and were in the process of being placed into manacles and leg irons by a mess of strangers!

All at once the aggrieved Indian Territory

rancher and posse were surrounded by ten very aggressive cowboys with leveled Winchesters with a number of fingers upon their triggers! Seeing that, Joe tried to get control of the situation by identifying himself in word and with his badge, as did the other posse members. But the ten drovers, loyal to their boss and truly not understanding or having 'a-word' of what they were seeing and hearing, stood firm with their leveled Winchesters. Then one of the cowboys demanded that the three Indians and their cattle boss be released or there would be hell to pay right then and there... That was when Joe observed a huge cloud of dust rising into the air and heard the thundering of numerous horses' hooves coming from the direction of the small town of Hendrix!

Joe then said out loud to himself, "I hope that isn't more Texas cowboys coming here to the ranch and their boss's rescue. If it is we have a problem in the making!"

It was then that Joe spotted Albert Brazinni and his brothers riding into view, leading a number of townsfolk and every one of them seemed to be sporting a rifle or shotgun of some sort! Moments later, the ten Texas drovers holding the marshals at bay with their leveled Winchesters trying to get their boss and his guardian Indians released from the lawmen, found themselves surrounded by a host of angry folks from Hendrix with obvious lynching on their minds if one 'could read' the looks on their faces! Not realizing Joe and company were lawmen and there to help, they were covered with the rifles from the angry folks from Hendrix as well, as were the Texas drovers!

Finally the rancher who had almost been killed by the Texas cattle boss and his four Indian cohorts, left his crying women folk, stepped out onto the porch and raised his hand to get the attention of his now very pissed off and ready to kill the first person who made an ill move, neighbors from town.

"Hold her, Folks," he choked out the words through his still damaged throat! "These guys are lawmen and just saved me and my women from further harm. You need to let them go and run off all these Texas assholes from storming over everything we locals own every time they are driving their cattle into the Indian Territory in the spring and then once again when they go back down to Texas in the fall. You also need to grab off these three Indians and that white cattleman standing there in manacles. They are the ones who tried to hang me and the ones who were raping my women folks when these guys arrived, stepped in and stopped it. We need to hang these bastards once and for all so they never again storm all over our ranches in the future, and in the process, cutting down our barbed wire fences meant to keep them and their herds of cattle out and off from our lands."

With those words from their fellow rancher and neighbor, the Hendrix folks disarmed the other drovers working for Potter and made for the white cattle boss and the remaining three Indians who had been responsible for all the raping that had occurred in the past and present, with the look of 'blood' in their eyes!

That was when Joe forcefully took over and let the Hendrix folks know that they were Deputy U.S. Marshals who had been sent there by Fort Smith's Federal District Court Judge, Judge Parker, to arrest the cattleman and his Indian cohorts so they could be taken back to his federal court to stand trial for their past and present deeds. For a moment there was confusion in the ranks of the townspeople on what to do with the Texas cattlemen at hand, then Joe and the rest of the posse flashed their badges once again and gained control over the soon to be a-hanging crowd of local townspeople!

That was when Joe announced, "Gentlemen, I need all of you to round up the rest of this cattle herd's drovers still at the front of the herd and have them drive their cattle back into Texas where they came from. That is, minus a number of cattle removed from the herd in payment to satisfy this rancher for the damage his ranch and surrounding croplands and property have sustained. Then all the rest of the animals need to herded back across the Red River, along with the rest of these Texas cowboys. The cowboys did no wrong in driving the cattle across this man's lands because they were just following orders from their boss. So let them go back across the river with their cattle and the understanding that if they ever do this again without the Indian Territory landowner's approval, you folks will fight back and stop it from happening!"

Seeing that the townspeople were listening to what the marshals were now saying, Joe continued with, "Lewis and Rufous, finish manacling those four 'hombres' and have Chino chain them to the chuck wagon bed to prevent them from any escape attempts. Then James, Lewis and Rufous need to take the written statements from these aggrieved women and the rancher for use in the Texan's trial in Judge Parker's court. That way, we won't need them to testify because we personally witnessed the felonious crimes being committed in our presence, but I want their statements anyway as backup in case they get a good defense attorney and want to fight the charges we are prepared to personally lodge against them."

Walking over to the white cattleman who was still bleeding from his ears and nose after being slugged in the back of his head with the butt of a pistol, it was then that Joe discovered his captured cattle boss was none other than Texan 'Horsehide' Charlie Potter! With that identification made, Joe advised Potter that he had a Writ of Arrest for him issued by Judge Parker in Fort Smith for previous murders, rape, arson and cattle rustling from a number of the local ranchers they had run over when they had driven their cattle across their ranches a year earlier. Additionally, Joe advised they were now also facing charges of attempted murder of the most recent rancher when they had driven their cattle across his lands and he had objected. Then they had tried to hang him for objecting over their trespassing cattle and getting in their way. Lastly, they were now also facing felony charges for the rape of the rancher's wife and teenage daughters!

Still somewhat in a daze over being struck so forcefully from behind by Joe, Potter finally acknowledged that he understood he was now under arrest, and then looking Joe right in his eyes, said in a sharp tone of voice heavy with his Texas drawl, "You will never make any of those charges stick. In fact, Cowboy, you are a dead man walking once my drovers get their crap together, come back across the 'Red', hunt your men down and hang the lot of you from the nearest cottonwood tree like the types of you and your kind deserve! And just for good measure, I intend to have my cowboys save a special treat for you, Marshal. I intend to have my men tie you up, wrap your miserable ass into a fresh cowhide and place you out into the direct Texas sun. That way when that cowhide begins to dry out, shrink in size and crush you to death, you can think long and hard about messing with us Texas cattlemen!"

"That threat of deadly bodily harm made in front of my men and witnessed thereof, will also account for additional charges that are going to be lodged against you, Mr. Potter, namely for threatening a federal officer with deadly bodily harm," quietly advised Joe. Potter just stared back at Joe, finally realizing to say anything further would just get him into even deeper trouble with the law, so to his way of thinking he would just bide his time and wait for his drovers to intervene on his behalf and take care of the pesky marshals…

With that, the locals gathered up the rest of the Texas herd's drovers and had them begin rounding up and driving their cattle back across the Red River, minus twenty head the aggrieved rancher figured he would need to cover the cost of damage to his farmstead and land. As they did, Joe quietly sat on his horse watching the sullen cowboys herding their steers back across the Red River under the urging eyes and threats of the Hendrix townsfolk. While sitting there on his horse supervising the cattle's return to Texas, Joe noticed a small group of three cowboys clumped together across the Red River sitting on their horses, looking back at him as their shackled boss was being loaded into the marshal's chuck wagon. Keeping a wary eye on their suspicious behavior, Joe lodged that bothersome fact into the back of his mind in case any trouble arose as a result of the three cowboys' suspicious-looking little 'confab' taking place on the Texas side of the Red River.

As for what had happened to the rancher and his family, Joe later assured them that since the marshals had witnessed the felony criminal acts being perpetrated by Potter and his renegade Indians upon the rancher's kin, there would be no need for him or his family to travel clear to Fort Smith to testify in the Texan's subsequent trials. That was unless they wanted to do so, because the marshals were prepared to lodge the appropriate charges themselves against the defendants and testify accordingly since they had witnessed the occurrence of the earlier heinous felony criminal acts. For that, the rancher graciously accepted Joe's suggestion of not requiring that he and his family travel all the way up to Fort Smith just to testify and in so doing, once again have to mentally and physically revisit what had just happened with the Texas cattleman.

Once things around the ranch had settled
down somewhat, Chino and the rest of the
posse drove their prisoners back to their dug-
out campsite. Joe on the other hand had further
important court business to attend to and rode
off in a different direction from the posse. Riding
back into Hendrix, Joe rode straightaway over to
The Lamb's Inn whorehouse and dismounted.
Moments later Joe confronted Mrs. Wilkins and
Mrs. Jackson, advising both women that the marshals would be by to pick them up early the next
morning and take them forthwith to Fort Smith
to testify against the Texas drovers for what they
had done to their husbands the year before. Joe
further advised that they would also be removed
from their current lifestyle in the whorehouse. A
lifestyle that had been forced upon them because
of the disastrous economic circumstances following the deaths of their husbands who had been
their sole providers.

Both women broke down and cried like they
had never cried before over hearing those words
of relief and the possibility of starting over in a new
and Christian style of life. About then, in walked
the whorehouse owner, one Dean 'Lambkins'
Mastel, demanding to know what was going on
with 'HIS' two women. Joe politely informed
'Lambkins' that the women were in the process
of being freed from their bondage as 'ladies of

the night' come the next day, and were now in the custody and care of the U.S. Government as federal witnesses for several felony murder and rape trials soon to be held in Fort Smith's United States District Court against the Texas drovers.

That was when 'Lambkins' asked Joe if the girls could work that night and at least until the next day, at which time they would be picked up by the posse and removed from his control. Joe sternly looked at 'Lambkins' saying, "If I discover either of these two women was touched in any way contrary to their desires, I will personally shoot you in a place where your name will be changed from 'Lambkins' to 'Mr. High Voice'! Do we have an understanding, Mr. Mastel?"

"Yes Sir," replied the heretofore physical and economic controller of the two women who had lost everything and were now going to get another start and normal lease on life. If those two women only knew what was in store for each of them in the immediate future, they would be in a state of shock...

With that 'bit of business' out of the way, Joe informed the women they would be on the road in the morrow at daylight, so be packed and ready to leave the area since they now had no reason to stay because of the earlier loss of their husbands and ranches to Potter's crew. Both women were very excited and informed Joe they would be more than ready to leave the next day. Joe also advised that they were now under the official care of the U.S. Government, since they were to become witnesses in a federal felony trial and to let him know if anyone messed with or mistreated either of them in any way. Both women nodded that they understood, then each gave Joe a hug of joy over their possibilities of starting over in a new life, and then he departed for the dug-out so he could help the rest of his posse make ready for the next day's trip heading back to Fort Smith.

Dismounting his horse back at the dug-out somewhat later, Joe was quickly made aware of the men's actions making ready to leave as they loaded the chuck wagon with their loose gear. Chino on the other hand, was putting together the evening meal of beans, roasted smoked elk meat, Dutch oven biscuits and coffee, as the men worked around him. Moments later, Joe pitched right in as well and soon the men had everything loaded into the chuck wagon and ready for the upcoming trip the next morning except for their evening's sleeping gear. Then supper was served to the posse's four prisoners and after they had finished, they were returned to their hay-filled rear section of the chuck wagon, manacled and then chained to the wagon's floorboards to preclude any thoughts or chances of escape.

Following that, the rest of the men had their supper and visited over their day's events and the upcoming and welcome trip back to Fort Smith. After supper, Joe and Lewis checked the state of their prisoners and then they like the rest of the posse, settled into their blankets and drifted off to sleep after experiencing another hard and dangerous day in the life as a Deputy U.S. Marshal in the Indian Territory.

Early the next morning way before daylight, Joe, who had been sleeping next to Chino, who was snoring away and sounding like a locomotive pulling a heavy load, awoke to the soft rumble-growling of Dog who was also lying nearby! Not moving hardly at all as his dad had taught him when he was a young man growing up on the Pennsylvania frontier when he awoke to any possible signs of close at hand and immediate danger, Joe carefully listened for what troubling mystery sound had awakened him even over Chino's 'locomotive' snoring sounds.

Then he heard that mystery sound once again that had originally awakened him! Joe was certain he could hear the soft rattling of a chain being abnormally exercised over by their chuck wagon! Slowly rising up on his elbows as if that would help him hear better, he once again could hear a chain making an unusual rattling sound coming from their chuck wagon holding all of their prisoners! There was no two ways about it, the chain-clanking sounds Joe was hearing were coming from their chuck wagon where they had their four prisoners chained to the floorboards! That was when a surprise hand was placed over his mouth from behind by his brother James, who had quietly sneaked up from behind his brother in the pre-dawn darkness!

Leaning over in the darkness of the dug-out to avoid the still burning campfire's fading illuminations, James whispered, "Joe, grab your gun! I think someone is trying to file through the chains of our prisoners!" Then in the feeble light of the campfire-illuminated dug-out entrance, Joe could see Dog slowly stand up and see that its hackles were standing high up clear across the full length of its back over the mystery events and sounds taking place around the nearby chuck wagon!

Quietly rolling out from under his sleeping blankets and not pulling on his boots so he could sneak more quietly, Joe and James 'Army-crawled' more closely towards the entrance of their dug-out. Lying down by its entrance, their bodies partially concealed by a side wall, both men peered out towards the darkened end of the chuck wagon where their four prisoners were chained. When they did, both men could see numerous suspicious shadows of movement in the darkness around the rear of the chuck wagon!

Seeing that and hearing Dog's very quiet warning 'rumble-growl' from deep within, Joe and James made their ways quietly back toward the rear of their dug-out and then crawled out the windowless opening in the back wall and dropped silently onto the ground on the other side. Then Joe and James, carefully sneaking barefoot and trying hard to avoid running the end of their feet into a clump of prickly pear cactus commonly found in the area, slowly peeked around the mud walls of the dug-out looking toward their chuck wagon and its mystery sounds. Sure as 'frog's hair is fine', both men could just make out the forms of several unknown humans moving around the outside of the back of the chuck wagon holding their prisoners, and also see the heads of several of the shackled men moving quietly and suspiciously around in the bed of hay in the back of the chuck wagon as well!

Joe took James's head in his hands and pulling it towards his mouth, whispered into his ear several instructions. When James's head nodded in understanding in Joe's hands, Joe quietly left his brother's side, crept back around the rear of the dug-out and disappeared into the darkness on the opposite side as he headed for the back side of the chuck wagon.

About twenty minutes later just as the mystery men managed to quietly saw through one of the prisoner's set of chains, James heard the booming voice of his brother say, "HOLD IT RIGHT THERE! MAKE A MOVE AND YOU WILL DIE IN YOUR OWN PEW!" Upon hearing those words of warning coming from out of the darkness, James heard someone in that group of mystery figures standing at the back of the chuck wagon yell, "RUN!"

Instantly upon hearing that command, an unknown cowboy came running around the end of the chuck wagon in the pre-dawn light and right into the rapidly swung end of James's .45 Colt's gun barrel and was instantly 'buffaloed' ('Buffaloed' is an Old West term meaning getting smashed in the head with a pistol barrel. A means of non-lethal control commonly used by Marshal Wyatt Earp when he was the law in Dodge City, as opposed to shooting someone)! That cowboy violently hit the ground in a cloud of dust even evident in the failing light of their nearby dying campfire and the pre-dawn light...

That movement was then quickly followed by James and Joe stepping into the picture right alongside the chuck wagon with drawn six shooters aimed at two more very surprised cowboys with a hack saw trying to quietly cut through the chains of their cattle boss prisoner still shackled to the floor in the back of the chuck wagon! "FIRST MAN WHO MAKES A MOVE

FOR HIS GUN WILL DIE RIGHT WHERE HE STANDS!" yelled Joe, with a very serious warning in the tone of his voice that was meant to be understood by all concerned with and around the activity in the back of the chuck wagon.

By now with all the yelling heard around the prisoners' wagon, the entire camp was now wide awake and moving into action. Out from the dug-out flooded Lewis, Indian Tom Johns and Rufous with Winchesters in hand, followed by Chino and Dog! Within moments, the situation was well in hand with two Texas cowboys in the process of being manacled and a third being revived with a pail of cold water tossed on his head as he lay on the ground at the back of the wagon after being violently whanged across the head by James's pistol barrel when he had tried to escape.

Moments later found the back of the chuck wagon now jammed with seven instead of just four prisoners. The three Texas cowboys were added prisoners who were now being held after being arrested by Joe for attempting to illegally release four federal prisoners who were wanted for a number of felony charges including murder back in federal court in Fort Smith.

Now that the entire camp was more than awake, Chino stoked up his outside campfire and began cooking up a hearty breakfast for his marshals and their now seven prisoners. An hour later, fried elk steak, stewed pinto beans loaded with onions and cloves of garlic, Dutch oven biscuits and coffee graced the men's breakfast table fare. The men ate heartily that morning because all of them knew they had a long ride ahead of them through the lawless Indian Territory, and who knew what additional Texas cowboys looking for their cattle boss lay ahead of the marshals in ambush along the trail. Then under heavy guard by the marshals, the prisoners were unchained from the floor of the wagon but remained in their manacles, while they were allowed to go to the bathroom and then eat their breakfasts. Following that, the seven sullen prisoners were once again safely ensconced in the back of the chuck wagon and remained under close guard as the rest of the men saddled up their riding horses, hitched up the reserve mules to the rear of the chuck wagon, and then the three-span of mules were hitched up to the front of the wagon and also made ready for travel.

Then with Joe and Rufous in the lead and Lewis and James riding alongside the wagon, Chino and Indian Tom Johns riding in the front seat of the chuck wagon, the odd-looking caravan made for the whorehouse on the eastern side of the small town of Hendrix. There they picked up the two ladies with their luggage and as Indian Tom Johns mounted his horse, the two ladies were seated alongside Chino on the front seat of the now very crowded chuck wagon. As the two very happy ladies rode up on the front seat with Chino, Dog cavorted around the moving wagon noticing all the new smells, and the marshals once again rode ahead and alongside as they left Hendrix and headed for the small town of Daisy.

Four days later found the marshal's posse and prisoner caravan entering the small town of Daisy. Then Joe headed the group up to the North Arm area and home of Deputy Rufous Barnes. There Rufous was once again happily reunited with his wife and small children. As for the other marshals, they set up their camp inside of Rufous's hay barn where he used to hide his bootleg whiskey in his earlier lawless days. Following that, the mules and horses were let out to pasture after Joe had made a trip into the town of Daisy and telegraphed Chief Marshal Fagan with the results of their trip and asking for any further instructions.

Marshal Fagan quickly replied with further orders and then Joe returned to the Barnes ranch. For the next two days the men rested and let their animals put on the 'feed-bag' in preparation for the long trip ahead back to Fort Smith. In the meantime, the two rescued ladies from the house of ill repute spent much of their time visiting with Martha Barnes and happily helping her with her small children, as well as cooking for the now large crew of posse prisoners and family. Early on the third morning after their arrival, found the marshals ready to head northeast to Fort Smith after eating a huge 'lumberjack' breakfast made by Martha Barnes and the Wilkins and Jackson ladies for all of the men and children.

However, as the marshals and their wagon full of prisoners and two ladies swung through the gate on the Barnes ranch and headed out toward Fort Smith, they found themselves riding without one of their own. Earlier when Marshal Fagan had telegraphed Joe back regarding his new orders, in them he had advised that Rufous was to remain behind! In those instructions, Rufous was to remain behind in that area and act in his official capacity as a Deputy U.S. Marshal. In that capacity he had been ordered by Marshal Fagan to pursue other known 'moonshiners' in that portion of the Indian Territory, arrest those caught in the act and in so doing, hopefully put them out of business after they had been subsequently transported back to Fort Smith and convicted. As Marshal Fagan correctly figured, 'it takes an outlaw to catch one', hence Rufous being assigned that southern area of the Indian Territory 'to put those 'moonshiners' in the business of making bootleg whiskey, out of the business' when it came to making illegal whiskey and selling the same to the local Indians and anyone who had a buck to purchase what he and Judge Parker called, 'the devil's brew'…

(Author's Historical Note: Rufous went on to a storied career as a Deputy U.S. Marshal, cleaning out a huge number of illegal stills and 'moonshiners' in the southeastern area of the Indian Territory and convicting the operators of the same. Sadly, Rufous Barnes died in the early 1930's of a massive heart attack after a much distinguished career! One of his sons, Otis, later went on to become the stepfather of this book's author. To this day, the author covets the last remaining Redwing five-gallon whiskey jug next to a picture of his grandfather standing beside a 1926 Reo touring car. Hanging all over the car on the fenders are four large mule deer bucks killed the same day by Rufous while out on a Barnes family hunting trip. However, he had to let the fifth mule deer buck of the bunch escape. That he did according to family folklore, because the smoke from a cigarette he was smoking was getting into his eyes. So much so, that he could not see to shoot the fifth buck in the bunch of five bucks running away that morning. Apparently it had been a very dry year in the forests and Rufous, fearing he would start a forest fire if he dropped his cigarette in order to see better to shoot, let the fifth buck get away. Once again, a testimony to the man's excellence with an open sighted rifle and his abilities as a reported crack rifle shot...).

The next seven days of travel to Fort Smith by the marshals and their prisoners were rather uneventful. That was if the friendships quickly developing between James and Mrs. Jane Wilkins, and Lewis and Mrs. Carol Jackson had anything to say about the issue! Joe began noticing during their trip back to Fort Smith, that every chance his two brothers had, they were riding alongside the chuck wagon talking to the ladies or come evening after supper, there were numerous long walks taken by the two brothers and the apparent lady of their choice...

Finally Joe had to put an end to the obvious fraternizations because all of the guard duties and care of the seven prisoners were constantly falling on his, Indian Tom Johns and Chino's shoulders. However even after admonishing his brothers, they still found or made time to spend with the two ladies of their choice. Finally with the arrival of the marshals in Fort Smith and the incarcerating of their prisoners within the federal jail facility, the two brothers found they had even more time to spend with the ladies of their choice, as they prepared for their next assignment and upcoming testimony in the U.S. District Court.

So much so, that Joe began realizing that his

two brothers were taking more than just a casual interest in the two now husbandless women, and the two women's building interest in his two brothers... But Joe somehow did manage to keep his two brothers at the tasks at hand as they prepared for their next assignment, which was rumored among the other arriving deputies from the field to be a really dangerous one!

Finally Mrs. Wilkins and Mrs. Jackson found themselves testifying in Judge Parker's court over what the Texas cattle boss and his renegade Indian cohorts had done to their lives a year earlier. The judge being a very religious man, after hearing the women's testimony of the gang rapes that had occurred upon their persons, was more than visibly touched. Finding Potter guilty for his crimes against the two women and responsible for the death of their two husbands, got him hanged four days later! As for his three Chickasaw Indian cohorts, they were turned over to the federal prison authorities after being given long jail sentences in which to serve for their parts in the gang rapes of the two white women. Lastly, the three Potter-loyal cowboys were tried for their acts in trying to release federal prisoners and were given three-year prison sentences to serve for their lapses in judgement.

CHAPTER EIGHT

"STEAMBOAT" CHARLIE,
A DEAD MAN WALKING!

TWO DAYS AFTER the Texas Trail Boss's trial, found the Dodson brothers in front of Chief Marshal Fagan receiving instructions on their next law enforcement assignment. That assignment involved running down and arresting a man named Charlie "Steamboat" Haskell and his gang of horse thieves, who were operating along the traditional cattle trails coming out from Texas that headed for the Kansas stockyards. According to Marshal Fagan, Steamboat's gang operated along the southern fringes of the Indian Territory just above the Texas border, waiting until the herds were out of Texas, then stealing the drovers' reserve horses used in pushing their herds of cattle across the Indian Territory. That way, Steamboat's gang avoided the dreaded Texas Rangers, being that the horse stealing crimes were committed outside of Texas and because of the lack of law in the Indian Territory. Henceforth, Steamboat's gang almost operated with impunity when it came to their horse stealing and subsequent illegal sale escapades.

According to Fagan, their method of operation when it came to stealing horses was fairly simple and yet bold. Steamboat's gang would lie in wait until a Texas cattle herd was passing close to their base of operations in the Indian Territory. Then come nightfall, several of his gang members would slip up onto the Texas drovers' reserve horse herds. There they would lurk until the rest of their compatriots were raising hell shooting up the place next to the chuck wagon in a fake attack designed to cause a distraction among the Texas drovers. While that was occurring, Steamboat's other men posted near the reserve horse herd, would then steal away with most of the valuable riding stock belonging to the Texans at the height of the distraction. Then according to Fagan, those horses would be brought back deep into the Indian Territory and sold to any Indians or white men who had the money to purchase such good and well-broken riding stock, without questioning the origins of the various brands.

Having said more than he wanted to at the

time during his briefing session, Marshal Fagan turned around in his chair, spit a stream of tobacco juice out his second story window and that was soon followed by what used to be a much slobbered over plug of chewing tobacco. Then ignoring the looks of amusement his men were giving him over his habit, Marshal Fagan removed another half-used plug of Brown's Mule chewing tobacco, chewed off a chunk, sloshed it around in his mouth until he found a comfortable place to lodge it between his cheek and gum, and then began once again with his briefing. "Alright you three, here are a stack of the latest known wanted posters with the men's pictures thereon to aid you in corralling the right men in this major horse thief ring of miscreants. I want every man-jack son-of-a-bitch from this gang alive so they can stand trial in Judge Parker's court and be hanged accordingly for their damn aggressive horse-stealing antics."

Then Marshal Fagan stopped almost in mid-sentence, spat out a couple loose leaves from his chewing tobacco plug that he had found annoyingly floating around in his mouth and then continued with the words, "Now, here is the information on the gang's ringleader and founder. The ring leader is one so named Charlie James Haskell with a well-earned nickname of Steamboat. Charlie was a steamboat captain during the Civil War running supplies on the Mississippi River hither and yon for the southern cause. He, from what I hear, was one hell of a damn good steamboat captain. His legendary reputation was one of daring and hellfire and brimstone when it came to getting his boat through any kind of Union blockades and delivering much-needed supplies to the Confederate troops and then bringing their wounded back behind the southern lines so they could be cared for by their own doctors. He remained a boat captain right up until the end of the war when he ran out of southern-controlled river waters and the 'Johnny Rebs' ran out of men and bullets. As I understand it, Charlie and his entire crew never surrendered and with a price on their heads by the Union Government for killing any and all helpless wounded Union soldiers they ran across, fled west into the lawless Indian Territory. There they laid low for a while and finally running out of money, began their dirty work of horse stealing, killing of anyone who got in their way and just in general, hell-raising when they came into any kind of a town big enough for them to celebrate their latest successful sales of their stolen horses from the Texas cattle drovers."

Then it was time for another stream of black-looking tobacco juice to be spit out his open second story window. Then getting up heavily from his much-used swivel chair, Marshal Fagan handed Joe a stack of wanted posters of Charlie and his fellow gang members with their pictures splashed across the documents. Listed in the fine print of those wanted posters were the individual rewards being offered by Texas cattle companies, local stage lines who had lost a number of their horses taken from their remote stagecoach stops, and several smaller short-line railroads in the Indian Territory, which had lost from their passengers and mail cars items of value during several train robberies by Steamboat's gang as well!

As the marshal shuffled about with his usual words of warning and preparation details for Chino and their Indian Policeman who by tribal regulation was a required participant in this posse, Joe took a quick look through the stack of wanted posters on his lap. They numbered ten in number and from the looks of the poster pictures, the men whose pictures were represented thereon appeared to be a pretty rough-looking lot. Then he noticed features of the man nicknamed Steamboat Charlie appeared to be more different than all the rest of his gang members. Steamboat was a tall, cadaverous-looking man, skinny as a rail, with a look of death warmed over in Joe's opinion, if the gaunt, sunken-in look on his face meant anything to the more than casual observer. That was when Marshal Fagan kicked in once again with his litany of instructions, and what he said that time more than stuck in Joe's memory.

"This here Steamboat fellow is never to be trusted and is reported to be a stone cold killer. He has a very nasty disposition and I think it in large part is because of his poor physical condition. He is a 'Lunger'! To any of you boys who have never heard that word being used, you are not alone. That word means he is slowly and painfully dying from an advanced case of tuberculosis. In short, it is not uncommon to see this man spitting up a lot of blood and coughing uncontrollably because of having such disease-damaged lungs. That ailment I am told is what makes him mean as a snake, very short-tempered and explosive in nature. If and when the time comes, make sure he is not only manacled but leg-chained as well while being transported. Additionally, for Christ's sake, don't let that bastard ever spit his diseased spew of crap from his lungs upon you! I sure as hell don't have any use for any deputies who are carrying such a disease and puking and coughing all the time! In fact, the last person of any reputation I have heard of who had such a disease was Doctor "Doc" John Holliday. Most of you have heard of him and he was one nasty and mean-tempered son-of-a-bitch because of his disease and his drinking habits, as was his woman, a woman named "Big-nosed Kate"," uttered Marshal Fagan in obvious disgust over the topic being discussed.

Then it was time for a spit of tobacco juice out his window once again and then he said, "Near as I can figure, you boys need to count on about a two-to-three-month trip into the area Steamboat and his gang are operating in, in the southeastern portion of the Indian Territory, near the small town of Harris. Also, since there are ten of those bastards that need to be rounded up and arrested, I am sending a jail wagon and two more deputies along with the three of you, just in case. How you are going to round up such a savage and numerous group of outlaws I don't know, without the lot of you being killed in the process. But being as short-handed as I am, that is all the qualified and experienced help I can spare and send with you lads," grumbled Marshal Fagan, obviously not pleased that he had to send such a limited number of under gunned officers into such a dangerous situation..

Turning and taking a quick spit out his open window, Marshal Fagan continued saying, "Now, there are also a slew of outside rewards offered for this bunch of outlaws besides the $1,000 federal award for Steamboat Charlie. With that in mind, all of you can collect those rewards offered for these men just as long as you bring them in alive. Additionally, you can not only collect your six cents per mile traveled and your $2.00 per prisoner capture fee paid by the federal government, but the outside reward money offered by the Texas cattle companies, stage lines and the railroad as well. So I suggest you get Chino in on what awaits all of you and make sure you take along enough ammunition just in case the lot-of-you get into a deadly faceoff with this bunch. Now I suggest you get going because in another month the cattle from Texas will be coming north along their traditionally traveled cattle trails as they head for the stockyards in Kansas. Bear in mind there were over 300,000 head of cattle delivered into the Kansas stockyards last year and many expect at least that many cattle coming in once again this year as well. With that in mind, that should give you lots of chances at intercepting this gang of horse thieves in action as they ply their illegal trade and nip them in the bud."

Then it was time to spit once again and then the Marshal said, "Oh, before I forget it, have Chino take a keg or two of cheap brandy along with you fellows. On five of those chaps running in this gang with Steamboat according to their reward posters, they are wanted dead or alive! If it just so happens that you have to kill those chaps carrying a 'dead or alive' handle on their posters, cut off their heads, brine them in the cheap brandy Chino will be carrying and bring those heads in when you come back to Fort Smith. That cheap brandy ought to preserve their facial features so they can still be identified and the reward money collected in the end. Sounds like a crude way to do something but that is better than bringing in a stinking and rotting carcass all the way back here. Then if you do it that-a-way, you have to find someplace to bury the carcass once the identification is done. So go the 'brandy' route and it will make you fellows a lot more acceptable in any town that you have to ride through. That way you can still collect the rewards on those chaps, unlike that which is under our federal system which requires the wanted men to be brought in alive! Keep in mind, I suggest bringing 'those dead or alive folks' in that way because bringing back a body from such a distance away will not make any of you welcome in any town you are passing through because of the smell a whole, long dead body emits." With those instructions out of the way, the men left Marshal Fagan's office with heads swimming over the preparations that needed to be made and the forces of evil that they would be facing, extra two deputies or not.

However, when the three brothers left Marshal Fagan's office, Joe found himself alone as he headed over to meet with Chino and the two new jail wagon deputies regarding the outlaw targets and the logistical preparations needing to be made. James and Lewis on the other hand, headed for the telegraph office in order to send a telegram to David, their younger brother back on their ranch in Arkansas, requesting that he come to Fort Smith to be with the other three brothers for several days. Well, that and some other business that involved David needing to be an integral part of another request in order for it to be successfully carried off...

Two days later, David showed up in Fort Smith in a buckboard with a hired hand riding a horse. For the next two days, the four brothers and Sam the hired hand had a celebratory 'blowout' over being united once again. Then when it came time for David to leave and go back to the family ranch and farm, Joe got a surprise he was in no way expecting!

When that day finally arrived for David and his hired hand to leave, Joe discovered that his younger brother had company. Seated on the front seat of the buckboard next to David were Mrs. Wilkins and Mrs. Jackson! That was when Joe finally realized throughout all those long shared walks and fraternizations on the way back to Fort Smith, that his brothers Lewis and James had fallen in love with the two young widowed women and they had in the offing, been asked to accompany David back to their family farm in Arkansas. There the two young widowed women would wait and live under David's care until Lewis and James could return and continue courting the two women with eventual marriage in mind! Joe, even though stunned down to his boots over this change in events, just had to smile and then laugh over how much 'wool' had been pulled over his eyes in such a short time. He then had to smile again when David left with the two women and his hired hand acting as a guard, especially when the moment arrived when the two brothers had to leave the two women. The moment was very touching and Joe, even though still surprised over the rapidly changing events in their lives, had to smile and hope his father and mother were 'looking down' and watching the wonderful events unfolding before his eyes with his two brothers and hopefully, their wives to come...

The following morning, the posse consisting of five deputies, a chuck wagon, a jail wagon, an Indian Policeman, and their extra stock animals headed for the extreme southeastern corner of the Indian Territory near the Texas and Arkansas borders. Joe had decided that their area for concentration of effort would be in the Harris area immediately adjacent to one of the most heavily traveled cattle trails in that day and age leading from Texas to the Kansas stockyards. Joe's plan was simple when it came to running across and hopefully capturing Steamboat Charlie and his elusive bunch of horse thieves. Joe figured that he and his posse would concentrate their capture efforts in the most heavily utilized cattle trail-use areas through the Indian Territory. This they did in the hopes that since that would be the general location where most drover-horse herds would also be located when the huge herds of cattle traveled north, that should also be the best general capture location for those who possessed evil thoughts of stealing the same.

Days later, Joe had the telltale sign of the law being close at hand, namely their jail wagon, dropped off in the town of Idabel at the local tribal headquarters for safekeeping until it would be needed. Then mounting their two riding horses that had been trailed behind the jail wagon, new deputies Jeff Walker and Fran Marcoux joined the rest of the posse as they headed for the Harris area near the historic Red River. There the group of men who were now posing as out of work cowboys looking for employment as drovers in a cattle herd moving north to Kansas, set up their campsite in a dense grove of cottonwood trees. There the men pitched several tents in which to sleep, built an outside firepit ringed with river rock, cut a stack of firewood to hold them through the many days they figured they would be in country, and settled in. The next day after Joe had left for the small town of Harris on an intelligence gathering trip, the rest of the men built a hell for stout corral for all of their riding horses and the chuck wagon's mules.

Meanwhile in the small, close at hand town of Harris, Joe spent time in the local store buying up some supplies of fresh meat, eggs, coffee and sugar, whereupon he also purposely visited with some of the local folks doing their shopping as well. In those visits, Joe let it be known that he and four more of his out of work cowboy friends were camped just west of town along the Red River waiting for a cattle herd in which to sign on as drovers. That way, Joe figured that story would forestall any rumors that might lead to tales of the law being close at hand among strangers camped along the Red River, which would eventually alert the very outlaws they had been sent to apprehend.

The next morning, Joe and Lewis took up their Sharps rifles and a pack mule, and began scouting along the western reaches of the Red River acting like meat hunters. In actuality, they were looking for any kind of a suspicious-looking campsite holding ten men near the much-used cattle trails who might be the Steamboat Charlie gang of horse thieves for which they now held Writs of

Arrest from Judge Parker. For the next three days the two men slowly worked their ways through numerous densely vegetated twists and turns of the Red River. This they did as they worked out the many hidden areas along the river that could hold such a number of outlaws, allowing them to remain out of sight and out of mind. Finding nothing of interest that might indicate such a gang of outlaws existed in the area now being searched, Joe changed his tactics.

The following morning, Joe took his brother James and a pack mule, and began acting like meat hunters once again as they began searching out the many twists and turns along the Red River as they began their search heading easterly towards the State of Arkansas. However, on their second day out near the small establishment of Tom in the extreme southeastern portion of the Indian Territory while pretending to be deer hunting, the two brothers ran across a large and well-used semi-permanent campsite.

No one was in sight in the newfound area of interest, so Joe and James rode into the campsite like a couple of lost rubes looking for some directional guidance. Finding no one at home in the campsite, Joe began surreptitiously looking around while his brother stood guard against inadvertent discovery by the camp's occupants. However, just in case the owners of the camp returned unexpectedly, Joe had James cut off a number of steaks from a deer they had recently killed, build a fire and began cooking the meat, while his brother took a better and more detailed look around the suspect campsite.

For the next twenty minutes or so, Joe nosed around the well-used campsite. Right away, Joe noticed the site's horse corral held 13 horses, all with different brands. That told Joe that those horses had come from many different owners and could have possibly been stolen stock. Then he began nosing around the sleeping quarters of the campsite. There Joe discovered the bedding sites of ten different individuals in two well-built, log and mounded dirt, lean-to sleeping quarters!

Then Joe heard the sounds of numerous horses near at hand and coming their way! Running from a lean-to and hearing his brother yelling for him to get his rear end back to the fire pit, Joe arrived just as ten surprised looking horsemen rode into their campsite seeing it occupied with two strangers! When they rode up, a number of the men reached for and withdrew their rifles from their scabbards and quickly surrounded the two strange men, ostensibly cooking several deer steaks over an open fire in their campsite's fire pit!

"Who the damn hell are you two?" yelled a scarecrow-like, cadaverous-looking man as he glared down from atop his horse at Joe and James cooking meat by his camp's fire pit.

"Good afternoon," said Joe, as warmly as he could sound under the now life-threatening circumstances the two brothers were facing. "My name is Joe and this here is my brother James. We were meat hunting in the area because we didn't have any food back in our camp and killed this here deer. Being especially hungry since we have not eaten for two days and seeing your campsite, we rode in to see who was here and see if we could use your campfire to cook up our meal since we are so hungry. Not finding anyone around to ask permission, we hopefully assumed that no one would care if we just used their fire pit and cooked our deer steaks," continued Joe as nicely as he could under the circumstances. Circumstances that now boded ill for both him and James because all ten of the riders appeared to be very upset over the two strangers being in their campsite, as was evidenced by a number of them who had withdrawn their rifles from their scabbards and were now pointing them at the two men! Second of all within the 'danger' department, Joe and James had recognized almost every one of the men as being those who were on their wanted posters safely stashed for the moment in their saddlebags. Wanted posters on each and every man in front of them that if discovered in those saddlebags, meant a violent and quick death for both of the brothers!

"The hell you say!" said the death-warmed-over, scarecrow-looking-like man leaning over the neck of his horse staring 'daggers' down at Joe.

"Yes Sir," continued Joe, in a gently and respectful tone of voice meant to diffuse the situation so 'he could get his legs under him' and try and figure a way out from the mess he and his brother found themselves. "We meant you good folks no harm. We just wanted to use your fire pit and fix something to eat because we are so hungry."

"Well, we do object to having our campsite invaded by two strangers and making themselves quite at home like they belonged here," continued 'Scarecrow' with an accusatory tone in his voice! "What should we do with these bastards? Kill them here as they stand all dumb and stupid-looking cooking some venison over our fire pit, or should we just take their deer and kick their dumb asses out from our camp?" Scarecrow loudly snapped like the foul-tempered chap he was appearing more and more to be.

"I say we kill them, toss their carcasses into the river for the fish and fowl to enjoy, take their horses and see what else they are carrying on their persons," said another rider still holding the barrel of his Winchester leveled at Joe's chest, with the hammer pulled back and his finger on the trigger!

A cold feeling went through Joe's body upon hearing those words. He knew that if the men searched their saddlebags, they would find all those wanted posters he was carrying. He knew if they did, both he and his brother were dead men! With that, Joe took a gamble, handed his cooking stick holding the deer steak on the end of it to his brother, reached into his buttoned shirt pocket and withdrew a twenty dollar gold piece.

Gambling that a bit of courage would go a long way even with these outlaws, Joe said looking right at the cadaverous-looking mounted rider who appeared to be the leader of the group, "Tell you what. This is my last twenty dollar gold piece and after that, I am a dead broke cowboy. That is why my brother and I had to kill a deer for food. I say I flip this coin and you call it in the air. If it lands on what side you have called, it is yours. If it lands on the other side, what say that we call our intrusion even and you just let me and my brother go with our apologies for being so rude in figuring use of your fire pit would be all right with you fellows?"

Leaning back in his saddle and surprised over the gall being shown by an out of work and apparently hungry cowboy, the Scarecrow laughed deeply, then began coughing uncontrollably over the strain of his deep laughter for a few moments, while the rest of his men remained respectfully silent. Finally getting control over his coughing fit, Scarecrow, also now known to Joe and James as the deadly Steamboat Charlie, wiped off the spots of blood and white foam on his lips and then said, "OK, Cowboy. Toss the coin and I am calling heads and you had better hope it lands the way you hope or you and your brother are going to be magpie and crow bait!"

With those words, Joe flipped the coin high into the air as all the eyes in Steamboat Charlie's band of merry outlaws watched the flashing coin sail high into the air. When it landed, it was tails, as everyone simultaneously leaned over in their saddles and looked down. With that, Joe boldly reached over to the coin, picked it up and then showed Steamboat Charlie that he had lost the bet.

"Well, I'll be a son-of-a-bitch. I lost that damn bet!" uttered Charlie in surprise Then Steamboat Charlie looking down at Joe from his perch upon his saddle as Joe blithely pocketed his coin, said, "You got more damn gall than all get-out, Stranger. What say I just take your deer for my men's supper and we call it even?"

"I would say you have a deal," said Joe, as he stepped over to their mule packing the deer, like he wasn't still, figuratively speaking, looking down the barrel of a leveled Winchester, untied its carcass and then turning with the deer hanging from his arms said, "Where do you want me to put it, Stranger?"

Charlie just shook his head over the gall Joe was showing and pointed over to a hanging tree graced with a much-used meat pole. "Put it over there and that would be fine," he said, still not believing what he was seeing in the way of 'sand' in the cowboy he and his men had cornered. "Mister, you got more damn gall than an African honey badger. Your father sure did a good job in raising you and putting into your spine a liberal dose of damn good grade gunmetal," he said wickedly impressed.

With that, Joe toted the deer over to the meat pole, made a slit between its tendon and leg bone and then began tying it onto the existing ropes used on previously hung animals being readied for butchering. Then without a single word of worry or show of concern, Joe hoisted the deer up so it would be ready for skinning and butchering. Then walking back to his horse, Joe mounted up and prepared to leave. "Come on, James, we need to leave these good folks to fixing up their supper and you and I need to go out again and find ours."

Not hardly believing the 'sand' his brother

was showing, James laid down his roasting stick with the deer steak on the end, walked over to his horse like it was a Sunday stroll, mounted up and rode over to where his brother was sitting on his horse.

"I thank you folks for your hospitality and may you enjoy the venison. Come on, James, we have some more hunting to do before we can make camp," said Joe, like he was back on their ranch in Arkansas going out for an afternoon stroll. With that, the two brothers rode out from the camp full of wanted men, turned and headed for home just like a pair of more than bold African Honey Badgers! As they did, both brothers could just feel the looks of ten disbelieving men over the gall shown by two hungry cowboys in the face of superior and angry odds...

For the longest time the two brothers rode on in silence realizing they had just cheated 'The Grim Reaper'! Then James who could hold his thoughts and tongue no longer over what had just occurred, said, "Joe, what the hell were you going to do if that 'Lunger' son-of-a-bitch or his men had decided to kill us right there on the spot for being in their campsite?"

For another long moment, Joe just rode along in silence upon hearing his brother's question. Then he said, "I was prepared to draw my pistol, kill that Scarecrow son-of-a-bitch and as many others of his men as I could before they killed me."

"That was your plan? You were just going to kill as many of them as you could before they shot the hell out of us?" gasped James.

"No, I expected that you would also be doing the same," said Joe quietly as he rode along. Then Joe stopped his horse, turned and facing his still incredulous-looking brother said, "James, you never bare your throat to a wolf!" The two brothers then rode back to their distant camp in silence after that short exchange. But as they did, James could only marvel over the courage his older brother had shown that afternoon in the clear face and defiance of death…

Riding back into their campsite just like nothing out of the ordinary had just occurred back at the outlaws' campsite; Joe lit down from his horse and requested that all the other lawmen gather around him. Once everyone was present, Joe detailed out the danger that James and he had just experienced. Then Joe detailed out what he had seen in the behavior, actions and looks of the men who were riding with Steamboat Charlie. In that following detailing of his observations, Joe made sure everyone realized that the men they were looking to serve Writs of Arrest upon were heavily armed and desperate-appearing men. As Joe described to the group of deputies what he had observed in greater detail, a deathly silence of determination settled over those gathered around regarding the now more than probable deadly challenges lying ahead of them.

Halting in his briefing of the men over the day's events experienced by the two brothers, Joe casually poured himself a cup of coffee from the coffee pot hanging over their fire pit, took a sip of the steaming hot brew and then commenced with the morrow's plans in a very matter of fact tone of voice. Therein Joe outlined that he and James would sneak back into the suspect campsite from its back side early the next morning. There they would hide themselves in the brush above the outlaws' camp and watch the men and all of their activities in order to better learn their daily pattern of activity. In the meantime, Joe ordered that all of the men be sure and clean all of their weapons and make sure they had an adequate supply of ammunition on their persons in case they became entangled in a prolonged fight with the ten outlaws needing to be arrested. Still not sure how such a large number of desperate men were going to be safely arrested, Joe advised the group that he would be 'stewing' over that problem throughout the next day, while observing the behavior and operations of their outlaws of interest at their campsite. Later that night after the deputies had finished with their supper and were lounging around their campfire holding their thoughts over what was to come once they became engaged in the tricky process of arresting ten deadly and desperate outlaws, Joe, James and Lewis wished they had a jug of 'moonshine' made by one Rufous Barnes in which to settle their nerves...

Way before daylight the following morning, found Joe and James safely hidden behind Steamboat Charlie's campsite awaiting what the day's events would unfold. Around eight o'clock in the morning finally found the outlaw's camp stirring below the two deputies and showing signs of life. Soon a number of the men were observed walking up onto the hillside and into the brush behind their camp and going to the bathroom. As they did, Joe took all of that morning activity by the outlaws into account and his planning for the action to come when their Writs of Arrests were to be served. Then several of the men began cooking the outlaws' breakfast and by nine o'clock the men were seen saddling up their horses in preparation for leaving and going somewhere. Somewhat later, all the men streamed out from their campsite on horseback and headed easterly along the Red River towards a number of traditional and well-used cattle trails utilized by Texas cattle herds being routinely pushed north towards the Kansas stockyards.

Waiting for about another hour to make sure the outlaws had left the area and satisfied that they were finally alone and it was safe to operate, Joe walked back to his hidden horse, removed its saddlebags and returned to where he and James had been hidden throughout the morning. There Joe instructed James to be on the lookout and listening for the outlaws' return and if so detected, whistle so Joe could be warned and have the time to safely leave the outlaws' campsite that time without being detected. With that, Joe left their place of hiding and hustled his way down to the now-abandoned campsite leaving a trail of dust hanging in the air.

As James watched out for his brother, he could see him doing something near the roofs of each of the log and dirt lean-to sleeping quarters utilized by the outlaws. Then James could see his brother gathering up some clumps of grass and stuffing it into the soft dirt of the lean-to in the area where he had been so intently working. Finally James observed his brother sprinting back across the outlaws' campsite and soon was back at their original hidden site where they could observe the outlaws below once again after they had returned from wherever they had gone that morning.

There the two brothers waited in hiding until about nine in the evening and were just in the process of leaving, when all of a sudden, they could hear the sounds of numerous horses coming their way! Moments later, a number of whooping and yelling riders rode into the now-darkened campsite and as they did, it became obvious they were pushing a large herd of horses ahead of the riders. That was followed with more yelling, as the men in the darkness below pushed about twenty head of horses into their corral adjacent their campsite, joining the 13 already there. Shortly thereafter, Joe and James could smell the dust and odor of dried horse manure being stirred up below at the outlaws' camp and floating into the air all around them by the milling horse herd. Finally several outside fires were started in their outdoor fire pits and as they grew in size, Joe and James could finally see what was going on below. From the now full horse corral illuminated below, it was obvious that the outlaws had scored big in the theft of some cattle drovers extra horses!

It was then that the two deputies observed several of the outlaws had just grabbed up their rifles and were running back towards the entrance of their campsite like the demons of hell were chasing them! Those riflemen had just barely made it back to their brush-covered entrance trail to their campsite, when three new riders riding hard, stormed into the campfire-illuminated campsite carrying their own rifles at the ready.

It then dawned on the two still-hidden deputies that the three new and hard-riding horsemen who had just ridden into the campsite, had to be drovers from the cattle herd which had just been raided for the extra horses held in their reserve as replacement mounts for those horses needing a rest from the daily regular drover duties.

Just as the three hard-riding riders stormed into the campsite compound below, Joe and James watched in horror as those riders were shot out from their saddles by the outlaws who had run to the brushy entrance and laid in wait to ambush any pursuers! As they continued watching the horror unfolding below, they observed the outlaw shooters emerge from the brush, walk over to the now dead three cowboys, and remove the weapons they carried, grabbed up their horses and led them to the horse corral. There the three horses were unsaddled and run into the horse corral with the rest of the still milling and confused just recently rustled drovers' horses. Following that action, six outlaws walked out to the dead cowboys lying in the middle of the trail leading into the compound and dragged their bodies off towards the banks of the nearby Red River. About twenty minutes later, the six outlaws returned to their campsite minus the three drovers' bodies which had been unceremoniously dumped into the waters of the Red River, in the hopes they would drift off downstream away from their hidden campsite and disappear forever!

Joe had seen enough of the outlaws' actions, as he and James then sneaked back to their hidden horses where they had been tied off earlier in the day and quietly left the area as they headed for their campsite. Arriving about an hour later, the two brothers were more than welcomed by the anxious and worried lot of Deputy U.S. Marshals, Chino and Tom Johns. After tiredly unsaddling their horses, Joe and James ate some left over supper and then discussed the day's events with the rest of their group of officers and men so they would be better informed as to the daily actions of the group of outlaws they were now stalking.

Then Joe outlined their next day's battle plan as it involved attempting to arrest Steamboat Charlie's band of horse thieves and now murderers! Sitting around in the light of their campfire, Joe took a stick and drew out the entire outlaws' campsite layout so the others would be familiar with the physical battle zone into which they would be venturing. Then he described what his plan of attack involved and the exact placement of each man the next day prior to the beginning of the anticipated deadly battle at hand. Finally, Joe rehearsed with each man his exact duties and the hand signals to be used and understood in their attack once the battle with the outlaws had been joined.

Realizing the next day was going to start early, Chino began laying out his breakfast preparation plans as the Indian Policeman, Tom Johns, began gathering up ten sets of manacles and leg irons and attached them accordingly to each man's saddle in a burlap bag in accordance with that man's involvement in the morrow's battle. The lawmen also laid out the rest of their gear needed for the next day's battle and went to bed early for whatever sleep they could get in the offing. Around two in the morning the next day, Chino's alarm clock went off and he began scrambling around making up the remainder of his previously planned-for hearty breakfast for the men. Breakfast was then hurriedly eaten and then the men saddled up for the day's events lying before them. Then with Joe in the lead and James bringing up the rear in the morning's darkness so no one would get lost en route the outlaw's campsite, the men ambled off single file towards the outlaws' camp and whatever destiny lay ahead for each officer and those dangerous outlaws they were pursuing.

Leaving Tom Johns and Chino back to watch over where the deputies would leave their hidden horses a short distance from the outlaws' campsite, since those two were not officially authorized to participate in the coming battle, the heavily armed deputies silently followed Joe off to their places of hiding in the numerically lopsided battle soon to come. Once on the site right next to the outlaws' camp, Joe quietly pre-positioned each man at his duty station in the expected battle to come so there would be no room for error once the anticipated shooting began and confusion reigned. Then the five lawmen quietly waited for the dawn and the destiny it would bring to each and every man in battle that day.

Come the morning's dawn, the sun peeped into the day and began illuminating the earth below as it traversed across the cloudless sky. Finally by around eight in the morning, the outlaws' camp began to stir and show signs of life. First sign of life was when one outlaw went to the outside fire pit, started a fire and set the coffee pot on the cooking irons over the now blazing fire to boil. Then that man headed up the brush-covered hillside behind the camp with a handful of paper so he could take his morning dump. Finding a suitable clump of brush where from other smelly signs, that area had been used previously for the execution of such bodily functions, the man dropped his pants, grabbed hold of a clump of brush to his front for support, squatted and began grunting hard to exercise his impacted bowels. As he grunted loudly to aid in relieving himself, he failed to hear the hammer being cocked on Lewis's Sharps rifle behind him, but the 'grunter' did feel the end of that rifle barrel being placed with authority against the back of his head!

Moments later that man laid face down in the dirt, manacled and leg-shackled with his shirt tightly tied across his mouth to prevent any warning outcries. When those duties had been attended to, Lewis made sure the now manacled man understood that to make just one sound of warning would be instantly followed by that of a Sharps .50 caliber bullet smacking hard into his body from just feet away! The same kind of bullet that would drop a buffalo dead at 300 yards with just one well-placed hit...

A second man then emerged from one of the sleeping lean-tos with paper in hand, wearing an inner urgency spread clear across his face, all of which was seconded by his fast walking up into the brush-covered hillside to take care of a matter of the utmost importance! Reaching a handy clump of brush none too soon, the man hurriedly dropped his pants, grabbed some sagebrush to his front for support, squatted and squirted out his 'sense of urgency'. Groaning in relief over getting to his clump of sagebrush just in time, that relief was quickly dispelled as the

man realized the person stepping out from behind a tree just several feet distant with a deadly
look in his eyes, was pointing a cocked Sharps
rifle right at his head! Moments later, that man
now laid in his own pew, manacled by hands
and shackled by legs, with his shirt tightly tied
around his mouth and eyes to prevent any undue
warnings being given to his unknowing cohorts
below. However, that man also had heard the
whispered words into his ear advising him that
to make any sounds other than still continuing to
finish his bowel movement, 'would lead to him
never again having to worry about having a bad
case of the trots'…

By now, the coffee was boiling out from the
long-abandoned coffee pot still hanging over the
fire, and soon another man was observed running from his sleeping lean-to to the coffee pot,
removing it and placing it on a flat rock next to
the fire pit to cool. Then looking all around for
the original coffee-maker culprit to give him hell
for letting the pot boil over, he was overcome
with nature's urgency caused by eating a greasy
supper the night before and without another look
or action at the campfire, took off for the much-
used hillside 'dump site'. Arriving at a place of
concealment somewhat later, the man grabbed
up several handfuls of grasses to be used when
he had finished, laid them alongside his chosen

place of action, dropped his pants, squatted and began taking care of the business at hand. As he did, he began looking around at the world that lay before him in a daydreaming sort of way, only to realize there was a kneeling, strange human being looking right at him from a large clump of brush not more than ten feet away! Surprised at what he was seeing, the man did a double take to make sure of what he was seeing! Then seeing the strange man draw down on him with a Sharps rifle caused the man to internally panic! In that moment of panic, the 'daydreamer' forgot where he was or what he had been doing and fell over backwards in extreme surprise! When he did, he 'married his bottom' onto what had just exited from that portion of his anatomy! Moments later, he too found himself manacled and shackled as he lay in his own pew with his dirty shirt tightly tied around his mouth so he could not sound any warning to his mates now stirring around their campsite below. He too, in addition to the discomfort he was suffering over having last night's greasy supper smeared all over 'his last part of the fence', realized his silence over what had just occurred was better than being silenced forever. An eternal silence that had been threatened by the presence of the nearby, deadly serious-looking man now holding the Sharps rifle at the ready and in a position from which he could not miss…

Realizing his time and luck were running out by waiting any longer, Joe began making his move to put the second phase of his capture plans into motion. As he did, he spotted who he now for sure considered to be Steamboat Charlie emerging from one of the sleeping lean-tos, coughing uncontrollably. Finally the coughing became so deep from within the man's frail frame and violent, that the man dropped to his knees in abject pain and misery, coughing all the way to the ground! When he did, the lean-tos of fellow sleep-mates emptied and the men realizing what a deadly and silent killer their boss carried within his being, just stood around him in fear of what to do, especially in avoiding contracting the deadly disease Charlie carried…

That was when Joe decided with a group of their suspect outlaws now gathered around their boss trying to decide what to do to help him, that it was time to pull the 'trigger'. "U.S. MARSHALS! DON'T ANYONE MOVE! ALL OF YOU ARE UNDER ARREST! ALL OF YOU SURRENDER AND JUST SIT DOWN WHERE YOU STAND UNLESS YOU WANT A BULLET!" shouted Joe.

For a moment, not a single surprised outlaw moved other than looking in the direction from whence had come the mystery voice carrying a command to surrender. Then the seven remaining outlaws in the campsite below, minus their captured compatriot 'crappers' on the hillside, exploded into their defensive movement and actions meant to preclude capture! All the men now broke running to their sleeping lean-tos for their rifles and pistols, since none were currently armed having just awakened and were in the process of trying to help their boss through his most recent violent consumptive coughing spell.

"I SAID HOLD IT RIGHT THERE! U.S. MARSHALS AND ALL OF YOU ARE UNDER ARREST FOR MURDER AND STEALING HORSES! STAND IN PLACE OR YOU WILL WISH YOU HAD!" yelled Joe.

Joe's words of warning and the cottonwood leaves being shaken by a slight breeze in the adjacent grove of trees, had the same force and effect over the stunned outlaws as to what had been just been commanded... That was when Joe decided he had better put the final part of his arrest plan into action. Earlier when Joe had surreptitiously ventured into the outlaws' campsite carrying his saddlebags, he was a man on a mission. Stopping alongside each sleeping lean-to, Joe had removed a number of sticks of dynamite from those saddlebags and hidden them at the corner of each lean-to. He then had pulled up several clumps of grass and had laid that over the exposed sticks of dynamite so the explosives would not be inadvertently discovered. To Joe's way of thinking, if the outlaws did not comply with his orders of surrender, the sticks of dynamite were going to become a crucial part of his 'Plan B' capture plans.

Seeing that his orders of surrender were not being heeded by the outlaws below as they all scrambled back inside their sleeping lean-tos for their weapons, Joe figured it was now time for his 'Plan B' to be instituted before things really got dangerously out of hand. Sighting across the open sights of his .50 caliber Sharps rifle, Joe took careful aim at a preordained spot at the end of the sleeping lean-to and squeezed off his first shot. BOOM! roared the Sharps and nothing happened as its bullet went barely wide of its mark and just struck the dirt on the side of the sleeping lean-to right next to the grass-concealed bundle of dynamite. Quickly reloading his single shot rifle, Joe took aim once more from his place of concealment just as both lean-tos erupted mad as hell outlaws, now armed up and loaded for bear, as they intensely looked for the person on the hillside with the commanding voice!

Immediately, bullets began slapping the earth, brush and rocks near where Joe was kneeling as he began taking careful aim with his Sharps once again at the grassy clump at the end of one of the lean-tos hiding the sticks of dynamite. He slowly pulled the trigger at his aiming point on the side of the lean-to, felt the heavy recoil of his rifle against his right shoulder and heard the booming sound of his rifle being fired.

With his second shot and that bullet smashing into the semi-exposed sticks of dynamite, there was a tremendous booming explosion as one of the sleeping lean-tos exploded into a thousand pieces of wood and a cloud of flying dirt! When that particular lean-to exploded as the high speed rifle bullet struck the nitroglycerin-laced dynamite, the men nearest it were scattered all over the place, finding themselves knocked silly and covered with wooden splinters and inches of flying dirt! But Joe did not stop there as he once again took careful aim with his hastily reloaded Sharps and carefully pulled its trigger only to feel the rifle's comforting recoil, hear its booming firing sound and once again seeing the remaining sleeping lean-to when his bullet struck the sticks of dynamite, exploding into a ton of flying dirt and a thousand board feet of blown all to hell wooden splinters!

With that second explosion of the remaining sleeping lean-to and the resultant physical scattering of its numbers of close at hand outlaws shooting onto the hillside in Joe's voice location, the results were immediate. Every one of the outlaws below in the campsite after that explosion now lay inert or highly dazed and crawling around on the ground like a gut-shot woodchuck. Not only that, but being in such close proximity to the two explosions, none of the outlaws could hear and all were physically disabled from the close at hand concussions from the exploding dynamite!

Then Joe saw Deputies Walker and Marcoux rising up nearby, still covered with the dirt from the blown all to hell sleeping lean-tos, and running forward towards the barely wiggling outlaws lying all strewn about on the ground. As they did, Joe saw his two brothers rise up from a ditch on the opposite side of the human wreckage still trying to untangle itself so they could fight back and in so doing, converged on the outlaws in a pincer movement towards oncoming deputies Walker and Marcoux.

Within moments, the remaining seven outlaws were all disarmed and in the process of being manacled by the deputies. Then as the deputies began shackling the still dazed and confused outlaws, an excited Tom Johns who just could not stay with the horses when the action was on going elsewhere, found himself shortly thereafter overlooking the scene below from his place on the hillside. Realizing the fight was now mostly over between all the white men, Johns took off racing for Chino and the horses so they could arrive shortly on the scene and at least take part in the duties of helping with the arrest and control of the outlaws at hand.

Soon the deputies had all seven of the men laid out on the ground like large gar fish lying in a quiet river's pool on a summer day. Then from up on the hillside, here came Chino leading all their horses and Indian Policeman Tom Johns pushing three rather stinky-smelling stumbling prisoners across the hillside towards the camp below with big grins on their two weathered faces. Twenty minutes later, all ten outlaws were laid out on the ground, with most of them who had been nearest the two explosions, starting to come around to their senses and realizing they now had a serious problem relative to their lack of freedom.

That problem became even more acute when the deputies were surprisingly confronted by a dozen hot-headed cowboys who had sneaked up from the Red River side of the camp after hearing the two explosions and were now confronting all of the men with raised Winchesters in hand and 'blood in their eyes'! It soon became apparent to the deputies why the cowboys with Winchesters in hand were so upset. They were upset because the cattlemen had discovered their fellow cowboys floating down the Red River the day before, and had taken it upon themselves to go looking for their killers and the horse thieves who had stolen a number of their reserve riding horses. Upon hearing the nearby explosions, the cattlemen had ridden their few remaining horses to the scene and now were in the mood for some frontier justice over the losses of their friends and favorite horses, which were now self-evident as they stood quietly in Steamboat Charlie's nearby corral…

The next few moments got rather exciting when the two forces of law and order and cattlemen almost went to blows over the situation at hand. However, once again Joe with his badge of authority in hand finally gained initial control of the situation. Then when the cattlemen discovered for sure that the ten men in manacles were the ones who had rustled their spare horses and had killed their three fellow drovers, it took Joe some more hide off 'his hind end' to get control of the situation once again before the area 'bloomed' into a mess of 'neck-tie' parties, or 'Texas Justice' as the irate cattlemen called it.

Once things were finally settled down and untangled, Joe took down the names of the cowboys who had been killed and after viewing their bloated bodies, searched out the men from Steamboat Charlie's command and made mental note of the extra charges they would be facing as murderers in addition to the horse stealing charges. With the cattle boss finally taking charge of burying his dead drovers and the rest of his men taking charge of the stolen horses from the nearby corral, things began settling down a bit after they had left the scene in order to get back to their herd.

Then Joe had Chino and Tom Johns remount their horses and ride for the town of Idabel so they could bring their jail wagon, which had been left behind earlier in order to not tip their hand that the law 'was in town', back to the outlaws' campsite. That way with that specially built wagon, they would have a safer way to transport all of their prisoners back to Fort Smith. With that chore out of the way, the deputies set about looking through Steamboat Charlie's camp supplies and soon they had supper on the way to being prepared. However, as that chore was being performed, Joe made sure there were always two deputies watching over their now mad as hornets, sullen and mouthy threatening prisoners. That included one furious Steamboat Charlie who was so mad and venomous over being captured in such a 'caught with his pants down' manner, that he was almost in a constant fit and state of coughing up bits and pieces of his diseased and bleeding lungs...

Later that evening, Chino rattled back into the outlaws' camp with the jail wagon, trailing the two men's riding horses. Then the deputies got all of their ten prisoners up from where they had been laid out manacled on the ground and loaded them into the now cramped jail wagon. Then Joe assigned the men to four-hour shifts watching over the prisoners to make sure there were no escape attempts. Joe also laid down the law that the prisoners when let out from the jail wagon to eat or go to the bathroom, they were to be watched over by no less than two deputies toting ten gage shotguns loaded with double ought buck with orders to 'shoot on sight' if any of the prisoners tried to escape! When Joe laid down those orders to his men, he made sure the prisoners were clearly hearing and understanding his words of instruction to his men as well...

The following morning, with the men riding and leading the prisoners' horses, followed by the jail wagon with Tom Johns riding 'shotgun', the party of lawmen began traveling back to their original campsite. There they loaded up all of their gear into their chuck wagon, let the prisoners out from the jail wagon by 'twos' so they could go to the bathroom, and later with Chino driving the chuck wagon and Tom Johns driving the jail wagon, the group of 'law dogs' headed out on their way back to Fort Smith so their charges could be jailed and tried for their crimes of murder and horse theft.

As the prison caravan moved out, Joe headed

them easterly to the nearby town of Foreman, Arkansas, which was just across the Indian Territory border. From there, Joe headed the caravan in a northerly direction to the town of De Queen where they holed up for the night. Locating a small meadow along their route of travel, Joe stopped the caravan for the night so the men and animals could eat and rest. Then as a campfire was built and Chino began making the men's supper, the prisoners were let out from the jail wagon so they could go to the bathroom, and then were allowed to stretch out on the ground near the campfire and relax from their long day riding in their cramped jail wagon. However, Lewis and Marcoux kept a close watch on the prisoners as they continued grousing about the manacles being too tight on their wrists and the uncomfortable ride they were experiencing in the jail wagon.

As Joe continued writing down in his case report the actions taken regarding rounding up Steamboat Charlie's gang of horse thieves and murderers, he heard Charlie, a man almost totally consumed by his consumption, begin coughing deeply and in a troubling frequency. Soon he began spitting up blood flecks in the foam around his lips and that was when Lewis requested that Joe take a look at their obviously very sick prisoner. Joe advised he would be right there just as soon as he completed the last part in his arrest report. Finishing just moments later, Joe put his paperwork away in his saddlebag and began walking over to the group of prisoners to check out Steamboat Charlie's physical condition.

As he walked over to the group of men now closely watching Steamboat Charlie bent over, retching up blood and coughing even more loudly, his 'sixth sense' began getting the better of him. However, with all the guards posted, Joe just shrugged off that sixth sense as a 'dry run' and kept walking toward the jail wagon and his group of prisoners and deputies. Just as Joe rounded the end of the jail wagon, he saw his brother walk to and reach over as if to help Steamboat keep his balance as he continued spitting up gobs of clotted blood due to his spate of violent coughing.

THEN IT HAPPENED! As Lewis bent over to assist Charlie, he immediately stopped his forced coughing which had been an act, quickly stood up, spun a surprised Lewis around and jerked his pistol from his holster! Quickly turning and facing Joe as he now approached, Charlie leveled his pistol, cocked the hammer and pulled the trigger! However, just as he did, Lewis now realizing what was happening, quickly shoved his butt backwards, causing Charlie to 'pull his shot', which had been aimed at Joe's midsection from just a few feet away!

Being only six feet away from Charlie, Joe was surprised when he saw what was about to happen and even more surprised when he saw the end of the handgun now being held in the prisoner's hand explode smoke and in the same instant, felt a searing hot pain in his side as the bullet struck home! However, save for Lewis's quick-thinking action in slamming his butt backwards into Charlie's belly throwing his aim off, Joe would have been a gut-shot and dying man just moments later! As it turned out, the bullet instead of striking him in the stomach, its flight path was jerked from off his dead center and tore out a six-inch slice into the soft tissue on Joe's right side!

When that shooting event occurred, five of Charlie's men having been pre-warned over what their boss was going to do if he got the chance, jumped to their feet still manacled and knocked Fran Marcoux to the ground! When that happened, several of the prisoners went to the ground with Marcoux in an attempt to get his pistol! Jeff Walker, realizing what was happening and standing nearby, went for his gun only to have it knocked from his hand by one of the other nearby prisoners who was also in on their pre-planned escape attempt! When that happened, both of the men dove for the dropped handgun, as the rest of the prisoners simultaneously rose to their feet in an attempt to disarm the surprised deputies, kill them and make good their escape!

That was when Chino, just moments earlier stirring a huge pot of beans and rice for the men's suppers, jumped into the close at hand fracas with his heavy, long-handled steel stirring spoon. When the prisoner who had knocked Jeff's pistol from his hand got to the gun first, he quickly grabbed the weapon and cocked it on his way back to his feet so he could shoot the closest armed deputy in sight, only to have Chino smash him in his face with his long-handled steel spoon! That prisoner being hit with the heavy stirring spoon, immediately grabbed his smashed-in face with both hands in excruciating pain and in the process, dropped Walker's handgun. Seeing that happening, another close at hand prisoner dove for Walker's pistol now lying on the ground, grabbed it up, quickly rose to his feet, took aim at a now fast closing in on the fracas James, only to have his face filled with a leaping, snarling and savagely attacking dog belonging to Chino! Down to the ground that screaming prisoner went as Dog savagely tore at the man's face and then his hands, which he had thrust onto his face to protect what was left after the dog had savagely bitten him several times!

BOOM! went another shot in amongst the

fighting men, which caused a pause in the escape attempt, as everyone's attention was instantly drawn to looking over at Joe standing in the middle of the fighting men with a recently fired pistol in hand and still ready for more 'business' if called upon! As that move froze the entire escape attempt in time, everyone could see Joe standing there with a recently fired handgun, his left hand holding a madly bleeding side where Charlie's near deadly, center of mass hit had gone astray. But that was not where their looks lingered. All the prisoners could tell by looking at Joe's face that his 'look' advised the next prisoner who even took a deep breath, it would be his last if Joe had his druthers!

That was when Tom Johns stepped in with his double barreled ten gage shotgun, fired one shot into the air right in amongst the recently fighting men saying, "Next outlaw son-of-a-bitch that makes any kind of a move, I will cut him in half with the remaining round left in this here 'Street Howitzer'!" Being that Johns was only six to eight feet from all of the action and the end of the barrel of his now leveled ten gage looked big enough to be the open end of a garbage can to the casual observing eye, 'rapt attention' to his command was paid by all!

However, Charlie, not to be denied freedom in his escape attempt, grabbed one of his men from behind and using him as a shield, thrust him forward towards Tom Johns thinking when he did, he would take the full blast from the Indian Policeman's scatter gun. Then he could make his next escape move in his heretofore failed escape attempt! That was when Joe smashed the end of his pistol barrel across the side of Charlie's head with such force, that the impact blow tore off Charlie's right ear from the side of his head and dropped him in his tracks like a head-shot buffalo hit with a slug fired from a .50 caliber Sharps rifle! With that and Chino pulling Dog off the now badly mauled face of one of the prisoners, the escape attempt had failed and was now history, as the scene around the camp now turned back to normal…

Moments later, all the prisoners were herded back into the jail wagon. That included the man who now lacked a nose, with only two holes in the front of his face where Dog had chewed it off, and a much-bloodied Charlie, inert form and all! That was the way Joe left the prisoners for the rest of the night as punishment for their ill-advised escape attempt. That is, without any supper or water or care for any of their wounds. He just figured a message needed to be sent to all concerned locked up in the jail wagon as well as any careless deputies who were along for the trip, that their tomorrows were not guaranteed in the business of law enforcement in the Indian Territory…

The next morning after the deputies, Chino, Dog and Indian Policeman Tom Johns had eaten their breakfasts, the horses were saddled, the mules hitched to the two wagons and Joe's painful but not mortal wound was dressed by Chino, the prisoner caravan again made its way in a northerly direction towards Fort Smith. However, the prisoners found that they were not included in any care of their physical beings, allowed any breakfast and were told if they had to go to the bathroom, pee through the bars of the wagon! As for any of the prisoners needing to have a bowel movement, well, they were on their own as far as Joe was concerned… Joe just figured since the prisoners 'had made their bed', they could now 'just lay in it'. By the noon mealtime when the caravan finally stopped to let the livestock graze and allow for the preparation of the dinner and dress Joe's painful side wound, the men in the prison wagon, although still sullen, were what one would call one hell of a lot more manageable. Whereupon, they were finally let out to stretch their legs, go to the bathroom and partake of the noonday meal. As for the blood-encrusted Steamboat Charlie where his ear had once been, when he began coughing up more blood-laced sputum, no one seemed to care since the sense was that he was now a 'dead man walking'…

But it was obvious that Joe and the deputies had learned a very valuable lesson and that being, regardless of prisoners in their care being manacled and shackled, the day wasn't safely over until all of their charges were safely ensconced within the confines of the jail facility located beneath Judge Parker's courthouse in Fort Smith. That survival lesson was also not lost on Deputy U.S. Marshal Joe Dodson either...

The caravan of lawmen traveled through the towns of Mena and Mansfield and as they did, drew many long stares from the townsfolk over the number of evil-looking men locked up in the jail wagon. Finally, into Fort Smith went the caravan of lawmen, chuck wagon and jail wagon without any further incidents involving escape attempts. Once at Fort Smith and after being incarcerated in the jail facilities, the men sporting any injuries, like losing an ear and most of one prisoner's nose from being bitten by the camp's dog during the ill-fated escape attempt, were tended to by the jail's doctor. Joe was also tended to by a local doctor but was soon turned away from any further care because the wound had only been a flesh wound and Chino had done a wonderful job on the trail of doctoring up the same.

After that and a trip to the local boardinghouse for a well-earned bath and some good ole down home cooking, the men shared the $2.00 paid for each prisoner brought in and six cents per mile for the distance traveled, and Marshal Fagan put all of the men in for the outstanding rewards offered for each of the men from Steamboat Charlie's gang by the local stagecoach companies, the railroad and the Texas Cattlemen's Association. Following that, the deputies later testified in Judge Parker's court over what they had personally witnessed in the way of any federal crimes being committed in their presence, and Deputies Walker and Marcoux were then assigned more duties by Marshal Fagan in the Indian Territory as his newest Deputy U.S. Marshal team.

It was then that Marshal Fagan released the Dodson brothers for a two-week respite from any further duties which they took advantage of by going back to their home ranch near the town of Booneville for some much-needed rest. Well, that and some damn serious continuation of the courting process by Lewis and James with the two ladies named Jane Wilkins and Carol Jackson. Two ladies that the deputies had rescued back in Hendrix from their lives in a brothel and had in turn, after a short courtship while on the trail, sent them to their home ranch to live and for their younger brother to protect and watch over. That was for their younger brother to watch over until Lewis and James could come home for some much-needed downtime from the Deputy U.S. Marshal business and spend more time in the courting department...

As for Steamboat Charlie, he died in jail from his tubercular consumption before he could have his day in court before Judge Parker. It was as Marshal Fagan had predicted to the Dodsons at the start of the Steamboat Charlie detail, that Charlie was a 'dead man walking'. That was just as well though, if what happened to the remaining members of his gang could be taken into account for all the horse stealing, murdering and raping they were responsible for over the years. The three men who had murdered the Texas cowboys trying to run down the horse thieves who had stolen their extra horses, died on Judge Parker's gallows together, as they had ridden roughshod across the lives of numerous others over the years. As for the remainder of the gang, all died violently at the hands of other inmates in federal prison years later while serving 30-year sentences for their roles as horse thieves and rapists in the lawless Indian Territory.

CHAPTER NINE

**"BUZZARD CREEK'S" LUCK RUNS OUT WITH
A 'BANG' AND HE 'RIDES' A WOODEN CHAIR
INTO ETERNITY!**

AFTER BEING TEMPORARILY released from duty as deputy marshals for two weeks' rest and spending that time back on their home ranch, upon the men's return to duty, found the Dodson brothers on their first day back again in Chief Marshal Fagan's office waiting to be briefed and collect their next law enforcement assignment in the Indian Territory.

Once Marshal Fagan had finished briefing two other deputies already in his office on their upcoming detail so they could make the necessary logistical preparations, he yelled for the Dodson deputies sitting in the outside waiting room to enter. Upon entering his office, the Dodsons found they were confronted by a very pleased Marshal Fagan over the success of their last assignment in safely rounding up the notorious Steamboat Charlie and his large gang of cutthroat outlaws without any fatalities incurred on either side. After finishing with his round of congratulations, Marshal Fagan beckoned for his deputies to take a seat in his cavernous office and get comfortable because he had some good news for the three officers. Then opening up one of his lower desk drawers, the marshal reached down, pulled out an obviously heavy canvas sack full of coins and with a loud metallic sounding 'CLUNK', plopped it onto the top of his desk.

"There she is boys! All of $5,050 in gold and silver coin reward money from the railroad and stage lines for capturing the Steamboat Charlie gang! It is all there except for the $1,000 reward offered by the Texas Cattlemen's Association for catching the horse rustling bunch of outlaws headed up by Steamboat Charlie, which I am told by my staff is on the way via the next stage. Seeing that most hard-working men in this country of ours make between $300-500 a year toiling in the fields, driving a three-span for the stagecoach company or working in the factories, I would say you boys have done right good in what your efforts for me, God and country have produced. I would hope the three of you men would find it in your hearts to share some of this reward money with Chino, Marcoux, Walker and Tom Johns, since I am told they had a hand in your successes as well," said Marshal Fagan through a much-satisfied grin of appreciation for the excellent law enforcement work recently performed by his deputies.

"That will not be a problem, Marshal. We had planned on splitting 'even-steven' whatever reward money we derived from this operation with Chino, Marcoux, Walker and Tom," said Joe with a smile on his face over the men's new-found fortunes.

Then the marshal got a serious look on his weathered old face, reached into his pocket and took out a plug of his favorite Brown's Mule chewing tobacco. A brick of chewing tobacco that was an ugly black-tar like-looking substance and possessed to the unwary 'chewer' a kick just like its namesake! Not even using his penknife this time to cut off a portion, Marshal Fagan just bit off a chunk and sloshed it around in his mouth until he found a comfortable place for the plug to comfortably reside.

Then turning so he could face his three deputies 'square on' as if to emphasize the seriousness of their next assignment, he took the time to look carefully at each man sequentially as if searching for any sign of weakness in their beings relative to what they would soon be facing on their next and most dangerous of assignments to date.

Satisfied at the 'dedication to the moment' look displayed in each of his three deputies' faces, he settled back into his chair and pushed his earlier worries aside. With that, Marshal Fagan moved his briefing notes on the deputies' next law enforcement assignment to the forefront on his desk so he would not miss any bits of information contained therein. Then with a loud "harrumph" and clearing of his throat, he began the usual in-depth briefing that he gave to each and every deputy sent out on their most dangerous of assignments.

"Gentlemen, your next arrest assignment involves a very dangerous individual named "Buzzard Creek" Jack Johnson and that of his three half-breed, wild as scalded cats sons named "Big Charlie" Johnson, Cherokee Bob Johnson, and the last son who goes by the moniker of Davis Johnson. We don't have any paper, drawings or pictures of the lot, just testimony from those who have unfortunately tangled with this bunch and have managed to survive those encounters," explained Marshal Fagan, as he began slurping his words because his mouth had since filled with chewing tobacco spit-juice from his new plug. Whereupon, Marshal Fagan turned heavily in his swivel chair and launched a long, black-looking stream of tobacco juice out his open second story window onto the bushes and ground below.

Turning back to face his three deputies and wiping off the residue spittle from his lips with his shirt sleeve, he began once again on his important briefing, made all the more critical because he only had second hand information and no pictures to provide his officers relative to their newest law enforcement assignment. "Let me start with the old man and leader of this mess of killing sons-of-bitches, namely a man named Buzzard Creek Jack Johnson. From a number of accounts by surviving witnesses who were there and observed firsthand the demeanor and personal looks of this gang, I can only offer the following information. Relative to Buzzard Creek, he is reported to be a large man who is powerfully built and has the agility of a 'tossed cat'. He has a fearsome-looking, heavily pockmarked face with a knife scar running from the bridge of his nose clear across the left side of his face. He has thick black hair with dark bushy eyebrows heavy enough to be a mustache on any normal man, which gives him the general look of a fierce animal! Additionally and one of the best facets of identification that I have is that Buzzard Creek has coal black eyes that are cross-eyed," advised Marshal Fagan, as it again became evident that he had to spit again.

Once finished with the spitting detail, Marshal Fagan continued his briefing without hesitation, like the spitting out his second story window was no big deal. "According to over a half-dozen witnesses, Buzzard Creek's demeanor upon any kind of confrontation was one of diabolical outrage and unrestrained savagery, almost like being one-half hell fiend! So much so that during several stagecoach robberies, surviving witnesses reported Buzzard Creek for no apparent reason, knifed or shot several people in cold blood without any kind of warning whatsoever! Several stagecoach employees, including two guards, reported that Buzzard Creek wore two revolvers and carried two Bowie knives as well. Additionally, one stage driver reported that his guard got off a shot at Buzzard Creek with his shotgun using double ought buckshot one time during a stagecoach robbery, and swore that the lead pellets just bounced off his chest! Then Buzzard Creek killed that man riding 'shotgun' and when the driver was stopped and ordered to throw down the strong box, he observed that Buzzard Creek appeared to be wearing a breastplate of thin boiler-iron around his upper torso and under his shirt! That explained why the buckshot just bounced off him when it hit him and made a strange metallic clunking sound!"

Pausing to thumb through more pages in his report, Marshal Fagan then continued with, "That same stagecoach driver had also advised

the previous investigating set of deputy marshals chasing Buzzard Creek, as advised from all
of their investigative reports, that he appeared
to be driven by stupidity, impulses and passions
beyond his control when interacting with the
passengers being robbed, at the same time the
strong box was being broken into by his three
outlaw and just as dangerous sons. After seeing
Buzzard Creek shoot down a woman stagecoach
passenger who could not get her diamond ring off
a swollen finger quickly enough, Buzzard Creek
displayed the utmost brutality and cruelty that
one would find exhibited only by the Blackfeet
Indians, when he knifed that dying woman to
death because of her slowness of action and then
cut the ring off her finger with his Bowie knife!
Several other folks robbed in post office robberies reported that Buzzard Creek, a known outlaw
in their area, would go into insane rages if those
being robbed did not move fast enough to his
commands! So much so, that even his three kids
and several other fellow outlaws who rode with
him in his early days, seemed to fear him during
those behavioral outbursts of being 'just one step
away from crazy'."

Then it was time for another stream of black-
looking spit to be spewed out the window before
he could continue with his briefing. "The other
thing being whispered about by those living in

Buzzard Creek's main area of operation is that he has two Indian wives that he won in a poker game, and they many times are reported to be working in concert with him, especially when it comes to being lookouts for their old man and three kids. Again, some of the whispers picked up by the previous team of deputies who tried running Buzzard Creek and his half-breed kids to ground, was that the gang lived somewhere in the Sans Bois Mountains in a secluded cabin off the beaten track. They had apparently picked up that information from a Mexican wolf and coyote trapper running his sheep in the area. Other case report information that my deputies picked up just before they were ambushed by Cherokee Bill's gang and killed, was that the gang's basic robbery standard is to ambush the stages just as they finish climbing a long steep grade or a stretch of road in the Sans Bois Mountains full of sharp curves where the stagecoach driver has to slow the horses and cannot see the gang awaiting them around the next sharp bend in the road."

Then shuffling his case reports and witness statement documents once more, Marshal Fagan cleared his throat and began by saying, "Those two earlier deputies who were riding one of those stages to get familiar with the road traveled by the stage line, found themselves by chance be-ing part of one of Buzzard Creek's coach robbery attempts. When the stage stopped, my deputies realizing a robbery was ongoing, bailed out and caught Buzzard Creek and his kids by surprise and arrested the lot on the spot. The entire gang was then brought to Fort Smith and held for trial for a number of their previously reported crimes. Subsequently, those two deputies who had witnessed the attempted robbery and were my main witnesses, were later killed in a shoot-out with Cherokee Bill's gang! Come the trial date, we found that six different souls from the gang's home area in the Sans Bois Mountains showed up and testified that Buzzard Creek and his sons were with them on a cattle drive when the deputies' case reports indicated it was them robbing the stage. Since my two deputies were dead and could not testify as to what they had witnessed during the attempted stagecoach robbery, Judge Parker had to let Buzzard Creek and his three sons off, and found them not guilty because the preponderance of evidence from the six other folks lying under oath outweighed my two dead deputies' written reports. Therefore they walked away from the courtroom 'scot-free' and continued robbing stagecoaches, post offices and general stores in the Sans Bois Mountains area. And my latest reports from the Pinkerton Detective Agency regarding this bunch of killers, is that they have graduated into robbing a few trains now as well."

Pausing to spit once again, Marshal Fagan with hardly any other hesitation continued saying, "I have since learned that the stage line operating in the Sans Bois Mountains area offered Buzzard Creek and his sons $5,000 to cease and desist in the robbing of their coaches and the killing of their passengers. I am further advised by the president of that stage line that Buzzard Creek graciously accepted their offer, agreed to stop his robberies of their coaches and then after being paid off in gold coin, promptly went right back to his robberies against the stage line. Well, that is one way those damn stage line fools can be parted with their hard-earned money," continued Fagan with a tone of disgust in his voice.

Then the marshal finding his mouth filled again with tobacco juice, spewed his stream of black-tar like-looking liquid out the window, joining numerous spots splattered along the wall below the window pane where he had previously aimed too low. Wiping off his mouth with the sleeve of his shirt again, he continued saying, "The other thing you lads need to know is that a number of the local folks in and around the Sans Bois Mountains look upon Buzzard Creek and his sons as kind of like a "Robin Hood" character of yore. Buzzard Creek has stolen thousands of dollars from all concerned, but he leaves alone his local ranchers and businesses in and around the area in which he lives. That he does to engender their loyalties and in keeping their mouths shut! That in mind, you men should probably not talk to any of the local folk because I would bet my next plug of chewing tobacco that word that you are on the hunt for him will promptly get right back to Buzzard Creek. But it seems any ranches, stores or post offices twenty miles or more away from what he considers his home ground, he robs and kills with impunity."

Then after another quick spit out of his open window, Marshal Fagan continued saying, "In fact, my two earlier deputies before they were ambushed and killed, discovered that Buzzard Creek and his kin have ranches where they stash extra horses in case they are being closely chased by my deputies or members from a local posse made up of aggrieved townsfolk. That way, their horses can outlast those of the officers of the law pursuing them. So when you three are nosing around in the area, be aware they have a number of friends that they leave some of their stolen money with on occasion, so that they will cooperate with the outlaws and keep their mouths shut. The other thing I failed to mention is that word is that Buzzard Creek is a sporting man. He likes fast horses, fast women, faro, cards and drink. So maybe if you pose as out of work cowboys or frequent the local saloons after hearing about another robbery, maybe you can catch Buzzard Creek and his kin with their 'pants down' having a good time with all their stolen money in a sporting house."

Finding his previous chew off his plug near pretty well dissolved in his mouth, the remains of that cud were then spit out the window and a new chunk of chew off the ever-handy plug was bitten off, inserted into his mouth and finally rested comfortably between the marshal's teeth and gums. Then he continued with his briefing with the words, "Now, as to those boys. About all we have on them is that they are typical half-breed Indians, medium height in stature, all weigh about 200 pounds, have coal black hair and dark eyes. However, those kids I am told are as mean as 'stepped-on snakes in July' during their robberies, many times shooting down the unarmed postmasters, store clerks and stagecoach drivers who they feel are not moving to their commands fast enough. Seems to me from everything that I have read is that those three boys are nothing but mirror images of their old man! So my suggestion to the three of you is don't turn your backs on any of them at any time unless you have a death wish. I also strongly suggest that the three of you keep a sharp eye peeled regarding any of their eye movements, because I imagine their next move will follow the directions in which they are looking and for Christ's sake, don't go off and catch them and then get yourselves killed before you get a chance to testify against this lot. I don't like losing their types in Judge Parker's court of law and neither does the judge."

Sitting back in his chair after such a long briefing, Marshal Fagan just looked at his men for a long moment as they continued looking back at him out of sheer habit, figuring there was more information still to come. Sure as 'shootin', there was more on the way with Marshal Fagan a moment later beginning by saying, "I would suggest the three of you leave Chino and Tom Johns here this time. Most folks in the Indian Territory have come to quickly realize that anyone with their own chuck wagon during these hard times or being trailed by a jail wagon with its obvious bars and all in plain sight for all to see is the law, and nothing but trouble for any of those who are running from it. I think since we have worked these outlaws previously, they will be extra cagey when it comes to any close at hand 'law dogs'. You may want to just take along a couple packhorses with your cooking and sleeping gear and go into the area as being out of work cowboys looking for a way to make a living in these hard times. Then keeping your ears to the ground, try and find out where these outlaws live or catch them in the act and put them out of business.

Just remember, they have a lot of local friends who may try to protect them once the word gets out that the three of you are the law and on the hunt for Buzzard Creek and his kin. Lastly, I don't think these four outlaws will go easily. You may have to bring them in lying across the saddle instead of riding in the saddle, more than likely! That being the case, I would much rather have the three of you reporting for duty than me having to attend your funerals over in Oak Cemetery here in Fort Smith and lay you to rest! A cemetery where we have already planted a number of my damn good deputies who were a bit slow on the uptake," said Marshal Fagan with a sharp edge in the tone and tenor of his voice. It was immediately obvious to the Dodsons that when the marshal spoke with such a deep almost sinister tone of voice, that such 'talking to' was not meant to be misunderstood when it came to dealing with any miscreant, and that included Buzzard Creek and his murderous kin...

With that, Marshal Fagan rose from behind his desk, walked over to his three deputies, shook their hands, bid them Godspeed and then grumbled, "Don't you men have something to do, like go out and catch some lawless son-of-a-bitch and his three sons and then get your tail-ends back here safely so I don't have to worry and can give you another damn assignment?"

Taking that good-natured 'grumble' in stride, the three Dodsons thanked the marshal for the work he did in collecting their reward money from previous assignments and then headed out the door. Half-an-hour later over at Ma Silvia's boardinghouse for lunch, the Dodsons, Chino, Marcoux, Walker and Tom Johns split up the reward monies previously offered by the stage lines and railroad for anyone apprehending Steamboat Charlie's gang and bringing them before Judge Parker's court for trial.

Then it was over to the general store where the three Dodsons stocked up on the food items they figured they would need for what promised to be a long and possibly dangerous trip ahead into the Sans Bois Mountains area after one Buzzard Creek Jack Johnson and his three sons, Cherokee Bob Johnson, Big Charlie Johnson and Davis Johnson. Four outlaws credited with several murders, robberies and the stealing of any number of horses from the stage line and a multitude of ranches in the outlying area that they could lay their hands upon, and sell the same in the next town over after they had used a "running iron" to alter the original owner's brand…

Oh by the way, the Dodsons also stocked up with a fresh supply of .50 caliber Sharps rifle bullets and a number of boxes of Colt .45 ammunition as well…just in case things got a little out of hand where they were going and who they were going up against. Joe also made sure he had several bundles of what he called his 'little play-pretties' just in case he needed to celebrate the Fourth of July a little early… Somewhat later after their shopping trip was over, Joe very carefully placed his 'play-pretties' into his saddlebags, as brothers Lewis and James cautiously moved off a short distance away just in case Joe had an unfortunate accident and 'celebrated' his 'last' Fourth of July a little too early…

For the next three days, the Dodsons, each trailing a heavily loaded packhorse carrying all of their 'necessaries' for a long trip into the backcountry, rode southwesterly in the direction of the Sans Bois Mountains, reported home of Buzzard Creek Jack Johnson and his three sons. On their third night along the trail, Joe once again took the time to review all the documents provided by Marshal Fagan during their earlier briefing regarding the stagecoach line that had been hit the hardest by Buzzard Creek and his kin. As near as Joe figured, most of the stagecoach holdups occurred along the stage line's route of travel between the towns of Lewisville to the north and Yanush to the south. In so doing, the stage line's route of travel led right through a portion of the Sans Bois Mountains, causing the coaches to travel through the purported operating area of Buzzard Creek and his kin. With that in mind, Joe geographically settled into the Robber's Cave area with his two brothers, figuring he would use that area most frequented by Buzzard Creek and sons as their jumping-off point when it came to working at apprehending their intended targets and bringing them to justice back at Fort Smith. With such actions, Joe was using an old trick Deputy U.S. Marshal Bass Reeves had taught him, namely working undercover centrally to those areas in which the outlaws historically operated when carrying out their evil trades.

Finding the site of an old Indian encampment adjacent a stream and small meadow centrally located to all the purported criminal action of Buzzard Creek and his kin, Joe figured that would be as good a place as any and the brothers began setting up their campsite. As Joe unloaded their three packhorses, Lewis and James using a large piece of canvas, built a sheltering lean-to under which would be the men's sleeping quarters and a place in which to store their provisions. Next up went their fire pit ringed by large stones removed from the nearby creek, and over it went several anchored cooking irons, a metal grate to be used as a cooking platform, and a soon to be welcoming pot of coffee bubbling away in the night's cooling air. Arranging their bedding in their individual sleeping areas under the canvas roof of their lean-to, the three deputies were then surprised by a shout from out of the darkness now softly creeping in around them…

"Hello the camp!" sounded a voice from out in the darkness. "Rider coming in on foot and I am a friend," yelled out the voice in the darkness.

Turning and facing the location of the mystery voice emanating from the darkness, Joe, Lewis and James made sure the leather retaining loops over the hammers on their handguns (used in the Old West to aid in keeping their pistols from falling out from their holsters) were undone in case a quick call for their use was in the offing. However, the deputies all soon relaxed a bit as a lone cowboy walked into the light cast by their fire, leading a slightly crippled saddleless horse with an obvious bad rear leg.

"My horse spooked over a bull snake a ways back and when he did, he 'crow-hopped' into a sharp stick, jabbing it into his right rear leg near his hamstring, crippling him up a bit. Man, these sore eyes are sure glad to see another heartbeat way out here in this God-forsaken country at this time of the night. I kind of figured I would be spending the night along the trail under the stars until I saw the light from your most welcome-looking campfire. My name is Nando Mauldin and what would be your handles, Strangers?" he politely asked.

Relaxing over their surprising visitor showing up from out in the damn middle of nowhere, all three of the brothers introduced themselves to the cowboy a-foot that they now knew as Nando Mauldin.

After handshakes had been made all around, Nando looked past the three brothers over at the steam now pouring out from the spout of their coffee pot sitting on a grate over the fire asking, "Say, if that coffee is ready, I shore could use some if you fellas were in a mood to share with a plumb wore-out cowboy a long way from his next meal and his bunkhouse."

"Let me dig out some cups and I will see what we can do," said Lewis. "We just got here our-selves and have hardly had the time to get all of our stuff unpacked," he continued, as he hustled over to their packs and panniers scattered all around their lean-to and shortly thereafter began noisily rummaging through their gear looking for some coffee cups.

As Lewis kept rummaging around in their packs for their coffee cups, Joe, always the broth-er in the group to take the lead in most situations said, "What the dickens brings you way out here in this place at this time of the night, Nando?"

"Well, until old "Buck" here jabbed that sharp stick into his rear tendon, I was stringing barbed wire for my boss, Jimmy Jenkins, owner of the

Flying J Ranch. Having a gimpy horse 'purdy-much' ended the barbed wire-stringing detail, since he could no longer pull the wagon carrying all the extra heavy rolls of wire and the rest of my fence stringing necessaries," said Nando with his Indian Territory nasal 'brush-Okie' way of speaking. About then Lewis discovered their coffee cups, walked back to their fire, poured a steaming cup full of coffee and handed it to a very appreciative cowboy and now their new friend.

Taking a sip, Nando said, "Brother, you boys sure can make good coffee. That coffee is as 'smooth as a schoolmarm's thigh'," he said with a sly smile over the 'funny' he had just uttered.

"Now that we are pretty much set up, how about joining us for some supper once we get it prepared, Nando?" asked Joe.

"I sure would be much obliged," replied Nando with a friendly look of relief spelled clear across his lightly whiskered face.

"Then pull yourself up a saddle to sit upon by the campfire, as I begin to throw together some Dutch oven biscuit mix and a mess of roasted venison back straps from a deer my brother killed while en route this campsite," said Joe.

During their evening meal, Nando asked the brothers what they were doing in that neck of the woods all by their lonesome.

Joe quietly replied that they were all out of work and looking for some kind of employment on any ranch that happened to be located nearby. Joe lied about the reason all of them were in country because it was necessary they maintain their 'cover', if they were to successfully run down Buzzard Creek Jack Johnson and his just as guilty three outlaw kids and arrest the lot, 'if they were willing and chose to go all peaceable-like'...

Upon hearing those words relative to being out of work and looking for employment, Nando said, "Why hellfire! My boss Jimmy Jenkins is looking for some cowboys to help me stringing some fence throughout his meadows near the home ranch. How's about tomorrow back at the ranch I introduce you guys and see if he is willing to take on some extra hands to help me get my fencing all done before the snow flies in these here parts?"

Joe looked at his brothers for their quiet acceptance of such a fine offer that would surreptitiously fit into their undercover law enforcement assignment, and then he said, "That sure sounds OK to all of us, Nando. Asides, it seems that you are going to need some help in getting your fencing wagon hitched up to a healthy horse and driven back to your ranch house anyway. We can do that for you with one of our packhorses. How about tomorrow you lead us back to your fencing wagon, we unload one of our packhorse's gear into the back of your wagon, hitch him up and let you drive him back to your ranch house, and we will follow so you can get another horse in order to continue your fencing work. Then while there, my brothers and I can see if your boss is interested in hiring us three out of work cowboys on the fencing crew."

Later the next day back at the Jimmy Jenkins ranch house, found a very happy owner over what the Dodsons had done in helping out one of his hands. Shortly thereafter found the Dodsons getting settled into Jimmy Jenkins's ranch's bunkhouse as three of his newest hired hands.

While the three brothers began unpacking all of their gear from their packhorses, Joe asked Nando what corral they could put their pack-horses into when they were not in use. Nando moments later showed Joe an empty corral where their horses could be housed. As he did, Joe noticed another large corral holding only four horses and asked if they should house their packhorses in that little used corral as opposed to using up another corral.

Nando gave Joe a funny look and said, "No, that corral has to stay almost empty with just those four horses in it." Then Nando leaned forward and whispered into Joe's ear, "That corral and its horses are reserved for friends of the boss when the law is hot on his friend's trail. Those are 'stash horses' that are used when the boss's outlaw friends' horses are about to give out from being chased so hard by the law or other ranchers. If the boss's friends can get to that corral without being caught, they can change worn-out horses for fresh ones and then outlast anyone chasing them who are still riding tired horses. Now, we best not talk about those horses in that corral no more and say nothing about what I told you to the boss," continued Nando. Upon uttering those words of warning, he looked over at the boss's ranch house to make certain that he had not been heard or seen divulging such secrets to a total stranger who did not need to know about the boss's secret 'stash horse' favor...

Later in the quiet of the bunkhouse with just his brothers, Joe shared his just-learned secret about the four 'stash horses' adjacent the corral holding their three riding and three packhorses. Being that there were just four 'stash horses' in that special corral, Joe wondered if those horses were the one and same horses to be used by Buzzard Creek and his sons if pushed too hard by a close at hand posse or an irate rancher who had just lost a number of his horses to horse thieves. Joe also wondered that because where they were now staying, they were only about a mile or so away 'as the crow flies' from the actual Buzzard Creek drainage and reported home site of the famous outlaw and his three sons...

For the next two weeks, the three undercover deputies kept up their ruse as they strung barbed wire fencing for the Jenkins ranch as part of his crew of hired hands, all the while keeping a cocked eye on the mystery corral holding the four 'stash horses' each evening when they came in from work. Additionally, when the Dodson brothers went into the closest small town on their day off to celebrate in the local saloon or take the ranch's wagon and a team of horses into town to reload it with more barbed wire, they kept their ears open hopeful for any kind of loose talk about the escapades or location of Buzzard Creek and his kin.

As they did, the brothers soon discovered that most everyone in the local neck of the woods were supportive of Buzzard Creek and his kin taking on the wealthy men who owned the stage lines and local railroads. It soon became very apparent that most folks, being as poor as church mice, appreciated it when Buzzard Creek and his kin struck either the stage or rail lines running through the area and through their robberies in the eyes of the locals, took those wealthy giants of industry down a peg or two.

With that kind of strong and approving local

support, the Dodsons found it hard to glean any kind of hard locational evidence as to where such outlaws actually resided or when and where they would strike next without generating a lot of suspicious looks from the locals. It was as Marshal Fagan had predicted earlier during their briefing, that the locals would be rather close-mouthed when it came to protecting their local 'Robin Hood' heroes! Especially in light of the fact that Buzzard Creek and his kin bypassed the locals in all of their killings and robberies.

Then one day the whole issue of Buzzard Creek and his kin came to a bloody head. The Dodsons returning from town heading back to the Jenkins ranch with two wagons full of new rolls of barbed wire and other needed ranch supplies, were brought up short and back to their original pressing undercover issue at hand. Rounding a bend in the twisting mountain road, both wagons were brought up short when confronted with a stagecoach sitting all by its lonesome in the center of the narrow mountain road. The stage was without any of its three-span of horses, all the doors of the coach had been left flung wide open, suitcases were opened and their contents scattered around, and there were five bodies scattered about on the road surrounding the now empty and abandoned stage!

Stopping their wagons in the middle of the now

blocked road and after setting their hand brakes, the Dodsons bailed off their seats and raced up to the stagecoach. They checked all the bodies lying scattered about and discovered that all had been shot at close range, if the telltale powder burns on their clothing indicated or revealed anything to the trained eye! Additionally, there was a dead woman lying along the roadside stripped of most of her clothing and showing signs of having been severely molested! Adjacent the dead woman in the ditch also lay a dead baby with a smashed-in head!

For the longest time, the Dodsons looked upon the raped woman and dead baby scene and then Joe slowly said, "Boys, we are through stringing fence in a passive effort in order to maintain our law enforcement covers while we cast about for Buzzard Creek and his kin. What we are seeing around this stagecoach to my way of thinking, is classic work of the Buzzard Creek clan, as has been reported to us by Marshal Fagan. We are now going on an active hunt for these killing bastards and like Marshal Fagan said, if they choose to resist arrest once we have located their hideout, they can ride back to Fort Smith 'across the saddle' if they so choose that way of travel! It's plain that the locals are going to protect these bastards, so we need to step up our game a notch and actively hunt these killers down ourselves, as opposed to passively waiting for their location information to come to us so we can then root them out and make the arrests when that time comes. Before what we saw here today happens again, we need to bring these rascals to justice and Heaven help any of these locals if they decide to try and stop us from doing what we are being paid to do."

With that, Joe rode back into the nearest settlement and told the Indian Police what had happened along the road to the stage and its passengers. Then Joe, several hands from the local stage stop and the Indian police rode back to the crime scene, carted off the bodies and moved the stage off to the side of the road so Joe and his brothers could continue on their way to the Jenkins ranch with their two wagonloads of fencing and other needed materials. Suffice to say, that was a very somber and long ride back to the ranch. A somber ride with the realization that they had been sent there to preclude such happenings by the likes of Buzzard Creek and his bloody kin and had failed to do so by choosing a more passive method in their efforts to discover the outlaws' hideout and make the appropriate arrests in that manner.

Once back at the Jenkins ranch, Joe advised Jimmy Jenkins as to what had happened with the stage and its passengers. When he did, he noticed a strange look coming across Jimmy's face, as well as observed that he had very little to say over the deadly events that had just occurred almost in his backyard. In fact, Joe figured from Jimmy's reaction to the stage robbery and killing that he somehow almost expected the same...

Then Joe advised that he and his brothers would like to collect their pay and then they would be on their way the next day looking for more steady work back in Texas. With those words and being pleased with the work of the Dodsons, Jimmy tried to get them to stay longer and even offered to pay them a dollar more for each day's work. Joe thanked their boss but advised they had best move on. Then when Joe turned, he noticed Nando taking an obvious three-span of horses still in their stagecoach traces from the 'special corral' into a nearby barn where they would be out of sight from anyone riding into the ranch house area. Joe also noticed that the four riding horses in the corral were not the same ones that had been there earlier in the day but had been switched out and replaced with other horses! Saying nothing over what he had just observed and suspected, Joe headed for the bunkhouse and his brothers.

Once there, Joe shared with his brothers what he had just observed and his thoughts that the three-span of horses he had observed Nando leading out of sight were those from the stage they had discovered robbed and sitting 'horse-less' back on the narrow mountain road... He then advised that if and when they were able to discover the whereabouts of Buzzard Creek and his kin and made their arrests, they would have some more official business back at the Jenkins ranch regarding the 'stash horses' in the special corral and the obviously stolen horses seen be-ing led by Nando Mauldin into the barn so they would be out of sight and out of mind.

The next morning bright and early, the Dodsons having collected their back pay the evening be-fore and with their packed horses loaded and ready to go, set out on their way as if riding for Texas and steady work. However that time, once out of sight from those back at the ranch house, the brothers began surreptitiously following four sets of fresh horse tracks heading directly cross country from Jimmy Jenkins 'special horse' cor-ral, the one now holding four different still-tired horses from the day before, directly towards the huge Buzzard Creek timbered drainage. A drain-age and reported home and hideout somewhere within of known outlaw Buzzard Creek Jack Johnson and his three equally guilty outlaw sons.

For the next six hours with Lewis who was the best tracker in the lead, the Dodsons followed the four sets of fresh horse tracks as they wound their way cross country from Jimmy Jenkins's ranch corral towards the vast Buzzard Creek drainage. Stopping because of nightfall at the end of that first day of 'cold-tracking', the three deputies made a cold camp and by daylight the next morning, were again following what they had suspected all along were the fresh tracks of Buzzard Creek Jack Johnson and his kin. Tracks of stagecoach horse thieving, robbing, raping and killing outlaws as they made their escape from their most recent stagecoach escapade towards their suspected and secluded hideout somewhere deep in the Buzzard Creek drainage system…

Then the three deputy marshals hit a snag in their efforts at tracking the four sets of horse tracks of the suspected Buzzard Creek Jack Johnson's group of outlaws. Early that second day on the hunt for 'the most dangerous game', the four sets of horse tracks led directly into the mighty waters of the fast-flowing Buzzard Creek and were lost due to the swiftly flowing waters washing away all evidence of their being. However, Lewis did not get his great tracking reputation by being 'last in line'. Without any hesitation, Lewis directed that James take one side of the creek and he the other, so they could continue tracking in the last known direction of the fresh horse tracks. In so doing, both brothers continued riding along both sides of the stream heading in the last known direction the four sets of horse tracks had taken them earlier in the day just before they had walked into the stream's fast-flowing waters and disappeared.

Later that day, James cut the four sets of horse tracks as they exited the waters further upstream and headed for a massive rocky slide area as if to hide their trail once again. Continuing on their faint trail, the three deputies slowly moved along, with Joe now in the lead as he looked for anyone lying in wait in ambush to see if the riders were being cold-tracked. However, the four sets of horse tracks were initially lost in the rocky slide area. It was now more than apparent to the deputies that the four horsemen on those horses, in case they were being tracked, did not want to be followed or blamed for what they had just done back at the scene of the stagecoach robbery! *Since stealing horses and murder were federal hanging offenses in the Indian Territory, no wonder the four horsemen and suspects did not want to be trailed, as was evidenced by the extremes they had gone through in order to hide their tracks*, thought Joe… Then Joe grinned as he rode along, knowing full well 'come hell or high water', the four suspect horsemen were being tracked by one of the best cold trackers in the U.S. Marshals Service — his brother Lewis!

If the four sets of horse's tracks belonged to

Buzzard Creek and his kin, they had apparently not reckoned with being tracked any further by anyone after their little walking the horses in a stream and then walking those same horses across a rocky escarpment. Normally those little ruses would have worked but the riders of those horses had not figured on being tracked by Lewis, who had been taught how to track by his 'almost part-Indian' father in their earlier years together. Stepping off his horse and handing his reins to James, Lewis began tracking the four horses across the now totally rocky escarpment. He did so by following the faint metal scrape and scratch marks left in the rocks by the horseshoes worn by all of the horses!

Finally riding up out from the deep draw and still on the trail, Joe and company stopped along a long timbered ridge and looked all around with their binoculars trying to get even a glimpse of the four mounted riders. None were seen but Joe did spot movement far below them that was of interest. Spurring his horse and still trailing his packhorse, Joe headed off the ridge they now occupied towards the movement of keen interest that he had spied moments earlier. When Joe spurred his horse off the timbered ridge, his two brothers quickly followed, knowing their brother's penchant for the chase when it was close at hand.

Twenty minutes of riding soon found Joe confronting a trapper setting his wolf and coyote traps below a den site in a jumble of rocks. Surprised over the arrival of three mounted horsemen in the forested outback, the part-time trapper and sheepherder backed away from his trap-setting duties. Knowing he was on to something good, Joe quickly stepped off his horse, gave the reins to Lewis and then briskly walked over to the much-surprised trapper still standing there with his mouth agape in surprise and a wolf trap in hand.

Taking out his marshal's badge and 'flashing it', Joe said, "I am Deputy U.S. Marshal Joe Dodson. I know that you, being an animal trapper know this country like the back of your hand. I am ordering you to show me where Buzzard Creek Jack Johnson lives in this here drainage! In short, you are hereby ordered by the U.S. Marshals Service to take me to his cabin and I do mean right now!"

Upon seeing a badge of authority displayed out there in some of the remotest country in the Indian Territory and aware of the almost total lawlessness in the land and just how violent and vindictive some of the local outlaws could be, the trapper was totally taken aback with fear over what he had just been ordered to do. So much so, that his eyes showed an inordinate amount of white ringing his pupils, knowing full well that if he did as he had been instructed to do, he may very well be killed for such acts of betrayal!

"I...I...I don't know what you are talking about," said the frightened trapper in response to Joe's demanding request.

"You lie to me and you will find yourself under arrest, and I damn sure will handcuff and take you forthwith to Judge Parker's jail clear back in Fort Smith, Arkansas, so he can hang you for disobeying a lawful order by a Deputy U.S. Marshal! If and when I have to do that, I will leave your band of sheep behind all alone for the wolves, eagles and coyotes to eat in the process. Do you understand?" said Joe, as he towered over the smallish in size sheepherder turned predator trapper in order to protect his band of sheep and livelihood.

"Yes Sir, I understand you and hear what you are saying. But if I show you where Buzzard Creek lives and he finds out that I informed on him, he will kill me and my family and if he is not around to do so, his three kids will! Then his kids will rape my wife, drown my kids and burn my home for letting you and your kind know where their Pa lives," replied a now trapped and thoroughly terrified little man over what he had just been ordered to do by a larger in size lawman with a determined look in his now very demanding stone cold and hard staring eyes!

Joe, upon hearing the little man bleat out his knowledge of Buzzard Creek and his where-abouts, said, "I will not ask you again. Lewis, hand me a set of manacles to be used on this man if he is not going to cooperate with an official re-quest from a deputy marshal of this here United States," bellowed out Joe in his most frightening sounding voice!

"I will show you! I will show you!" yelled out the now frightened sheepherder, as the heavy smell of lanolin from the close at hand band of sheep rent the warm afternoon air. "But if I show you, I cannot be seen by Buzzard Creek and he cannot know that I was the one to betray him and his kind. If he sees me, he and his kin will kill me just as surely as that damn old wolf did my sheep last night," the frightened sheepherder bleated out with the tone and tenor of terror ringing in his words!

"Fair enough!" said Joe. "But you lie to me or lead me and my men astray, I will hunt you down and throw you so far back in Judge Parker's stinking jail back in Arkansas, that the jailers will never find you and the rats will eat you alive! Additionally, I will tell everyone that I meet in this area that you told me where to find Buzzard Creek and even if you get away from me, he and his kids will hunt you down and probably eat you alive after they have raped your wife, killed and eaten all of your children and stampeded all your sheep off the nearest cliff!" When Joe uttered those 'threatening' words aimed at the poor cowering sheepherder, he almost had to laugh. There was no way in which Joe would ever do such a mean thing to anyone or his family, but the poor damn sheepherder did not know that...

"I will show you! I will show you, I promise!" said the now frightened out of his skin sheepherder.

"Let's get going then. We are burning daylight and I mean to have that Buzzard Creek bastard and all of his kids in chains before sundown unless you lead me astray. However, if you want to see another sunrise, you had better not lead me or my men astray," said Joe in such a steely tone of his voice that even a maddened grizzly bear would have hesitated not to obey what had just been commanded!

Two hours later from high atop another long timbered ridge, found the marshals and one scared all to hell sheepherder looking down the ridgeline leading directly to a fortress like-looking, deeply secluded log cabin surrounded by several small barns and a corral holding a number of horses and one milk cow. Running through the cabin site area ran a small feeder stream leading to Buzzard Creek many yards below in a nearby draw and the entire immediate area was surrounded by heavy timber. As Joe sat there on his horse looking at the site below that greeted his eyes, he couldn't help but figure never had he seen such a cleverly laid out, fortress-like, sturdily built log cabin and well laid-out defensive perimeter that he could ever remember.

"There is where Buzzard Creek and his three boys and his Indian wives live. Now may I go before they find me here and get back to my sheep?" asked the terrified little man.

"You may go and get back to your band of sheep before the wolves eat you out of house and home," said Joe. "But, if you are lying to me about who lives down there, remember what I told you earlier. You will either be eaten alive by the rats in Judge Parker's jail back in Arkansas or killed by Buzzard Creek and his kin once I let the word get out that it was you who informed on him and gave away his home site location to the marshals," said a very serious looking and sounding Joe, for the effect it would have on their unwilling and scared as a jack rabbit in front of the hounds, reticent guide.

"Thank you! Thank you! Thank you, Sir! Now I must go before I am found out!" said the sheepherder, as he scampered off out of sight into the heavy timber like a cottontail rabbit being chased by a damned hungry long-tailed weasel!

Waiting out of sight from anyone below in the

cabin who might be looking on, Joe made sure the sheepherder had not turned tail, gone down to the cabin via another route and 'let the cat out of the bag'. Seeing that their presence still remained unseen or unknown to those in the cabin below, Joe and his brothers melted back into the timber and spent a cold night without any sign of a fire waiting for the next day's arrival. While there, Joe laid out his plan of attack to his brothers in case Buzzard Creek and his kin refused to surrender. To accent his plan of attack, Joe then visited his saddlebags, pulled out several small flour sacks containing his 'play-pretties' and made sure each brother had an adequate supply of Joe's special 'outlaw convincers'. But not before he had inserted a fast burning and shortened fuse into a number of his teeth-crimped blasting caps! Then taking a small sharpened stick (it is not safe to do the following with anything that is metal), drilled a hole into the end of each stick of dynamite, inserted the fuse with its blasting cap into the hole and tied off the other end of the length of fuse around the end of each stick holding the blasting cap so it could not inadvertently pull free. Then each brother was allocated a number of Joe's 'play-pretties' in case their use became necessary the following day while trying to extract the outlaws from their fortress-like cabin.

Come way before sun-up the following morning, found Joe, Lewis and James secreted around what was alleged to be Buzzard Creek Jack Johnson's cabin. About seven o'clock in the morning, the front door to the cabin opened and out walked an Indian woman over to the outhouse, entered and then she shut the door. Minutes later, that door opened and the woman walked back out and over to the front of the cabin, picked up a pail and headed for the nearby creek. There she dipped out a pail full of water, walked back to the front of the cabin, poured some water into several wash pans sitting on a bench and then took the rest of the water inside presumably to help in fixing the morning meal.

Moments later, an older man matching the sketchy description the deputies had of Buzzard Creek Jack Johnson and three younger men exited the cabin. Once outside and a fair piece from the cabin's outside living space, the men unbuttoned the flies on their pants and urinated onto the ground. Then the four men retreated back to the cabin, washed up out in front of the cabin in the two wash pans, and then re-entered the cabin and shut the front and only door to their cabin. Being that the four men had been heavily armed when they were out in front of the cabin and very alert to their surroundings, Joe did not chance a shootout out there in the open without better cover for the three deputy marshals.

So Joe quietly waited for a better opportunity in which to announce their presence and effectuate an arrest of the four men in question. Finally an opportunity arose when someone from inside opened up the front door and the two windows on the side of the cabin to let in some fresh air. It was at that moment in time that Joe decided he would announce to those men and women inside the cabin of the presence of the Deputy U.S. Marshals and give the cabin's occupants a chance to peacefully surrender if they were of a mind…

"BUZZARD CREEK JACK JOHNSON! THIS IS DEPUTY U.S. MARSHAL JOE DODSON SPEAKING! YOU AND YOUR THREE SONS ARE UNDER ARREST FOR STEALING HORSES, ROBBERY, MURDER AND RAPE! SHOW YOURSELVES OUT THE FRONT DOOR OF YOUR CABIN WITH YOUR HANDS RAISED AND UNARMED! YOU ARE SURROUNDED BY OTHER U.S. MARSHALS AND WE HAVE BEEN ORDERED TO BRING YOU AND YOUR SONS TO JUSTICE, EITHER DEAD OR ALIVE. WHETHER YOU LIVE OR DIE IN THE NEXT FEW MINUTES, THAT IS YOUR CALL!"

BOOM-BOOM-BOOM! went three quick shots moments later fired out the two sets of now opened windows in the direction from whence had come the sound of the voice ordering their surrender, followed by the words, "YOU CAN GO TO HELL, MARSHAL! IF YOU WANT THE FOUR OF US, YOU CAN COME IN AND GET US! OTHERWISE, YOU CAN ROT IN HELL AFORE ANY OF US SURRENDERS TO THE LIKES OF YOUR KIND!" shouted Buzzard Creek defiantly!

Then only the deep woods silence followed, other than that of the sounds of a faraway wood-pecker hammering away on a dead, lightning-struck pine tree limb. Then all of a sudden out the front door stormed four men and two women with rifles in hand, shooting in every direction into anything that could act as a hiding place for any U.S. Marshals! When they did, there was such a hail of bullets flying through the air that instinctively the Dodsons ducked down behind the surrounding two barns and a woodpile where they had sneaked behind for cover. Places of cover behind which the three marshals had been hiding in the pre-dawn darkness so they could safely surround the cabin and all of its occupants in case anyone tried escaping.

Then Buzzard Creek and his kin with now empty rifles, stormed back through the open doorway into their fortress-like log cabin to await the next line of action. Once again Joe announced who they were, that the cabin was surrounded and that now all of them including the women were under arrest for the attempted murder of Deputy U.S. Marshals! All those words drew in response was desultory rifle fire being fired from within the cabin out the still open front door and two open side windows... After that, only more silence followed, once again competing with the faraway woodpecker for any attention-generating sounds.

For the next six hours there was no discernible movement around or inside the cabin now under siege. Then all of a sudden, out the front door streamed four men and two Indian women once again with rifles blazing, aimed at every point on a compass where a marshal could possibly be hiding! To the Dodsons, there were so many shots fired and bullets filling the air from the multi-shot Winchesters being fired by the outlaw shooters and the Indian women, that the air sounded like it was full of angry bees around an overturned hive!

That was when the shooters who were so intent upon shooting their rifles at everything and anything that could hide a marshal, failed to hear someone giving out a loud whistle, then moments later seeing three smoking, light tan like-looking sticks of 'something' being hurled in their direction. BOOM-BOOM-BOOM! went the blasts from the three just thrown sticks of dynamite near the front of the cabin wherein stood the six shooters. Six shooters who were totally oblivious of the thrown danger at hand, as they continued the deadly serious business of discharging their Winchester rifles at any real or imagined targets near their cabin!

When the smoke and flying clouds of dust and debris from the three quick explosions of dynamite had drifted away, two Indian women lay sprawled dead across the ground where the dynamite had landed close by their feet! As for the four men, they found themselves in various stages of disarray and discombobulation, as they tried slowly returning to their feet and continuing to do battle, albeit from somewhat wobbly stances. In fact, when the four outlaws' Winchesters 'ran dry', they continued standing out in the open and began confusedly fumbling at reloading their rifles, as if to continue with the fight at hand regardless over what had just exploded around their feet!

Once again, there was a loud whistle from Joe and moments later, that was when three more fuse-smoking sticks of dynamite landed near the men attempting to reload their rifles so that they could continue the fight with their largely unseen targets!

For Cherokee Bob Johnson, oldest son to Buzzard Creek, he began a reaction on his part that would lead him ultimately to a 'river of no return'! Spotting a close at hand smoking stick of dynamite landing near his feet, he instinctively quickly reached down, grabbed up the stick of dynamite and prepared to throw it back in the direction from whence it had come. However, in the emotion of the moment, he fumbled and then dropped the stick with its furiously burning short fuse! Undeterred and pissed off that he and his kin were being challenged by what appeared to be nothing other than a few mere mortals, he reached back down and picked up the stick of dynamite. Cherokee Bob then turned and tossed the stick of dynamite back in the direction of its thrower Lewis, who had thrown the dynamite from the side of the barn behind which he was been hiding. As it turned out, that stick of dynamite had just left Cherokee Bob's fingertips when it exploded! When it blew up, Cherokee Bob disappeared in a rainbow-hued spew of human mist, as his Winchester rifle was simultaneously blown spinning through the air and ultimately splashing into a nearby horse trough full of water!

Almost in the same instant that Cherokee Bob had turned into a rainbow-colored spew of human mist, the other two sticks of thrown dynamite that had landed nearby the furiously reloading men, went off with almost simultaneous blasts! Moments later after the dust had cleared from those two close at hand blasts, the deputy marshals could see Buzzard Creek, Big Charlie Johnson and Davis Johnson confusedly crawling on their hands and knees back towards the still open doorway of their cabin. Joe realizing what they were trying to do, stood up and fired his Sharps rifle into the dirt in front of the crawling and dazed men as a warning and an attempt to stop them, so an arrest could be safely made outside of the protective walls of their fortress-like cabin on the remaining three still very dangerous outlaws.

Walking out in the open from behind the barn, where he had been hiding to take his shot with his rifle in an attempt to stop the three crawling and dazed outlaws from getting back into the protective walls of their cabin, exposed Joe's exact location for the first time. Even in his dynamite-caused haze of the moment, Buzzard Creek seeing his assailant for the first time, staggered to his knees, drew his revolver and 'fanned off' five quick shots in Joe's direction! When he did, two bullets sped by Joe's head so closely that they caused him to duck back behind the barn for the cover it offered immediately after getting his warning rifle shot off! Then sticking his head back out to where he could see what was happening, Joe managed to see the last of the remaining three outlaws disappearing back inside their cabin in such a hurry to escape any flying bullets or blasts from sticks of thrown dynamite, that they left the front door to their cabin wide open!

Joe now found himself and his two brothers in a quandary. The three outlaws were now once again back inside their fortress-like, massive pine and fir log cabin and not showing any signs of a lack of fight. *Perhaps it was the thought that a hangman's noose awaited the three men*, thought Joe, over the outlaws' intransigence as to why they still remained hidden behind the cabin's protective walls and full of fight. Joe then tried two more times by shouting out surrender instructions and only received several more rifle shots fired in his direction as a response to his order to lay down their arms, cease and desist...

Later when darkness fell over the land, Joe and his brothers were finally able to leave their places of hiding and safely get their heads together to plan another route of attack to gain the surrender of the three outlaws being held at bay. As they did, they made sure that the front door and the two side windows were carefully watched, so that none of the trapped outlaws inside could effectuate an escape under the cover of darkness.

Soon other plans were discussed in order to safely capture all three remaining outlaws and put into motion, because they did not have enough dynamite between them to blow down such a well-built cabin unless they could get such explosives to go off inside. In order to do that, that meant approaching an open front doorway or the two windows in plain view of anyone inside the cabin and that would not do if one wanted to live to see the next sunrise…

Finally James came up with a plan, and moments later he had drifted off into the darkness as Joe and Lewis continued watching the open front doorway and the two windows. Two hours later, James returned all covered with sweat but happy to report the next part of their plan was ready to be put into operation. Then the three deputy marshals remained awake and hidden throughout the remainder of the night watching the front door and side windows of the cabin in case anyone inside tried to escape using the cloak of darkness as their protective shield.

Come sunrise when there was enough light to see, Joe tried one more time verbally to get the occupants of the cabin to surrender, and that time he gave the trapped outlaws an ultimatum of surrender or be destroyed. That time the sound of Joe's warning voice again drew very heavy rifle fire from the now dynamite-blast-recovered trapped outlaws within their cabin! Then Joe yelled over at where James was now hidden and told him to "get her done"! For about the next ten minutes nothing unusual could be seen or heard. Then from behind the cabin where there were no windows or doors to cause any safety concerns about rifle fire coming from inside, long curls of heavy dense white smoke began billowing upwards over the rooftop announcing to the world that the outlaws' cabin had now been set afire!

Soon the blazing fire behind the heavy but very dry logs making up the cabin 'got its legs', and now very thick curls of black smoke began storming skyward as orange and yellow flames began licking all over the rear of the cabin's roof and walls! With those plumes of acrid heavy smoke came the loud crackling sounds of the cabin's demise and with that, Joe and his brothers made sure they had the open front doorway and the two windows more than covered if the three trapped men inside tried to make a run for their horses which were standing in a nearby corral.

Twenty minutes later, fully one-half of the cabin was ablaze and still there was no sign of anyone inside coming out and surrendering to the three deputies. Soon, over two-thirds of the cabin was now covered with roiling dark clouds of smoke with long licks of flame dancing into the heavens! In fact, the smoke and flames were now rolling out from the two side windows, and one could clearly hear the window glass shattering and breaking from the fire's intense heat.

However, that now made it easier for the three deputies standing at the ready looking for signs of anyone trying to escape the now roaring like 'the hubs of hell' cabin fire. Since the window area was now ablaze, that meant no one needed to watch that area for any escapees, so all of the deputies' attention could now be affixed on the still open front door and only escape avenue left, which at that very moment was emitting billows of black smoke rolling outward as well!

Then all of a sudden out from the front doorway burst three desperate men with their shirts and pants smoking from all of the intense heat experienced earlier from within the furiously burning cabin! However, every one of them was still carrying their 1876 Winchesters and were soon blazing away at the last known hiding places they had observed the marshals secreted behind from the day before! Then when their Winchesters ran dry, those rifles were quickly discarded and the men drew their pistols and stood there defiantly out in the open, frantically looking all around for any kind of a target that said 'deputy marshal' to shoot at. Seeing none and sensing their freedom was close at hand, the men broke for their nearby horse corral, grabbing bridles off the corral posts as they ran by and then tried running down a horse on which to bridle and ride out from the area bareback and into their freedom.

However, when the three desperate outlaws stormed into the horse corral, a combination of the nearness of the burning cabin and the men stampeding into the horse corral caused the horses to explode in panic and flee from the hard-charging and now very desperate outlaws. Soon a circus of sorts of running horses and three men chasing after them ensued within the confines of the horse corral. Finally the three outlaws had caught and bridled their horses of choice and it was then that they noticed the clear danger at hand...

Kneeling by two corners of the horse corral and another from behind a horse trough full of water, were three very determined-looking marshals with Sharps rifles leveled at each outlaw! Seeing the riflemen had drawn down on each outlaw at such a close in and killing range caused a temporary halt in the horse round-up and then the outlaws' hands rose slowly into the air, realizing to do otherwise would result in sure death for each and every one of them. However as the outlaws began surrendering, Joe noticed that the older of the men, the one he considered to be Buzzard Creek, was absolutely foaming white spittle from his entire mouth he was so violently and almost inhumanly outraged over the events at hand he was facing. Like Marshal Fagan had warned during the earlier briefing back in Fort

Smith, Buzzard Creek was just a short hop and a jump away from being crazy in thought, word and deed...

Then Joe instructed the men to SLOWLY reach for the buckle on their individual gun belts with their left hands, all the while keeping their right hands high into the air. When those instructions had been followed, Joe then instructed the men to unbuckle their gun belts and let them drop to the ground. After the three outlaws had complied with that set of orders, Joe instructed each man to keep his hands high and then walk away from their gun belts over to where he stood at the edge of the corral with his Sharps rifle still leveled dead at who and what he considered was Buzzard Creek's chest. The way Joe figured it, control the head of the snake and it can't bite you...

That was when Buzzard Creek, not able to contain the crazy fury building up inside of his person, 'went off' swearing at Joe and challenging him to a fair fight with rifles, pistols or a knife... his choice! Joe just looked at Buzzard Creek's now flaming red-flushed face and mouth covered with a dirty white spittle foam, remembering again Marshal Fagan's words about Buzzard Creek Jack Johnson's penchant for running on the razor edge between sane and crazy, and not to trust him...ever!

That was when Joe told Buzzard Creek to drop to his knees and lay out face down in the horse manure in the corral and when he did, to spread his arms out to his front. For the longest time Buzzard Creek just glared at Joe with a killing look in his eyes and did not move or respond to Joe's instructions. Finally Buzzard Creek looked Joe straight into his eyes with a wild look on his face saying, "I ain't laying in any horse shit for any son-of-a-bitch and that includes you, marshal! You want me to do that, you just drag your ass over here and make me," he continued with a look on his face that clearly read, "Herein lies a killer!"

With that, Joe walked boldly into the horse corral and right up to Buzzard Creek. As Joe neared within arm's length, Buzzard Creek became a blur of movement whereupon he instantly bent over, grabbed a hidden Bowie knife from the inside of his boot, stood up lightning fast in order to stab Joe and in so doing, violently met the steel butt plate from Joe's Sharps rifle being smashed into his face at a high rate of speed! Upon impact with the butt of Joe's rifle, Buzzard Creek's face exploded into a splash of blood and the savage outlaw dropped instantly and face down into the horse crap in the bottom of the corral! When Buzzard Creek hit the dirt and horse crap lying on the floor of the corral, he lay bleeding like a 'stuck hog' and out like a light as a result of the impact from Joe's rifle butt!

"Lewis and James, the next outlaw who tries anything funny, anything at all, KILL HIM WHERE HE STANDS!" yelled Joe. Upon hearing those words and seeing their old man, a man considered just one notch away from being crazy as a loon and a killer at heart lying in his own expanding pool of blood in the horse corral, the 'message' finally got across to the two sons as to what they were facing. Instantly, both men dropped to their knees and then lay face down in the horse crap and moved not a single wit from that position once assumed!

With that and Lewis and Joe 'drawing down' on the two remaining outlaws with their rifles, James went back to the barn where he had been hiding, retrieved the manacles where they had been stashed earlier in preparation for the arrests to follow and returned with those restraints to the corral. There still under the rifles covering the two men lying in the corral, James tightly manacled each man as he formally identified himself and the others as Deputy U.S. Marshals and then placed them under arrest for murder, robbery, rape and the stealing of horses. Next, James searched Davis Johnson and Big Charlie Johnson and removed Bowie knives from the insides of their cowboy boots as well. Then Joe said, "James, remove both of those men's boots and toss them out of the corral and away from them so they can never again use them as a hiding place for deadly weapons." Moments later, two sets of cowboy boots could be observed sailing over the corral railings and out of reach of the prisoners as Joe had ordered.

Then James walked over to Buzzard Creek who was still out cold from being so violently smashed in the face with Joe's rifle butt, manacled him and then searched him. In so doing, James discovered another Bowie knife hidden in his other cowboy boot and a concealed .44 caliber derringer tucked away in a homemade groin holster on Buzzard Creek! Both weapons were removed and then with Joe's urging, James did an even more detailed search of the inert man, whereupon he discovered another smaller knife strapped to Buzzard Creek's left leg under his pant leg. Joe then instructed James to remove Buzzard Creek's boots and toss them over the corral fence as well so they could not be used as a place to hide any more weapons. From then on, it was Joe's intention that none of the three outlaws would be wearing any boots for the rest of the trip back to Fort Smith, 'come hell or high water'!

James then left his brothers and went to fetch their horses for the trip out from the Buzzard Creek drainage outlaws' hideout. As he did,

Lewis saddled up three horses for the outlaws to ride and then turned the rest of their horses in the corral out to roam free. As for the milk cow in the corral, Joe affixed a long lead rope onto the animal, figuring he would drop the cow off at the nearest farm or ranch they ran across since Buzzard Creek and his remaining kin had no further use for it. Besides, to leave a milk-producing cow out on its own would be cruel and inhuman. Cruel and inhuman in light of the fact the animal needed milking at least daily or its udder would become painfully extended, causing extreme misery. Finished with that bit of 'milk cow' business, Joe walked over to the burning cabin and one at a time, lifted up each of the dead Indian women killed by the blast from the dynamite and tossed their bodies into the inferno that used to be their cabin! As he did, Joe realized all of the money that Buzzard Creek and his sons had robbed from the various stages was now for naught, as it all went up in smoke inside the burning cabin...

Two hours later, with Joe leading two of their three packhorses, Lewis leading a packhorse and a milk cow needing to be milked as evidenced by the milk leaking from its teats and James riding in between his two brothers for the extra protection they offered to the odd-looking caravan as he led three horses carrying three heavily manacled prisoners as their riders. As for Buzzard Creek, he rode dizzily along on his horse with his head covered with bloody foam from a badly smashed nose and with a face now covered with blood-soaked horse manure. Maybe Buzzard Creek would not sprawl out in a horse corral when arrested but he sure as hell would be wearing a face covered with blood-soaked horse manure for all to see if Joe had his way all the way back to Fort Smith and the hangman's gallows.

By late afternoon as the caravan made its way slowly back towards the Jenkins ranch, they ran across a homesteader and his family scratching out a living adjacent a small plowed field. The homesteader was sure surprised and pleased to be a new and proud owner of a damn fine milk cow to say the least, especially a fresh cow that arrived and in the need of being milked... Following that bit of business, Joe turned his group of riders back towards the Jenkins ranch for what he considered some rather unfinished official business.

Walking his group of deputy marshals, prisoners and the associated pack string down the local stagecoach road toward the Jenkins ranch after leaving the homesteader, Joe all of a sudden became aware of the sounds of a number of horses coming their way. Looking back and making sure by eye contact and with a nod of his head so that his brothers were hearing the same sounds and were alert in case a number of the locals had somehow gotten word of the capture of Buzzard Creek and his kin and were coming to take the law into their own hands, Joe kept looking back towards the sounds of horses' hoof beats. Moments later Joe could hear the sounds of chains jangling like that from several spans of horses pulling a heavy wagon. Then around the corner in the road behind them came the daily run of the stagecoach.

However, once the stage driver and his man riding shotgun became aware of the group of unidentified men on the road ahead of them, the driver turned and said something to the man riding shotgun. Moments later, Joe became aware that the man riding shotgun had leaned over and warned the riders in the coach of the men ahead and then turning back around, lifted up his double barreled ten gage shotgun, cocked both hammers and kept it in a ready position in case he had to make quick use of his scatter gun!

Seeing that ominous movement of the man riding shotgun, Joe reached into his shirt pocket, withdrew his Deputy U.S. Marshal's badge and held it high for the stage driver and his 'man' riding shotgun to see. Seeing that badge displayed, the stage driver slowed his three-span to a walk and cautiously approached the group of men who had just now pulled off the road so the stage could pass. Then the driver apparently recognized Buzzard Creek Jack Johnson, stopped his stage altogether and made a move for his handgun. As he did, he quick-looked over at his man riding shotgun, said something and then turned his attention back to his prancing horses in order to keep them under control. However, his man riding shotgun, upon seeing and identifying Buzzard Creek as well, kept his shotgun at the ready in order to protect himself, the stage, the U.S. Mail, and its riders inside the coach.

Then the stage driver and his 'shotgun' saw that Buzzard Creek and two other men with him were in manacles and by then, Lewis and James had their badges out and held high into the air so no one would mistake the group of them as stagecoach robbers. Then with a whoop and a holler, both the stage driver and his man riding shotgun stood up and let out a shout of recognition as well as joy upon seeing some of their worst 'nightmare highwaymen' obviously under arrest and in chains sitting on horses before them!

Joe then slowly rode back to the men operating the stage and said, "Driver, do you recognize any of these men who are sitting there on those horses in manacles and chains?"

"Damn right I do! That dark-haired one in the red flannel shirt is the one who robbed me and this stage 'twiced' over this past year! You need to let me get off this box, come down there and kill that son-of-a-bitch for what he did to two women who had been riding on my stage in June of last year! Damn, I can hardly believe it! You boys caught Buzzard Creek Jack Johnson and his sons. Wait a minute. One of his sons is missing," said the happy as could be stage driver.

"No, we didn't miss him," said Joe. "He was killed when we tried to arrest the entire bunch back at their hideout," continued Joe, as he shifted his weight in his saddle to a more comfortable position in order to talk to the stage driver more easily.

"Well, I'll be a 'sombitch'," said the man still holding his shotgun at the ready just in case its need was called for in 'short order'. "You boys 'catched' the worst son-of-a-bitch in this here valley," said the now happily grinning man riding shotgun. "Hot diggity! I can't wait to spread the word of their capture and the killing of one of his evil damn sons," continued the man riding shotgun.

Joe, ever the professional said, "Driver, I need you to dismount and come over to my horse. I need to get some papers out from my saddlebags and have you write down what you know about when you were robbed, who did what, and what each and every one of Buzzard Creek's bunch of outlaws did to you and any of your coach's riders."

"Damn straight, Marshal. That I can and will gladly do," said the driver. Then turning to his man riding shotgun. the driver said, "Bill, get our passengers out from the stage so they can see this killing son-of-a-bitch in chains up close and personal like and on his way to a hanging I would suspect. That way, they can stretch their legs, go to the bathroom and see some history in the making. Just make sure the women go to the bathroom on one side of the stage and the men on the other side," he continued.

An hour later and behind schedule for the stage, the stage and horsemen parted company. But not before the driver, his man riding shotgun and a previously raped female who remembered Davis Johnson as her rapist during another stage robbery, had provided written testimony for Joe to use when back in court in Fort Smith. As for Buzzard Creek, all he did was threaten everyone who stepped forward to put to print what had happened to them at his hands or those of his pack of outlaws on previous occasions. However, Buzzard Creek's threats rang hollow when everyone took the time to look upon Buzzard Creek's face covered in blood and all smeared in horse crap...

Then as the passengers loaded back into the stage and it proceeded on its way to its next stage stop and a fresh change of horses, the three marshals observed a lone rider slowly riding down the road towards them trailing a loaded packhorse. As the rider got closer, Joe recognized Nando Mauldin from his earlier days when he and his brothers were working under-cover stringing fence wire for Jimmy Jenkins. Recognizing Nando and realizing he had some official business with him as well, especially as it related to his leading the previously robbed stage's three-span of stolen horses into Jenkins's barn days earlier, Joe just quietly sat there on his horse awaiting Nando's arrival.

Nando slowly rode up and recognizing his friend Joe, broke out into his characteristic big smile. Then that smile turned to a look of amaze-ment when he also recognized Buzzard Creek and his two sons quietly sitting there on their horses, all decked out in the manacles and chains of arrest! "Holy Cow!" said an amazed Nando over what he was observing. "You guys have Buzzard Creek Jack Johnson, Davis Johnson and his brother, Big Charlie Johnson in manacles! What the hell happened and who the hell are you guys, seeing that you can arrest people?" asked Nando, clear full of surprise and wonder over what he was seeing!

"I might ask you the same," said Joe looking intently at his former friend and now possibly another arrest for being in the possession of sto-len stagecoach horses in the making.

"I guess I don't know what you are implying. You know me, Joe. I am Nando Mauldin and the one who got you and your brothers a job over at the Jenkins ranch," drawled Nando in his Indian Territory, almost southern way of speaking.

Looking directly at his former friend, Joe said, "Nando, how do you explain away the day I saw you taking that obviously stolen three-span of horses belonging to the stage line still in their traces and leading them into Jenkins's barn in order they not be seen by anyone casually riding by the Jenkins home place?"

"That is one of the reasons why I am leaving the Jenkins ranch and Jimmy Jenkins's employment and heading for better pastures. Pastures where just because I am a hired hand, I am not obliged to be involved in things illegal just because my boss orders me to get involved. You were right. Buzzard Creek and his kin had stolen those horses from the stagecoach they had robbed earlier in the day and had brought them to the Jenkins ranch for Jimmy to hide them out. Then Jimmy Jenkins would take those horses after things had cooled down and sell them to any willing Indian or white man buyer miles away from where they had been stolen so no one would be any wiser. Jenkins also harbored Buzzard Creek's worn-out horses by keeping 'stash horses' in that special corral so they could be traded out for fresher horses and continue outrunning any posse that happened to be chasing them. I just finally figured out what crooked things Jenkins was involved with, got a gutful of that kind of behavior because my Ma and Pa did not raise me up that-a-way, and just decided to get the hell out and away from such illegal going-ons," quietly replied Nando.

"Nando, I am glad you just said what you did. That tells me something about you and your honesty and lack of real involvement with Jenkins other than doing what you had been ordered to do. That being said, I need you to turn your horse around and follow us. I need you to do so because it is just a matter of time before the cat is out of the bag, and the word gets out that the marshals are in town and have captured Buzzard Creek and what is left of his kin. I would imagine once Jimmy Jenkins hears that his friend and partner in crime is in irons, he will leave the country and be a devil to chase and catch. So we are heading there as we speak, just as fast as we can to the Jenkins ranch to arrest Jimmy for the possession and sale of stolen horses and collusion in aiding and abetting a known outlaw like Buzzard Creek and his kin. So we need to get our rears in gear and get to Jimmy's before the word of the capture of Buzzard Creek gets out and becomes common knowledge. But in order to close the ring on all the illegal things going on with Jimmy, I will need to get your written statements on what went down regarding your boss and his collusion with Buzzard Creek and any other of his crooked dealings. Once I have that written testimony down on paper and with what the three of us observed regarding Jimmy's illegal activities, we plan on arresting him and hauling him before Judge Parker in Fort Smith for his day in court, right along with Buzzard Creek and what is left of his kin," said Joe.

"Be glad to do so, Partner. I can't think of anything I would rather do than help put that crooked ex-boss of mine away for what he enabled Buzzard Creek and his kin to do to the folks around here, especially when it came to the killing and raping they did during that robbery and killing spree when those three-span of horses were brought into the ranch to hide, later sell and split the profits with that gang of outlaws," said Nando.

Later that day, Joe and his group of outlaws and deputy marshals rode into the front yard of the Jimmy Jenkins Ranch. Jenkins, upon hearing a number of horses reining up in front of his ranch house, walked out onto the front porch with a huge smile over having some company, when all of a sudden he recognized the return of Nando, Joe, James and Lewis. However, a split second later, Jimmy also recognized Buzzard Creek and his sons sitting glumly on their horses all manacled up and obviously under arrest. When he did, his smile turned to a combination of panic, concern and then moments later, a mean-assed looking sneer!

Without a single word upon now understanding the situation before him, Jimmy turned and briskly walked back into his ranch house like a man on a mission before any of the marshals could make a move. However when he did, Joe had Lewis jump off his horse, run up onto the front porch of the ranch house and position himself alongside the now closed front door. As Lewis did so, he quietly drew his revolver and just stood there as if expecting some kind of violent action soon to come from the ranch owner still inside the house.

Moments later as the rest of the horsemen sat silently on their horses in Jenkins's front yard, out the door burst Jimmy Jenkins holding a double barreled shotgun with both hammers cocked and blood in his eye! Putting the shotgun to his shoulder and pointing it in the direction of Nando and Joe, Jimmy said, "Alright you sons-a-bitches, get off those horses, drop your gun belts and step away from them. Then whoever has the keys, let my three friends go or I will blow your asses clear to kingdom come," snarled an obviously now very deadly and feeling somewhat cornered Jimmy Jenkins.

That was when an unseen Lewis standing alongside the now open door, forcefully reached out and shoved the end of his pistol barrel onto the side of Jimmy's head saying, "Drop the shotgun or you will die right here in your own pew before you can take another breath, you outlaw son-of-a-bitch!"

Jimmy, totally surprised over having a pistol barrel shoved onto the side of his head with such 'authority' and upon hearing the cold steel in Lewis's voice, flat 'exploded' in surprise! Instead of dropping the shotgun, Jimmy in total terror knowing what was coming next if he failed to obey Lewis's command, tossed his shotgun out into his front yard in total terror! BOOM-BOOM! went the tossed shotgun when it hit the hard ground, having being tossed cocked and ready to fire! When the tossed shotgun went off, the close at hand explosion shocked the nearby horses into bucking and 'crow-hopping' all around in the front yard! When they did, Davis and Big Charlie Johnson, surprised as much as were their horses, were immediately bucked off and fell beneath the horses' flashing hooves! However, Buzzard Creek, just waiting for any chance to escape, kicked his horse hard in its flanks and broke away from the rest of the bucking and milling horses!

Down the road fled Buzzard Creek, as Joe found himself unhorsed in the melee and subsequently tossed onto Jimmy's picket fence in the front of the ranch house yard. However, Nando being a better horseman than most and having been in the saddle since age three, broke from the pack of 'exploding' horses and went right after Buzzard Creek like greased lightning! Down the road thundered Buzzard Creek and right behind him streaked Nando on his fast moving bay. Rounding a bend in the road leading out from the Jenkins ranch, Buzzard Creek found himself all of a sudden being violently unhorsed when Nando swung the end of his rifle barrel onto the back of Buzzard Creek's head! That crushing blow knocked Buzzard Creek out cold and launched him from his saddle into a mess of brush lining the side of the road, landing him in a cloud of dust with a hard-sounding WHOOMP!

Meanwhile back at the ranch house, as Joe recovered from being unhorsed onto the top of a picket fence, hurriedly mounted up and took off down the road after Nando and a fleeing Buzzard Creek. Lewis and James however, stayed back at the ranch house holding the rest of their prisoners at bay. Moments later, Joe rode up onto a scene that made him smile and further convinced him of Nando's innocence when it came to Jenkins's nefarious activities while in cahoots with Buzzard

Creek. There he found Nando dragging an inert and still out like a light Buzzard Creek over the saddle of his horse for a return trip back to the ranch house…

Riding up, Joe said, "Need any help, Partner?"

"Nah, just loaded this son-of-a-bitch like one would do a 'tote sack' of corn, and he didn't seem to mind or object in the process. So I just figured since he wasn't too full of fight with a busted nose from an earlier fight in which he lost and a cracked skull at the end of my Henry rifle just now, I would just load his miserable carcass like one would do a sack of field corn," said a grinning Nando Mauldin, pleased over his 'capture accomplishment' of one mean son-of-a-bitch.

Somewhat later and back at the ranch house while Lewis cooked supper from the victuals he found in Jimmy's ranch house kitchen as James stood guard over their prisoners, Joe had Nando write down his statement of testimony regarding what he knew about Jimmy's nefarious illegal activities with Buzzard Creek. Later after supper was had by all, Buzzard Creek, Davis Johnson, Big Charlie Johnson and now Jimmy Jenkins, all had their manacles checked, making sure they were locked but not too tight on the wrists of the prisoners. Then Joe made sure each prisoner was leg-chained to each other so none could run without one hell of a lot of difficulty, even if they found a way to rid themselves of their manacles…

Taking four-hour shifts watching over the prisoners, the men slept in Jimmy's ranch house that evening. The following morning as Lewis cooked breakfast using some more of Jimmy's foodstuffs from his kitchen and some farm fresh ranch eggs from the hen house, breakfast was had by all. Then the horses were grained and watered, all of jimmy's livestock were let out to roam free as were his chickens, and then the marshals headed out on their way back to Fort Smith with their prisoners. As for Nando, he had other plans and headed north to return to his folks' ranch to see if they needed a 'good hand' during their fall round-up.

However, before Nando left the company of the prisoners and his three friends, Joe made him promise to telegraph Marshal Fagan at Fort Smith, leave information as to his whereabouts in case he was needed to testify or be located, and at the same time request the federally offered rewards on Buzzard Creek, Davis Johnson and Big Charlie Johnson. That he was urged to do because Deputy U.S. Marshals could not collect rewards offered federally. Rewards offered by private entities like banks, stage lines, railroads and the like, Deputy U.S. Marshals could collect. However, since they were on the federal payroll, they could not collect any federal reward monies offered for the arrest and convictions of federally wanted men or women. Joe did so with Nando because there was a federal reward of $10,000 for Buzzard Creek and $5,000 each for his sons for the killings, robberies, stealing of horses and rapes that they had committed. Bottom line, when Nando telegraphed Marshal Fagan with his request for the reward monies, Joe, Lewis and James had paved the way through their recent case reports for Nando to collect such monies. In so doing, since most working men made only $300-500 per year, Nando stood to receive a rather princely sum. When he did, that meant he could purchase the needed lands for his own dream ranch… (Author's Note: Today, Nando's family ranch is still a working cattle ranch in the State of Oklahoma.)

Two days later found the Dodsons dropping their prisoners off at the Fort Smith jail facility, turning in their case reports to Marshal Fagan, and then heading to Ma Silvia's boardinghouse for some welcome hot baths after just bathing in creeks, along with some of her great home cooking. Also planned after the meals was their reunion with the always happy Miss Betsy Davis, her great personality and a plan to keep her busy serving a number of Sylvia's great, 'never could get enough of them' homemade pies!

A week later, the Dodsons appeared in Judge Parker's court and offered their testimony as to

Buzzard Creek, Davis Johnson and Big Charlie Johnson's criminal activities. All three of those men were found guilty of their crimes and were hung five days later for murder, robbing stages, stealing horses and their several cases of rape. Come the day of their hangings, all three men wilted in the face of meeting their maker and had to be carried up the 13 steps onto the gallows, and since none could stand on their own due to their forthcoming fear of dying, had to be dropped through the opening and hung while tied down in a sitting position in wooden chairs! Watching the event, the Dodsons just shook their heads over the three men's behavior in the face of meeting there 'Maker'. It appeared from all of their actions while up on the gallows, that they weren't so tough after all unless they could bully other less fortunate souls with their numbers and using the business end of a Winchester rifle to get their points across... As for Jimmy Jenkins, he was sentenced to 30 years in federal prison for his collusion with Buzzard Creek in the horse theft and sale operations. He died many years later from a congenital heart condition while still in prison.

CHAPTER TEN

THE DEPUTY U.S. MARSHAL ODYSSEY ENDS BECAUSE LIFE IS NEVER PROMISED

While at the U.S. Marshals' Fort Smith blacksmith shop getting all their horses and mules reshod and their chuck wagon refurbished in preparation for their anticipated next assignment, Joe was summoned out from such work by another Deputy U.S. Marshal who had a serious look spelled clear across his face.

"Joe, Marshal Fagan sent me to fetch you and your brothers. Something very serious and unusual has come up and he told me to run you fellas down and send all of you over to his office immediately," said the deputy. Joe, realizing that Marshal Fagan was always 'serious business' when it came to his law enforcement operations, called forth his brothers and they hustled their way over to the marshal's office.

Arriving at Marshal Fagan's office somewhat later, Joe knocked on his door and was asked in by the Chief Marshal's booming voice. As Joe and his brothers walked in and sat down in front of the Chief Marshal's big oaken desk, they all could see that he was clearly searching their faces as if looking for something. Looking for 'something' that would tell him that what he was about to do, was wise or even justified under the unusual circumstances he now found himself facing.

Realizing that he could think better with a chew of tobacco between his teeth and gums, Marshal Fagan removed a small brick of Brown's Mule chewing tobacco from his vest pocket, bit off a chunk and sloshed it around in his mouth so that it finally fit comfortably therein. Putting the remaining chew back into his vest pocket, he decided to let the Dodson deputies hear what he had to say straightaway and without any 'flowers' in the tone of his voice, so he could better judge their reactions and so, he 'let her' fly.

"That Confederate son-of-a-bitch Colonel Jackson and a number of his men, the ones who killed your Pa, Ma and two sisters several years back, have recently escaped from their federal prison and are now on the run in the Indian Territory and up to their usual mischief! The one and same damn gang of outlaws the three of you brought into Fort Smith under citizen's arrest for murdering your kin and stealing a herd of your cattle. If that isn't enough of an issue, those dolts over at the federal prison failed to notify this office right away when that occurred! Instead, they went looking for those desperadoes by themselves thinking they were hiding somewhere close at hand, and because they were so embarrassed over the fact that so many of them had escaped all at the same time and manner. The fact is, by those prison dolts messing around with that escape and then trying to round all of them up, all that did was allow the escapees time to put a lot of country between them and the long arm of the law. Now our work is made doubly difficult because those bastards have had another taste of freedom and are reportedly running amuck breaking every federal law in the books. Additionally, I have my suspicions that the ex-Confederate military officer who is also an attorney and had originally defended his previous commanding officer, your Colonel Jackson, had something to do with those escapes. As we speak, I have dispatched a couple of marshals over to where that attorney lives so that he can damn well answer some questions regarding this surprisingly well-planned escape. An escape which I am told included horses and trail provisions ready for them, so when they overpowered their guards and fled the scene, their get-away would be successful."

Upon hearing those surprising words, the Dodsons sat slowly upright in their chairs and the collective looks upon their faces spelled trouble with a capital "T", for both sides, especially if they were the deputies asked to pursue, arrest and bring before Judge Parker the recently escaped federal prisoners just identified!

"I hesitated to call you boys and put you on this case because of the history you have with a number of that bunch of killers, but who better to put on their trails than several of my deputies who have an agenda when it comes to bringing this bunch of miscreants back to justice once again?" said Marshal Fagan, as he continued seriously studying the faces of his three deputies looking for any signs of emotion or reactions over the information he had just relayed to them.

Seeing just looks of determination and a showing of distinct signs of a 'hunter of humans' serious look creeping across the faces of his three deputies, Marshal Fagan made up his mind to go with the three men on this assignment and with that decision, set his capture plans into motion. "Boys, the information I have just received from a Tribal Elder from the Caddo Nation, is that this bunch of escaped outlaws has just set up their base of operations in the Smithville area in the southeastern part of the Indian Territory. A piece of geography that just happens to be conveniently

adjacent to the gang's newly reported area of livestock rustling predations. Additionally, word is
they have teamed up with six known and rather
ruthless Caddo Indian renegades and this entire
bunch is now into the cattle rustling business in a
very serious sort of way. However, there is a new
twist to their method of operations. According to
several local Arkansas sheriffs, these outlaws are
preying on local isolated ranchers in their state,
killing the owners, rustling their cattle and then
spiriting the stolen beeves back into the Indian
Territory or all the way down to Texas. Once
there, they are selling the same to anyone who
has the money and is not too keen on asking any
questions as to where the cattle came from, their
lack of having any Bills of Sale or the brands they
are wearing."

Turning in his chair, Marshal Fagan then spit
a long, black-tar like-looking stream of tobacco
juice out his open second story window onto the
bushes below. Then turning back in his chair so
he could face his three now quietly determined-
looking deputies, he commenced once again with
his briefing on the Confederate Colonel and his
new Caddo Indian renegade partners. "I have an
old family friend named Larry Davis who lives in
the Smithville area who is also a rather prosperous cattleman. I have made secret arrangements
with him to make it look like he has taken you

three men and your partners on as out of work cowboys to help manage his rather extensive herds of cattle. Now hold your questions on my mention of your 'partners', for that information will soon be in the works. In that capacity as cattlemen for Davis, I expect the three of you to gather what intelligence you can from the locals in the Smithville area and use your own discretion and judgment as to when to 'drop the hammer' on these cattle rustling sons-a-bitches once you have them in your sights."

Pausing in his briefing and not seeing any sign of concern in the faces or eyes of his three deputies, Marshal Fagan continued saying, "Now keep in mind, these six Caddo Indian members of that cattle rustling ring, as reported to me by my friend the Tribal Elder, are as mean and vicious as any nest of trampled-upon snakes in the hot west Texas July sun! With that extra danger in mind, if those Indians give you any trouble during this investigation, between you, me and the outhouse, don't be afraid to burn a little 'serious' powder in order to keep them in line or making sure that the three of you stay alive! Also, my Caddo Tribal Elder does not have any problem if those renegade 'war-hoops' ever return to his Tribal rolls and neither do I." Then Marshal Fagan quietly said, "Just make sure any Indian killing that is called for is done all legal-looking and proper-like," with a measure of stone cold steel and frontier justice in the tone and tenor of his voice… Then, it was time again to spit out the window the amount of tobacco juice he had accumulated in his mouth while going through the briefing machinations with his deputies.

"Now according to several of those local Arkansas sheriffs, these ex-Confederate Colonel-led cattle rustlers are working primarily in the areas immediately adjacent to the Dutch Creek Mountains of Arkansas. They are using the forested cover of the mountains to hide not only their campsites but to mask their stolen cattle movements across the State of Arkansas and into the Indian Territory. As I am also told, these rustlers' method of operation is to move along hiding in the Dutch Creek Mountains, locate a small isolated rancher adjacent those mountains, swoop down, kill the rancher or his hired hands, and then drive the cattle along several well-used backwoods trails westward into the Indian Territory. Then if the rustled cattle herd is large enough or are valuable registered stock, they drive them all the way deep into Texas where they are sold for the highest dollar to less than discriminating buyers. Then it is into several of the towns along the way in the Indian Territory or in western Arkansas to celebrate and spend their money on drink, the faro table and women.

Then when they are almost broke, it is back into the Dutch Creek Mountains scouting out the next promising herd of cattle they are aiming to rustle, and so forth and so on," continued Fagan with more than just a lilt of disgust in the tone and tenor of his voice.

Then it was time to again 'dust' the bushes below his second story open window with his powerful Brown's Mule chewing tobacco juice. Turning to face his deputies once again after spitting out his window, Marshal Fagan gave his men another warning about the dangerous law enforcement mission they would soon be facing saying, "Boys, I expect that sooner or later, you will be moving about in some of your old stomping grounds near your home of Booneville pursuing these ex-Confederate hombres and their Caddo Indian renegades. That being said, you need to keep your heads down so the locals who know of your new law enforcement roles don't give you or your presence away by spreading the word that you three are 'U.S. Marshaling about in country'. With that in mind, I have taken the liberty of not even informing the local sheriffs of your whereabouts in their own backyards for your safety and the success of your latest assignment. However, that can be a double-edged sword. By not informing the local law enforcement, they may mistakenly think you and your partners are the rustlers or in your time of need, may not be close enough at hand to help out. Like I said, that can be a double-edged sword! So the three of you and your partners will be pretty much on your own and facing at least nine or ten cattle rustlers and killers of the most dangerous kind."

Pausing to let those words of warning sink in, Marshal Fagan commenced saying, "Bear in mind that the Colonel had made it known before he escaped that he would never ever again return to a Yankee prison! Saying that he would die first before submitting again to Judge Parker's Yankee justice system or incarceration in some stinking federal prison! With those words from your main subject of law enforcement concern, I would suggest that all of you head down to the marshals' armory here in town and make sure you requisition whatever you think you might need in the way of added firepower for this mission and then some."

Pausing to get his 'wind', Marshal Fagan began once again by saying, "Now about your mystery partners on this detail that I glossed over earlier in our briefing. Since you will be facing the possibility of arresting some renegade Caddo Indians and in accordance with Tribal arrest policies, I am assigning two Indian Police Officers to accompany the three of you on this assignment. I know you know and respect Indian Policeman Tom Johns and he will be one of the Indian officers that I will be sending along with the three of you."

Then it was once again time to spit out the window, only that time most of the tobacco juice ended up on the window frame and wall... Making a loud 'harrumph' sound over his obvious miss on his stream of tobacco juice, Marshal Fagan continued along like nothing out of the ordinary had just happened saying, "Then there is another Indian Policeman I would like to send along with you fellas as a little extra insurance. That Indian Policeman I have in mind to send along with you fellas is known among his kind as not only an excellent tracker but a damn 'good hand' when it comes to using a Winchester rifle, knife or his favorite choice of weapon, his tomahawk! Not only that, the man I have in mind is not very big in size, but is quick as a 'tossed cat' and strong as a double-span of oxen when it comes to feats of physical endurance or even having to use his fists. This Indian Policeman's name is Chief Many Hats Peltier and he is a Turtle Mountain Chippewa who is far from his home in the Dakota Territory. But how he got here and is working as an Indian Policeman in the Indian Territory is a story for another time. Just remember, put your trust in him because his reputation as a truly dedicated and competent lawman is nothing short of outstanding, even by white men's standards!"

Pausing once again to spit, then realizing his cud of previously chewed tobacco was now just about worn out, he spit it out the window, reloaded with another fresh chaw and then commenced with, "Here are your Writs of Arrest from Judge Parker for the Colonel and his fellow escapees. Being that these men, if you are able to bring them back alive, are going to face Judge Parker once again, I doubt many if any will see many more sunrises when he gets through with them! Tom Johns and Peltier already have the Writs needed issued by their own people for this detail pertaining to the six Caddos, providing those renegades survive the arrest procedures as well. Additionally, here is the name and address of my friend and cattleman you five will be using as your cover who lives near the Smithville area. Just bear in mind, these men one and all are very dangerous outlaws and with their being on the run, I doubt any will surrender or submit to your arrests. With that in mind, I am authorizing you three deputies an extra allotment of ammunition for your rifles and handguns of choice. I would also suggest since you three deputies are only carrying a single pistol apiece, that you consider carrying two handguns each at the very least for this assignment."

"Now, don't you damn men have something to do other than stand around all day in my office, cluttering it up and looking like a mess of crows sitting on a telegraph line waiting for a long-dead jack rabbit to show itself along the road as their next meal?" grumbled Marshal Fagan. Then as an afterthought, Marshal Fagan said, "Oh by the way, don't forget to draw an extra allotment of riding horses and pack mules for this detail from the marshals' livery as part of your provisions. Since Chino will not be making this trip because his chuck wagon would be a dead giveaway, you men need to count on taking your own provisions along, especially if part of the detail is spent camping out or on a long stakeout waiting for this mess of rustlers and killers to show themselves and cross your paths."

Then there was a knock at the Marshal's Office door and in walked Indian Policemen Tom Johns and Chief Many Hats Peltier. The marshal made the introduction of Peltier to his three deputies and then the five men headed for the armory and livery to requisition what they figured they would need in the way of fire and horse power for their dangerous and upcoming law enforcement assignment.

Two days later found the five lawmen heading south to Smithville and the Larry Davis ranch so they could use it as a 'cover' to explain

away their physical presence in a strange community, until word came down that the Colonel
had struck once again and then the hunt by the
lawmen would be on. Trailing behind the five
'out of work cowboys' were five hell for stout
packhorses fully loaded for what the men figured
would be at least a full month's law enforcement
detail in the outback. Two more days of travel
found the 'out of work cowboys' arriving at the
Larry Davis cattle ranch and after introductions
were made all around, the men were shown a
bunkhouse they could call their own for the duration of their assignment that could be used to
further their cover while 'on the hunt'.

For the next two weeks, Joe and his crew of
lawmen helped Larry Davis with his cattle as a
means to provide for their cover, being that they
were strangers in the area and all. Then come
the weekends the five men scattered to the four
winds, using their covers as cowboys working
for local rancher Larry Davis, with their noses
to the ground hoping to pick up clues as to the
whereabouts of Colonel Jackson and his bunch
of rustling and rancher-killing outlaws. As part
of their plan, Joe had the white men of his group
frequent the boardinghouses, saloons, stables
and any other places frequented by the public,
looking for any clues as to the whereabouts of
the men they were hunting. As for the Indian

Policemen operating undercover, they visited those places frequented by the several tribes of Indians in the area, looking for any leads on the six Caddo Indians allegedly running with Colonel Jackson and his bunch of cattle-rustling and murdering outlaws.

At the end of that first two-week period and without any results leading the lawmen any closer to the outlaws they were hunting, Joe came up with another plan. One Saturday morning after the men had finished eating their breakfast meal, Joe sat all of them down in their bunkhouse and advised there was a change of plans in the offing. Sitting around their breakfast table with cups of coffee in hand, Joe laid out his proposed plans by saying, "Gentlemen, we have not made much headway in the intelligence gathering department over the last two weeks regarding Colonel Jackson and his band of merry outlaws' location or most recent operations."

Pausing to let that change of direction comment sink in with his men, Joe continued saying, "That being the case, I would like to suggest a radical change in our operations. Being somewhat familiar with the area where Colonel Jackson and his bunch are operating, I would like to change our current means of operations for a different strategy. When me and my brothers lived in Booneville, Arkansas, it was standard practice for some of our fellow cattlemen and neighbors to move their cattle to the Indian Territory's markets by driving them westward in the large valley between the Dutch Creek and Caddo Mountain ranges toward the town of Mena. From Mena, those smaller herds from the area would be driven to market, not to the stockyards in Kansas, but westward into the local markets that supplied either the U.S. Army and/or the always hungry tribal markets."

Pausing in his dissertation, Joe could see that all of his men were intently listening to the plan's rollout, so without any questions coming his way, he kept going saying, "I would like to suggest that we establish a campsite somewhere either at the southern edge of the Dutch Creek Mountains or on the north side of the Caddo Mountain range that allows us to observe any cattle movements occurring across the valley floor between those two ranges of mountains. Marshal Fagan's intelligence was that the men we are hunting would ride along both mountain ranges seeking out the smaller cattle spreads, kill the local ranchers and make off with their livestock heading westward towards the Indian Territory. In so doing, those cattle rustled would more than likely be driven straight down the valley between those two mountain ranges, being that would be the shortest and easiest route to travel to the Indian

Territory or even further south to the Texas markets."

Then 'running dry', Joe took a sip of his now cooling coffee and then continued saying, "Therefore, I suggest we establish our campsite as out of work cowboys just east of the town of Mena near the settlement of Board Camp. That way, we will be smack dab in the middle of the large valley that 'drains' the areas between the Dutch Creek Mountains and those of the Caddo Mountain range. There would be no way that any herd of cattle, no matter how small in number, could be moved by us if we occupied a campsite in that area, without us observing the same. That way we could surreptitiously monitor any herd of beeves moving toward the Indian Territory via that valley and ascertain if it is the Colonel and his band moving them. Then upon their discovery, we could tail them and when they made camp for the night, pick off their night herders one by one. That way we could lessen the numbers of opposition that we would be facing when we finally decided to spring our trap. Following that picking off of the 'nighthawks' guarding the resting herd, we could then approach the remainder of the men in camp, hopefully surprise them as they slept and arrest the lot without any serious incident. What do you guys think of that plan?" he asked.

Upon being asked that question, there was a murmur of obvious approval by all the men except from Chief Many Hats Peltier. He remained very quiet as if digesting every aspect of Joe's proposed new strategy. Then Peltier looked Joe straight into his eyes saying, "I like the plan but would make one modification to it."

"Yeah, what would your modification be regarding any changes to that plan, Chief?" asked Joe, remembering what Marshal Fagan had said earlier about that Indian Officer's expertise as a well-respected lawman.

"If anyone is assigned the job of picking off the 'nighthawks' guarding a suspect stolen herd come nightfall, I would suggest that be me. My specialty is that of not being seen no matter how hard one looks out for me. If we are successful in locating the Colonel and his men, that job of removing the threat from those riding 'nighthawk' should fall to me," stridently said Chief Many Hats.

Upon hearing those words and again remembering Marshal Fagan's report on the law enforcement and Native American survival abilities of Chief Many Hats, Joe just smiled and nodded his head in the affirmative saying, "Chief, if we are able to get an angle on the Colonel and his men, the detail of 'molly-hocking' the 'nighthawks' will be your baby…"

That afternoon as the lawmen prepared for the next portion of their journey as per Joe's suggestion, Joe met with Larry Davis and explained that they would be leaving the next day in their attempt to intercept the Colonel and his band of outlaws, and put them in the business of terrorizing the local Arkansas cattlemen out of business! Larry asked if there was anything that he could do to help rid the area of the cattle rustling scourge and Joe replied in the affirmative. In response to Joe's request for aid, Larry had his ranch cook provide several sacks of pinto beans, white rice, flour, coffee and sugar. Additionally, Larry's cook provided a gallon tin of lard for cooking and a host of spices to the lawman for their anticipated detail that lay ahead.

Daylight the next morning found the lawmen's string of horses and pack animals strung out along the trail as they headed, led by Joe who knew the way, towards the small Arkansas town of Board Camp. Two days of travel later found the horses of the lawmen drawn up in front of a long-abandoned and run-down homesteader's shack just to the east of the Board Camp settlement. The homesteader's shack was somewhat run-down but it would do in a pinch, thought Joe, as he looked the structure over. However, what had really caught Joe's eye in the out of the way location was a hell for stout corral suitable for holding all of their horses.

By nightfall, the five lawmen had cleaned out all of the wood rat leavings inside the long-abandoned homesteader's shack, had built an outside firepit for cooking most of their meals, laid out a bedding area for all of the men, and had unloaded all of their valuable packs holding their provisions inside the shack where they would at least be under a roofed-over area in case of the occurrence of any afternoon thunderstorms.

Then the routine and rotation stakeouts of the lawmen began on a dawn-to-dusk set of assignments. Every day, different teams of two men each rode to the northern and southern reaches of their valley's cattle trail constriction point before it opened up, leading directly into the nearby Indian Territory. Once there, the lawmen would set up their concealed observation points allowing them to oversee any cattle traffic moving along the established trails. That left one man always back at their abandoned homesteader's shack and campsite to watch over their extra horses and their stacks of provisions. Additionally, the man left behind was the designated camp cook for that day and expected to have the evening meal planned out and prepared for the returning men, who because of their isolated situations, had not eaten anything since breakfast in order to maintain their 'out of sight because they were strangers in the area' presence.

However, Joe's stakeout plan proved to be a good one. The valley floor was worn to dust by several old cattle trails leading out from the many small cattle ranches located along the eastern reaches of the valley between the Dutch Creek and Caddo Mountain ranges. Cattle trails which were all heading westerly toward the Indian Territory and the major north-south routes of travel leading from Texas to the Kansas stockyards. It soon became apparent that if anyone trailed any cattle along the now watched established cattle trails, they would be spotted and then the surreptitious trailing of each herd by the lawmen could begin until the identification of its owner and drovers could be made.

Then the long and boring wait began and did not end until the morning of the thirteenth day of their joint stakeouts. During morning's breakfast on that thirteenth day, the thundering sounds of many nearby horses' hooves could be heard off in the distance of the valley. Scrambling for their binoculars tied to each man's saddles previously tossed over the corral's rails to dry out from their use the day before, the front yard of the old homesteader's cabin for a quick moment looked like a rat race to their burrows with a hungry hawk circling high overhead! Finally the men were able to grab their binoculars from off their saddles and observe eleven riders riding hard into the western end of their valley and then into the Dutch Creek Mountains on another well-used trail leading north to the Waldron area!

Then Lewis was heard to exclaim, "By damn, it's the ones we are looking for! Look at that tall skinny guy leading the pack. Sure as shooting, that is that damn ex-Confederate Colonel that we hauled into Fort Smith several years back after they had raped and murdered our kin back at our home ranch! Now that son-of-a-bitch is going to pay for his boldness, if I have my say."

Then Tom Johns was heard to utter, "There are at least six Indians riding with that bunch of white men and if I were a betting man, I would bet they were the Caddo renegades reported to be riding with the Colonel!"

Looking through his binoculars, Joe was then then heard to remark, "Those riders are the ones we are looking for, that is for sure! Having those six Indians riding with them confirms that is our group as well as having that tall drink of water leading them, which more than matches my recollection of what Colonel Jackson looked like when we arrested him the first time!"

As the lawmen watched from a distance with their binoculars, the now identified Colonel and his men quickly moved off from the valley floor and into the timber of the Dutch Creek Mountains and then shortly thereafter, rode out of sight. "Chief Many Hats, I need you to saddle up and trail that bunch from a distance and ascertain where they are headed," said Joe in a now excited tone of voice. Continuing as Chief Many Hats ran to his saddle and then to the corral holding his horse so he could saddle up, Joe shouted out, "We will load the packhorses and follow the trail those men are leaving. Chief, we will stay on their trail until we meet up with you later on somewhere along their trail. Once we all get together again, we will put a 'capture' plan into play if at all possible," said Joe over his shoulder, as he began packing up their panniers and hurriedly loading all of them with their provisions. Within minutes Chief Many Hats was saddled up and then he was out the gate and riding hard towards where he had last seen the eleven riders entering the Dutch Creek Mountains timbered area.

An hour later, Joe had all the men and pack animals loaded and on their way towards the Dutch Creek Mountains as well. However when they moved out, Joe had assigned Indian Policeman Tom Johns to lead the rest of the lawmen and their pack strings because he was the second best Indian tracker in the group, and had already memorized what Chief Many Hats's horse's hoofprints looked like so he could more accurately track their 'point man'.

Riding across the valley floor and into the Dutch Creek Mountains, the lawmen rode with Tom Johns in the lead tracking the horse of Chief Many Hats and the group of eleven men's horses as well. Following closely along behind Tom Johns, who was mostly looking down at the tracks from atop the back of his horse, was Joe. As Joe was riding along behind Tom Johns, he remained alert to the surrounding country the lawmen were entering, on the lookout for any sign of an ambush by the eleven men they were now tracking and in so doing, protecting Tom Johns from being the first lawman killed if such an ambush was to occur.

It was now obvious to all of the concerned lawmen that the eleven riders were riding fast and heading in the direction of Waldron like they knew exactly where they were heading. Soon the lawmen had left the trail running through the forested area of the Dutch Creek Mountains and entered upon the main road running directly into the town of Waldron. Since darkness had now descended upon them, the lawmen slowed trailing the eleven men and were soon intercepted by Chief Many Hats, who had been waiting for the rest of his party just south of Waldron on the road's turnoff, which led northeasterly towards the hamlet of Danville, Arkansas. Being that it was now not possible to track the eleven outlaws due to the onset of darkness, the lawmen pulled their horses off the road a short ways and set up their cold camp out of sight from any casual nearby traveler. However by daylight the following morning, the chase was resumed with Chief Many Hats doing the principal tracking and Joe riding 'drag' to his Indian counterpart, as a guardian against any ambush by those being tracked in case they had left someone behind their route of travel to ascertain if they were being followed and if so, by whom.

Only this time, Joe had changed their pursuit plans slightly because he remembered what had happened to the Dodsons when they had originally set out to catch those who had killed his family back at their ranch house years earlier. On that occasion, the Dodsons had cold camped along the way only to awaken in the morning and discover that their horses were missing, having been taken by two of the Colonel's men who had been left behind to ascertain if their group was being followed. The killers, upon discovering they were being hotly pursued by the Dodsons, the two ex-military men left to ride 'drag' behind the main group of outlaws pushing the stolen cattle, took matters into their own hands. When the Dodson men were naively fast asleep, the two men from the Colonel's band of cattle rustlers had slipped back into their camp, stolen the

Dodsons' horses and left them afoot and unable to continue their pursuit and apprehend the thieves of their cattle and the killers of their kin!

Joe, remembering those series of sad events and lessons learned by the novice brothers from several years earlier, had turned Chief Many Hats loose on the day's tracking. However, he had also undertaken the simultaneous pursuit acting as his Indian tracker's extra set of eyes to preclude such a series of events from recurring when the main party of lawmen arrived and made camp that evening. This time if Joe discerned that they were being watched from afar by the Colonel's men riding 'drag', he wanted to make damn sure those men found Joe and others of his kind waiting for them when they tried to steal their pursuers' horses...

Sure as 'shooting', the Colonel, wise beyond his years because of his military experience, had once again dispatched two of his best outriders to remain as lookouts, before the main group of outlaws made camp for the evening further down the road. The purpose of those outriders left behind was to ascertain if they were being followed and if so, lay back until nightfall when the pursuers were fast asleep, slip into their camp and steal their horses, leaving those pursuers afoot and unable to further pursue the main bunch of rustlers!

Somewhat later as Chief Many Hats continued with his tracking duties, he all of a sudden stopped his horse in the middle of the road and dismounted. Then in a clear voice, Chief Many Hats said, "Damn, Joe, my horse is not acting like himself." Then Chief Many Hats inspected the horse's left rear leg's hamstring and then once again declared that his horse was starting to go lame and could not be ridden any further. Then with a nod of his head, Chief Many Hats turned his horse around and began walking it back in the direction they had just come. Joe, surprised over his tracker's actions but suspecting something was afoot, said nothing, turned his horse around as well and the two of them then walked their horses back out of sight around a bend in the road from whence they had come.

Once out of sight from the area where they had turned around, Chief Many Hats said, "Joe, a pair of horse tracks broke off from that main group we have been following and slipped off into the deep timber back where I stopped. I think that was a ruse on their part in order to watch their back trail and see if they had been followed. Seeing that, I pretended to have my horse go lame and that is why I walked him back around this bend where we could not be seen before we stopped and talked over what we now need to do. Thankfully you did not make an issue of what I was doing and I think our trick worked. Now, I will bet come dark, those two riders will come back this way on their horses to make sure we are no longer in country. If they do, you and I need to be waiting for them and capture that pair if at all possible. If we can do that, we will only be facing the odds of nine of them against the five of us, plus spoil their little 'watching their back trail' plan. What do you think?" said Chief Many Hats.

Joe just smiled over what had just taken place. Sure as Marshal Fagan had said, Chief Many Hats was one hell of a good lawman! Leaving Chief Many Hats there out of sight, Joe sped his horse back down the road to where the rest of his party was plodding along waiting for Joe and Chief Many Hats to return to them with the evening's battle plan. There Joe had the party hold up, ride their horses off the road into the timber and out of sight. Then advising the men to wait until he and Chief Many Hats returned, back Joe sped to where he had left his best tracker hidden in the dense brush lining the edge of the road.

Once back together, Joe hid his horse and then joined Chief Many Hats in the dense brush along the roadside and waited. Sure as predicted once darkness settled over the land, Joe and Chief Many Hats could hear the almost muffled sounds of two horses coming their way down the road! Soon softly muffled voices could be heard discussing the two unidentified riders with the horse that had gone lame. Additionally the voices could be heard discussing what they would be having for their supper once back with the Colonel and the rest of their band…

With their suspicions confirmed about the identity of the two riders now approaching their locations where Joe was hidden alongside one side of the road and Chief Many Hats on the other, the two men waited to spring their ambush on the approaching and now having been identified as two riders from Colonel Jackson's band of murderous and cattle rustling outlaws.

When the two riders were alongside where Joe and Chief Many Hats lay in wait, Joe exploded from his place in hiding in the brush and using his rifle stock, smashed it into the side of the head of his rider! "OOOFF!" went the rider in the dark on Joe's side of the road, followed by a loud WHOOMP! when his crumpled body left his saddle and hit the roadbed!

"WHAT THE HELL!" yelled the rider on Chief Many Hats's side of the road, followed by his yell, "RUN, WE ARE BEING AMBUSHED!" With those words, the man in the dark still on his horse on Chief Many Hat's side of the road spurred its flanks and exploded into a hoped-for escape from the ambush! WHACK! went the crunching sound of what could only be interpreted as the sound of metal on bone, followed by a very audible groan and then another loud WHOOMP! as a large body hit the roadway! Then Chief Many Hats quickly got control of the man's spooked horse as Joe did the same with his man's horse on the other side of the road. However, it took Chief Many Hats a few minutes to pry the deeply sunken blade of his tomahawk from the side of the man's head that he had just killed. When he tried to escape on his horse, Joe's star tracker had seen to it that it was that man's last run...

Joe and Chief Many Hats carried the two dead men off into the timber far enough away from the road so their eventual decaying body smells would not be noticed by other travelers. Then with the two outlaws' horses in tow, the two lawmen rode slowly back to where the rest of their group was cold camped. Joe made the mental observation that both men they had just killed when they were approaching the 'ambush' site, were speaking in soft southern drawls. To his way of thinking, just further affirmation that they had the right group of outlaws in their sights. That evening, the men rested uneasily for what the morrow would bring. However, the outlaw odds against them were now a manageable nine outlaws to five lawmen...

The following morning found the lawmen

and their packhorses heading down the road towards Danville. However, just before arriving at the burg of Danville, Chief Many Hats riding in the far lead, noticed that the remaining nine suspect men turned off just past the small hamlet of Blue Ball and were now heading north on the road leading toward Waveland. Keeping to the brush and timber along the roads so they would not run into any locals or backtracking men from the suspect bunch of outlaws on the road looking for the two now dead men who had been assigned to ride drag on the lookout for any pursuers the day before, the lawmen bypassed Waveland. However, the lawmen doggedly continued following the outlaws tracks as they headed in the direction of the small settlement of Blue Mountain.

Then it dawned on Joe, Lewis and James almost at the same time as to where their cattle rustlers might be heading! "Damn," said Lewis, "do you suppose those bastards are heading for Joseph Meek's place in order to rustle his herd of cattle? In fact, the same herd of cattle Dad had us boys drive to his place and sell to Joe years ago?" he asked almost randomly of those around him, as if wondering himself over such a possibility.

"Meek was the only cattleman in the area when we were here several years ago," replied James. "Do you suppose those bastards are going to steal Meek's cattle and then drive them across Arkansas towards Poteau in the Indian Territory to sell?" he asked himself out loud.

"Guys, if that is our outlaws' plans, that means they will have to drive them right past our father's home ranch before they can make their escape into Indian Territory! The last time we knew, our brother David and his hired hand Sam are the only men on the ranch with the two ladies that James and Lewis hope to marry when they finish with this being a marshal 'thing'," said Joe. "Do you suppose they are going to sweep across our little valley, strip all the local ranchers of their cattle in one giant sweep and then drive them into the Indian Territory to be sold? Remember, this is where all of this started with Colonel Jackson stealing our dad's cattle, killing him and then moving on to our home ranch and raping and killing our mother and two sisters," said Joe quietly, in a tone of voice that now carried a deadly tone of suspicion of what might be coming!

"Damn! If that happens our two fiancés are staying at our home ranch with David until we can come home and marry them!" loudly exclaimed James and Lewis all at the same time, after hearing what Joe had to say and then had put 'two and two together' themselves!

"If that is the Colonel's plan, sure as all get-out,

that means he means to eventually steal all of our cattle that David is keeping for us, after he takes all of Meek's livestock as well. If that is what is going to happen, then his group will probably kill David and Sam, then rape and kill your wives-to-be, if he follows his old pattern of murdering and raping all those he steals cattle from," said Joe softly with the deadly realization over the possibility of what he had just 'unearthed'!

"Follow me, Boys," said Joe, as he led his horse off the road and into the dark timber alongside the road. Soon, all of the lawmen had hidden and tied off their horses in the darkened wooded glen where they would be out of sight from any-one else traveling along the nearby road. Then Joe gathered all the men around him saying, "I know a shortcut over to Meek's ranch. I sug-gest we head that way, wait for the Colonel to start stealing that man's herd of cattle and then ambush him in the act of rustling. I figure with the element of surprise, we can shoot a number of those outlaws out from their saddles from ambush with our Sharps rifles before they even know we are anywhere close at hand! That way, we can even up the odds even further, round up the Colonel and what is left of his command, and take the bunch back to Fort Smith so Judge Parker can hang the lot so the world is rid of their kind. Any questions?" asked Joe. Moments later, the lawmen were picking their ways through a dense mountain forest on their way over to Meek's cattle ranch so they could ambush the Colonel and his kind and be done with what needed doing...

༚◦ؤ

"Colonel, what do you reckon happened to Darrel and Len? You dispatched those two days ago to watch our backsides and now look what has happened. I'll bet them two rode into the nearest saloon, got drunk as skunks, then got throwed into the 'hoosegow' for being drunk and disorderly, and now there they sit," said 'Corporal' Black.

"I suppose you are right, Corporal," said Colonel Jackson. "I never should have let those two go off on an assignment without you riding along to keep them in line," he continued. "However, that was then and this is now. We are reduced in numbers but I think we can still steal this man's herd of cattle, drive them down the road to that damn Yankee's home ranch where we killed that old man some years back, and steal his herd as well. Then we can ransack the ranch house for whatever we can find of use and then be on our way toward the Indian Territory and then out of harm's way from any law wanting to chase us," replied Colonel Jackson.

A half-hour later, Colonel Jackson and his

group of outlaws and renegade Indians rode up into Meek's front yard and then sat there on their horses waiting for him to come out from his ranch house and be 'hospitable'.

Hearing a passel of horses out front in his yard, Joseph Meek got up from his table, walked down his ranch house hallway and out onto the front porch. Seeing three white men and six Indians quietly sitting on their horses looking at him, Meek said, "Good Morning. What can I do for you men?" he asked. His question was answered by a single shot from the Colonel's pistol, dropping him where he stood on his porch being 'hospitable'!

"Now, let's get them beeves and be on our way afore them local 'law dogs' get wind of what we are a-doing and get on our trail," said the Colonel as he holstered his still-smoking pistol, whirled his horse around and started out into Meek's south pasture to help his men round up the cattle and start driving them down the back road toward the Indian Territory.

Just at dusk, making slower time than he had counted on in getting Meek's cattle gathered up and on their way, the Colonel rode ahead of his men to another fenced pasture, jumped off his horse, unlocked the gate and helped wave Meek's stolen herd of cattle inside its protective fences. Then standing there for a few moments, the Colonel's memory drifted back to the morning several years previously, when he and his men had first invaded that same pasture to rustle the cattle contained therein. There they had cut the fence, hell bent on rustling the landowner's herd of registered cattle before he even knew it was happening. However, it just so happened, the landowner, one Albert Dodson was in the same pasture looking his cattle over and checking out his new cow-calf relationships. Seeing the ex-Confederate Colonel, the one still 'fighting' the Civil War, and his men cutting his fences, Albert, an ex-Yankee Captain, rose to the occasion and intercepted the men trying to rustle his cattle. In so doing, he managed to kill two of the ex-Confederate cattle rustlers but paid the price with his life! Angry over the loss of two of his men, Colonel Jackson had his men raid Albert's ranch house and in the process, they raped his two young daughters and wife and then killed the same so there would be no witnesses!

Then the Colonel's face clouded over as his memory once again took him back to those days thereafter. As it turned out, Albert had four grown sons, three of whom pursued him and his men and eventually caught a number of them including the Colonel, had them prosecuted in Judge Parker's court and subsequently sent to prison! Then the Colonel's face brightened in the fading daylight as he looked down at the distant ranch house as he had done from that very spot where he now stood years earlier when they had initially rustled Albert's cattle. Here he was taking not only Meek's cattle but planned on taking Dodson's cattle in the pasture where he now stood the next morning as well. Then ironically, his eyes fell upon the distant ranch house as a sinister look slowly crossed his face. As his men finished running all of Meek's stolen cattle into Dodson's pasture, the Colonel with his sinister smile returning and now slowly crossing his face said, "Come here, Boys. I think I have a treat in store for the lot of you."

"Boys, when some of my boys and me hit this pasture some years back, we ended up with all of the owner's cattle that time as well. Then we headed down to his ranch house after killing the landowner and raided the place. While there, my men also raped the three good looking women who occupied the ranch that evening several years back. What say we pay that place a visit, since we can't push these cattle no more this evening, and see what pleasures that place will yield this time around?" said the Colonel with a sinister smile.

Closing the gate to the cattle pasture, the Colonel mounted up and turning said, "Follow me, Boys, and let us see what kind of treasures we find in that ranch house this time." With that, he set the spurs to his horse and the three white men and six Caddo Indians rode their horses down to the ranch house and into its front yard. As the men dismounted, they could see through the front windows of the ranch house illuminated by oil lamps, two women in the kitchen happily making homemade pies and bread.

As the men bunched in behind the Colonel and headed towards the front porch and the door leading into the kitchen, Dale Black, an original rider with the Colonel said, "Last time I was here I managed to bed all three of the women in this house before we kilt them all. Tonight, I am going to bed those two women before those 'Injuns' get to them and despoil them in such a manner where a white man would be turned away from partaking any of what they would leave when they are through."

Then the nine men burst through the front door from out of the darkness, sending the two surprised and now alarmed women screaming and running down a hallway for the safety of their bedrooms! As the men entered the warm and great-smelling kitchen of homemade bread and pie smells, the group mass-gathered around the table holding the numerous cooling loaves of bread and pies and like a mess of wild hogs who had not fed for a while, descended upon the baked goods and began gorging themselves...

After a few minutes of gorging down huge chunks of hot, just from the oven, homemade bread, Dale Black and Donald Rice, two of the Colonel's original Confederate sidekicks, left the kitchen table and began unbuckling their gun belts as they headed for the women's two bedrooms with hope for the 'womanly treasures' that lay behind those two closed doors…

"Won't do you no good to hide behind this closed door, Little Miss," said Black as he approached one of the closed bedroom doors. "I aim to come in and have whatever you are hiding from me, come hell or high water!" he bellowed. Kicking in the bedroom door, all accompanied to the screams of the woman in that bedroom, Black just grinned a leering grin, dropped his gun belt on the floor that he had been carrying and said, "Come here, you little vixen, for I aim to have whatever you are hiding from me," as he made for the shadow of the woman cowering behind her bed.

Down the hallway in the next bedroom, Rice had already kicked in the door and without a word, dropped his gun belt and made for a woman who was standing there in the low light of a whale oil lamp looking right at her would be 'suitor' with 'fire' in her eyes.

Back in the first bedroom, Black made his move for the woman cowering behind her bed but in so doing, he forgot to look behind the bedroom door he had just kicked in... BOOM! went a ten gage shotgun, blowing Black almost completely in two! Over in the second bedroom, Rice, like Black, had forgotten to look behind the bedroom door he had just kicked in. Hearing the explosive sound of shooting in the first bedroom, Rice turned in amazement away from what had just seconds before could have been a magical moment with a woman, only to see a Colt .45 aimed at his head from just two feet away! The last thing he saw was a flash as the gun was discharged, blowing his head into dozens of chunks of bone, blood and brain matter all over the bed he had planned on using just moments earlier with the scared woman in mind!

Racing out from the first bedroom after killing Black with his shotgun, Lewis blew the head clear off of an Indian standing in the hallway awaiting his turn at one of the two women previously chased into their bedrooms! Racing out from the second bedroom after killing Rice with a shot to his head from just several feet away, James fanned off two quick shots from his Colt .45 into an Indian who had just walked into the bedroom hallway still stuffing his mouth with freshly baked bread and looking for 'his share' of more 'specialized tastes' in the second bedroom. Both shots fired from about eight feet away struck the

Indian in his chest with such impact, the previously swallowed bread just gorged down, flew out his mouth in a long 'chunky' spew!

Joe, who had been hiding in a clothes closet, upon hearing the shooting coming from the bedrooms, burst out from his place of hiding and almost stumbled into an Indian urinating on the floor near the pantry! BOOM-BOOM! went Joe's two quick fanned shots from his Colt .45, which blew the Indian taking his last piss in the corner of the hallway into a sprawled-out and bleeding heap on the floor!

Then BOOM! went a single shot from a pistol fired by a surprised Indian just emerging from a raid he was making on a nearby pie safe in a second kitchen pantry! Emerging from that pantry with a whole pie in hand, that Indian was surprised over Joe's closeness to him in the hallway and recognizing him in an instant as an enemy, tossed that pie into Joe's face from just feet away! That Indian's surprise was quickly followed up with one shot from his rapidly drawn pistol into Joe's pie-covered face, killing him on the spot!

James's face was then splattered with the brains and blood from his brother Joe's head being blown apart by the Indian's close at hand shot, because the two brothers were close together at the time of the shooting! Stepping back in shock over what he had just experienced in his older brother's death, James quickly regained control over his emotions in the immediate face of danger from the close at hand, still-armed Indian standing in the open pantry doorway, pulled down on the killer of his brother and shot him squarely between the eyes from just six feet away!

The Colonel, still stuffing his face with homemade apple pie fresh from the wood stove's oven, upon hearing that first shot, stood there in frozen surprise and amazement! However, his two remaining Caddo Indian cohorts, carrying 20,000 years of genetic instincts when it came to survival, lunged for the front door and escape from the close at hand shooting. However, at that moment, the front door burst open and in streamed Indian Policemen Tom Johns and Chief Many Hats with guns cocked and in hand! BOOM-BOOM-BOOM! went three quick shots from the Indian Policemen, nullifying those 20,000 years of survival instincts lodged in the genetics of the two Caddo Indians, who were now in the process of crumpling dead to the kitchen floor as a result of receiving deadly .45 caliber pistol slugs into their chests from such close range!

All of a sudden, the Colonel realized that he was all alone and without a single friend in the room. All of his men were now obviously dead in the face of what he was now facing... Those thoughts were buttressed by his looking at Lewis and James, both covered with blood and brain parts, holding Colt .45s on his person from just a few feet distant. Then turning, the Colonel realized that there were also two serious-looking Indians holding down on him with their pistols from just ten feet away! No matter how he looked at it, he had two chances looking him in the face, 'slim and none' when it came to taking his next few breaths if he made any kind of a move!

Lewis, now the oldest living son, stepped forward and took charge. "Chief Many Hats, would you please disarm the good Colonel and when you do, if he even breathes too deeply, KILL HIM ON THE SPOT!"

Without saying a word, Chief Many Hats stepped over to the Colonel, placed the end of the barrel of his pistol up under the man's chin and said, "Colonel, would you please drop your gun belt by using your left hand to undo the buckle. Looking over there by the wall and seeing my friend Deputy Marshal Dodson lying there dead, would you please resist this arrest, Colonel?" said Chief Many Hats with iron in the tone and tenor of his voice, and the end of his gun barrel not shaking one single bit as he uttered those words!

About then, the marshals heard about a dozen horses reining up in front of the ranch house. Moments later, David, Sheriff Del Garrison and the rest of his posse burst through the front door and entered the kitchen area with drawn guns. Then the booming voice of Sheriff Del Garrison, after quickly surveying the scene, barked out orders saying, "Put your guns away, Boys. The work that needed doing here has been accomplished!"

For the next two hours, the ranch house was slowly cleaned up and put back into order. Joe's body was put into the spring house and the bodies of the eight dead Indians and ex-Confederate soldiers were hauled off in a wagon and dumped into a deep nearby draw known to be a den site occupied by a female black bear and her three cubs...

Then sitting around the kitchen table holding a gallon jug of corn liquor, the men solemnly toasted the life and times of Joe Dodson, Deputy U.S. Marshal, brother and good friend to all, who was now in the hands of his Maker. Daylight the following morning found the two women fixing breakfast and replacing the now empty whiskey jug with a full one from the spring house... After a hearty breakfast had been eaten by all of the men, Joe's body was removed from the spring house and carried up to the family cemetery wherein lay his father, mother and two sisters. There Joe was laid alongside his mother, as his three remaining brothers said what they wanted to say, and then Deputy U.S. Marshal Joe Dodson was laid in to rest for all eternity...

Then it was back to the ranch house and now there were two gallon jugs of corn liquor sitting on the table, as the two women prepared a feast befitting the celebration of a good man's life. It was then that Sheriff Del Garrison asked Lewis, "How the hell did you come up with the idea to ambush the Colonel at your home place, instead of taking him on at Meek's ranch when the Colonel and his men were rustling the cattle?"

Pouring himself three fingers of good corn liquor, Lewis sat back in his chair and quietly said, "The idea to ambush the Colonel at our home place was all Joe's. He realized that to take on the Colonel's nine heavily armed men would more than likely get a mess of us killed. So he put 'two and two together' and came up with this plan to ambush him here at our home place. Joe figured the Colonel would take the Dodson herd of cattle along with those from Meek and in so doing, backed us off from Meek's herd of cattle and hustled us back to our staked-out horses. We grabbed them and all of us raced back to our home place. There we hid all of our horses in the barn so the Colonel and his men would not realize we were here, and then we got the two wives-to-be of me and James to act out the part of surprised women baking in the kitchen. By their doing so, the outlaws would be lured into the house where we could come at them from two sides as well as individually when their guards were down, and they had nothing but thoughts of getting at and compromising our women. Joe just figured they would be so interested in taking the women that we could even up the numerical odds using the element of surprise, round up the whole bunch and save ourselves in the process. He just didn't figure a damn Indian being in the pantry stealing a pie out from the pie safe and then confronting him from such a surprising location. All of you know what happened next, so no use in going over those details. But the credit goes to Joe. He always had a head for figuring out ways around the impossible and in doing so this day, probably saved our bacon, us being so outnumbered and all by a mess of killing sons-a-bitches."

The next morning, the Dodsons helped sort out Meek's cattle from theirs and took them back to Meek's home ranch for the benefit of his wife and kids. The following day, with Lewis in the lead followed by James trailing the now man-acled Colonel, and with Tom Johns and Chief Many Hats in van, the posse made its way up to Fort Smith where the Colonel was once again incarcerated in a 'Yankee' jail. Five days later, the good Colonel had his day in court, with Lewis and James testifying to the fact that they had observed the Colonel killing Meek and rustling his cattle. Judge Parker immediately found Colonel Jackson guilty of murder and cattle rustling as well as escaping from a federal prison. Moments later, Judge Parker sentenced Colonel Jackson to hang by his neck until he was dead! Three days later, James and Lewis had the satisfaction of watching the unrepentant Colonel swing from Judge Parker's gallows. As for the Colonel's attorney friend, also from the late Confederate Army, the one who had helped in the Colonel's escape from the federal prison, he 'swung' with his friend on the same day! In that man's trial, Judge Parker found since he had helped the Colonel escape, that had allowed for the death of one of his Deputy Marshals to occur. Therefore, the attorney was just as guilty for that murder of his Deputy Marshal as if he had pulled the trigger on the killing shot and he should 'swing' as well.

Later that afternoon of the hanging, found the two Dodson brothers standing in front of Marshal Fagan. There Lewis and James tendered their resignations as Deputy U.S. Marshals, collected their $2.00 for bringing in Colonel Jackson and were paid their six cents per mile for all the riding they had to do in order to run Colonel Jackson to ground and bring him forthwith to trial in Judge Parker's court…

That same afternoon, Lewis and James had lunch with Tom Johns and Chief Many Hats in celebration over their friendship, the time on the trail they had spent together, and then said their good-byes. Days later, the Dodsons returned to their family ranch and resumed their lives as gentlemen farmers and ranchers. Lewis Dodson was married to the little gal he had saved from an unwanted life in a whorehouse some five months later, and six months after that, James married the little gal he had saved from an unwanted life of sin that had been forced upon her. They both went on to have large families, as did their younger brother, David who was married a year later.

One week after the Dodson brothers had tendered their resignations as Deputy U.S. Marshals, a rainy and gloomy afternoon found Marshal Fagan quietly sitting at his desk and pondering life around him. It was then that he truly realized the modern world had betrayed most of the subjects he oversaw and tried to protect in the Indian Territory as the Indian Territory's chief federal law enforcement officer. Native American subjects who were displaced from the lands of their forefathers with their love of heritage being replaced with a life of often times despair surrounded by much lawlessness.

Then his mind shifted to those officers who

served under him in and for the United States of America. Always outnumbered Deputy U.S. Marshals, who many owed a profound debt of gratitude for their humanity and selflessness. Marshals who went into a lawless land, riddled by many broken promises, broken treaties, broken hopes and lives, all with their hopes for the humanity they protected and served. Officers who with little compensation and support, sacrificed their lives for little recompense other than a great love for those around them holding little hope, while every day facing much violence in the belief and hope in their abilities in maintaining the rights of all humanity. Federal Law Enforcement Officers one and all, who shared the bonds of brotherhood and had no time to cry or for their emotions of loss, but just the hopes for those they served and the duty they collectively shared.

Shaking his head over the challenges he and his men still faced and the losses that came with 'carrying the badge', Marshal Fagan turned in his swivel chair and spat a stream of Brown's Mule tobacco juice out his second story window onto the bushes below. Then turning back around, he quietly thought, *Damn, I am sure going to miss those Dodson brothers. Now they were Deputy U.S. Marshals of the cut and caliber of Deputy U.S. Marshal Bass Reeves...*

CROSSED ARROWS: MOUNTAIN MEN

(THE MOUNTAIN MEN BOOK 1)

BY TERRY GROSZ

IN 1829, JACOB AND MARTIN left Kentucky to become Mountain Men, trappers of the Rocky Mountains. The rugged mountains that lay beyond America's frontier remained mostly unexplored. In those days, when beaver were plentiful and the buffalo roamed freely, the killing was good. The two young men would also find that life would be hardscrabble in the high frontier. They would face grizzly bears and hostile Indians. And they would risk horse wrecks and mountain storms to trade their furs each year at "rendezvous." Crossed Arrows is the story of two adventurers who lived hard in the earliest days of the Wild West.

Available now from Terry Grosz and Wolfpack Publishing.

ABOUT THE AUTHOR

WHETHER AS A PROFESSIONAL in the field of wildlife law enforcement or as a prolific writer, Terry Grosz has distinguished himself with a kind of passion, dedication, integrity and professionalism that often exemplify Humboldt State alumni. The beginning of his 32-year career in wildlife law enforcement came in 1966 with the California Department of Fish and Game in Eureka. After several years and a transfer to Colusa, he was hired by the U.S. Fish and Wildlife Service (FWS), moving into increasing responsibility for conservation and wildlife law enforcement in successively larger geographic regions, from jurisdiction over the central half of Northern California to finally Assistant

Regional Director for Law Enforcement where he supervised FWS's wildlife law programs covering 750,000 square miles.

When Grosz became the FWS Senior Special Agent, he wrote regulations, policy and procedures, responded to congressional inquiries, provided advice, guidance and expertise. But it wasn't just a desk job. He also traveled throughout Asia assisting foreign governments in curtailing the smuggling of wildlife and establishing cooperative international law enforcements programs. In all the various positions held by Terry, he supervised agents who protected wildlife from being smuggled or imported illegally into the US, protected eagles from being poisoned or trapped, and more.

In 1998, Grosz retired from the FWS and began a second career as a prolific writer, and has since authored and published fourteen wildlife law enforcement memoirs and seven historical novels. Clearly, he's got a lot of material to work with. Many of his stories have hilarious moments and hair-raising adventures, some others are sad and tragic, they are all about the men and women who work as wildlife conservation officers trying to preserve our natural heritage for future generations.

৵৽

Find more great titles by Terry Grosz and Wolfpack Publishing at http://wolfpackpublishing.com/terry-grosz/